RESISTANCE

END OF EMPIRE

Book Two

RESISTANCE

END OF EMPIRE

Book Two

by

ALEX JANAWAY

First published 2018 by Fantastic Books Publishing

Cover design by Gabi

Artwork by Kirsty O'Rourke

Map illustration by Fez Baker

ISBN (ebook): 9781-912053-76-6

ISBN (paperback): 9781-912053-74-2

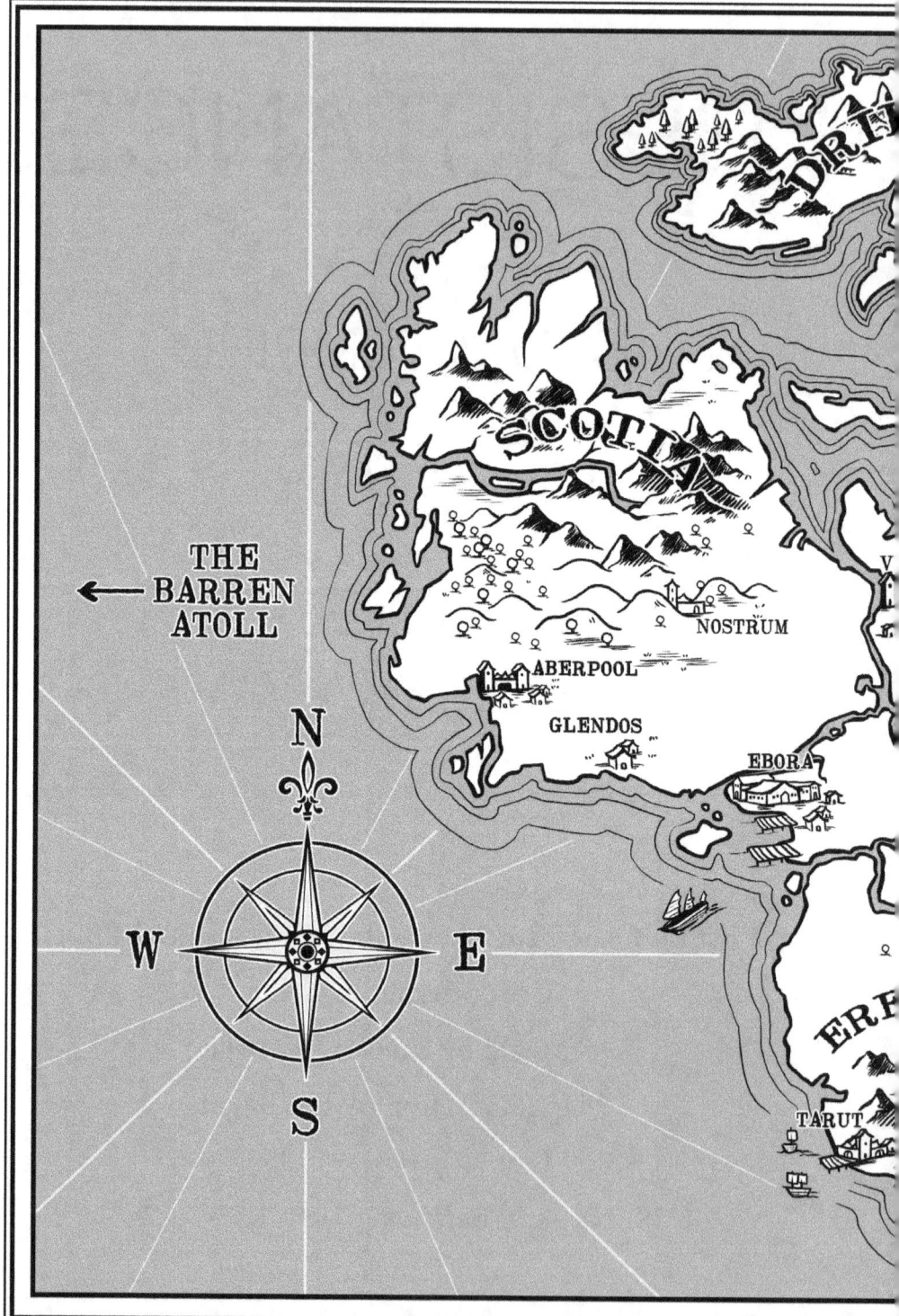

The Tissan Empire

DEDICATION

To Siobhan, who tells me when I've got the words wrong ...

DRAMATIS PERSONAE

The Expedition

Father Michael – ex arena champion, protector of the Emperor
Emperor Tigh – ruler of the Tissan peoples
Ellen – a Gifted, and friend of Father Michael
Bron – woodsman
Uther – squire to the Emperor
Cadarn – a Leader of the Eagle Riders; rides Hilja
Bryce – an Eagle Rider; rides Nukka
Corporal Fenner, Beautiful, Wendell and Coyle – marines
Eilion – a Gifted, commander of the Emperor's bodyguard
Raspa, Loras, Grieg, Leisha, and Mercer – the other Gifted with the expedition

New Tissan

Father Llews – counsellor to the Empress
Cardinal Yarn – head of the Schools of the Gifted
Arch Cardinal Vella – head of the Imperial Church
Empress Alana – the Emperor's mother
Admiral Lukas – commander of the Imperial fleet
Japes – a marine
Malik – a Gifted
Jenna – an Eagle Rider; rides Lissa

The Heartlands

Captain Sabin Fillion – Imperial officer and half-elf
Patiir – a Member of the Elven Parliament
Nadena – daughter of Patiir, wife to Fillion

Brynne – daughter of Fillion and Nadena
Hedra and Alica – son and daughter of Patiir
Kanyay – Servant from the wood elf tribes
Marmus – ambassador of the Dwarf Nations
Reygar – Dwarf guide / warrior
Rabi – of Patiir's household
Tekla – a Member of the Elven Parliament
Ezra – Servant to Member Tekla
Kefe – a member of the Elven Parliament
Lenard – elf historian

The Dwarf Nations

Cade – Crew boss and slave
Devlin – ex Imperial officer and member of Cade's crew
Issar, Meghan, Evan, Krste, Miriam, Anyon, Emerich and Trent – members of Cade's crew
Vidar – dwarf and mine owner
Geir – Accounter working for Vidar
Gwillem, Sent and Winders – slaves
Rula – slave and midwife

The Highlands

Owen Derle – Eagle Rider and Head of Eagle's Rest; rides Arno
Murtagh – second in command of Eagle's Rest
Naimh – Murtagh's sister
Jenni – Murtagh's wife
Larsen and Saul – trappers
Jussi – Eagle Rider; rides Ayolf
Erskine and Ernan – Eagle Rider and brothers
Anneli – Eagle Rider; rides Taru
Skeet and Breege – Highlanders

The Nidhal

Nutaaq – Father of his tribe
Arluuq and Immayuk – Nutaaq's brother
Weguek – a Nidhal warrior
Gantak – a Nidhal shaman

The Erebeshi

Major Killen Roche – Imperial officer commanding the Third
Erebeshi Scouts
Captain Jehali Rashad – Erebeshi Scout
Hassan and Sadad – Erebeshi Scouts

Scotia

Gerat – resistance leader from Scotia
Bedwyr, Hosen and Dill – Scotians

CHAPTER ONE – KILLEN

Killen shifted uncomfortably. No matter where he lay his head he encountered bare, uneven rock or lumps of stone. None of it was flat. He should have made more of an effort to clear the ground beneath him. He'd been living this life for long enough it should have been second nature, but some part of him must still be hoping it was all temporary. He sighed and rolled on to his side resting his head on his hands. In the shadowed gloom he watched the rise and fall of the camel's rib cage, expanding and contracting at a slow measured pace. At least someone was sleeping comfortably. Its thick patchy hair, covering mottled skin, was coarse to the touch. Red patches tracked where some insect had feasted upon its flesh; perhaps one of the big ugly spiders, all hues of yellow, brown and cream, aggressive and bitey. He'd been warned of the horror of the scuttling bastards injecting venom to dull the pain, biting into the skin, and leaving their eggs to hatch into baby horrors that would eat their victim from the inside out. He'd believed it too; for a good six months until a grinning scout put him right. Humans were never their hosts. Still, every night he made sure the edges of the blanket were weighted down with stones, the thick fabric stretched taut, creating a cocoon of space; dark, cool and stinking of camel scent.

He hated his camel.

He hated it with a passion that defied logic. It was the embodiment of everything that was wrong with the world. Everything that had gone wrong for him. He should have stayed in the capital. His banishment to the south was unwarranted. He was not the first imperial officer to share a courtesan. Lucy had been a fine woman, a little older than him in her early forties (she wouldn't say which year exactly), worldly-wise and a little jaded perhaps but with a body that was the envy of girls half her age. Just because she'd

1

chosen to lie with his colonel, it all went to shit. He was fine with it but that self-important idiot wanted her all to himself. He remembered the colonel's smug look, his smart uniform, his preening superiority the day he'd issued the summons. 'Congratulations, Major Killen Roche, your first independent command. The Third Erebeshi Scouts. Good luck to you. I'm sure your career will know no limits when your five years are done.'

Five years? Five. Fucking. Years?

Killen hand had itched to draw his sword, but he was not a fool. His good times were coming to an end. Twenty happy years working in the headquarters shuffling paper and passing messages, out of the way of any real military action, had ended. He'd always nursed a hope that the ending might coincide with his mandatory retirement. That hadn't worked out. It was cold comfort that this chain of events had kept him alive when everyone else was likely dead. Including that vindictive colonel and poor Lucy too. He didn't blame her. She was a professional.

His wildest imaginings had never seen him spending nights in the desert. And he'd never known it would get so cold during the winter months; that he could be baking in the sun one moment then shivering his ass off the moment he stepped into shade. And if he thought that was cold, it was nothing to the nights that came in fast and hard with a cold that could kill a man if he wasn't prepared. Such was life in the Jebel, the high country of central Erebesh.

The camel whined and snorted, its whole body shuddering as it began to wake, rising slightly then settling back down.

He hated that camel.

It was lighter in his little hole now. The morning sun was making the edges glow. He'd have to get up soon, even though he'd had no sleep. He was in charge. There was an image to maintain. Even though the whole bloody trip was a waste of time.

He heard the scuff of boots, footsteps drawing near.

'Major?'

'Yes?'

'You are awake.'

'Yes. It would appear so.'

The blanket was ripped upwards, his small securing rocks flying all ways, many falling on to him.

Killen blinked at the burst of light. He was facing almost directly eastwards, right towards the sun. A figure stepped into his vision.

'Sir, come and look!'

'Yes, Hassan. Right with you.'

Hassan spun away, cloak billowing, his camel skin boots kicking up small dust clouds as he stalked off. Killen took in the air of excitement on his young features.

Pushing the collapsed blanket shelter away from him, he stood up. His camel, its long neck turned his way, seemed to regard him with mild contempt.

'I hate you,' he said, forcefully.

The camel stared back, its jaws working. Killen suspected the camel didn't care.

He stretched his arms and gazed around the camp. Everyone else was already up, packing away their blankets, taking a quick breakfast of dried meat or a sip of water. Each man wore light leather breastplates over their traditional off-white robes, and sleeveless, striped aba coats over the breastplates. No one wore their pointed helms, preferring a kufeya, a square of fabric folded into a triangle with a point on each shoulder and held in place by camel wool. He'd resisted at the start, preferring the helm, with its long chainmail neck and cheek guard. But his head had started to boil sufficiently for him to change his mind. He pulled his kufeya from under the blanket and settled it on to his head, arranging the material around his shoulders. His own breastplate was steel and he'd elected to go without its protection for now.

He, Killen Roche, officer of the imperial army, had gone native. His sun-bleached beard was long (the shaving had stopped very early on), his skin a dark brown. At a distance he might pass for one of the Erebeshi, the only anomaly being his standard issue cavalry sabre, rather than the scimitars and bows the scouts carried.

3

Killen worked his jaws and ran his tongue around his dry gums as he walked to the saddlebags piled next to his beast, and reached for a waterskin. Pulling the stopper, he took a swig, sluicing the cool liquid around his mouth and spitting it on to the ground where it was absorbed fast, leaving a dark patch on the rocky ground. He ran over it with his foot, feeling small stones, no bigger than the rivets in his armour, roll underneath. When he lifted his foot the patch was gone; no evidence of it ever having been there. The desert had swallowed it, like it did with anything humanity tried to impose. There was no permanency to be had here, no stability, no growth. That's why the tribes moved on. It was impossible to stay in one place, the desert wouldn't let you. He lifted the waterskin again and took several deep gulps. They had a good supply back in the caves. They'd been there longer than anywhere since they'd retreated into the high country. At first, he had been in daily fear of running out of water and food, doomed to wander the wasteland until madness and death took them all. Yet the Erebeshi were not bothered in the slightest. They had been born to this life and saw no future where they were not the princes of the desert. It was an alien culture but in the last year he had learned to trust their ways when it came to survival.

I may be a fool, but I thank the Emperor he granted me the wisdom to hide the worst of it. When word had reached them that the last Erebeshi city had fallen, that all pretence of imperial control had been lost, his command could have left him to fend for himself. God's above, they could have slit his throat, and he wouldn't have blamed them. Happily, they decided to bring him along and treat him like he was still their commanding officer. He had Jehali Rashad, the native captain of the scouts, to thank for that. And now, due to Rashad's urging, they had embarked on an expedition to the northern borders of Erebesh, on the flimsy excuse of an uncorroborated report of signs of life. A whimsical adventure indeed.

If Killen wanted out, away from the desiccated earth and the heat, now would be the time. Strike out for more temperate climates. Perhaps the Riverlands. But he hadn't and he wouldn't. Because then he would be alone.

'Major. Come along. You must see!' Hassan beckoned to him from the top of a small rise. Others were heading in that direction, a hubbub of excitement building. Killen stoppered the skin and returned it to the saddlebag. The camp lay empty around him, only the camels left, so he quickened his pace, kicking up small puffs of red dust, climbing the slope, part of a gaggle of scouts. At the top, he found himself at the back of a group, who to a man were looking at the skies, hands raised to shield their eyes. He did the same, scanning the blue. Far away to the east, high in the sky, he spied the smallest wisp of a cloud.

'What am I looking at?' he asked no one in particular.

A few heads away Captain Rashad looked at him and smiled.

'You are looking in the wrong place, Major. Look up there.' Captain Rashad raised his hand and straightened his index finger.

Killen followed the line. He felt his eyes squint, his muscles pull his mouth into a frown.

'Do you see it, Major?' asked Hassan, his grinning teeth sharply highlighted against his dark skin.

Yes. He saw something.

'What is it?'

'Sadad.' The Erebeshi officer called to their best scout. 'You have the best eyes. Tell us what you see.'

Sadad, a wiry, moustachioed man of indeterminate age tugged at his beard and looked thoughtful. 'I see a bird,' he said.

'He sees a bird, Major,' stated Hassan.

'A bird?' How utterly unremarkable. Now that he had a name to give the dark shape in the sky, it made sense. The creature was little more than a dot, yet he could begin to make out a slight flaring to either side. A suggestion of wings. 'Yes, it's a bird. What of it? There are many predators out here.'

Rashad shook his head. 'Not like this.'

Was this what had dragged them out to the wilds, a rare bird? When some of their scouts had returned saying they'd seen signs of life, a thought he had not dared to entertain with all the evidence to the contrary, he had assumed they had meant human life. Now he was angry at himself for allowing a spark of hope. This was a waste of time. There could be no life the way he understood it.

He sighed heavily. It was a clear enough day to see the far ranges to the north; a week's travel at least to even get close. North. That way lay home. Half a continent away, before his assignment compelled him to the barren wastes of the Jebel.

'Right. We've seen the bird. Let's return.'

'No. Major Killen, you don't understand.' Captain Rashad turned to look at Killen. His sparsely bearded cheeks were taut, hollow. He shook his head, his lips still turned upwards into a wry, knowing grin.

'That is not just a bird. That's an eagle.'

CHAPTER TWO – THE NIDHAL

The sun stood alone in a deep blue sky. Far off to the horizon, there was the suggestion of cloud, but perhaps it was nothing more than the eddying of the snow that rested upon the tallest peaks. The spring heat was bringing plenty of meltwater down from the mountains, and the rivers provided a cooling relief to the Nidhals' work. Not that Nutaaq was in any position to enjoy it right now. His head was hot and beaded with sweat, but he resisted the temptation to run his hand over his brow. Better the water run down his face than movement give away his position. He had already given a mighty effort to this hunt. It would have been better if he had removed his bearskin jacket, but he had neglected to cover himself in goose fat this morning. Their prey was too good at sniffing out his kind, and it was only the bearskin that disguised his scent.

His eyes moved left and right, scanning the undergrowth. His brothers were close, but he could not see them. That was good. After the snows, the trees had yet to recover their leaf and the bushes and grasses provided minimal cover. His family were wise to that, the cycle of the world was constant change and they adapted as necessary. What never changed were the ways of the beasts that shared their world. They were predictable, their needs driving them to the same habits. Nutaaq smiled.

And we of the People are no different.

On each passing of the sun, each changing of the season, they had their habits. The warmer months were the time to hunt, to gather, to prepare for the cold to come. Battles were fought, brothers died. Then the days grew shorter, mediation ended conflict, and minds turned to making babies. As the snows came, the shamans would tell the families stories of the old times, of legends and myths. And with the new sun

7

came fresh hopes, new desires and a chance to right old wrongs. Nothing changed, everything was predictable.

And I would change all that.

His brother Arluuq thought him mad for believing it, while young Immayuk told him every day that clearly he had been smoking too much of the weluck leaf. Only shamans had the power to harness its effects and Immayuk was eagerly awaiting the day Nutaaq's topknot turned orange. But he was neither mad, nor a Singer in waiting. As the eldest of the three, he was the Father now, since the passing of their sire during the winter. In many ways he was only continuing what his sire had begun, taught as he had been to think beyond what was expected, to range further and look for opportunity in the wider world. And just look what those travels had brought back. He was glad his sire had lived long enough for Nutaaq to show him his discovery. There had been pride in those eyes, even as the life had faded from them. His sire had approved, and now he was Father, his word was law and the family would follow. But even he could not have dreamed that other families would have so quickly embraced his vision.

'Nutaaq.'

He felt the odd pressure in his head even before his name was uttered. It no longer scared him, nor caused him discomfort, but it was a strange sensation. To hear a thought in your mind that was not your own. Even the shamans could not do that.

'Nutaaq. *We are ready.*' The voice was light, soft, a gentle timbre. Like the kiss of a breeze upon the skin. It was the voice of Ellen, a female, but it was nothing like that of the females of his family. She was no more than a child to his eyes but she had power, that was obvious, and this Ellen was no fool. He respected her for that.

He took a deep breath through his wide-ridged nostrils, then blew it out slowly and deliberately, gathering himself for the chase, focusing his thoughts on the task at hand. Twenty spans away, a small herd of oreqs gathered at the bank of the river to drink. One of the animals, the alpha male, had already filled his belly and now stood watch. The oreq was forever moving its head, the two spikes that emerged from its forehead pointed forwards, which helped to show which way the creature was looking. And you never wanted a male oreq looking at you, because those spikes would soon be aimed at you. He had seen one of the family's hunters taken in the back. Those spikes had punched clean through his chest.

Nutaaq tightened his grip on his spear and stood upright in one fluid, silent movement. His stare was fixed on the alpha. There were other males in the herd, but that one was the most dangerous. He pulled back his arm and released his spear in one smooth, practised action. The moment it left his hand he grabbed his second spear, and charged forward, letting out a bellow, a loud guttural challenge. His shout was joined by those of his brothers, the noise echoing in the clearing. The oreqs reacted immediately, their bodies tensing, ready to flee or fight, as they looked to the source of the sound. Nutaaq broke cover, knowing his brothers were with him, their spears flying ahead of them. Tissans appeared out of the brush to flank them, their weapons glinting in the sun. Escape routes blocked, many of the herd began to ford the river. It would do them little good, as more of the Tissans, along with Ellen, were waiting to receive them.

Nutaaq kept his focus on the male. His spear had struck the oreq in its flank and drawn blood, but it was not a clean strike and the spear had been shaken free. The creature howled in pain and fury as it turned to face him, its powerful hind legs tensing, readying to leap. Nutaaq closed the distance to a few spans and levelled his weapon. The oreq launched into the air, its spikes aimed at his chest. Nutaaq followed the leap, raised his weapon, and thrust it forward into the alpha's belly, even as he fell to his knees. Hauling back on his spear, he used the beast's forward momentum to carry it up and over his head. The spear was almost torn from his grasp but he held firm and pulled it free.

He swung round. The alpha had rolled and was scrabbling to regain its feet. Blood spattered the floor, pouring from the hole in its gut. It would die of its wounds but it wasn't done yet. It bellowed, saliva dripping from its mouth as it lunged to bite him, Nutaaq struggling to keep the spear between them.

A black shape entered his vision from his right side. It took a moment to register it was Immayuk. His brother drove his weapon deep into the alpha's side. The oreq fell to the ground, snapping at the haft of the spear that held it pinned.

'Finish it, brother!' shouted Immayuk. He was grinning, though his face showed the effort of trying to keep the beast down.

Nutaaq dropped his spear, pulled free his wide-bladed falchion, and leapt to the other side of the writhing alpha. He gripped his weapon with two hands, raised it high over his head and brought it down, chopping deep into the exposed, thickly muscled neck of the oreq. The head was half severed from the body, and the beast's movement ceased as a pool of blood spread outwards, staining the ground.

'You missed your throw,' taunted Immayuk.

Nutaaq knelt and wiped his blade free of blood against the oreq's flank.

'I did not miss, brother,' he said, keeping his voice calm. Immayuk was deliberately baiting him, as he always did. 'I simply wished to make the fight more interesting.'

'Thank the Fathers I was here to help you then,' replied Immayuk, as he pulled free his spear.

'I thank them for you every day.'

Nutaaq stood and looked at the outcome of their hunt. Most of the herd were still in the water, splashing away from them, following the river's course south. He walked towards the bank and watched them get on to solid ground beyond the range of the hunter's weapons. They would be allowed to go, they needed to survive and replenish their numbers. On the far bank, two more oreqs were down. His sharp eyes could see small arrows, bolts they called them, jutting out from the corpses. Fired from the mechanisms some of the Tissan warriors carried, they were deadly at shorter ranges, but Nutaaq had already decided that the People's bows were more accurate and had a far greater range. The mechanisms, crossbows, took time to load. A good archer could loose a dozen arrows and guarantee many strikes in the time it took the crossbow to be readied. But arrows were rarely used to hunt oreqs. It was a mark of pride and expectation that in honour of the oreq's great strength and ferocity, a warrior must face this enemy with spear and axe and club. The Tissans had no such scruples but then the Tissans were strange folk.

'Nutaaq!'

He looked towards his brother, running toward him, his spear levelled. An eruption of sound alerted Nutaaq to the oreq emerging from the water. He had no weapon, no time to react, could only brace for the impact. Another spear flashed into his vision and took the beast in the side with such force it knocked it back into the water. Then Immayuk was by his side. Another warrior stepped forward and brought his axe down hard on to the skull of the oreq, the crack audible as bone and brain were crushed.

The warrior stepped back and Nutaaq realised his saviour was his brother, Arluuq. Tall and powerfully muscled, even for one of the People, Arluuq's topknot was coloured yellow and had been allowed to grow down around his ears. It contrasted with his dark green skin and ensured he stood out in any melee.

'It was the alpha's female. She wasn't happy with you, brother.'

'I should have been more careful,' conceded Nutaaq.

Immayuk let out a long sigh.

'Oh brother, where would you be without us to look after you?'

Long dead. He conceded that even as the Father, he was not the mightiest warrior, nor the most cunning. *Truly one is never so strong as with Family, and never so weak without it.*

He clapped Immayuk on his back and stepped forward, gripping Arluuq's hand.

'Good throw, Arluuq.'

Arluuq shrugged.

'It wasn't me. That spear was on the ground ten spans away. It was one of them. The arrogant ones.'

Arluuq pointed at one of the Tissan warriors, a tall, well-built male that wore ornate armour. His name was … Eilion? He was one of the Gifted, one who possessed power, so Ellen had told him. Arluuq had the right of it. That one carried himself like he was a great one, a hero, like all the Gifted did, except for Ellen. If she had not been present at their first meeting, their fledgling alliance may have swiftly met a short and bloody end.

Nutaaq reluctantly nodded his thanks. The Tissan inclined his head slightly in return. Nutaaq owed the Tissan a debt, no matter what he may think of him.

'*Nutaaq? Are you alright?*' A voice sounded in his head. Ellen stepped forward from the group of Tissans, her face radiating concern. She wore armour too, though Nutaaq found it hard to imagine she could fight well in it. She looked too slight. Water dripped from her legs and waist from where she had forded the river.

He grunted in response.

'*I am happy.*' She smiled at him.

He inclined his head. There was no lie in her eyes. She was as she seemed, though it still unsettled him that she spoke in his mind that way. It was strong magic. And one of the reasons he had trusted to ally his people with hers.

'Nutaaq!' another Tissan called to him from across the river. It was the leader. They called him Emperor. Nutaaq likened him to a Father, the Great Father, Father of all. There had been no such person in all the history of the People.

'Grace.' Nutaaq used the word they all used to greet this man. It was getting easier to speak their words, though his voice growled out the sounds. The Tissan's language was so soft to hear, to make the words come out properly he had to whisper them. He was also prudent enough not to reveal just how many words he had learned in their short time together.

The Emperor crossed the water, flanked by two of his Gifted. He clapped Nutaaq on the arm and pointed at the carcasses. He said a few words and grinned.

'He says that the hunt went well. The Family will feast tonight,' sounded Ellen.

Nutaaq grunted. He had understood well enough.

'Brothers, let us go home,' he commanded.

He stood by and watched as the Tissans on the far side hauled up the oreq corpses and dragged them to the riverbank, their smaller frames making it heavy work for them. In contrast, his family easily gathered their share of the slaughtered, tied their legs together to thread on to poles which were in turn hoisted on to two sets of shoulders.

The Emperor was still by his side so Nutaaq reached for the small waterskin attached to his belt, and took out the stopper catching the pungent smell of the fermented chaga within. He passed it over to the Tissan. The Emperor had taken a liking to it, and Nutaaq watched with approval as the man took a long drink, wiped his lips and passed it back. Nutaaq took a large swig. That oreq had caught him off guard and rattled him a little. He savoured the sour and sweet liquid and enjoyed the heat as it ran down his throat.

The Emperor clapped him on the back. He did not mind, he liked the Emperor, he liked his energy, his passion. More importantly they shared a common bond and a common purpose.

'Good,' he said with a smile, his attempt at speaking Nidhal, odd and delicate.

Yes, a good day. But there will be better days to come. Bloody days.

Nutaaq smiled back and nodded.

'Good,' he said.

Three cycles from now he would face the Fathers of all the Families and he would tell them of their future. He would tell them they were going home.

CHAPTER THREE – MICHAEL

Father Michael stood with his arms folded across his sleeveless leather jerkin and allowed his breathing to return to normal. There was a surprisingly cool breeze coming down off the mountains, but he barely felt it. His body was still warm from his exertions and he stood comfortably watching the deep blue sky ahead of him. His opponent, a Nidhal called Weguek, sat on his haunches just to his left, taking a long drink from a crude wooden tankard. Steam rose from his body, his upper torso bare to the elements. His grey-green skin was covered in old scars and fresh scratches. His topknot hung at an untidy angle, where one of the braids had frayed loose. It had been a real challenge to best the old warrior. Say what you would about the Nidhal, they were good fighters. Father Michael's size – and there were no bigger among the surviving Tissans – matched the average Nidhal warrior's build, and that meant he could go toe to toe with them. Ellen had told him that the Nidhal had observed his daily training, and wanted to see what he could do. He had been happy to oblige. For too long he had raised his weapon to strike a man down, to kill. Even his sparring back in the pits had stopped once it became clear no one would face him. With Weguek, however, it took all Father Michael's efforts to defend himself, and in the end he just wore the Nidhal down.

I must be getting old.

Or perhaps it was his years of devotion to the Living God that had taught him wisdom. In truth he was not as sure as he used to be. All he knew was that the Emperor did not confide in him as much as he used to, preferring the protection of the Gifted. Father Michael had no problem with that; they were his bodyguard after all. Yet it galled him a little that the Emperor no longer expected Father Michael by his side, and that meant he could not fulfil the charge laid on him by the Arch Cardinal. So he did the next best thing, he trained. He practised his art, honed his body and polished his skills that had diminished in the long journey from Tissan. Now he was almost back to his best, his muscles had regained their strength and their speed … almost. No doubting it, he was older, and could feel the passing of the years. He had to make the remaining years count.

I serve the Emperor, my Living God, until the day of my passing.

A distant shout drew his attention to where a knot of Nidhal were gathered, gesturing to the sky. He looked up. An eagle approaching from the east. He looked around at the encampment, as more Nidhal came to witness its arrival.

Weguek stood up next to him, eyes fixed on the bird. The spectacle of the visit of a giant eagle had not worn off among the Nidhal. Father Michael understood and shared their sense of wonder, even after such a long time being among the Riders and their mounts. The power of the Tissans to tame such mighty beasts inspired a respect in the Nidhal which had certainly helped pave the way for the alliance of the two species. The eagle passed low overheard and he spied black spots that dotted the wings. It was Hilda, Cadarn's bird. There was a hubbub of interest interspersed with the howling of vargr, the creatures the Nidhal used a mounts. He and Weguek watched in companionable silence as the eagle's wings flared and it touched down on the edge of the small encampment that the Tissan party called home. With the spectacle over, the Nidhal started to drift away. Father Michael clapped Weguek on the back. 'Thank you, friend.' The Nidhal responded with a tight nod. Father Michael left the small area between yurts they used for sparring and made his way towards the Tissan camp, keen to speak with Cadarn, eager to find out if the Arch Cardinal had sent him any messages.

Walking between the Nidhal yurts he passed a vargr stretched out on the ground, it had clearly lost interest after the eagle had passed by. He paused a moment to admire the animal. All muscle and teeth, it was as large as a pony, with powerful hind legs, a coarse, shaggy hide and furry pointed ears, more like a bat's than anything else Father Michael could think of. Its breath was deep and even, clearly at rest, but it regarded him with curious, if not a little suspicious, eyes. *Easy there, just passing through.* He had been here long enough now for his scent to be familiar and the many vargr scattered around the yurts to not instantly bare teeth at his passing. They had been fortunate not to encounter the wild packs that roamed these lands, there would have been bloodshed. He nodded to the creature and continued on. Why had he done that? No harm in keeping friendly, he supposed, he'd had his fill of fighting wild animals.

As he approached the Tissan tents he saw Cadarn was already in discussion with Bron. The Rider looked over and waved to Father Michael. He raised his hand in return as the pair left Hilda and headed towards the cookfire that Bron had permanently ablaze.

He joined them at the fire where Cadarn was leaning over the cooking pot and filling his bowl with stew. Since setting up this permanent camp, the quality of food had improved, and the Nidhal had shared some of their knowledge of local herbs to add some welcome flavour to Bron's cooking.

'Father,' acknowledged the Eagle Rider.

'Leader,' replied Father Michael. 'What news?'

'Forgive me, I am starving. Can we eat and talk?' said Cadarn, in his usual calm and steady manner.

'Of course, I could do with a meal myself,' said Father Michael, trying to sound gracious.

'Father Michael is always hungry these days,' added Bron with a grin.

Father Michael ignored the jibe and, collecting another bowl, helped himself to a large portion. Together both men settled on to a selection of Nidhal blankets scattered around the fire. Father Michael took a mouthful and chewed, he was desperate for news, but he let the Eagle Rider settle down to eat and tried to find his patience. Bron took a spot opposite them, leaned forward, picked up a small stick, and prodded the fire. Father Michael took another mouthful and chewed it faster, his frustration growing. *Damn it all.* He opened his mouth to speak.

'Things are getting busy back home,' said Cadarn at last.

Father Michael shut his mouth and nodded, his attention fixed firmly on his bowl.

'Is that right?'

'The Admiral has the place in a frenzy. I don't think I have seen any man happier since this all started.'

Father Michael grunted. Happy was not something he would think to describe Admiral Lukas. He looked with unconcealed cynicism over at Cadarn, whose mouth was quirked in a smile beneath his thick, grey-speckled beard.

'Hard to believe, I know. But there is a real sense of purpose about New Tissan. Everyone is working towards a common goal. There are more buildings; many of the families have a wooden roof over their heads. The Admiral has his shipwrights and carpenters working night and day.'

'I would like to see that,' said Father Michael. They had been away for so long, at least four months, and yet it would seem things were moving quickly everywhere but here.

'Oh, my apologies, the Arch Cardinal sent this for you,' said Cardan, reaching into a leather satchel by his side. He produced a small, folded piece of paper that he passed over.

Father Michael nodded his thanks.

'It has been a good few years since I had to do messenger duty,' said Cadarn. 'Not that I ever had to fly so far in one mission.'

'Are the waystations in place now?'

'Yes, that was part of the reason I made this journey. I wanted to inspect them myself, make sure my Riders are in good order. Speaking of which, is Bryce about?'

'I saw him leave a couple of hours ago. He was escorting the hunting party.'

'Right. That probably means he's found a spot to lay low and sleep,' said Cadarn. 'I imagine they will not be back for some time yet. So, if you'll excuse me, Father, I might close my eyes until they return.'

'Of course.'

Father Michael waited until Cadarn had settled down under the lean-to shelter he had built next to where his eagle lay. He looked for Bron and saw him a little way off working on a haunch of meat. Beyond that, the Nidhal camp lay sprawled out to the west, a mess of hide tents and canopies that reminded him of their own first few weeks after arriving in this land. Yet the Nidhal had been here for centuries and had not appeared to make any attempt at a permanent settlement – they were more like the Erebeshi in that regard. Always on the move. He looked at the paper in his hand and broke the small wax seal, unfolding the single sheet to find the words that were indeed written in the familiar script of his mentor.

Father Michael, I hope my words find you well. It has been many months since we saw each other and yet so much has changed for all of us. Winter has given way to Spring and New Tissan grows thanks to the grace of our Emperor and Living God. Our people all miss Him terribly but the good works He has done in forging our new alliance have filled all of us with hope for the future. And did I not say that it would be so? Who could have imagined that in such a short space of time we would have seen such a change in our fortunes? The Council, under the Emperor's edict, has bid the Admiral to focus on a ship-building endeavour that will see our fleet double in size by the end of the year – which, I am informed, would be more than sufficient to transport all of us back home if we so desired. Though, as the Emperor has intimated, we will need as much space again if we are to realise his vision.

And what of these Nidhal? We have yet to see one and only have the briefest of descriptions to go by – they sound brutish. I would welcome your thoughts on our new friends. Naturally, that the Emperor has chosen to befriend them is evidence enough of their value and trustworthiness, yet having been so recently betrayed by the other races, it would be rash of us to relax our vigilance. I take comfort in your presence by His side, Father Michael – I am sure you have become a voice of solid counsel. Rest assured that I continue our good work, here in New Tissan. In the months since you have gone, the Church has made great strides in returning the authority of rule to the Emperor's most devoted.

Remember, Michael, you must be the Emperor's strong right arm. Guide Him and protect Him, then return Him home to us.

Vella

Father Michael held the letter before him and folded it gently. He had not struggled greatly with the words, and had even noticed he no longer mouthed them as he read. He felt a warm glow inside. It was good to know that the Arch Cardinal still trusted in him and encouraged him to continue in his task to guard the Emperor. And though Vella was not explicit, it was clear to Father Michael that the purge of the old ruling class from the Council was continuing. He wondered how it was being done, if the Arch Cardinal had other devotees who would act like Father Michael had. He felt a flicker of emotion, a sour taste in his mouth. He shook his head. When he had choked the life from Baron Ernst he had done so willingly, in the name of his Blessed Emperor, yet thinking back on it, Father Michael had come to realise that each time he took a life something became … detached from his soul. He dismissed the thought. There was no room for doubts, no matter how insistent. All that mattered was that he served the Emperor with whatever tools he had at his disposal, and those tools were obvious. *I am a killer. It is what I do.*

CHAPTER FOUR – CADE

'Oh, for fuck's sake!'

'What is it?'

'Look at this shit.'

Cade walked over the rock pile that had been deposited outside the mine entrance and joined Anyon, who was pointing at the pile with one hand and scratching his balding pate with the other. Cade stood next to him and folded her arms.

'Yeah?' she asked.

Anyon looked at her askance. 'C'mon Cade, what are we supposed to do with this?'

Cade turned from the entrance and scanned the canyon, flanked on all sides by steep mountain slopes, and full of Tissans labouring in the summer heat. 'Hey, Devlin!' Cade shouted.

Devlin stood by a cart that was facing away from the mine entrance. He glanced around, acknowledged Cade's hail with a wave, and handed over a manifest sheet to Miriam, who held station on the driver's bench of the cart. He then approached Anyon and Cade, his thumbs tucked into the rope tied around his waist, and leaned forward to inspect the rocks, his shaggy, greying hair falling forwards. He stood back upright, swept his unruly locks behind his ears, and looked at them both.

'So?' he asked.

'Anyon wants to know what to do with this,' Cade said.

Devlin shrugged, matter of fact. 'What do we normally do.'

'Oh come on, really?' responded Anyon.

'You heard the man,' said Cade.

'But there ain't nothing in that!' protested Anyon.

'Since when have you become the expert?' asked Devlin.

20

'Since about a year ago when we started humping this stuff up,' stated Anyon, heatedly.

'And in all that time has anyone ever listened to you?' asked Devlin.

'Well, no but that's–'

'That's because if you pulled this whiney shit with the dwarves you would have had your balls cut off.'

Anyon's face went red, and his lips pursed.

'I think that means you break these up just like you have every other bloody rock you've broken up since you got the job,' said Cade.

'Right, fine,' muttered Anyon, and picked up a sledgehammer.

Cade met Devlin's eyes and flashed him a grin. He tilted his head indicating they should talk. They moved off to the sound of metal on rock merging with the other sounds of labour echoing off the canyon walls.

'Everything alright?' asked Cade.

'Yeah, reckon. Just checked the output numbers. Three more carts and we'll have met the target for today.'

'Good. I guess we can ease back.'

Devlin nodded, but raised his eyebrows and looked towards the pair of dwarf guards standing at the entrance to the mine shaft.

'But not too much, ay?'

Cade waved a hand.

'Those two? They couldn't give a rat's ass. They're the laziest of the bunch, they don't even look for a reason to beat us down anymore.'

'Suppose so,' admitted Devlin. He was quiet a moment. 'I haven't seen Geir today.'

'Uh-huh.'

He was the one they had to watch; the Accounter was fine if the work was regular and productive, but anyone he caught slacking they would all be in for it.

'We see him less and less now. Guess the boss has got him doing other stuff,' she suggested.

'He can't complain we haven't got things running tight.'

'Hells no. Vidar knows when he's on to a good thing,' agreed Cade. For the last three months Cade had been schmoozing the bastard so hard that he now trusted Cade and her crew to run the whole show. And that meant less oversight, fewer guards, fewer beatings and less chance of being gutted for backchat. After all, she knew what strings needed pulling on their dwarf master. He was a greedy son of a bitch, and if she could promise him better output at reduced cost, she had him right where she wanted him.

'Speaking of which, you wanna hop on the cart with Miriam?' asked Devlin. 'He'll be wanting his update.'

Cade ran her hand through the mop of hair gathered up on top of her head and scratched her pate.

'Suppose. I'll see you back at the homestead,' she said.

Devlin clapped her on the back and strolled away.

Cade turned and spat. She wiped her face and looked at the ordered industry going on around her. Things had gotten better of late. There were certainly worse jobs, and her crew were getting the best of the work. She walked over to the cart and climbed aboard, nodding to the driver, Miriam, who nodded back. Miriam clicked her tongue and the pair of draft horses strained a little before the momentum built and the heavily laden cart started to move at a gentle pace, following the track around the draw and through the crowding slopes on either side. As they travelled, other routes opened up leading to different mines and workings. Most, Cade knew, were owned by different dwarf concerns. Ahead of them two more carts were making their way onwards, heading roughly north and west. A few more minutes and the track, now well-worn and rutted from the constant traffic, opened up on to a wide plateau where a number of warehouses, smelters, workshops and stables were scattered and grouped, each one its own separate enterprise. Cade's cart cut left and headed towards a larger grouping of buildings on the edge of the plateau. From there they could see down the slope where a route led into a wooded river valley which swept north.

Around them a number of dwarves went about their business, many grimy from a day working in heat, others armed as guards, and a few who wore finer, cleaner clothes, and carried ledgers. Since getting permission to use her people to drive the wagons, Cade had been paying close attention to how the plateau functioned. Most of the mine owners employed fellow dwarves to do their work, at least up here, away from the mines. But she had seen at least two other mining outfits using carts manned by humans, though both also carried dwarf guards. It made her wonder just how many other human work crews were in these mountains.

They arrived at the warehouse, and were met by more of Cade's crew emerging from its cavernous, shaded interior.

'Afternoon, Cade,' said Evan. The lad had filled out some in the last few months and was looking the better for it.

'Evan,' she acknowledged.

He beamed up at her with something akin to hero worship. She was damned uncomfortable about that, she didn't want anyone worshipping her. Respect and obedience would do just fine. Behind him came Meghan, who smiled at her warmly but with a different look in her eye. Cade knew what that was too, and it was just as strange – no one had actually *loved* her before, she wasn't even sure what that felt like. But, well, she could live with that, it certainly had its benefits. She pushed herself off the cart and made her way inside as the others started to unload the unrefined ore to be stored until it was taken to the smelter, then she headed towards a set of stairs leading up to a balcony that led to the office overlooking the warehouse interior. She nodded to the two guards at the bottom of the stairs. One stepped back with a crossbow aimed point blank at her while the other stepped forward. She knew the drill and raised her arms high. The dwarf ran his hands down her sides and around her back. She then lowered her arms and opened her hands. He nodded and gestured to the stairs, and in return she gave him a beaming smile. He snarled at her and growled something out in dwarvish. She stepped past him and walked up the stairs.

She shook her head. *Did he just call me a whore?* She was pretty sure he had, her dwarvish was getting better and she was specialising in swear words. She reached the balcony and stopped a moment to look down on her people bringing in the rocks and sorting them into rough piles. She went and knocked at the door.

'Enter,' came the gruff reply.

Cade turned the handle and stepped through, having to lower her head somewhat. Before her sat the boss, Vidar, his head bowed over a ledger as usual. He did not look up and she knew better than to speak first, so she closed the door and waited.

'Well?' he asked, after a moment, still not looking up.

'All good, boss.'

Vidar looked up and fixed her with his best icy glare. Four months ago that would have meant a swift and savage beating.

'And what does that mean?'

'It means today's target will be met, as promised.'

'As expected.'

'Yes. That too.'

'And what about the smelting crew?'

'We've got four working on that, each with two apprentices. Give me another couple of weeks and I reckon you can stop using your people completely.'

Vidar tapped a finger on the desk.

'No. I'll keep my own working on the precious ores.'

'As you say, boss. Can't see why you'd be concerned about theft. What are we going to spend it on?'

'A thief's a thief. You can't help yourself,' he said dismissively and stood up. She clocked the dagger he always carried. He walked over to the window that looked out into the warehouse.

'It hasn't escaped my notice that I now have you humans working in every aspect of my operation out there.'

'I like to provide a good ser–'

'Nor has it escaped the notice of many of my colleagues up here on the plateau,' he said, shooting another sharp glance her way. 'And some are questioning the wisdom of it. They say that I am being a fool. Some say that I am too soft, others that I am taking work away from my own kind. One even had the audacity to say I was being disloyal and questioned my patriotism!' He placed the sheathed dagger on the table, then after a pause, withdrew the blade and inspected it. 'The one thing I hear the most is that I need to crack down, to keep you in your place. To remind you that your lives belong to me. They say I need to make an example.'

He turned and looked towards her, the dagger held horizontally, ready to thrust. Cade swallowed. *Oh, this can't be good.* She raised a warding hand and took a step back.

'Now see–' Cade began to protest.

He barked a harsh laugh over words.

'Is my example made?' He replaced his dagger. 'They are fools. All of them. They forget what our business, what my business, is.' He turned his back and returned to his desk.

Cade briefly closed her eyes and breathed deeply. *Steady girl, remember the world you live in.*

Vidar sat down and placed a hand on his ledger.

'Using your kind in the mines and taking on work here will reduce my costs. You get injured, it costs me nothing; you die it costs me nothing.' Vidar shrugged. 'I make more money by using you and when you are used up, then I'll go back to employing dwarves again.'

Cade bowed. 'Sounds like a plan.'

'You know there are other mines using humans out there?' he asked tilting his head to the window.

'I noticed some,' she said.

'Of course you did. I know that about you, Cade. Always keeping an eye open.'

To Cade the warning was clear. *And you think you are on to me, do you? You haven't a clue, you short-arsed bastard.*

'I've got plans to expand here. There are some here who have rather more business vision than those who question my methods. You've got a smart mind. You've put it to work staying alive, winning your folk some concessions off me. Well done. You want to keep them?'

'I'm guessing that's not a trick question,' Cade muttered.

'There will be more demand for your kind up on the plateau soon. I'll need you to keep them in line. Organise them, train them as needs be. You do that right and your life won't end so soon or so dismally.'

'Now there's an offer I can't refuse,' replied Cade, wryly.

'No, you can't.' Vidar returned to his ledger. 'Get out.'

Cade resisted the urge to curtsey and opted for a tug of the forelock.

She backed out of his office, closed the door and walked down the stairs ignoring the two guards at the bottom. She left the warehouse and took her spot back on the cart.

'Almost done,' said Miriam, climbing up next to her. 'Everything alright?'

'Hmm,' Cade looked over. 'What? Oh yes, the boss is really pleased with us. Gonna give us a day off.'

'Really?' asked Miriam brightly.

'No, you daft cow.'

'Oh,' Miriam responded, her eyes downcast.

Cade shook her head. Not the sharpest tool, Miriam. But truth was, things were happening, *change* was happening. Life was going in her direction and she was still proving useful. More humans in other mines, all needing her to give them direction. Now that was something she was looking forward to.

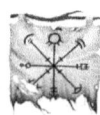

Cade barely noticed the jolting of the cart on the journey back, or the chatter of her crew, returning with them for the end of day's Accounting. Her mind was mulling was over the latest development in her fortunes; success was proving to be a real ball-ache. As she clambered off the cart, Meghan walked over and touched her shoulder.

'You alright, Cade?'

As always, Meghan was sharp enough to have picked up on Cade's mood, but she wasn't prepared to share just yet. 'Yeah, just thinking some things through,' Cade replied.

They joined the stream of people entering the mountain, following the tunnels leading to the Downside Gate. As they arrived, a discrete glance showed a dozen guards flanking them on either side while another four stood on the walkway over the gate, covering them with crossbows. Always the same number, always the same faces. They said dwarves were inscrutable, that no race was so hard to tell apart. Well, that wasn't true. There were all different kinds and different types of dwarf: sour, mean, angry, cruel, arrogant, indifferent. But as far as she could tell they were all greedy.

The gate opened and the crowd filed through and on to the parade square. Cade took her time. Having been outside all day meant her vision would need to adjust; not so those in the mine shafts. The gloom of the cavern was luxury compared to the single flickering candle flames they were used to working by. Everyone moved quickly, drilled and practiced over many months. Cade took her assigned place, a piece of unremarkable ground as familiar to her as her own bed space. She felt that familiar little knot of tension growing in her stomach. In the silence, the creaking sound of the gate opening once more seemed overly loud. She flinched despite herself. It was in these moments that she felt most vulnerable, most exposed. She tracked the arrival of the Accounters, three of them, and six guards. She recognised Geir, back from whatever errand he'd been sent on. And then the dwarves disappeared, moving quietly among the assembled crowd, making marks in ledgers. Her hand drifted to her arm and traced a finger over the brand that marked her as one of Vidar's. Not that it made much difference these days, Vidar had taken them all on to his ledger. In fact she was one of the lucky ones: she hadn't had to endure a second branding like those belonging to other owners. One was quite enough. She quickly dropped her hand as Geir and two of the guards appeared at the end of her line. She stood a little straighter, kept her eyes fixed forwards. The older dwarf stopped, looked her up and down, inspecting her for any injuries or signs of sickness that might make her a liability, then made a downward stroke on his ledger and moved on. She squeezed her eyes shut and took several long breathes. A few minutes later she heard the gate creak shut and felt a tangible release of the crowd's shared tension. None had been singled out. No deaths this day. A single horn sounded one long note and the gathering splintered. Cade made straight for the long upward curving path carved into the cavern walls towards the area known as the Heights. Around her several others fell into step, an honour guard of sorts, all members of her crew, all living in the caves that led off from the path.

'So, what are you thinking about?' asked Meghan, sidling up close.

'Just had some news from the boss. He's planning on expanding again.'

'There's a surprise,' Meghan muttered.

'It's an opportunity.'

A queue of folks was forming at the water cave; pots, buckets and sundry other containers were in their hands. Issar was already in place controlling the flow. The thin-framed Erebeshi waved as they passed.

'They better hurry up – I need a piss,' said Cade.

They reached a cave entrance half-way up and ducked inside. She went straight to her pile of blankets at the rear of the cave, checking to see if anything had been disturbed. Satisfied that all was in order she settled down and watched Meghan busy herself by the firepit, where she made a noise and lifted something off the ground, it dangled from between her fingers. Cade leaned forward. A rat? No doubt one of the guys had found it and dropped it off. 'Who's cooking tonight?' she asked.

'You.'

'Are Devlin and Issar coming round?'

'You want Issar to cook?'

'He's good at it.'

'So are you.'

'Yes, but I'm lazy.'

'Ain't that the truth.'

Cade stretched and lay down on the blankets, putting her hands behind her head. She watched as, unbidden, Meghan began to build a fire. That was Meghan, far too giving for her own good.

'You said something about an opportunity?' Meghan prompted.

'Uh-huh. Vidar wants me to act as his, I don't know, go-between? Turns out that I was right, there are a whole lot more mines out there using humans as a workforce. Vidar has a mind to offer up his services as a manager for the whole damn mountain range.'

'And how do you figure?'

'Wants me to organise any other groups whose owners take him up on the offer. Get them cooperating, get them working, sort out any artisans, get others trained up.'

'Overseer.'

'What?'

'Overseer. That's the name you are looking for. The title.'

'Oh, right. Sounds good. I could work with that.'

Meghan stood up and came to lie next to her, propped up on her elbows.

'Means you'll need Devlin and the others to step up.'

'It's not like Devlin doesn't run the show already. I'm more like the figurehead, you know, the acceptable face of cooperation with our oppressors.'

Meghan bit her lip and nodded.

'And that's what I worry about. Everyone here knows you, knows what you did.'

'And things are better, right? Everyone gets to use the water, nobody has to pay for it. And hardly anyone gets beaten to death now.'

'Yes, Cade. Things are better. But you start becoming the mouthpiece of the dwarves, folk aren't gonna take it well.'

'Sweet Emperor on his privileged arse, Meghan! I'm doing them a solid! Can't they get that?'

'Yeah, everyone here does, and you have our crew. We'll all back you. But no one outside of here knows you.'

'Look, I get it. I'll just be real charming, like always. People'll figure it out. The more work that we can take off our masters means less of them around and a chance of a better quality of life. Everybody wins.'

'Preaching to the converted, Cade.'

'Thanks.'

Meghan reached out and played with Cade's topknot.

'You know, we've been working topside for a while now.'

Oh, I know what's coming. 'Yes?'

'Just think it might be good if we took a turn down below.'

'Really?'

'Yeah, we don't want people to get resentful or think that you are making favourites of your crew.'

'Even though I am?' Still, Cade felt indignant, it was true she had moved those of Vidar's branding mark who had supported her up into the Heights, but not exclusively, there were still plenty of groups she'd let stay.

'Yes. Like it or not, you are in charge up here, but you took the role by force. It would do no harm to show you are no better than any of them.'

But I am.

'Fine! Okay. I'll speak to Devlin.'

Meghan leaned across and kissed her cheek.

Cade closed her eyes. She wanted to speak to Devlin anyway, they had some planning to do. If they worked this right, Cade could see a rosy future. One in which they could start living topside, at least herself at any rate. Maybe Meghan and a few others. Hells below, she couldn't save everyone, right? Saving herself sounded like an excellent start.

CHAPTER FIVE – KILLEN

Killen was so pleased to be away from his camel, he was willing to suffer the pain four hard days riding was giving him. He raised his arse off the saddle and tried to stretch his muscles.

'How are you doing?' asked the Highlander, Larsen.

Killen whistled. 'Not going to lie, my sores have got sores.'

The older man grinned. 'You and me both.'

'I thought you were the horse master,' said Killen, gently settling back into the seat.

'Not really, I'm just one of the few who actually knows how to manage them,' said Larsen, leaning forward and rubbing the neck of his animal. 'Most of us have never owned a horse let alone ridden one. I was lucky, my father lived in one of the lower valleys, he kept a few and taught me how to ride and take care of them.'

'I suppose you all owned eagles,' said Killen staring into the distance.

'Hah!' barked Larsen, breaking into a laugh.

'What?'

'Is that what you think? We all got birds?'

Killen shrugged. 'I thought that's what you did.'

'And everyone in the Riverlands owns a vineyard, right?'

The man had a point. 'Alright, if you put it like that.'

'Most of us don't own eagles, either,' Larsen explained. 'That's reserved for the Riders. Don't get me wrong. I'm damned proud of them. But you can keep all that flying shit. It terrifies me.'

Killen had to agree with him. He was perfectly content to be on the ground and away from the smell of camel. His unit were making their own slow way towards the Highlands. The camels would find far more sustenance as they reached the borders but they'd still go at their own

Emperor-cursed pace. He leaned forward and patted the neck of his mount, a grey mare with a gentle disposition. They were covering ground at a speed the camels could never match, over territory far more suited to horses. This wasn't the Jebel or the sands of Erebesh, this was the foothills of the southwest Highlands and the lowlands of Celtebaria. Damn but it was good to see green again. He leaned back and gathered a skin, taking a sip of water. He replaced the skin and sat back.

'How much farther do you think?' he asked.

Larsen pulled at his ear and made a face.

'Depends. They were looking at hitting a gnome camp somewhere west of here before I headed out to find you. Most of our folk are on foot apart from the Riders. Might be the gnomes have moved on. The lad will find them.' He looked up and Killen followed his gaze. High above them an eagle described a wide circle. Damn but the kid must have some cast iron balls to do that. Apparently, he was Gifted to boot.

Killen thought again about the Eagle Rider who led these folk. This Owen lad had asked to meet with him, and Killen was happy to oblige, but he didn't really understand the urgency. Larsen was an affable companion but didn't have much to offer in the way of explanation. The best he could fathom was this bunch of Highlanders were conducting minor raids to protect their borders. That seemed like a risky undertaking, it drew attention to their existence, though Larsen claimed the gnomes couldn't be credited with over-thinking these things. Even so, he would counsel caution, they were in no fit state for any kind of military operations. Best to do what he and his were doing; hunker down for a few years and let the storm pass.

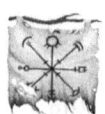

Four days later Killen realised maybe the storm wasn't going away. Jussi had spotted the columns of smoke first and had put down to point them in the right direction. As they made their way through the rolling wooded landscape, the scale of the skirmish started to worry him. Those smoke columns were mighty large. And a perfect marker for anyone who might want to investigate further.

'Looks like a scrap,' he commented, as he rode next to Larsen.

'Maybe,' agreed Larsen. 'Owen's probably burning the bodies. Might be one of their hunting camps, that means their shacks and such will be going up too.'

Killen shook his head. He had thought they were killing small parties of gnome hunters. Numbers that could be explained away or at least not provoke a significant response.

'How many gnomes in one of these camps?' he asked.

'Oh, depends. Usually twenty, thirty. Think there was one with fifty we hit a while back.'

Fifty? 'That's … audacious,' Killen commented.

'Audacious? Fancy word. Does it mean having big balls?'

Killen raised his hands. 'It just seems a bigger target than mere hunting parties.'

'Ah, the gnomes are vicious bastards, I give them that. But they spook easy too. We hit them hard and they tend to run. As long as you don't give them a chance to regroup. And the trick o'course is making sure none of them get away.'

Killen did not respond. This was definitely not what he had expected. This was a campaign. 'How many fighters did you say you've got on the ground?' he asked.

Larsen looked up and thought. 'About thirty of us. Depends on who is free, who we need back home, hunting parties and so on. We've pushed out a long way from the Rest and it takes a while to backtrack. And it depends on how many eagles we got with us. Owen's got them flying all hours and days. If they're not fighting with us they are scouting for camps or going further, looking for survivors. Like you.'

Thirty. If this crew have been doing this for a while, chances are they must be competent. Or very lucky.

'Casualties?' Killen asked.

'We've had a few. More than we can spare, less than we might have expected.'

Killen thought that an interesting perspective. 'And do you agree with the plan?' He kept his tone light, conversational. It was a leading question, but he needed to know what he was riding into.

'You want to know if we are a bunch of lunatics, right?'

Killen turned and saw Larsen looking right back at him with a wry smile. Obviously he was not as subtle as he thought. Might as well play it a little straighter then.

'The Highlands are that way,' he said, pointing. 'This is border country at best. For all I know we are in Celtebaria. It's a long way to go to keep your country safe.'

Larsen nodded.

'Yeah, I suppose you're right. Owen's got us out on a limb. But it's working and it ain't nothing we aren't willing to do. He's kept us together. Given everyone a sense o'purpose. He's just a little more driven than others.'

'I'm concerned you are over extending. If you stray too far from home, you might never make it back,' he advised.

'I reckon you lot might be able to help with that.'

'The war's over,' Killen stated.

'That depends on who you ask.'

Killen figured he already knew what the answer would be with these people. So be it. He would keep his counsel for the moment and see how the land lay.

They rode on in silence towards the smoke. He spotted circling birds just over the site, yet something struck him as odd. They were describing a very wide arc, some distance beyond the smoke. And their size … eagles then.

'Looking for survivors?' he asked.

'On the hunt. Could take a while. We have to be sure.'

Killen was pleased to hear it. Overhead Jussi passed by, keeping low. He raised a hand in greeting before he sped onwards.

The hunting camp, or what was left of it, was set amidst a cleared area just on the edge of a stand of trees. Killen spied three separate smouldering piles describing a crude triangle upon ground that was trampled, bare of earth and smoking in patches. One, the smallest, was a cookfire, with stones encircling the smoking embers. The second, the remains of a far larger fire, looked like a structure that had collapsed in on itself. The final was large again, lumps were piled upon each other and flames flicked over the shapes, struggling to maintain a constant burn even as black smoke curled upwards.

'Wind's a little fitful today,' said Larsen.

On cue, a gust blew against Killen. *Gods.* The smell! It was the scent of burnt meat, but merged with a sickly, disgusting odour like vomit.

'Not sure they smell better or worse when they are dead,' observed Larsen. He climbed off his horse and Killen followed suit. He stretched his back and sighed. Why did everything ache so much?

Two figures, two humans, appeared from the edge of the treeline and walked towards the fire. One, a female carried an unstrung bow in one hand. The other, a man, carried a gnome over his shoulder. Killen thought it looked like an adolescent child, its arms dangling freely behind the man's back: thin, a dirty mottled brown in colour and bearing several crude bracelets. The man, broad-shouldered and wild-haired, nodded at Larsen as he passed and unceremoniously dumped the gnome on top of its equally dead brothers. At least, Killen presumed it was dead.

'Alright, Larsen?' the man asked.

'Yeah. Not too bad, Skeet.'

The woman, perhaps in her mid to late twenties, stooped down and held the arrow head into the flames, only allowing its head to be kissed by the heat.

'Don't want their filthy blood staining my arrows,' she said defensively, noticing Killen watching her. She stood and tilted her head. 'Who's this?'

'Nice to see you too, Breege. New recruit,' said Larsen. 'Proper military man.'

Breege turned and spat into the flames. 'Didn't do too well in the war, though, did you?' She blew on the arrow and stuck it back into a bag hanging off her belt.

'Be nice. They had it as bad as the rest of us,' replied Larsen.

Killen had nothing else to add. He was not in a position to judge.

Breege gestured behind her. 'The others are still out hunting. They shouldn't be long.'

'Anyone hurt?' asked Larsen, dismounting.

'No. Another good day. Got a score of eighteen. A few more to come maybe.'

'Smaller group than usual,' observed Larsen.

'Maybe they're getting the message,' grinned Skeet.

'A good haul, then?' inquired Larsen.

Skeet, pointed towards a small group of pack animals and the piles of furs and a number of skinned and cured carcasses piled next to them. 'We were stacking these up when that one made a run for it. Thought we'd got them all.'

'Spoils of war,' said Larsen, indicating the goods. 'We'll take that back, always helps. We are growing after all.'

Killen watched the two men get to work loading their spoils. He imagined it would be a long trek.

'Hey, you want to sort your horse out?' Larsen asked Killen.

Killen looked over to where the man was unsaddling his mount. 'Oh. Yes, of course.' He got to work on releasing the cinches and straps and was dumping the saddle when his mare snorted, her head picking up as she took a few steps back.

He stood up and looked around. About fifty yards away an eagle was coming into land, taloned feet extending, and wings stretched wide as it touched down. He stepped close to his horse, placing a hand on its flank to try and calm it.

'She'll be alright,' advised Larsen. 'They are getting used to the fact the eagles aren't hunting them.'

'What about us?' muttered Killen.

Larsen snorted and carried on with rubbing down his horse.

Killen gathered up a handful of long grass and followed suit. He continued to watch the eagle and its Rider. They were taking their time, seemingly conducting a similar process to Killen. Finally, the Rider started walking their way, removing gloves and headgear as he approached and extending his right hand in greeting. It was a firm grip. Killen looked into the Rider's face. He was younger than he had expected. The skin was coloured, flushed a little and the beard was full but there was an obvious smoothness to the features. He looked into the eyes. There was warmth, and intelligence. And steel.

'Owen Derle,' said the Rider.

'Major Killen Roche, formerly of The Third Erebeshi Scouts.'

'It goes without saying but it's damned good to see you,' said Owen.

'Likewise. Though I had not expected to walk into a fight.'

'Sorry about that. We couldn't wait any longer, they were getting ready to leave.'

Killen rubbed the back of his neck. 'Larsen was telling me about your operations. You've been hitting the gnomes hard. And you are a long way from home. It looks to me that you are on a mission.'

Owen's glance flitted to Larsen, an unspoken moment of understanding. Killen appeared to have hit the mark on his assumption.

'Come and say hello to Arno.' Owen tilted his head towards the eagle. Killen nodded and fell into step. The walked in silence for a few moments.

'How was the journey here?' the younger man asked.

'Relentless.'

'Sore ass?'

'You have no idea.'

Owen nodded. 'That was my fault. I wanted to see you before I left.'

'Left?'

'I'm going to look for more survivors. My eagles are the best equipped for the search although there's not as many of those as I'd like.'

'And a lot of ground to cover. Your lad was lucky to find us. It was only because my scouts knew what they were looking at that we showed ourselves,' said Killen.

'That's the problem,' agreed Owen. 'I can send riders out and they could spend a lifetime without finding anyone.'

'Do you have any ideas where to look?'

'Some.' They drew close to the eagle. It turned its head in a swift motion to watch their approach. Owen stepped up to the bird and placed a hand against its neck. He looked at the bird's eye and it seemed to Killen they shared a moment. Owen looked back at him and smiled.

'Just introducing you. Major, meet Arno. The finest eagle in all of the Empire.'

Killen nodded at the bird. 'Pleased to meet you, Arno. Don't mistake me for prey, will you?'

Owen laughed. 'It's fine. He knows the difference and he remembers who my friends are.'

Killen smiled warily at the bird. *Good. Let's stay friends.* Last thing he wanted was those damned talons slicing into him. But if the bird ever fancied some camel …

Owen pulled his hand back and folded his arms. 'You are right, of course.'

Killen didn't always like being right. 'About …?'

'I'm not just protecting our home. It's more than that. I don't want the gnomes coming anywhere near us. They have to learn to fear the Highlands. To spread the word that it's haunted or that there are monsters or whatever story they come up with to explain their missing hunting parties.'

'And you leave no survivors. That way they have no idea that your people are behind this.'

'Exactly. As far as every other intelligent species is concerned, humanity is extinct. I want to keep it that way.'

'To what end?' As he asked, Killen took a step towards the eagle. In spite of himself he wanted to pet it. After all, would he ever get another chance? Owen nodded his understanding. 'Go ahead, Major. Arno won't bite.'

'It's not the biting I'm afraid of,' said Killen, resting his hand against

Arno's soft flank. He pressed a little, felt the power of the eagle, its steady breathing. He thought it would be a fragile thing. But there was nothing delicate about this creature.

'Major?'

'Yes?'

'I thought I was the only military left. That I would have to fight this war on my own.'

Killen raised an eyebrow. He had been right. 'We're still at war, are we?'

'Only because we have no choice.'

'You sure? Last I looked we were routed and our cities burned to ash. Don't get me wrong. I am pleased we have found your people and, trust me, I have no desire to end my days living in a cave in Erebesh. But fighting back won't end well for us; we simply don't have the numbers.'

Owen rocked back on his heels and sighed.

'I understand, and I get it. I want my home to survive. For my people to rebuild. And I want to find as many as I can to bring them home, to give them a future.' Killen noted the look in Owen's eyes. There was no warmth now, just the steel. 'But for us to do that, we have to be strong. We have to fight for our right to exist free from violence or persecution. The elves and the dwarves and all the rest of them took us apart and we barely scratched them. One day they will understand there is a price to pay.'

A price. Killen wondered just what that looked like, how large it would have to be.

'Rider Owen. I'll give you an example,' Killen said, using his most formal voice. He noticed Owen stood a little straighter. No bad thing, even if Killen really didn't consider the lad a soldier anymore. 'I have a camel. It is an ugly, mean-spirited bastard. It does what it likes when it likes and doesn't give a damn about me. And it attracts flies. Even in the Jebel. And you know what? The camel doesn't care. It really doesn't give a shit. It keeps chewing. And, a few days later that fly will be dead. And the camel keeps chewing,' Killen finished.

'I understand, Major. And I am not a fool. That is why I want the borders of the Highlands secured. Of all of Tissan, it is the most defensible. That's why so many of us survived the war, there are plenty of places to hide. But I want to do more than just survive, we need to thrive. To become strong. And when someone, someone more organised than gnome savages, comes visiting, they had better play nice. Or we will teach them a lesson they'll respect. The Empire thought itself better than everyone and never once thought about how the other races would react to that. We have to prove we are as worthy as any other race to exist. And those races respect only strength and violence.'

Killen closed his eyes. The lad spoke with emotion and passion. But he was advocating a continuance of the war. Was that something he wanted? Was he duty bound to fight for a dead emperor and an empire crumbled to dust? If not, could he even call himself a soldier anymore?

'Major. I want you to join us. But I can't make you. These people here are my family and they have all chosen to follow my lead. But I would never make any of them take up arms if they did not wish to. And I will not ask it of you and your soldiers. But, by the Emperor, you could really help,' he said, with a hopeful smile that showed his true age.

Killen puffed his cheeks and blew out the air loudly. He had really not expected to be reunited with fellow Tissans in such a manner. But then, what had he expected? The world had changed. He had just been ignoring that for the last year and was there really any going back? *Shit.*

'I'll need to speak to my soldiers. I'll not order them; they have the right to decide for themselves.' They had damn well earned it keeping his useless backside safe.

Owen nodded his assent. 'Fair enough. Thank you, Major.'

'Don't thank me yet,' he grumbled. 'I suppose I had better go find my troops.'

'Stay tonight. Rest up. We'll be cooking up one of those haunches.' That sounded good. Killen felt his mouth start to water. 'Larsen can go with you and lead you all into the Highlands. But I can't afford to send Jussi to find your soldiers.'

'It won't be an issue. They are Erebeshi scouts. They'll find us.'

Owen smiled. 'Very good, Major. Please excuse me, I have some Riders to wrangle. It is truly good to have met you.'

'Likewise, Rider,' replied Killen with a dip of his head. He watched the lad walk back to his eagle then returned to Larsen.

The man was sitting on the ground rubbing his bare feet. 'We heading out already?'

'Yes,' nodded Killen. 'Owen wants everyone heading south for a few hours until nightfall.'

'It's to make sure anyone tracking us doesn't think we are heading west.' Larsen pointed up. 'The eagles always hang back to see if anyone follows.'

Killen made an appreciative grunt. That was smart. The lad seemed to know his business. Killen corrected himself. The lad knew his business; otherwise he'd never have all these folks following his lead. 'Did any gnomes ever do that?'

Larsen scrunched his face in thought. 'Nope, nor anyone else either.' He tilted his head towards their grazing mounts. 'We'll wait for the others to get back; give our horses some more rest time and we'll walk 'em to wherever we set up camp.'

'Fine with me,' replied Killen. Larsen folded his arms and looked at him. 'What?'

'You going to stick with us?'

Killen opened his mouth to reply then stopped himself. Well, yes. For all his weighing up of Owen and his concerns about what his intentions were, it had never occurred to him that they wouldn't. After all, they were other people, and there was always strength in numbers. He realised Larsen was looking at him expectantly. Killen nodded.

Larsen gave him a thin smile. 'Good.'

'Good,' agreed Killen. *Yes. Good.* He supposed so, even if they were joining a war, and a small one at that. But he was still a soldier, what else was he going to do?

Owen pushed his way through the thick brush and found himself on the edge of a shallow sided bowl. At the bottom a small fire was blazing and the shadows danced and played against the wooded canopy surrounding it. It was good to see that even with friends nearby the Riders still practiced good concealment out in the wild. He worked his way down, using his spear as an aide. Though much of the soreness had gone, he favoured his other leg, and it was unlikely he'd ever be able to walk without a limp. It was a good thing he was made for fighting from a saddle.

Three others were waiting. Owen accepted a mug of tea, and cradled it with both hands, feeling the heat penetrate his gloves.

'Sorry we don't have anything stronger,' said Erskine.

'You're sorry,' muttered his brother Ernan. When Owen had first met him, he had gone clean-shaven but now sported a sharp pointing goatee, still quite refined when compared to his better-natured brother's shaggy growth.

Owen blew on the tea and took a sip. It was sweetened with honey, a luxury.

'We can hardly have young Jussi trying to keep his bird up if he's hungover, can we?' said Ernan.

'I've had stronger before now!'

'Ah, but you've never been drunk before,' pointed out Erskine.

'No, but–'

'Then trust me when I say you want to be somewhere warm and comfortable when you do,' advised Erskine.

'Being with *someone* warm and comfortable would also help,' added Ernan.

Owen didn't need night vision to know the heat coming from Jussi's cheeks had nothing to do with the fire. It reminded him how young the lad was. *But not that young.*

'Fat chance of that with your ugly face,' observed Erskine.

Owen sipped the tea and listened to the banter. It was something he had grown up with as an Eagle Rider, a lifetime ago. He remembered Cadarn sitting back, as the ritual abuse did the rounds, allowing his squadron the chance to relax, to bond. Owen could still see in his mind's eye Bryce laying into Harwen about something the lad had done wrong, Jenna laughing and telling Bryce to stop being such a grumpy old bastard. Now he was in Cadarn's place, and he let his Riders prattle on for a while longer.

His Riders, such as they were. Of the three only young Jussi was Gifted, but at least the brothers had worked hard to build a relationship with their birds, and they shared a natural familial shorthand which helped them coordinate in the sky. The test would come when they had to fight together, when they faced a swarm of buzzers. Owen had done what he could to prepare them, by matching them against Jussi and himself. Their ability to talk to their birds and each other had beaten the brothers every time. Even when they tried to bully Jussi, Arno and Owen were always able to take them out before they could catch the lad. Still, there was much to be taught from understanding why they were defeated, as long as they were willing to learn it.

There was one member of his small squadron missing: Anneli was on station at Eagle's Rest. She and her eagle, Taru, had taken longer to gel and he did not want her ranging as far. The eagle may have training, but Anneli was not Em. And the eagle remembered. Perhaps they may never work. The time was coming soon to decide, if he was any judge.

Owen finished the tea and handed the cup back to Ernan, all of them falling silent, waiting for him to speak.

'Were there any problems today?' he asked.

Ernan made a face. 'We're all still here, aren't we?'

Owen closed his eyes. Gods, but the man made it difficult.

'I spotted some manticores,' offered Jussi.

'Did they see you?' asked Owen.

'I don't think so. I kept high, like you told me.'

Owen shook his head. 'You have to be sure. We can't afford any mistakes. If they track you, they find us. If they track us, they find Eagle's Rest. You all know better than that.'

'Sorry, Owen.'

Ernan made a face. 'Since when has a manticore ever chased? They're lazy sons of bitches.'

'Since when have you ever got close to one?' countered his brother.

'Just remember, all of you, we don't get second chances.' Owen left it at that. Ernan was probably right. Manticores would have gone for the easy kill, but that wasn't the point. They had to play this smart. They had to be sure. 'Alright. Let's recap on the search, again.' He had been over this before but he wanted it straight.

'I found nothing to the north,' said Erskine.

'How far did you go?' asked Owen.

'Brevis. Not much left of it mind, just a shell.' Erskine leaned forward and retrieved the pot suspended above the flames and poured out a measure of the tea into Owen's empty mug.

Owen nodded. He looked at Ernan.

'I went west to the river, like you said. Nothing.'

Owen nodded and tried to keep his frustration in check. They had to do better.

'I found the soldiers!' added Jussi.

'Yes, we know,' said Erskine, landing a punch on Jussi's upper arm.

'Ow!' complained the lad.

'Good work, Jussi, well done,' said Owen. Jussi beamed his triumph at the brothers. Soldiers. The first they had found. And if one group had been hiding out in the Jebel, there could be others. 'Jussi, tomorrow I want you to follow me home. Resupply, rest up, and then the next day I want you heading back towards Erebesh again. Go straight for the high country. Just conduct a search for as long as you can. But don't expose yourself, or run out of supplies. Keep safe, and try to avoid any manticores, alright?'

'Yes, Owen. I won't let you down.'

Owen nodded. 'I know you won't.'

'What about us?' asked Erskine.

'The lands directly to the west are empty, the cities to the north laid waste. That shouldn't be a surprise, their armies rolled right through that territory and it was the most populated.' He had hoped they might find people scavenging in the ruins, but there was nothing left to scavenge. The enemy had seen to that.

'Then where are we going to look?' asked Ernan.

'Jussi here had the right idea,' replied Owen. 'We have to push out further, out to the edges of the world. When they destroyed Aberpool there was nowhere else for them to hit, but there were still thousands of leagues of coastline, countless forests, and tracts of wilderness that they wouldn't have bothered with. The cities and settlements are the wrong places to search, the enemy focussed on them, we've proved that now.'

'We do what we did with the Highlands,' said Ernan.

'Yes, we scour the valleys and the forests and the mountains.'

'It's gonna take a long time to do that. There's a lot of ground to cover,' said Erskine, picking at his teeth.

'Are you two provisioned?' asked Owen, ignoring Erskine's remarks.

'Yes, we both swung by Eagle's Rest before coming here,' said Ernan.

'Good. I'm loath to say it but I need one of you to push on and head to the far northeast, head for the Plains. The folk there were mobile, it's possible some got away from the initial advances into Tissan.'

'I'll do it,' stated Erskine.

'And me?' asked Ernan.

'Angle southwest, head for the water separating Erebesh from the Riverlands, then follow the coastline. When you hit Aberpool head back. I'm going directly west then turning for Scotia. It was a long time ago, but that was the last time I saw anyone outside of the Highlands making a fist of it.'

'Are you sure you should be heading out yourself?' asked Erskine.

'It's not as if we have Riders to spare, is it? Murtagh has the Rest in hand. There's nothing else I can do for now, other than looking for ways to make us stronger.'

'I thought we were entering the campaigning season,' said Jussi.

'There's no such thing as a season anymore, Jussi,' replied Owen. 'We need to work hard all day, every day if necessary.'

'Those are some journeys you are asking us to take,' said Ernan.

'Good thing I bought my hunting bow,' said Erskine.

'There's nothing else for it. We'll meet at home. Make it eight weeks from now,' said Owen.

'Fair enough. What about those Erebeshi?' asked Ernan.

'Jussi and I will let Murtagh know he's going to have guests. He can arrange a welcome party.'

'It's good news, us getting some real soldiers back into the fight,' said Erskine.

'I'll drink to that,' said Ernan, withdrawing a small leather flask from the folds of his cloak.

'Hey! You said you didn't have anything!' protested Erskine.

'I never *said* anything, you idiot,' said Ernan. 'Now do you want some or not?'

'Can I?' asked Jussi.

Ernan raised his eyebrow at Owen. He shrugged. *Why not?* Ernan graced him with a wolfish grin and took a pull before passing it to his brother who in turn gave it over to Jussi who took a healthy swig and almost spat it out again.

'That's not ale!'

'It's Murtagh's special spirit.'

'It's horrible!'

'You'll grow to like it,' laughed Ernan.

Owen waved the proffered flask aside. Murtagh's wife, Jenni, had warned Owen very early on of Murtagh's attempts at distilling. He wasn't in the mood to deal with a hangover, despite the good news. A success on their first proper scouting mission beyond the Highlands; better than they could have hoped for. Eagle's Rest had thus far gathered a host of scattered survivors, found by a systematic search of their homeland, flying in pairs over sections of the high country. Larsen and Saul were still leading parties into the deeper valleys looking for any still out there. The winter months had been hard and he'd had the brothers to train and he had been tempted to keep searching in pairs; there was safety in having a second pair of eyes. But time was moving on and they needed to cover more ground. He needed as many people who could contribute as possible. Spring was making its way towards summer and he wanted to be ready for their first offensive.

CHAPTER SIX – FILLION

'Sabin!'

Captain Sabin Fillion , last survivor of the Tissan Imperial Scouts, looked up from his desk. 'Hedra? What are you doing here? How did you get in here? I thought Parliament didn't allow youngsters inside.'

The younger elf, his brother in marriage, grinned.

'It pays to be my father's son.'

'I suppose so,' admitted Fillion. 'And you don't have to toil here in your father's office every day to get it.'

'Exactly,' laughed Hedra. 'You are welcome to this job. I have no interest in it.'

'Are you telling me that you are not following your father into politics?'

'Why would I want to? It's boring. No, you can do all that stuff now you are family. Me? I'm for the army.'

'Really? Where has this come from?'

'All thanks to you, Sabin. You inspired me.'

Bullshit.

'I don't think I was ever an inspirational warrior,' Fillion said.

'I wouldn't know about that, Sabin. You never talk about it. I was referring to how diligently you have applied yourself to the task of Servant. You'll be a Member next.'

'The Gods forbid!' cried Fillion, throwing up his hands.

'Anyway, all the late nights and paperwork and politicking. You can keep it. I want a more exciting life.'

'And you think you'll find that in the army? Who are we at war with? You missed it.' *At least for now.*

Hedra put his hands on hips. 'You should listen to father more. He has plenty to say about that sort of thing.'

'Oh I know.' Fillion was sure his father-in-law, Patiir, would have a great deal to say. He stood up and stretched. 'Anything else I can do for you?'

'Oh me? Nothing. But my sister wants a word with you.'

Fillion raised an eyebrow. 'My wife's here?'

'Hardly! She is so big with your child, she can barely stand.'

'She'd smack you if she heard that.'

Hedra grinned and turned to leave. 'See you at home, brother.'

Fillion shook his head and puffed his cheeks in mock frustration. He sat down and closed his eyes. Damn it but he was tired. He opened his eyes and looked at the documents laid out before him. The words swam, his vision blurred. Time was running out and he hadn't achieved one fucking thing. Nothing to show for his efforts other than marrying a damned elf and siring another one of them – quite literally sowing the seed of his own potential discovery if it was born displaying its human heritage. If this was his attempt at gaining revenge he was doing one poor fucking job.

He had maybe six weeks of freedom left and was no closer to working out how he was going to bring the elven kingdom down. It was just too big a task for one man. He wasn't a politician, he wasn't a schemer; he was just a soldier. Increasingly his thoughts turned to a far simpler plan. He now had unfettered access to the Parliament and the Members and their staff. He could, if he wished, embark on one glorious day of violence. It would be easy to take down one of the guards, steal his weapons and armour and march bold as brass into the Chamber. He was sure he could wreak havoc among the cream of elven politics, sending a shockwave through the Homelands. They'd take him down soon enough, but before they did he would die shouting 'For Tissan and the Emperor!' The vision helped calm his nerves, brought him a small moment of pleasure. Yes, that would be some moment. But it would be a short-lived act. The guards and mages would soon bring him down and the Parliament would recover, replacing their dead members with other worthies. And they would commemorate the day and clap each other on the back for being right about the barbarous humans, and wasn't it good that they had all been exterminated. Fillion sighed. If it came to it, he would do it rather than risk discovery and execution. But he mustn't give up hope. And things were not as bad as they appeared. He just happened to be related by marriage to one of the most influential Members in living memory (which was long for an elf), the actual elf who had instigated the genocide in the first place. He was his trusted Servant, husband to his daughter. That was impressive in anyone's book. *Right, get over yourself and get to work.* He stood, gathered up the sheets in front of him and placed them into the satchel hanging off his chair. He looked towards the closed door of his father-in-law's private office. The Member had meetings elsewhere and would not be returning today. He stepped out on to the main concourse and shut the outer door. There was no lock. There was no need. This was the Parliament of the elves. The might enjoy the cloak and dagger of politics but they never condescended to outright skulduggery, a fact that Fillion kept close to his heart. There might well come a time he could use that against them.

He walked along the concourse towards the entrance, nodding at acquaintances and colleagues. The hour was late and the building was almost empty. Parliament itself was in recess and many Members had already returned to their home estates in outlying provinces. Fewer of the Servants who continued to maintain the administration of government bustled about. He would have liked to go for a drink, but Kanyay had already returned home to his people in the east, and without him, Fillion would end up having to deal with the other patrons of The Silver Chalice alone. It would only sour his mood. Instead he made straight for home, hurrying along the parade. He heard the night dirges from the Temple echo through the warm air. The low male tones intermingled with lighter, female ones, mixing and swirling around each other, creating a hypnotic sound, so unlike the loud, bright prayers of the Imperial religion. Fillion breathed deep, the warm evening air helping to divert his thoughts. If he ignored where he was, it could even have been a pleasant evening.

A short time later he entered the house and made straight for the inner courtyard. As expected, Nadena was reclining in a large wicker chair, gazing at the water fountain that was the centrepiece of the courtyard. A large whiskered fish wound its way around the central pole hunting a smaller fish. The water erupted around both, giving a frantic, dynamic feel to the hunting scene. It struck Fillion as something of a metaphor, though it may well have escaped his elven family. He walked quietly behind Nadena, leaning in close to kiss her cheek.

'I can hear you,' she said with a mock-stern tone.

He closed the distance, placing his lips on her skin for a moment, and moved round to face her. She was wearing her hair loose about her shoulders and was dressed in a simple white shift – a tradition among pregnant elven women. Her hands moved slowly over her stomach, the bulge pressing against the fabric. She smiled up at him warmly.

'You need to stop working so late,' she chided.

Fillion crouched before her and placed a hand on the bump.

'I'm trying to get the hours in now so maybe your father might let me enjoy the birth of our child.'

'I think you know him better than that. Even so, I want you here.'

'Yes, mistress,' Fillion said, bowing his head.

'That's better.'

Fillion stood and helped himself to the decanter of iced water.

'Talking of which, I was speaking to father today,' she said.

'Uh-huh.'

'We are leaving for the estate the day after tomorrow for the summer. Father is keen that you come with us; he is anxious you do not miss the birth.'

How very gracious of him.

'So I don't have to stay here?'

'The privilege of marriage to me, my love.'

Fillion leaned forward and kissed her again. He had not been sure what Patiir would have him do. If they were away from the capital and their child was born a human, he would lose the opportunity to act.

A male voice behind him. 'Sabin?'

Fillion turned around to see Rabi standing respectfully behind them. 'Yes, Rabi?'

The master would like to speak to you. He is in his study.

'Very well, thank you, Rabi.' He watched the old retainer disappear and turned back to his pregnant wife. 'Your father calls me,' he said.

Nadena reached out a hand and he took it.

'When you are finished talking, can you persuade him to come to dinner.'

'We'll be there.'

He let go and walked back into the house proper, heading for the east wing. At the end of the corridor Patiir's study door was closed, though as he drew near he could hear voices within. He paused to listen, and recognised the gruff tones of Marmus, the dwarf ambassador. An unlikely late night visitor but no doubt he would still be all business, dressed as he always was in his trademark brown robe of office and his wide leather belt embossed with the geometric shapes that marked the dwarf style. He knocked.

'Come in,' came Patiir's muffled response.

Fillion opened the door to find Patiir sitting behind his desk and Marmus to one side, dressed as he had envisaged.

'Come in, Sabin, shut the door,' said Patiir.

Fillion joined Marmus and nodded a greeting.

'Ambassador, it is good to see you.'

The dwarf returned the nod, his usual scowl in place. Despite the fierce shrewdness behind his eyes, Fillion doubted that this dwarf elder realised the extent to which Patiir distrusted him. 'Sabin,' he growled back.

'Sabin, I have been discussing some trade and business matters with our honoured guest,' said Patiir. 'As you probably know, we are returning to our estate for the summer recess, but the Parliament is keen to continue cementing our new trade relationships. To that end, a deputation has been asked to travel north to inspect some of the new mine-workings that have opened up since the end of the war.'

'I see,' said Fillion. In truth he had no idea where this was going.

'I have been tasked with selecting the members of that deputation. I would like you to go.'

Oh.

'In fact, the Ambassador was most pleased when I suggested you.'

Fillion looked at the dwarf, who tilted his head in acknowledgement.

'I am honoured, truly. But what of Nadena and the child?'

Patiir raised a placating hand.

'Sabin, I understand. It pains me to risk you being absent for the birth of your first child and I know that Nadena will not be happy. But I cannot afford to go and in my stead must go someone trusted and valued. The dwarfs would expect nothing less, is that not so, Ambassador?'

'Aye, quite so,' the dwarf agreed.

Patiir smiled reassuringly. 'Nadena will remain at the estate with her sister as company when I return to Parliament. It is my hope that this will be a short trip. If it goes well you will be back in less than three months, just in time for the birth. Believe me, the Ambassador and I are in agreement that this is nothing more than an exercise in due diligence. I am sure our dwarf friends are conducting their affairs as … honourably as they have always done.'

Fillion was filled with conflicting emotions. There was every chance he would be caught and imprisoned if the babe was born human. He could use this chance to escape, to accept the fact that, despite his best efforts, no plan he could come up with was going to work. But neither had he come this damned far to just give up. It took every ounce of control for Fillion to maintain a straight face but he had no choice but to accept the assignment. He bowed low and said, 'Then I will do so gladly, I am honoured to be asked.'

'Thank you, Sabin. You are a good Servant and by representing the interests of the Parliament in this matter you do our house a great service,' said Patiir, smiling indulgently. 'If you will be so good as to see the Ambassador out, you and I can discuss the details of the trip after dinner. You will be leaving tomorrow.'

'Of course.' Fillion opened the door and ushered the Ambassador through. Together they walked in silence, through the house and out into the entrance courtyard.

'Just so you know, I asked for you. Patiir just agreed,' said Marmus.

Fillion raised an eyebrow.

'Really?'

The dwarf shrugged.

'I'm heading back with you. Affairs of state have to be attended to and I have got to report back to the Council. If I have to share the road with an elf, I'd rather have one I can at least tolerate enough to have a drink with.'

Fillion took that as high praise indeed. He had cultivated a relationship with the dwarf over drinks at The Silver Chalice facilitated by an introduction by the wood elf Kanyay. The three of them all outsiders, drawn together for support; not that they knew the truth of it as far as Fillion was concerned.

'Are we taking ale with us, then?' asked Fillion with a smile.

'We better bloody be,' grunted Marmus. He stood by the gateway and inspected Fillion. 'Get yourself some proper travelling gear. It's hardy country where we are heading, not all pretty forests and the like. But, if you are lucky, when we get back to my lands, you'll get a chance to drink some proper beer.' With that, Marmus headed off into the dusk.

Fillion closed his eyes and took a moment to take stock and move beyond his conflicting thoughts of earlier. He was going to the Dwarf Nations. This was unexpected. He had to embrace the opportunity it offered. If he were to do well during this trip, it would further cement his reputation. It all had to head towards that. If he could prove just how invaluable he was then surely an audience with the King became that much more possible. There was just the one small matter of the pregnancy. Always that.

'Sabin.'

Sabin turned. It was Patiir.

'Are you well?' the elf asked.

Fillion forced a sigh.

'Sorry, I find myself a little tired today.'

'Then it is the right time for us to take a break from the city,' replied Patiir. 'Come, let us go to dinner.' He beckoned Fillion to join him and placed an arm around his shoulder. 'There is another reason I wish you to go.'

'Oh?'

'It has come to my attention that the dwarves are using humans to work their mines.'

Fillion stopped in his tracks.

'What?'

Patiir lowered his arm and looked at him gravely. 'I understand your shock. I felt the same thing when I discovered this. If this proves to be true then it concerns me greatly. It was never part of the terms of our alliance. The dwarves were welcome to any wealth and goods they could acquire from the campaign and the humans were to be wiped out. That was the agreement.'

'How could they have hidden this from us?'

'When the war ended we withdrew quickly. There was no need for us to remain; we had no interest in booty. It was left to the dwarves, gnomes and our other allies to scour over the remains, to seek out those last pockets of human life and eliminate them. If they chose to hold humans captive, it would have been possible to hide this from us.'

Humans left? Working for the dwarves? Fillion had started to believe he was the only one left.

'And what do I do if that this is the case?'

Patiir folded his arms.

'This trip is genuine. You are there to inspect the mines and their produce. If you see any signs of human labour, do not acknowledge that they have strayed from their agreement, but return and report to me any truth in this matter. I will relay this information to the Parliament, to the King himself. The dwarves will no doubt feign outrage and deny all knowledge, but raise it with them we will.'

'And what will we do?'

'That much should be clear, Sabin. We will demand that the dwarves act in good faith and respect the spirit of our original terms. We will demand they put down every single human they have in their employ. We cannot risk them building some kind of slave population, breeding them as a workforce. Because, believe me Sabin, I wouldn't put it past them if it profits them to do so.' Patiir leaned in close and studied Fillion. 'Sabin, you have gone quite pale.'

'Forgive me … It's just … I thought it was all over.'

Patiir reached out and squeezed his shoulder, a fatherly act. 'I understand. I too had thought we had put this unpleasantness behind us. It is alright, we will deal with this in due course. Come, let us eat.'

Fillion allowed himself to be guided inside. Once more his mind was in turmoil. Humans, maybe hundreds of them. There was no way would he assist in their final annihilation. He could never betray his own kind. In fact, Patiir had just handed him a gift.

CHAPTER SEVEN – MICHAEL

'We are heading home.'

Father Michael looked up from his bowl of stew. 'Home, Your Grace?'

'Yes, I believe it is time,' said the Emperor, thoughtfully stroking his beard. It had grown thicker in the course of their mission and gave him a nobler visage.

'Home to Tissan?'

The Emperor laughed and shook his head.

'Not quite yet, Father Michael, though I am pleased you are so keen to return. No, we are heading back to New Tissan. We have been gone far too long and I wish to speak to my Council in person. There is only so much progress to be made via missives carried by Riders. No offence, Leader Cadarn,' said the Emperor quickly.

'None taken, Your Grace' said Cadarn, placing his bowl down and warming his hands over the fire in the Emperor's tent where the three men were taking their evening meal.

'We have so much to do and I wish to be on hand to inspect the ongoing construction of the fleet.'

'That is good news, sire,' agreed Father Michael.

'And what of the Nidhal?' asked Cadarn.

'I have consulted with Nutaaq. Most of the tribes have been contacted and are sending representatives to the gathering. We already have an accord with several of the largest tribes and Nutaaq believes the others will agree to put aside any differences for the greater good. I will speak to them two days from now. If all goes well then I propose we leave the day after that.'

'All of us?' asked Cadarn.

The Emperor paused a moment. 'I was of a mind to take us all back, but now you ask the question, do you believe there is value in retaining a presence here?' he asked.

'It would make sense, Your Grace. This fledgling alliance needs to be nurtured. But who would we keep?'

'What do you think, Father?'

Father Michael rubbed his chin. It appeared to him a simple answer. 'There really is only one person who can do that. The Speaker, Ellen.'

Cadarn nodded his agreement.

'You are right, of course,' said the Emperor. 'I must admit that even after all these months, much of their language escapes me. I have little aptitude for it.'

'Whereas Speaker Ellen has proven to be most adept,' said Father Michael. He had learned a little Nidhal in his time among them. His years in the arena had exposed him to all the cultures of the Empire and their mother tongues so he was used to picking up the basics quickly, but Ellen was a natural linguist.

'Yes, she has proven to be a valuable member of our expedition. Father Michael, would you be so kind as to find the Speaker and bring her to me?'

'Of course, Your Grace.'

Father Michael pushed himself up and exited the tent, his mind full of thoughts about returning to New Tissan civilisation. He considered how simply they had lived on the expedition west, the thick, animal-hide shelters provided by the Nidhal had made the Tissans far more comfortable than they had expected to be when they set out, but nothing compared to an actual roof, or a soft bed. He walked through their small camp where the main cookfire blazed merrily. Young Uther trotted past, heading for the pot.

'Shall I get you another bowl, Father?' he asked. 'The Emperor asked me to fetch more so it's no trouble.'

'Thank you,' said Father Michael. 'I'll be back in a moment.'

He nodded to Bryce, who sat outside his tent making repairs to a leather harness. Behind him, Father Michael could make out the crude wooden shelter that had been erected to house their two eagles. One appeared to be asleep while the other was preening its wings. On the far side of the camp, the Gifted had two larger tents erected. Several of them were sitting outside, gathered around their own smaller fire.

'Father Michael,' called Eilion.

Father Michael approached them and placing his hands into the wide arms of his robes, he nodded politely. It was the best he could muster. Six months with this man had done nothing to modify Father Michael's low opinion of him.

'I am looking for Speaker Ellen.'

'She is not here, I am afraid. Have you seen her, Mercer?'

The big Gifted, another Shaper, shrugged.

'She does have a habit of wandering off,' sighed Eilion, shaking his head. 'I would suggest you head over to our Nidhal hosts, you might find her there.'

Father Michael bowed his head again and turned to leave, but something about Eilion's tone stopped him.

'You don't approve?' he asked.

Eilion raised an eyebrow.

'She would be better served spending time with her fellow Gifted, developing her skills, learning how to fight. Instead she spends it mixing with the Nidhal.'

'She is obeying the Emperor's wishes,' said Father Michael, forbiddingly. What more needed to be said?

Eilion tilted his head in acknowledgment. 'You are right, of course, Father. I am over-protective of our young sister; she has so much to learn.'

Father Michael bowed his head and left the group. Not for the first time he wondered at the Gifted and their ways. Such arrogance was unseemly. But, for a time, in his own way, he had been just as arrogant, believing he was better than everyone else. And, in his own small world, fighting in the arena, he had been.

He left the camp and made his way across to the larger settlement of

Nidhal. It was growing even bigger now, as more and more arrived in preparation for the gathering. Dozens of fires blazed against the dusk light, and the hubbub of hundreds of voices drifted across to him. He spied a figure walking towards him, its dark form framed against the firelight. As he drew closer, he saw the figure wore a robe, the hood down, and was shorter and slenderer than he. The figure stopped and raised a hand in greeting.

'Father Michael, I knew it was you,' said Ellen. 'Have you come to speak with the Nidhal?'

'The Emperor sent me to find you.'

She reached him and slipped her arm through his, turning them around. If it had been anyone else but her he would have flinched away, but he had grown quite fond of her and tolerated the physical contact.

They walked back to the camp in silence for a few moments.

'So why does the Emperor want to see me?' asked Ellen.

'Ah, it is not my place to–'

'Let me guess. He is going to ask me to stay here when you all leave?'

Father Michael looked down on her in surprise. 'How did you know?'

'Oh, it's not hard, Father. I know the Emperor has been planning to return home and it makes perfect sense to leave someone behind to maintain our relationship with the Nidhal. And who else can speak their language so well?'

'Your Gift is your burden,' he acknowledged.

'It's no burden,' she said, tapping his arm. 'Just as yours is not.'

'My gift?'

'Don't think I haven't been watching your bouts. I'm no expert but you are proving a match for your formidable opponents.'

'It's just a way of keeping sharp,' he muttered. In truth he had started to look forward to his time training with the Nidhal. The braves who came to see him spar appeared to enjoy watching him fight and some had even started to place bets on him to win. Old memories were re-emerging of his time before his conversion, when he had been at his most brutal, most savage best. He believed the Nidhal could see that in him. That was good. He had grown soft since their departure from Tissan. 'I need to be ready if the Emperor needs me.'

'And it sends a message to the Nidhal. They can see they are dealing with people who know how to handle them. They'll think twice before trying anything.'

Father Michael stopped. So she had the same concerns as him? Ellen was looking up and smiling at him, that twinkle in her eye. He shook his head. *My but she was a smart one. What on earth did she see in him?*

'Also, and don't you dare tell anyone this,' she said, her face serious, 'I've been getting Corporal Fenner to put bets on you for me. Most of the other Gifted are either sitting out or betting against you. So I'm having to keep it quiet.'

Let me guess, Eilion.

'You shouldn't be betting at all,' he chided her. 'You are Gifted and I am a member of the Imperial Church. It is beneath our dignity.'

'Yes, Father, of course.' She squeezed his arm. 'And this isn't the arena.'

It was not. That time had passed. They arrived at the Emperor's tent and Father Michael stood to one side to allow Ellen in.

'Just keep winning,' she whispered, before she entered the cool interior.

Keep Winning? He had never lost.

CHAPTER EIGHT – OWEN

The cityport of Aberpool. Owen circled high above it, looking down on the remains of the last city to fall in the war. He hadn't been back since the day of that final rout and had not known what to expect: perhaps nothing more than bleak, lifeless rubble. Yet from up here he could see that the walls still stood. Within, he could still easily trace the routes of the main streets marked by the structures that helped define the layout of the city. He bid Arno make a slow circling descent. The wind was blowing in from the sea and with it came the sound of crashing waves. The call of birds, hunting and diving among the waves, added to the ambient noise, their circling and wheeling echoing that of Arno. Life. And yet directly below him, he expected none. Owen kept his eyes scanning the horizon, mindful that an attack could come from any direction. He remembered their terrifying escape over the city, hunted by gryphons. And the rescue of that burly priest they'd found on a roof. Did he make it to the ships? Did they get away? Maybe they did, maybe they didn't. Who knew what was beyond the far oceans?

As they spiralled lazily, Owen recognised familiar landmarks: the Council Hall, the Roosting Tower next to it, the main square, the prison. All of them built of solid, thick stone, though they were surrounded by angular spaces where adjoining wooden structures had been destroyed in the firestorm. He could pick out the districts that could afford that more robust construction. The wealthier merchants' quarter appeared the most intact, and a number of the harbour properties. Of the rest of the city, there were whole swathes of empty ground punctuated by surviving buildings. Nothing remained of the Rookery, not even ash. He pulsed to Arno to take a wide turn out to sea, the wind now buffeting his face and ears so it drowned out all other sounds. Then another turn and a long run back toward the city, giving them the best chance of spotting and reacting to any enemy presence.

Arno took them in on a slow, low glide, the sun sparkling off the sea as they sped past. Owen watched a shoal of fish zigzag under the water, light glinting off their scales. Behind them a group of dolphins chased, their fins rising and dropping, slicing through the water. As they cruised over the harbour, the spaces enclosed within the moles were empty. Once across the wharf, they were into the city proper. Owen tensed, alert and ready for a fight, but with so few buildings left standing, Arno had plenty of room to manoeuvre and there were no signs of any potential dangers. They swept past the Roosting Tower – or what was left. It had been reduced to perhaps a half of its size; the top taken off by some kind of blast or missile, a pile of rubble surrounding its base.

On reaching the square, Arno extended his claws and flared his wings, touching down in a field of green. Owen unwound his face scarf and looked around in surprise. Everywhere the ground was covered in plant life: weeds, flowers and tall grass pushed their way up through the gaps in the cobbles and amidst the piles of detritus. Elsewhere vines and creepers were establishing themselves in the shells of the standing buildings. Owen shook his head. *Life goes on.* Even in this silent tomb.

Owen took his feet out of the long stirrups and swung down on to the ground. Collecting his crossbow, he took a moment to load it. A rustling noise from the undergrowth made him stand to, his weapon raised. Arno swept his head round, keen eyes centring on the source of the sound. A large striped cat bounded out of some nearby bushes, startling him. It had a mouse clamped in its jaws and stared at him warily for a moment before stalking off to enjoy its prize. Owen exhaled through his nostrils and eyed Arno, shaking his head. *You can let that one go.*

Keeping his finger on the trigger, he walked over to the central structure, a large stone platform, which like everything else was draped in green. Yet amidst the growth was a huge pile of bones, yellowed, pitted and in many cases broken. It was only on the top of the platform that he could see whole or partial skeletons, with arms, heads, ribcages still held roughly together. Yet more bones spread around the platform and beyond. Not far from his feet what looked like an arm bone lay by itself on a bed of weeds. He walked over and knelt. The bone was chipped and marked with irregular indentations. It had been gnawed upon. Owen stood up straight.

'We're still here!' Owen shouted. 'You bastards. We're still here!'

His voice echoed across the square. A small flock of birds burst from hiding, taking to the sky, the sounds of their flapping carrying clearly to him. And then silence returned. Owen waited. Willing something to emerge.

Nothing did.

He returned to Arno.

He took them north, tracing the route they had followed on that last night, over a year and a half ago. They flew over the beaches where thousands had tried to reach the ships lying out at sea, where small craft, almost capsizing, saved who they could; and where those thousands remaining had been driven by the advancing dwarf warriors into the water to drown. Then he was among the sandy bluffs and hillocks overlooking the beach, and from there he and Arno turned northwest, heading into the wilds beyond, hoping to recall the landmarks before him, trying to pinpoint the valley where Gerat and his people had been holed up. Yet it had been so long ago that none of it looked familiar. Owen chewed his lip. What had he been expecting? This was never going to be easy. *Alright, Arno. Time for you to hunt.*

That night they made camp in a cavern in the side of a hill. Though it was summer, it was still damp and cool within, so they kept to just under the lip of the cavern where it was dry and allowed them a decent launch position if need be. The night was warm and they needed no campfire. Arno was happy with his freshly caught rabbits and Owen had his trail rations. Chewing on a piece of dry-smoked meat, he walked outside and looked up at the cloud-streaked, darkening sky. He picked up a stick and used his foot to clear a bare patch of earth. Hunkering down he scratched out a crude map of the coastline and country. Once done, he drew a series of parallel lines running west to east and then another set running north to south. He had to get more precise in his search method so he had to apply some common sense. Using the grid, he situated his own approximate position in relation to the key landmarks and started to reason out the route he had taken. Finally he was satisfied that he had put together a sensible search plan. The sky was growing darker, it was time to bed down. He patted Arno on his flank before he settled. *You get first watch*. The eagle cocked his head and blinked. Knowing Arno would keep him safe, he was soon out like a light.

On the second day of his search he found what he had been looking for, the old steading and barn, the place he had first met Gerat and his people. Flying low, heading west to east, he cut across the valley, covering the ground in seconds, barely registering the building to his left before he was beyond it. Arno banked to the right and Owen took them on a slow run up the valley, landing next to the large barn. If anyone was here, he wanted to announce his presence without any preamble. He was willing to take the risk that a non-human had taken up residence. He leaned back in his saddle and took his time to look around. The steading looked even more worse for wear than last time, which was understandable, but the barn was in a better state. He studied the trees that flanked it closely on either side, waiting for any hostiles to emerge, knowing Arno would likely spot something before he did. After a minute, it was clear that nothing or no one was coming. He dismounted, loaded his crossbow and made his way cautiously to the barn. The door was closed but unbarred. He opened it and stood just outside the threshold peering around, waiting for his eyes to adjust to the gloom. A low wall of hay bales faced him. He waited a moment. Nothing. He stepped inside and made his way past the hay barricade. Above his head cobwebs obscured the roof, a few lacklustre beams of light coming through holes in the planks. He hunkered down and played a hand over the bare ground. There were tracks of footprints all over, but there was no way of knowing how long ago they were made. On the left-hand side of the barn was the cattle pen and some stalls for horses. Owen walked over to look inside them. Rusty hooks lined the wall beside him and he absently raised a hand to run his fingers over the metal. Flakes came off at the touch.

'Never thought we'd see you again.'

Owen jerked back and raised his bow as a man emerged from the far stall and faced him, his appearance obscured in the shadows.

'Likewise,' replied Owen.

'You can drop that bow, unless you intend to shoot me,' the man offered.

Owen did so and the man, dressed all in furs, stepped forward out of the shadows. Owen saw changes in him; the wild hair was familiar but the beard was now streaked with grey. A vague smile played on the man's lips. Owen also noted the long hunting knife at his belt, the expected hand axe to his side. He carried a spear, but leant on it as a prop.

'Good to see you again, Gerat,' said Owen.

'We spotted you two days ago, to the north of here. You were too far away for me to be sure, but being as we don't see many eagles round here anymore, I figured I'd come here, just in case.'

'I was hoping you might,' acknowledged Owen.

'You know the next question.'

'Why am I here?'

Gerat nodded.

'I made it back to the Highlands. And I found survivors. We are rebuilding. Now we are looking for other groups. I hoped that you and your people would have made a go of it.'

'Yeah, we have, I suppose. After you left though things got rough. More of those bastards came through, a whole pack of gnomes, more than we could handle so we got out of here and went north. That's when a bunch of wood elves hit us.'

'How bad were you hit?'

'I lost half of my people.'

'Emperor's grace,' swore Owen, shaking his head.

'We got lucky there weren't more of them, those crazy bastards attacked us even though they were outnumbered. We got them all, which gave us a chance to get away, but it cost us.'

'Your daughter, Myra?'

'She didn't make it.'

Owen opened his mouth to express his sympathy, but found that he had no words. She had been young enough to still be innocent, perhaps she had died that way too, not truly understanding how wicked the world could be. Like Em.

'They'll pay,' he said. It was the most honest thing he could say.

'You got room on that bird for a passenger?' asked Gerat. 'I'm getting too old to walk everywhere.'

Owen smiled. 'I reckon he can carry us both, as long as you don't mind heights.'

'It's not the heights so much as the falling.'

'Yep, the falling bit hurts like hell.'

'Then keep it low.'

Together they walked out of the barn, towards Arno.

'Where are we headed?' Owen asked, as he pulsed to Arno, '*We have an old friend flying with us.*'

'Not far, you head north and when you hit the stream follow it upriver.'

'Alright.'

They reached Arno and Owen pointed to the rear saddle straps.

'See those things that look like long saddle bags? Just climb up and put your legs into them. Then just tie yourself up with the straps.'

'I see,' said Gerat, and he hauled himself on to Arno's back.

'I'm impressed you want to give it a try,' admitted Owen.

Gerat fixed him with a stare. 'Things change.'

'Yes, they do,' agreed Owen. 'Yes, they do.'

Owen followed suit and settled on to Arno.

'Sorry, old friend. Heavy load for you to carry.' Arno shook his head in response and extended his wings. Owen turned him around to take advantage of the gentle southern slope.

As they took to the air, Owen felt Arno toil against the extra weight. He hadn't had to carry more than Owen and his kit for some time and, though the eagle was bigger and stronger now, Gerat was a test. Owen kept them low and on a northerly track. Their speed through the air reduced, and Arno had to battle a headwind. Owen turned his head so he could be heard against the rush of air. 'I haven't seen any hostiles since I came back.'

'There isn't much of anything this far west. There's no one here but us now,' shouted Gerat.

That was interesting.

They flew on for a short while before they saw a line of water flowing south west. Arno tilted his wings and started to follow it back to its source: a range of craggy, forested slopes. Gerat tapped him on the shoulder.

'Head to the highest point, there's a small plateau that you can land your bird on.'

Owen nodded. Arno flapped his powerful wings, matching his position relative to the rising ground, and cruised over the treetops, aiming for the tallest point of the range. The trees did indeed give way to a bare peak: uneven and strewn with rocks and boulders. Owen felt a wave of relief, he was starting to worry for his bird. Once Arno had settled, Owen climbed down quickly to help Gerat off.

'How was that?' Owen asked.

Gerat looked at him askance. 'Don't know; I had my eyes shut for most of it. Come on, there's a way down over here.'

Owen raised a hand. 'Gerat. A moment.' He turned to his saddle bags and collected his crossbow and spare bolts.

Gerat nodded his approval with a grunt then started leading them down.

'We used to use this as a lookout point during the day,' said Gerat. 'You get a good view from here.'

'Not anymore?'

Gerat didn't turn to respond. 'As I said, things are quiet round here now.'

Fair enough.

As they went into the treeline, they followed a path that navigated rocky outcroppings. Owen passed by a pile of detritus and bones. A midden? He glanced at Gerat, felt himself hold the crossbow a little tighter. It was probably nothing. Further on a number of openings within the outcroppings marked the entrances to caves. Clothes and several sheets hung suspended from the trees crowding round those cave mouths, and now he saw dark, grimy faces peering silently out from the gloom within. He had to step over an animal carcass, the size of it suggesting a small dog or a fox. This unsettled Owen. The eerie silence didn't help either.

'No fires during the daytime. And only in the caves,' said Gerat simply. 'No reason to advertise our presence, even now.'

'Gerat.'

A familiar looking man appeared from behind a tree.

'Bedwyr. Look who decided to show his ugly face again.'

Owen nodded at him, recalling his dislike for the stout Scotian.

Bedwyr eyed him for a moment with unconcealed suspicion.

'You get lost?' he asked sourly.

Gerat laughed.

'Bedwyr's humour has not improved I'm afraid. Come on.' Gerat tilted his head at Bedwyr. 'Come see me later.'

Further down they went, passing crude shelters made of thick branches and covered with earth, their roofs spouting carpets of moss and thin grass. Men and women gathered by their homes to watch them pass. Owen felt uncomfortable as they regarded him with suspicious, even hostile eyes. Children peered from behind their parents with a mixture of fear and curiosity. The worked their way down in a zig-zag fashion, arriving at a sheet of rock set into the hillside with a narrow cave entrance. Here Gerat stopped and motioned Owen inside. The entrance was little more than a slit, and Owen had to turn himself to the side to squeeze in. Within, the space opened into the size of a large room. A shaft of daylight from high up allowed Owen to make out a pile of furs against the far rock face, and a low table stacked with weapons. Gerat brushed past him and settled down on one of the tree stumps by the table, placed there in lieu of chairs, waving to Owen to sit on another. As he did so, Gerat pulled forward a couple of beakers on the table and fished out a waterskin, pouring something that didn't smell like water into the vessels. He pushed one across to Owen then raised the other in salute. Gerat downed his in one large gulp and gave Owen an expectant look. Owen picked up his beaker, brought it to his mouth and flinched. Emperor! The smell! He tipped it back and swallowed, the liquid running like fire down his throat. Gerat grunted, slammed his beaker down and wiped his hand across his mouth. Owen placed his down as well, focusing on containing the burning heat that was now rising back up his throat. He sucked in some air and swallowed a few times before blowing out, and the sharp, sour taste lingered unpleasantly on his tongue.

Gerat's grin was feral.

'It's the best we can do, but it works.'

Owen could only nod.

Gerat placed his hands on the table and eyed Owen. 'It's maybe not what you were expecting.'

'This place?' asked Owen. 'I don't have any expectations. Only hopes.'

Gerat barked a harsh laugh. 'Hope? You still spinning that wheel of bullshit?'

Owen placed his hands on the table, mimicking Gerat, and leaned forward. 'Yes, Gerat, I am. And I'm hoping that you've still got some fight left in you.'

Gerat's eyes narrowed. 'Careful, lad. I've got more than enough fight for anyone who cares to question it.'

Owen raised his hands. 'I didn't mean it that way. I told you we are rebuilding. I've even got other Riders now. There's a community, back in my old home Eagle's Rest. But that's not why I'm here. I'm looking for folk that are willing to fight.'

Gerat raised an eyebrow. 'You've changed your mind, then?'

'I just had to learn a lesson. We won't be safe until they realise they have to leave us alone. They have to learn a lesson too, that they must pay a price for what they did to us.'

Gerat rubbed his chin.

'Do you know all that we had to do to survive?'

'What you had to,' replied Owen flatly. He didn't care to judge; it didn't matter to him.

'Aye, we did what we had to,' said Gerat. He inclined his head to the exit. 'You see how many people I got out there?'

'More than you had.'

'A lot more. I've got maybe two hundred, give or take. We did what you did, what was left of that first group you knew. We started looking for other survivors. I said to you back then there would be. This place is the ass end of nowhere: tough country, tough people.' He stopped and poured them both a refill. 'We also found some other groups of refugees that never made it to Aberpool, or never even tried. They were in a bad way. We gave them a choice, join us, pull their weight and survive, or don't.' He took a drink. 'Not many of them made it through that first winter, when we were on the move, living hand to mouth. We found this place last summer. I liked it straight away. Problem was the folk already staying here didn't want to share.' Gerat stopped and looked intently at Owen, his eyes dark, challenging. 'I took it from them.'

Owen held Gerat's gaze. *He wants to see if I judge him? Who am I to judge?*

He reached for his beaker. Then thought better of it. 'You did what you had to do.'

Gerat pursed his lips, then nodded his head and emptied his beaker. 'What do you have in mind?'

'It's simple,' said Owen. 'It's the same message I'm giving to anyone we find. Join us. Come to the Highlands. There is space, there is safety. There is strength in numbers.'

'And in return?'

'You fight. Everyone fights.'

'No more living quietly?'

Owen shook his head. 'It's not going to work. I don't want it to work. Not yet. They have to pay for what they did. All of them, the elves, the dwarves, all those bastard races who judged us. They have to bleed.'

Gerat hissed and leaned in close. 'Now you understand, don't you? They wanted what we had and tried to take it from us. They damn well took near everything from me. Now I do the taking.'

'I get it,' said Owen nodding. 'I know what we have to do.'

Gerat placed a hand on Owen's shoulder.

'Alright, then. Tell us where we need to go.'

CHAPTER NINE – FILLION

As the expedition gathered at the northern gate of Apamea, Fillion rubbed a hand against Amice's flank. He'd barely had time to prepare and had given little thought to the logistics of the journey. He eyed the other members of the deputation: three staff to take care of their living arrangements and drive their attached wagons, two clerks of the Parliament, both riding on the wagons and his fellow Servant Ezra who possessed a fine-looking mare. He'd been surprised to hear the older elf had been picked to go, Fillion did not have him pegged as the type who would enjoy a field trip. But as the Servant to Member Tekla, it made sense. She was second only to Patiir in her political influence and the two were often thick as thieves in their machinations.

He nodded to Ezra and the elf hurried over.

'Well, this is going to be a tedious trip, isn't it?' said Ezra, looking put out.

'If you say so.'

Ezra caught his tone.

'Sabin, you look unhappy … oh, of course. You wife is soon to give birth. My apologies, no wonder.'

'Yes, that's it,' agreed Fillion, longing to punch his tactless elven face.

Ezra reached out and patted his shoulder.

'Don't worry, you'll be back before you know it. Excuse me I just need to talk to the clerks.'

He bustled off to the other elves in the group. Fillion watched him go, working hard to contain his annoyance. They were all so full of their own self-importance. He turned away to inspect their travelling companions. It appeared that Marmus had decamped with almost his entire Embassy staff: eight more wagons, some thirty dwarves, of which a good score of them were guards. Fillion appraised them with a professional interest; arrayed in column, two abreast, they wore a full set of chain and leather armour topped off with thick black angular helmets, their faces hidden behind the cheek and nose guards. Each carried a halberd resting against their shoulders. Fillion was grudgingly impressed. He could ask for no better protection on the road. The guards were the only ones on foot.

As he readied Amice for the journey he was alerted to the sound of hoof steps behind him. He turned to find Marmus astride a solid-looking mountain pony. Fillion felt his eyebrow rise in unbidden surprise. The ambassador fixed him with a surly stare.

'Is something amiss, Sabin?' he asked, sharply.

Fillion raised a hand.

'No, my friend, on my honour. I just don't think I've ever seen a dwarf mounted upon a horse.'

Marmus shifted in his saddle and grunted.

'It's not that unusual, we have cavalry and I'm too damned old to be walking everywhere. But it's true, my people have more affinity to the soil than the sky,' he conceded. 'We like to keep our feet on the ground. Gives us a good sense of perspective.'

'That makes sense,' agreed Fillion, affecting a sly smile. Marmus shook his head, his suspicion evident. Fillion knew Marmus well enough now to know the dwarf understood teasing, even if he didn't appreciate it. 'It's important to know where you come from and where you are headed.'

Marmus let out a sudden loud bark of laughter. 'That is why I like you, Sabin. You have a twisted view of the world that I can sympathise with. Quite unlike your kin.'

Fillion acknowledged the compliment with a gracious bow of the head. Yet, even as he did so he realised his mistake – be too different and his travelling companions might start to question just what was going through his head. He had to be cautious; he was still a Servant and had to conduct himself as such.

That need for caution was further brought home two weeks into the journey. Vineyards and tended fields and forests had turned into the wilder foothills of the borders between the two realms. As the elves and dwarves settled around their respective campfires, Ezra took a seat next to him.

'Young Sabin, it is good of you to grace us with your presence tonight,' Ezra said lightly, making a show of warming his hands against the fire. An unnecessary act considering the time of year. It was a calculated attempt at being comradely. Surely Ezra didn't expect Fillion to fall for that shit?

'Oh, you noticed?' he said lightly. Try as he might to mix with his fellow elves, his evenings were mostly spent with the dwarves; Marmus was just better company.

Ezra smiled.

'Oh, it's alright, Sabin. I do understand. Member Patiir is keen to have someone close to the ambassador and it seems you have made great strides in that regard.'

Fillion smiled.

'He does seem to tolerate me more than most of my kind. And, yes, you are right. I see no harm in being gracious and forging links.'

'Quite so, quite so. Member Tekla is equally keen to ensure our interests are looked after and our alliances … well-tended.' He stretched his legs out and waved to one of the staff. The elf reacted quickly, bringing him a cup of wine. Ezra nodded his thanks and cradled it in his hands. 'It's never easy dealing with the Dwarf Nations. They have no King, just a cabal of lords – merchant princes if you will – who make up a council, and they get a little agitated if someone of high importance comes calling. They get competitive, falling over each other to gain advantage, constantly wary of who of their number might be making deals and agreements behind their backs. Makes it dreadfully hard work to get anything done.' Ezra stopped for a moment to take a sip.

Sounds just like Parliament to me, thought Fillion.

'So, in a way,' Ezra continued, 'we, that is you and I, are doing them, and Marmus, a favour. We can conduct our business at a lower key. The council can accommodate our visit, knowing we are just functionaries; in ourselves we do not possess any real power.'

'Of course, we just happen to represent two of the most influential Members of the Parliament. Both of whom could be said to have the ear of the King.'

'Inasmuch as any has,' said Ezra. 'You are learning fast, Sabin. Why if we wanted to, either of us could cause all sorts of trouble if we allowed our personal agenda to get in the way of what is best for the Heartlands.'

And there it was, the veiled threat? The friendly warning? Ezra and he may be on the same mission, but their loyalties were clear. At least as far as Ezra understood it.

'You know me, Ezra. I like to keep it simple. I am just happy to serve and play my part. Besides, I'm going to be a father soon.'

'Yes, you are, young Sabin,' Ezra said, somewhat patronisingly. 'Is it still weighing upon you, the imminent weight of parental responsibility?'

'It is,' agreed Fillion. He didn't have a clue what might be happening back there and the thought was quite terrifying.

'I am sure we will be done with our business and back in no time. And then you can get on with the serious work of fatherhood. Keeping Patiir's family line going, eh? And it'll mean less time for you and your two cronies at the Chalice.' Ezra chuckled and took another sip. 'Honestly, Sabin. Of all the two individuals to tie your flag to, a wood elf and a dwarf. If it tells us Servants anything, you are definitely not a political animal. You are an odd fish!'

Yes. And another reason to watch my step. No matter how hard I try, there will always be questions about my behaviour.

Fillion waved at the staff elf. He fancied a drink himself.

It was another full week of travel before they saw their first dwarf settlement, towards the end of that seventh day. Fillion hadn't been sure what to expect and was curious. He stared ahead at the cluster of buildings sitting at the confluence of two rivers coming down out of the mountains. From here it looked like a human town. He felt a hollow ache inside as he moved forward again. He'd assumed it would be all high walls and grim aspects, given dwarven nature, but as they came closer and began to move in amongst the shops and dwellings, he found himself in a bustling community that could have been a twin of Vyberg, but for the absence of humans and albeit at a slightly smaller scale. As they entered the town, Fillion was bemused by how everyone appeared almost nonchalant at the arrival of a heavily armed caravan. A few stares at the elvish contingent and then folk just carried on with their business.

As they proceeded along the main street, his eye was caught by the craftsmanship of every structure. His gaze alighted on a smithy. No ordinary, functional human construct was this. Every piece of timber was shaped to fit, every block of stone carved to match its partners with an even level of mortar between each one. Looking up to the rooftops, the rafters and eaves were covered with embellishments of swirling patterns of sharply-angled symbols. And as his eyes moved on, in each building he studied, there was artistry and individuality, and that was the most surprising thing. It did not seem to matter what was the purpose of the building, each one had been lavished with care and attention. It wasn't like the elven design, which he found garish and cloying to look at; these dwellings were what every town of the Empire could look like if all its citizens was treated as equals, where it wasn't just royalty or the Imperial Church who could afford the finest masons and carpenters.

'Welcome to Bar-Ras. By your open mouth and surprised expression I'd say that this was not what you were expecting,' observed Marmus, as he rode alongside Fillion.

'Yes, you could say that.'

'What were you expecting?'

'I don't know, but I'm impressed.' Fillion quickly raised a hand. 'My apologies, that came out wrong.'

Marmus grunted. It was, Fillion was relieved to hear, his amused grunt.

'Most of your kind have an opinion of our culture. Few of them ever get to experience it.'

'I'm amazed at the quality of build. I do not see one structure that has any disrepair,' said Fillion. It would be far too much to say so, but he actually *liked* it.

'We dwarves are a practical people, and we have pride. A lot of it. And that means even the most humble of dwellings are given much consideration in their design and construction. As a nation, it is the thing that brings us together and gives us a sense of who we are. It doesn't matter which merchant house you claim allegiance to, there is not a dwarf alive who could bear to see a shoddy piece of work.'

'I can see that, my friend. And are your cities like this too?'

Marmus nodded.

'We don't have cities on the scale of the elves, or the humans for that matter. But our larger towns, yes, they are sights to behold.'

'Is it true they are built into the mountains themselves?'

'Yes. As I said, we are a practical people. We make our wealth and livelihoods from the rock, and it makes sense to live where we work.'

They reached a bridge that crossed one of the rivers. On the upstream-side a number of tree trunks, lashed together, were carried by the current towards several workers who splashed around, gathering them up. There was much shouting from the workers and some seemingly aggressive encouragement from an on-looking foreman as they secured the trunks against the bankside.

'This is a big logging town, amongst other things. Plenty of good forest further up east in the hills,' observed Marmus.

'Are we heading up that way?' asked Fillion.

The dwarf shook his head.

'Not quite. We are following the course of the northern river, we call it the Bar.'

'And the other is called the Ras,' Fillion mused. He was busy looking at the Bar, tamed in its descent by a series of locks, like giant steps down the mountain. And going up that canal were barges, almost at every level, piled high with covered cargo, and plenty of the tree trunks.

'Yes, puts things in context for an elf, doesn't it?' said Marmus. 'The Dwarf Nations have been around a long time. We've learned a few things along the way.'

Fillion was inclined to agree as they crossed the bridge, then turned on to a well-worn, paved road.

They rode alongside the canal for a short while. At the lowest point, six barges awaited their turn to enter the first lock, and a number of ponies were allowed to roam free, cropping at the grass verges. A barge was within the first lock, slowly rising as the waters gushed in from above. The noise was like being close to a waterfall, a splashing, echoing thunder of sound. On the far side a dwarf led two ponies to the top of the loch, ready to pull the barge into the next waiting area.

'We've got sixteen locks,' said Marmus loudly, drawing close to Fillion. 'We have ponds, dwarf-made lakes, to hold the water needed to fill the chambers and house the barges going up and down. There are locks further on where the slope is so steep, each chamber gate leads on to the next chamber. Other places we've built further along the route have switchbacks and viaducts. The barges are able to penetrate into the higher valleys and peaks where the true dwarf settlements are clustered. The ones you were expecting to see.' He eyed Fillion. There was definitely a sparkle of pride there, and why not?

'This is truly most impressive,' said Ezra with a sincere tone that Fillion rarely heard.

'I'll take the compliment,' acknowledged Marmus. 'These locks don't stop. We have produce and materials flowing continuously into the dwarf lands from here. During the day they go up and at night they come down.'

'And yet it is undefended,' pointed out Fillion, with his soldier's perspective.

'We are well inside dwarf territory, who would dare attack us? Perhaps you are sizing us up for an invasion, lad?' said Marmus, with a raised eyebrow.

'My colleague is hardly the finest military mind!' laughed Ezra. 'No offence, Sabin.'

Fillion felt himself flush, the guilt of getting called out for scoping out potential weak points for an attack was nicely disguised as embarrassment.

'None taken, Ezra, it just struck me how vital this settlement is.'

'Oh, I'll give you that,' said Marmus. 'But hundreds of years of peace and stability will lower your guard somewhat. No, there's no risk to us this far in. It's not as if the Tissans are coming for us, eh?'

Fillion nodded quietly. *Already here.* He watched a dwarf insert his windlass into the winding gear and begin opening an upper-lock gate, allowing the water to flow in.

'We'll follow the canal to the top. There'll be a waystation a few miles further on. We can lodge there overnight and then tomorrow onwards into the mountains themselves. That will be where we part company.'

'What? I thought we were travelling together?' Fillion exclaimed, caught off-guard.

'No. I said that when we planned this trip I had messages to deliver. Messages that have to be personally relayed. Ezra is travelling with me, and you will be heading to the mines with a contingent of my guards as guides and company.'

'Oh, that is a shame.'

'Don't get all dewy-eyed on me, elf. We'll meet back here in ten days' time.'

'I'll try and keep myself amused,' said Fillion with a smile.

Marmus grunted and kicked his pony forward.

'I'm sorry, Sabin. I thought you knew the arrangements,' said Ezra.

'Patiir was clear in my task, I just didn't stop to think that there would be a division of labour,' replied Fillion.

Ezra shrugged. 'Member Tekla is always interested in the politics of any and every nation. Your Member often takes a more focussed view on matters.'

'I can't deny that.'

'It does him credit, and his knowledge and views have always carried great weight. We are lucky to have him.'

Fillion chose not to reply.

Early the next morning Fillion mounted Amice and took a moment to gaze back along the canal and follow its course downwards. A gentle breeze was blowing down from the mountain, making him shiver slightly. The Ras was only a few yards away and a barge was moving sedately past, heading upriver, the conversation of its crew easily reaching him over the sound of the water. He breathed deeply, from here on in he was on his own. Almost. The sound of hooves on cobbles made him look back at the waystation. The building was more like a fortified coaching inn, of the sort that could have been found way out west, back in the more remote parts of the Empire. Marmus was leading his pony towards him.

'Don't fret, lad,' said Marmus, as he climbed on to his mount. 'Do a good job and I'll make sure next time I'll have you accompany me into the Dwarf Nations proper.'

'I'll use that as my incentive,' Fillion replied, with a polite smile.

'There are your companions.' Marmus pointed as, with a degree of grumbling and clanking metal, a half dozen guards emerged from the building. A moment later one of the dwarven wagons rumbled into view from the stables to the rear of the waystation. 'Reygar is in charge,' he said. One of the armoured dwarfs raised a hand. 'He knows the way, and anything you need, you just ask him. He's already been told to treat you with respect. More than your lot normally get.'

Fillion took that as a rare acknowledgment of friendship. Marmus nodded and guided his mount away. 'Now what is keeping the rest of my malingering party?' he shouted.

The six dwarves took up positions in front of the wagon. Still on foot, even though there would be room in the back.

'Good morning, Sabin!' said Ezra as he appeared out of the waystation.

'I trust you slept well?' inquired Fillion.

'Well enough, thank you.'

Fillion gestured towards their dwarf companions. 'I suppose I'll have to get used to some one-sided conversations for a while.'

'Oh, enjoy it. It will be nice not to have one's opinions questioned and analysed at every turn. Consider it a holiday from the politics of Parliament.'

A holiday? What in all of Tissan was that?

Ezra held his hand up and Fillion took it.

'I'll see you soon,' Ezra said with a bright smile, then he leaned in close. 'Keep your counsel my friend, I know a little of your task and I bid you to be careful.' He stepped back, the smile still in place, and patted Amice on the flank.

Fillion pondered their parting, not surprised that Ezra knew something, but surprised at his words of caution. Perhaps being away from the capital had lightened the elf's usual disposition somewhat.

'Servant,' said Reygar, drawing Fillion's attention.

'Ah. Um. Reygar. How long to the mines?' asked Fillion.

'Two days.'

'Very good. Are we camping under the stars? I rather liked the waystation.'

Reygar fixed him with a hard stare. There'd be no idle banter with this fellow.

'Stars,' the dwarf replied.

'Excellent. Shall we?'

Reygar nodded and set his men marching. Fillion fell in behind them and the wagon brought up the rear. He spotted a barge slowly making its way towards them. Its cargo was covered with tarpaulins, but the barge rode heavy in the water. *Rocks?* Either that or it was laden with gold. There would have been a time when had no interest in such things. Now he was concerned with the task at hand. If there were humans working these mines, what was he to do?

CHAPTER TEN – MICHAEL

Michael fingered the fringe of the cloak draped over his shoulders, savouring the warmth of the fur against his body and the stout thickness of the hide that no doubt would protect him against the harsh winters of this land. The garment had been presented to him after his run of victories and Nutaaq had offered it with genuine pleasure. A practical gift, from a practical people. In another life, he might have grown up in a tribe like Nutaaq's, fighting for his kin and for his own pleasure, not the whims of a master. But then he would have never have met the Emperor.

He stood to one side as the rest of the party bustled around, preparing to set off. Finally, after months away, they were heading home. There was a sense of excitement and purpose among the Tissan contingent, and in truth, he was just as eager. He wanted to see the Cardinal, to tell him of all the wonders he had seen. He wanted to share just how much the Emperor had achieved. He wanted to see the Cardinal's face when he learned of their new allies and that the dream of returning to Tissan would be realised in their lifetimes.

'You are not going to wear that, are you? It's boiling!' asked Corporal Fenner as he strode past carrying a basket of bread.

''Course he is! It's good to see the champion is back,' called Beautiful, from the wagon that Fenner was heading towards.

'Yes, it is. But it's still bloody hot,' said Fenner as he handed the bread up to her.

Father Michael experienced a wave of self-consciousness. Yes, it was a warm day. There was no need for the cloak and to wear it was a mark of another life. He reached to free the horn fastening.

'Father. Wear it if you wish. You earned it and you have done us proud in doing so.' Father Michael turned at the sound of the Emperor's voice. 'I think your efforts did as much to win the Nidhal to our cause as any of the promises and diplomacy.'

Father Michael shrugged. 'I'm not much of a diplomat.'

The Emperor laughed and clapped him on the back.

'I'm glad of it. I have enough of those waiting for me back at New Tissan. The Nidhal, I think, much prefer your honest and straightforward approach to negotiations.'

'I admit I was pleased to do something more physical.'

'Keep it up, Father. You know, I might even suggest to the Arch Cardinal that we should consider forming a new martial force from the ranks of the religion.'

'I thought that was the Gifted?'

The Emperor nodded, conceding the point. 'They are my finest warriors, but they are too few. I need a larger force to win the wars ahead, and brawn would strengthen our ranks.' He clapped Father Michael's shoulder and moved off. After a few strides he turned around. 'Besides, Father, wouldn't you like to be a general, one day?'

He laughed lightly and continued on. Father Michael watched him move among the party, his manner easy, every inch the ruler of all. Never had he seen the weight of rule carried as effortlessly by his Emperor. If nothing else, to see that, made the trip worthwhile. As for being a general? He sincerely hoped the Emperor truly had been joking.

The Tissan expedition formed up, pointed south and east. The Emperor was mounted, the rest were walking or riding in the two wagons, one a replacement for that lost to the river during the winter. An honour guard of twenty Nidhal, riding vargrs, would accompany them part of the way and this group waited to one side, their mounts shifting and growling restlessly.

Behind the Tissans was a gathering to wish them well. Yet it could not be more unlike the one the residents of New Tissan had given them last year. It seemed all of the Nidhal tribes had gathered to watch them – it was a staggering sight. It evoked memories of the arena, of vast crowds clapping, cheering, shouting his name. But this was no crowd baying for blood. It was a horde of warriors, thousands strong, dressed in leather, metal and bone. They were terrifying and glorious. The hope for their future. Every single tribe represented at the gathering had pledged their support to Nutaaq and the Emperor's promise of new lands when they helped him reclaim the Empire. Nutaaq, flanked by his two brothers, stood before the throng. Directly behind them gathered the other tribal leaders and their shamans. He spied Ellen, standing to one side, her hands clasped in front of her. Her eyes met his and she grinned.

Just saying goodbye to my brothers and sisters. I'll see you soon, Father. Keep the Emperor safe.

He would truly miss her. He raised a hand and she waved back. Father Michael eyed Eilion and saw the disapproving look on his face. Father Michael smiled. He could not help himself.

He watched the Emperor ride towards Nutaaq, dismount and hold out his hand. As the two grasped each other's wrists in a ritual farewell, Father Michael felt a surge of regret, yet also pride. A hush fell over the vast gathering.

Once remounted, the Emperor pulled his sword from his sheath and raised it high in salute. As one, the Tissans followed, raising their fists into the sky.

'The Nidhal!' shouted the Emperor.

'The Nidhal!' cried Father Michael in chorus with the rest.

Then pandemonium erupted as Cadarn and Bryce flew their eagles low over the massed Nidhal who roared their approval and waved their weaponry aloft.

The roar echoed across the huge camp like a rumble of thunder as the Emperor turned his skittery mount around. Father Michael fell into line with the rest of the Tissans and they began to move off.

'That went well,' observed the marine, Wendell. The four marines had taken control of the second wagon, Father Michael walking alongside them.

'And here we are heading back into the wilderness, all alone again,' said Coyle.

'Not quite yet,' said Fenner, pointing to their left flank from his position on the front of the wagon next to the driver, Beautiful. Shadowing them at a distance of a hundred yards loped their Nidhal escort.

'How many bolts to take down one of those things?' asked Wendell.

Fenner scratched his beard.

'A vargr? I dunno. You hit it in the side, chances are it'll keep coming. No good treating it like a deer and waiting for it to bleed out. Maybe hit a hind leg. That should hobble it.'

'And it'll be moving fast. Tough shot for one,' added Beautiful.

'And if it's coming straight at you–?' asked Coyle.

'You take it straight in the face,' interrupted Father Michael.

'Well, yeah, o'course,' agreed Fenner. 'But you gotta wait 'til it gets close, just to be sure. That way you get the punch from your crossbow.'

'I'd shit myself,' observed Beautiful.

'I'd still like to see that,' said Coyle.

Beautiful responded with a gesture that sent a ripple of laughter through the group. Father Michael smiled.

'You reckon you could take one, Father?' asked Wendell.

'Like I said. Coming face to face with a wild vargr, you take it head on, it's too fast, too manoeuvrable, so wait for it to come to you, then you strike. You get one shot at the thing. Make it count, disable the beast, and you have the advantage.'

Fenner whistled. 'A *wild* vargr? Those the Nidhal ride aren't particular friendly as it is and they are the tamed ones! Your idea sounds great in practice, but I think I'll let you take that on, Father.'

'I'd rather not.'

'Now that's a tactic I agree with,' said Beautiful.

'Either that or you stand in the line with your fellow marines and unleash a storm at the thing,' said Fenner.

'That's the usual way,' said Wendell. 'Cut 'em down before they ever reach you. Strength in numbers.'

'Not many of us left to do that kind of fighting anymore,' mused Beautiful.

'So we do what we do best,' said Fenner with a touch of pride in his voice. 'We fight dirty.'

'Hey, Father!' Coyle tipped his head towards the front of the party. 'Reckon they could take one?' Father Michael knew he meant the detachment of Gifted, who marched in column just behind the Emperor. A Shaper could certainly come up with something to distract a vargr, a powerful Gifted could even cast something sharp right at it, perhaps right through its eyes.

'I am sure they could. They are the Emperor's chosen warriors,' he said loyally.

'Yeah, but they've never had to face one of those things charging right for their balls,' Coyle replied.

'I'm sure they would fight bravely,' Father Michael added.

'Hmm, I sense a bet coming on,' said Fenner.

'What you thinking?' asked Beautiful.

'Oh, who would come off best in a fight with a vargr. Our Father here? Or one of the Gifted?'

Father Michael shook his head. Did they ever stop with the wagers?

'You have a view, Father?' asked Fenner.

'Like I said, I hope it never comes to it,' said Father Michael.

The marines fell silent and he could swear he could actually hear their minds doing the calculations. He also found that a part of him was also weighing the odds, old habits that died hard, a professional detachment that was keen to measure his own skill against it.

'Hey, Father,' said Fenner, breaking the silence. 'Didn't I see you a few years back? Sweet Emperor, maybe it was even ten years ago, doesn't time fly? Anyway, I saw you in the arena, in Vyberg and you were the big finale. What was it you faced?'

Father Michael sighed.

'It was a manticore.'

Fenner slapped his knee and nodded. 'Yes! That was it. I swear, I'd never seen the like. One minute you were all over it, then the next thing, you sidestepped, cut its tail off and then leapt on its back and strangled the life out of the fucker. Honestly, I've never seen the like.'

'I'll take ten on the Father,' said Wendell, quickly.

CHAPTER ELEVEN – CADE

Cade yawned and stretched. It had been a long night and she had barely slept. Vidar was working them harder for some reason. Or maybe there was no reason at all, and he was just being a cruel bastard. Either way, here was their first delivery of the day, and it was barely past breakfast. The cheek of it. She gazed lazily out towards the north of the plateau and the route leading off it. If she had someone to complain to she might have done. As it was, most of her people usually blamed her. What was that about? She was the one who made their lives easier, after all. She was minded just to give it all up and let someone else do the thinking and leading. Devlin. Yes, he could do it. He'd like that. She could retire. Find herself a nice, dark tunnel and just get back to chipping bits of shit off other bits of shit. Anonymous. But dangerous. But then, what was new?

'Visitors,' murmured Miriam, from the driver's side of the wagon.

'What?' Cade looked ahead. 'Oh.'

As their wagon arrived at Vidar's complex, with another five in convoy behind them, Cade spotted a line of ragged looking individuals, about a dozen or so. All huddled against the wooden wall of the warehouse, guarded by four of Vidar's goons. Miriam drew the wagon up to the main doors and applied the brake. Cade hopped off and shook her legs as the warehouse doors opened and some of her crew walked out to meet them. She saw Evan amongst them, along with Emerich and Trent, a lank Riverlander.

'New faces,' she said to Evan as he wandered over. The lad had started to fill out. It was good to see.

'Yep. They arrived an hour ago. They haven't spoken yet,' he said.

'One did but he got a smack for his trouble,' offered Trent.

She looked closer at the prisoners, studying their faces. Most were dirt-streaked, thin, worn and possessed of that brow-beaten look she was used to seeing on her own people, although less so these days. A couple of the newcomers eyed her with interest, standing a little straighter, holding themselves with dignity. That was good. It meant they were people who could help her get things organised. In another way it could be bad. It depended on how they got to be here and the kind of system they were running – she didn't need any more thugs or wannabe gang masters. She had done too much to get where she was.

Her crew had climbed aboard the wagon, so she slapped its side. 'Alright, get to it.'

Seeing a figure she recognised emerge from the shadows of the warehouse, she moved to intercept him. Geir. The grey-bearded little shit was carrying a small leather book in his hand rather than the ledger that she always thought of as an extra limb.

'Morning!' she said brightly. 'I see we have some guests.'

Geir did not acknowledge her greeting. 'Here.' He thrust the book into her hands, walked past her and stopped in front of the line of prisoners. 'These are the representatives of the other workings and mines that make up this concern. You know what you need to do?' he asked.

'So the boss finally got the others to agree to let him manage operations, huh? He's a smart one,' Cade replied.

Geir scowled from beneath his bushy eyebrows and facial hair. 'You have the day to elicit the required information from them. The book contains the necessary information regarding population sizes, work routines and outputs. At dusk, Master Vidar wants a full report. And he expects the first tranche of workers to be inducted and trained tomorrow morning.'

Cade scratched her head. Vidar really didn't hang around. She caught Geir still staring at her.

'Um, yes?'

'Do you have any questions?' he asked.

Cade screwed up her face.

'Nope. Happy.'

Geir eyed her silently for a moment, then shook his head.

'The guards will remain outside the entrance and will collect them when you have finished.' As he departed, he waved a dismissive hand.

Cade watched him stalk off, then turned to face the gathering. She put on her sunniest smile.

'Morning, all. Congratulations. Your day has just gotten a little better.'

A few of them looked confused. Cade glanced at the four guards.

'Any of you boys speak our lingo?'

The guards stared at her with open hostility but only one acknowledged her with a shake of his head.

'Fair enough,' she replied, and turned her attention back to the line. 'As I understand it, you lot are representatives of the various mines and quarries dotted hereabouts. And you'll note we all wear different brands.' She raised her arm. 'But from here on in, they don't mean squat. We all work for the dwarf that sits in the office just inside this building. He's smart enough to realise we ain't just cattle, leastways, we got more latitude than some of his compatriots would like. Now we play this right, we get a tiny piece of our lives back. But don't get cocky!' she said with a stern finger raised.

She watched their expressions. Some were still confused, others downright sceptical. One, a man who she had clocked as one of the brighter ones, narrowed his eyes thoughtfully. A woman with a shaved head grinned at her and spat. Yep, she'd have to watch that one.

'Now, what I need from you is your best guess of the talent pool you each have. I'm talking about skills, trades and the like. Especially those who might have smithying experience or an associated job – Hells, I'm looking for woodworkers, farriers, drivers. Anything you can think of that will fill a function that the short-arses would normally fill.

'How about gaol warder?' said the man. He had a thick beard and a length of blond hair tied up in a bun on his head.

Oh, funny guy.

'Hilarious.' She fixed him with a look and he looked right back. 'Let's see what else you can come up with. Firstly …' she craned her neck and looked into the warehouse. 'Hey, Miriam! You got that sack?'

'Yeah?' came a shouted reply.

'Good. Break it out. We have some folks who need breakfast.'

Again, glances were exchanged.

'If you'd like to follow me inside, we've got some food and water for you. Nothing fancy, bread and cheese, but it's pretty fresh.'

Some of the faces broke out into hopeful smiles.

'So if you'd like to come on inside …' She ushered the group along and glanced back at the guards. 'As you were, boys.'

She followed the others in and looked up towards Vidar's office. Do this job right and she'd be sitting pretty. She opened the book in her hands. The first few pages contained neat writing and a bunch of numbers, all in the Imperial language. That's as much as she recognised. She couldn't read for shit. She'd pass it to Devlin later; he had a mind for this kind of crap. She moved on into the depths of the warehouse, away from unwanted attention. Already the new arrivals were gathering around Miriam, who was dishing out the food. Cade had expected this day was going to happen, that Vidar was close to taking control, so she had made sure to have a welcome package ready for when it happened. Hearts and minds. Seemed only right she should be prepared. She scratched her neck and yawned. Time to get to work.

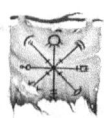

As bidden, Cade released the others as the bright blue sky started to fade to black. They walked out, their heads a little higher if she was any judge, to be met by their guards who, through some less than gentle cajoling, got them back into a line and then marched them off. Cade allowed herself a moment of satisfaction. It had been a productive day. And interesting as well. Through her discussions with the others she had discovered that there was a damned sizeable population up here in the mountain range. Many thousands if those folks had their numbers right.

She'd have to check that tonight with Devlin. That meant there was a wide base to draw from for the work required on the plateau. She could get this stitched up nicely.

The dwarves must be importing a shit-ton of food, even if was crap. Feeding that many was quite the effort. There was a bakery on site, she could smell it sometimes. Maybe there were kitchens too. She had people who could work in those as well. That would mean better bread, not the tough, stony shit the dwarves made. Damn, they could even start brewing ale. *Oh my lords, that would make me a happy lass.*

She turned and made her way to the steps leading to Vidar's office. The two dwarves watched as she approached, barely reacting, their caution not as clear as it had once been. She was a familiar sight after all. One covered her with his crossbow while the other made her raise her hands and patted her down. It was only then that she caught a waft of something inviting and looked outside, seeing a small group of dwarves waiting by the entrance. They were gathered together, talking quietly and sharing a skin. These were not local boys. They were dressed in fancy armour and carried themselves like professional soldiers. An important visitor, perhaps?

The dwarf checking her stepped back and jerked his thumb at the stairs.

As Cade began the ascent, her mind moved back to the day's business; the other mine representatives were a mixed bunch. One or two were a sorry excuse for community leaders – things must be real bad at their workings. The others were in a better state, certainly after she'd spent an age bringing them round to the new way of things. Blondie, the sarcastic one, proved to be alright. He didn't let on who he was, or what he'd been before, but he was shrewd and smart and more importantly, happy to follow her lead – for the moment at least. The skinhead, well, she'd be a problem. She reminded her of Anzo, long dead, who'd seen an opportunity to seize control through thuggery yet had been too stupid to see where that would lead. She'd tell Vidar that Baldie would have to go, along with most of whatever crew she had. As for the others, well, once they got a taste of the good life, some of them might make a play. She'd just have to make sure they never got the chance. *Queen of Tissan. That's me.*

She reached the balcony and saw the door was open, light spilling from the room within. She stepped forward and was about to raise her fist to knock when Vidar opened the door.

'Ah,' she said.

Vidar raised an eyebrow.

'Wait inside. I'm just saying goodbye to a guest.'

'Right you are,' she replied with a nod, and stood aside to let him pass.

Vidar walked out followed by his guest, and Cade took a small step back in surprise. This was no dwarf. An elf! If the height didn't give it away, the fancy clothes, long hair, fine features and pointy ears certainly did.

The elf turned to look at her. By the open-mouthed expression on his face, he was even more surprised than she was. For a moment he missed a step, almost halting. He stared at her as if he wanted to say something.

Cade looked the elf straight in the eye. 'Take a good look. Might be the last chance you get,' she said softly.

'Get inside,' growled Vidar.

The elf closed its mouth and swallowed.

Vidar ground out some words that were not dwarvish, and the elf nodded and started to follow him down the stairs. He turned to look at her once more as he disappeared.

That was a turn-up. Today was a day for surprises. The familiar stomping of Vidar's boots encouraged her to take a position in front of his desk.

Vidar entered and closed the door, walking past her to settle down once more in his chair.

'What have you got?' he asked. *Ever the one with the small talk.*

Cade gave him the lowdown on what she had learned and what he could expect from his new workforce.

'And they are being prepared?' he asked.

Cade nodded. 'Yes, I've given instructions that those most suited are to make themselves known and be ready for transport here at dawn tomorrow. We should be able to take over most of the work you require within a few days.'

Vidar studied a ledger, running a finger down the page.

'Good,' he acknowledged. 'It costs me money every day smelters stand idle.'

'I understand, boss,' she said. 'Speaking of idleness. I can see there being a few problems with some of the civic leaders you found.'

Vidar glanced up, an eyebrow raised.

'Some of them might not want to play fair,' she said.

Vidar narrowed his eyes. 'You'll need to put better leaders in place,' he said.

'I'll make that a priority.'

'Speak to Geir. He'll arrange their removal,' Vidar said with a dismissive wave of his hand, and returned to his ledger, making a note on the page in his blocky scrawl.

'Right-oh, boss. Anything else you need?'

'No, you can go.'

'Thanks. Who's the elf, by the way?'

Vidar looked up sharply. 'That's none of your damn business.'

'Yes. Of course not,' Cade replied quickly. 'I'll leave you to it then.' She backed hastily out of the office, closed the door and walked slowly down the steps. *That was a moment.* Last thing they needed was the elves getting involved in her action. She was almost thankful for Vidar's stubbornness – personal greed and gain always came up trumps.

She passed the guards and walked outside into the dusk, seeing shadowed figures moving among the line of wagons that were parked up.

'Hey, Miriam,' she called.

The woman emerged from the rear of the wagon. 'Yes?'

'We all set?'

'Five minutes, I reckon.'

'OK, I'm just going for a looksee at something. Wait for me.'

'Right.'

Cade walked around the warehouse and Vidar's complex towards the centre of the plateau. It was not lost on her that already, with Vidar's commercial ascendancy, she could now walk unguarded. She approached a cluster of structures related to the logistics of the mining operations. Following her nose, she located a stone-walled building with a large chimney. The smell of baked bread filled her with a sense of comfort and pleasure, but started her stomach rumbling. She walked to the entrance to the half-opened door, peeking in to have a look – several dwarves wearing leather aprons covered in white powder were engaged in the business of baking. At the rear was a large oven radiating so much heat she could feel it flowing over her even from this distance. The dwarves were busy pounding dough and warm loaves were stacked on a rack right by the door. She'd seen all she needed to. As she withdrew, she held one in each hand. Her crew would eat well tonight – perks of having a boss who's a thief.

Moving swiftly, she rounded the side of the bakery and started to head back to the wagon. Suddenly she felt an arm snake around her neck.

'What the fu–!' Dragged into the shadow of the building, she struggled to batter her assailant with the loaves.

A hand covered her mouth and an urgent voice hissed, 'Be quiet!'

She fought on, raising her foot, aiming for the shins.

'Ow! Fucking stop,' the voice was in her ear, a male voice. Krste. The voice was speaking to her in Krste.

Cade stopped. 'Alright, alright. Just let me go.'

'OK. Just don't run.'

Cade felt the pressure on her throat release. She spun round, still holding up the bread.

'You're lucky I didn't bite your fingers off, you bastard,' she growled.

'Sorry, but see how nice it is when you don't struggle?' The man stepped away from the shadows. And Cade took a step back. It was the fucking elf!

'You! What do you thin–'

The elf raised his hand to quiet her. 'Please, I'm a friend. Can we just stay in the shadows? I only have a moment.'

She cocked her head.

He spoke in perfect Tissan. There was the hint of an accent, maybe from the east of the Empire.

She eyed him cautiously, but followed him back into the shadow of the bakery.

'You must listen to me,' he said. 'You have to know what's going to happen to you.'

'Yeah, I know. You lot are pissed off. The dwarf already told me.'

'The dwarf knows nothing. The elves know about what's going on here. They want it ended. They want you all dead.'

Cade shrugged. That was hardly news. Every other race on earth wanted them dead.

'What do you care? Who the hell are you?' she demanded.

The elf leaned in close.

'My name is Fillion. *Captain* Sabin Fillion. Of His Majesty's Imperial Scouts.'

'Bollocks you are.'

The elf sighed.

'I know, you look at me, you see one of the enemy. I get it. That doesn't change who I am. My mother was an elf, my father was human. From the borders.'

Ah, that made sense. She was right about the accent. Even so.

'Prove it,' she demanded.

'How? I can tell you anything you want to know about the Empire. Just listen to me. Do I sound like an elf?'

'Not sure, I've never heard one.'

'Look. I was part of a group sent to save Prince Tigh, to get him to Aberpool before the fleet sailed.'

'Fleet?' she asked. 'I was at Aberpool. Didn't see a fleet. I was in a cell though, so I guess I might have missed a few things.'

The elf, Fillion or whatever his name was, shook his head.

'Look, you must have gotten out. What did you see? The city. It was deserted, right? No citizens, just soldiers?'

'Yes,' she said. 'What of it?'

'That was deliberate. A means of helping the escape, to buy time. Everyone was either put on the ships or forced outside.'

Cade chewed the inside of her cheek. That's pretty much what she'd heard from other survivors. Either way, what would this elf ... human ... half elf-man, gain from talking to her if he wasn't on the level?

'Say I believe you for one second. So what? And how in the Seven Hells are you here? Dressed like that?'

Fillion reached out and touched her shoulder. 'I'm surviving. Just like you. And I'm looking for a way to fight back. To make them pay.'

'Good for you. We're a little busy right now keeping our heads down and trying to stay alive.'

'Listen to what I am saying. Your dwarf can't protect you. You can't just live out your lives here. The elves will come or they will make the dwarves do it. They want you all dead.'

There was a tone in his voice that told Cade that he was telling the truth and a chill went through her.

'How long do we have?' she asked.

Fillion shook his head. 'Worst case scenario? I'd say you have three months.'

'Three months?!' That gave her no time.

'As I said, that's worse case, you may have longer. It depends how much of a fight the dwarves want to put up to keep you.'

'They can be stubborn when it's in their best interests,' Cade assured him.

'But then there are the elves, and the one I work for? He won't delay – he'll do whatever has to be done.'

The one he worked for. Yeah, she'd love to talk to him about that little nugget. But that would have to wait.

'What can you do to help?' she asked.

He thought for a moment. 'I'm not sure yet. I can't hide the facts. But maybe I can cause some delays. I have my own plans.'

'Oh, well, far be it from me to get in your way.'

'Look, I'm sorry. It's just been a while since I've spoken to another human.'

'You've been with them since Aberpool?' she asked.

'Yes.'

'Shit.'

Fillion smiled ruefully. 'Indeed. But I know you'll have had it bad.'

'At least we could be ourselves.'

A cough, coming from somewhere nearby, caused Fillion to whip his head round.

'We're out of time. What are you going to do?'

Cade scratched her head. Good question. 'You came to the right girl. I reckon we'll have to rethink our future. Might be time for us to blow this place.'

Fillion nodded. 'Good. Head west. There are no remaining enemy outposts in Tissan lands, as far as I know.' He paused, a pained expression on his face. 'I wish I could do more.'

'Hey, don't sweat it. Happy to get a heads up, all things considered. I haven't put up with this shit just to be slaughtered by a bunch of uppity, pointy-eared bastards.'

That brought a smile to his face. Fillion nodded. 'Good luck.'

He turned away and vanished into the night.

Cade stayed where she was, leaning against the wall. She looked down at the loaves still clutched in her hands. It was times like this she really could do with a bottle of something red. Or white. Or a small keg of something. She wasn't fussy. She closed her eyes and rested her head against the stone behind her. If this Fillion was being straight with her, then they needed to come up with a plan. Things were taking a turn she'd never expected, but maybe not everything she had helped to engineer would go to waste. She looked out over the plateau. She wondered how many dwarves were left in the mountain range. And how many humans there were for each one of them.

'Right.'

She stepped out from the shadows, making for the warehouse.

She had work to do.

CHAPTER TWELVE – FILLION

Fillion sat with his back against the waystation, the sun warming his face. He watched the barges pass by on the Ras, their dwarf masters calling to one another, sharing information. No one paid him any mind as he observed, no one questioned his purpose for being there, even though he was an elf. The dwarfs were a remorseless and implacable enemy, yet again he was struck by the notion that what played out before him could have been a scene from any Tissan community. But it only took a moment for him to remember what they had done to his people. What they were still doing. Branding human beings, using them as slave labour, treating them like cattle. That put things back into perspective and made his purpose sharper. The question, however, remained: what should he do? What could he do? It was a cruel fate that he was chosen to be the instrument of their demise. Should he keep up the charade and keep focused on the bigger picture? If so, he was condemning them all to death.

The young woman he had spoken to had come across as smart and seemed to take on board what he said to her. He wished he'd had more time, but he'd acted on the spur of the moment. Meeting her on the stairs like that, locking eyes with her. He had seen intelligence as well as stark loathing. Even though his mission was to seek out human slaves, it had shaken him to his core to bump into one so soon.

The dwarf, Vidar, had taken pride in his business, had flaunted his use of Tissans, had confirmed all that Patiir had suspected. Vidar had even referred to that woman by her name, Cade, called her his fixer. So again, the question: what could he do? There was, he supposed, one option. He could say nothing. Tell Patiir that there was no truth in what he believed. There were no humans in bondage, and the dwarves worked the mines. That might wash. The dwarfs had never admitted to it, they were happy with the way things were. He could plead ignorance – say that the dwarves had just lied to him. Deceitful, untrustworthy and greedy, it's what they were known for after all. It would buy him time. *Idiot.* Did he really think he could get away with that?

'You made it, then?' asked Marmus, emerging from the waystation's doorway.

'Yes, it appears I did,' replied Fillion. The dwarf and his entourage had arrived late in the night. Fillion was already in his cot when they had showed up, but he had heard the ruckus they'd made outside and the stamping of their boots as they had traipsed upstairs.

Marmus grunted and scratched his beard.

'Did you get what you need?'

Fillion nodded.

'I believe so.'

Marmus moved his scratching to his chest, rummaging around under his shirt.

'Good. Then you are ready to head back?'

'Yes, I just need to saddle Amice.'

'Right, I'll get the lads ready.'

Marmus disappeared off to the stables. Fillion stretched his neck and pushed himself off the ground. His peaceful repose was at an end.

'Ah, Sabin, my friend!' declared Ezra, emerging into the sunlight. 'At last, someone I don't have to look down on to speak to.'

'Careful, Marmus might hear.'

Ezra waved a dismissive hand. 'That old curmudgeon has so much hair growing out of his ears I'm shocked he can hear anything.'

'Have a care, Ezra, he is a crafty one. I wouldn't put anything past him.'

'As you say. All I know is the conversation has not been scintillating since we parted ways.'

'And how was your business?' Fillion asked.

'Quite acceptable. I met with a number of merchant representatives, passed messages to various politicians and functionaries, and got treated as dirt by all I came into contact with.'

Fillion simply smiled.

'And did you see them?' pressed Ezra.

'See who?'

'The humans, of course.'

Fuck.

Ezra barked a laugh.

'Oh, Sabin. I'm sorry. It's just the look on your face. Please, do not take it personally. Your innocence does you credit, just as much as it makes you terrible at statecraft.'

Inwardly Fillion cursed his foolishness. It was obvious that if Patiir had wind of something then so would Tekla. For all he knew he might have heard it from her in the first place.

'I can't hide anything from you, can I, Ezra?'

The Servant shook his head. 'Not in this case. Member Tekla and I had half expected the dwarves to pull something like this. It is fortunate that there are several dwarves who value gain over patriotism. I was passed information regarding the matter some time ago and duly informed both our respective masters. But, this is Member Patiir's particular area of concern and it was only right that you were given the task of confirming the veracity of the intelligence,' Ezra smoothed out his robes and then looked up at him, a quizzical brow raised. 'And?'

'It's true,' said Fillion with an exaggerated sigh. 'The dwarves have thousands of them. In fact, it's just one dwarf. He has taken over the management of the whole area, and he's got the humans working almost every element of the mining operation. Now the other owners just reap the benefits.'

Ezra nodded his head approvingly.

'A sensible business decision.'

You cold bastard.

'I will inform Member Patiir of my findings. But I must admit, I don't know what he expects to achieve,' said Fillion.

Ezra leaned back and stroked his chin, contemplating. 'I doubt very much this will be allowed to continue. If it's one thing that Patiir is known for it's his thoroughness. He would not suffer there to be any humans this close to the Heartlands. He'll make a special petition direct to the King. Member Tekla will support him in this, as will many others. We had all expected the humans to be eradicated.'

Fillion felt a hollow sense of defeat. There goes any hope of trying to stall.

'Even so, there must be survivors still in the west?' he ventured.

'Perhaps, but not in any great numbers. None that we need concern ourselves about. No, the threat lies in what the dwarves may decide to do. They say that they will let the humans slowly die off. But what if they get a taste for having this slave nation? Encourage them to breed?'

Fillion hadn't thought about that, but it was obvious now he did.

'The response to this will be quick,' Ezra continued. 'The dwarves will be put under the strongest political pressure. There will be the threat of sanctions, tariffs and the like. They won't like that.'

'I suppose so,' agreed Fillion.

'Come on, you two!' announced Marmus, rounding the building astride his mount. The sound of tramping feet announced his guard, and behind them the creaking of wagons. 'The sooner we get going, the sooner I don't have to look at your faces any longer.'

Fillion waved in response.

'Was that dwarf humour?' asked Ezra, clearly not sure whether to be outraged or not.

Knowing Marmus, it depended on who he was referring to. As Fillion went to fetch Amice, his mind was racing. Thousands of Tissans were living on borrowed time. He needed a new plan.

A few days later Fillion joined Marmus who sat on a log apart from his entourage, gazing out into the wild. Fillion was on edge, aware of the risk he was about to take. Behind them the cookfire was starting to burn low and on hearing soft words spoken he turned, a little too abruptly, to see Reygar lean forward and place two branches on to it. Fillion watched the sparks drift lazily into the star-strewn sky. *Calm down.* He had to play this right. Beside him, Marmus puffed on his long-stemmed pipe. He appeared calm and unaware of Fillion's unease.

'Nice night,' he ventured.

Marmus blew out a few smoke rings. 'It is that.'

He took another puff and offered the pipe to Fillion. This was a first. Fillion nodded and accepted the pipe. The tobacco smoke tasted surprisingly sweet. He made an appreciative noise and passed it back.

Marmus watched him and smiled.

'Not what you were expecting?'

'Not really.'

'Well, you elves aren't known for your palates. But good for you for trying it.' He replaced the pipe in his mouth and took another draw.

They sat in silence for a while. Fillion rubbed the back of his neck. He looked across at the far side of the camp where his elven colleagues were gathered. They couldn't hear them over here. Now was as good a time as any.

'Marmus. We are friends. At least, I know you dislike me less than most of my people,' Fillion said, keeping his gaze fixed on the fire.

Marmus murmured his agreement.

'And you know I fought in the war against the humans. So I have no love for them.'

'Hmm.'

'I find myself possessed of certain knowledge. I am … conflicted.'

Marmus pulled the pipe from his mouth, finally interested. 'Continue.'

'I am a loyal Servant. I serve my Member and my King and my people. But if I did not share with you what I know, it would be a betrayal of our trust. Something I have come to value a great deal.'

Fillion glanced at Marmus. The dwarf was looking at him keenly, his eyes glowed sinister in the reflected embers of his pipe.

'What is it, lad, spit it out,' urged Marmus.

Fillion sighed loudly, letting his shoulders droop as if in defeat.

'You know Member Patiir asked me to accompany you to act as his agent to inspect your new workings, to ensure it was a viable concern. And that I did. But my secondary mission was to discern whether there was a workforce of enslaved humans.'

'No discerning needed, I gather,' said Marmus.

'It was something of a … surprise to me to discover just how many were employed. We are not talking a few hundred humans. There are thousands, Marmus.'

'And your point is?' asked Marmus, his voice betraying no sense of shock at the news.

'Patiir will not suffer this situation to continue unanswered. He will press for their annihilation.'

'And why does he think he has any say in this matter?' responded Marmus. 'It's none of his damn business.' The tone of his voice had changed. It was challenging and officious, like he was back at the Parliament.

Fillion shook his head.

'It violates the terms of our treaty, Marmus, as you well know. Patiir will bring all of his considerable influence to bear on this. He will petition the King to force the Dwarf Nations' hand in this matter and I believe he will succeed. One way or another Patiir will ensure the humans are eradicated like the vermin they are. He will not rest until that happens. You know him, you know how driven he is.'

'He can try, Sabin. He can try,' said Marmus, flatly.

'Marmus, I do not like being used as a spy. I warn you of this because I do not wish to see you ambushed or manipulated in any way. The number of friends I have in the capital would be exactly halved if you were to be expelled.'

'No fear of that, Sabin. I will not be bullied. Nor will the nations of the dwarves,' Marmus growled.

Fillion waited for more but Marmus had taken to his pipe once again. He turned to look at Marmus directly.

'Will you keep this discreet? Between us?' he asked.

Marmus nodded, the pipe held in clenched teeth. Then he pulled it free and met Fillion's gaze.

'I understand the delicacy of your situation. You're stuck right in Patiir's web. You are wed to his daughter, you have sired his grandchild. I will not betray your confidence.'

Fillion sighed again. Relief causing shoulders to sag, this time for real.

'Thank you, my friend. What will you do?'

'Do? Nothing for now. I'll wait for Patiir to play his hand. But forewarned is forearmed. I will think on how to counter his machinations.'

'Very well.' Fillion made a play of forcing himself to stand. 'I will take my leave of you and bid you goodnight.'

'One last thing,' said Marmus. Fillion stopped. 'If you hear anything else on this matter, I would appreciate it if you let me know. Naturally in a manner which serves your continued discretion.'

Fillion hesitated a moment then nodded his assent.

He turned and walked back to his companions, feeling Marmus's eyes burning into his back. He smiled despite his caution. The play was in motion.

CHAPTER THIRTEEN – OWEN

Owen looked up from his fire. Arno was awake, his head tilting to the side. Had something spooked him? Owen corrected himself. Hardly anything spooked Arno. He looked around and listened for a moment but nothing seemed amiss. '*Close your eyes, my friend, rest,*' he pulsed softly. Arno looked at him, blinked once or twice, and then shifted himself back into a comfortable position. Owen smiled and returned his gaze to the fire, stoking it a little with a stick. He leaned back and looked up into a night sky that was clear, cloudless and bright. He felt something close to contentment, which he had not felt for some time. Although he still felt the same joy whenever he was in the air, on the ground his mind had been fixed on his purpose for so long. In this quiet moment, however, surrounded by the slopes of a Highland valley, the smells familiar, the landscape comforting, he had no reason to deny himself a moment's respite. The war carried on, it had never really ended for him, but just for tonight he felt he could put it out of his mind.

Perhaps it was the excitement of going home. He was longing to get back there, because there was a home to go back to, and it was full of people living their lives. The expectation had started to creep over him the previous evening, when he entered the borders of the Highlands proper, and espied the fire of a human hunting party. It was incredible to see life, human life, returning to the land. And to think, he had played a part in making it so! He'd made a show of gliding low and sweeping over the campsite a few times, just so they would know they had a friendly visitor.

He found a suitable landing place a short distance to the west of the camp and had put down, leaving Arno settled. Then, forging his way through the dark trees, he had sought out the light, a clear and obvious beacon, and with it, a hunting party from Eagle's Rest, led by Saul. He was welcomed in by the leathery old hunter and joined his group of ten, an equal number of men and women, around the fire. He shared their meat and told them his news. Another gnomish incursion had been dealt with, his fighters victorious with no serious casualties. A much smaller party this time, that had required little effort or numbers to deal with. It seemed the gnomes were either finally learning their lesson or being weeded out. They had toasted his success and Owen settled back to an evening of good company. Saul confirmed that Gerat and his people had arrived shortly before he'd led his group out.

'I have to say, Owen. I've not seen a more bedraggled lot than them since the early days. To be fair, they looked pretty overwhelmed by the Rest. It all seemed a bit much for them.'

'They have just walked a thousand miles to get here,' said Owen with a laugh. 'You were no different when I first met you.'

Saul waved his hand dismissively. 'That's horseshit, I looked exactly like I do now. Rugged and lived in. Perfectly at home and suited to the hunting life.'

'You smelled just like you do now as well,' one of the group added.

'I didn't know things that weren't dead could smell like that,' chimed in another.

Saul sniffed loudly. 'It's called *blending in*, something you shits have still to learn.' He leaned in close and Owen had the opportunity to enjoy the odour first hand. It did smell a little like something had died. 'Don't listen to this lot of wet-behind-the-ears. A whole year I've been trying to teach them about woodcraft and they still insist on washing every morning. They'd have brought beds if we'd had mules to spare.'

Owen had settled back to listen to their friendly banter, perfectly at his ease, returning to bed down with Arno a couple of hours later.

He smiled at the memory. And he was surely looking forward to those beds Saul had mentioned.

He and Arno had left at dawn to continue the journey, finding his current campsite later that afternoon.

Owen awoke to spats of rain falling on his face. He screwed his nose up and shivered despite himself. It was time he was up and about, the idea of getting rained on, even for the short trip home, was most unwelcome. And, like an idiot, he had not thought to pack his oil skins. Too much comfortable living campaigning in the low country. He pushed back the blanket and sat up, looking into a grey sky. The seasons were changing. Definitely no time for breakfast. He looked sadly at the gently smouldering remains of his fire, an occasional droplet of water sizzling against the hot stones that ringed it. He set to breaking his very modest camp. He rolled up his blanket, tied it off and then packed his remaining gear. As the rain continued to fall in a desultory fashion, he hurried over to Arno who was, naturally, already awake.

'Morning, old friend. No time for a hunt.'

Owen stowed his belongings and fished around in one of the saddlebags, retrieving a small haunch of meat and unwrapping it from its cloth package.

Arno eyed this with interest and followed Owen as he placed the meat in front of the eagle.

'Field rations for you.' He stepped back, and Arno cocked his head watching him go. They had done this a thousand times and Arno needed no more encouragement, darting his head downward quickly, gobbling the meat in one go.

'At least someone gets breakfast,' said Owen, ruefully. Wasting no more time, he climbed aboard and settled into the saddle.

'Let's go home,' he said aloud, and pulsed directions. Immediately Arno responded and they were in the air and climbing.

Owen pulled his woollen cap a little lower over his face. At least it looked like the cloud cover was breaking up further west and beyond it the skies looked a lot friendlier. Arno made a turn, swooped over the top of a lower-lying peak, and there, directly ahead, was home. They followed the ridgeline that led to the gateway. A couple of figures were walking along the trail that wound its way down to the valley below.

Then he was over the settlement proper, the hall, the outhouses, and the roost. A number of folk were about, and some pointed at his approach. A figure stood by the entrance to the hall, wrapped in dark furs. Was it Murtagh? He had missed the big Highlander. No, Murtagh would not be wearing furs at this time of year, he was far too hardy a soul. Whoever it was raised a hand in greeting. Arno took them in a wide curve before angling his way back for the roost. The gate to his stall was open, they all were, and Arno made an easy glide inside.

Owen climbed off and got started into the routine of unpacking his gear, and removing the saddle from Arno. He looked around the roost as he loosened straps; the place was empty of both eagles and people. That was odd. He would have expected someone to be along to give him a hand, it wasn't that early in the morning. Finally, the door opened and in stalked two men, neither of whom he immediately recognised. Following them was Gerat, wearing a set of dark furs. It must have been him by the hall.

'Morning, lad,' said the Scotian.

'Gerat,' Owen said, dumping a saddle bag and extending a hand.

The man took it in his and shook it firmly. 'Good to see you, Owen.' Gerat looked, if anything, hairier than before, his exposed skin tanned and leathery.

'And you. I heard you had arrived, so I came ahead of the others.'

'Good of you,' said Gerat. 'These two will help get your kit stowed,' he said, indicating his two companions.

Owen nodded. 'Where's Murtagh? Naimh?' Even if the big man was not about, Naimh, his sister, would have come to see him. She had arguably more influence in how this place ran than her brother.

'Oh, I said I'd come and see to you. Everyone else is still inside, breaking their fast.'

'A little late, isn't it?' asked Owen.

Gerat was quiet a moment then shrugged. 'More mouths to feed.'

Owen scratched his chin. He supposed so. 'How was the journey? Jussi wasn't big on details.' He glanced at Gerat's men. Neither appeared to be doing much.

Another shrug. 'It was a long, damn trip, Owen, but, I have to say,' he looked up and around, 'this place. It's perfect.'

Owen smiled. 'Yes, I think so.'

Gerat beckoned him forwards. 'Come, you'll want to say hello to your people.'

That was an odd way of putting it. 'Your people too, now,' responded Owen.

'As you say.'

As they made their way towards the hall, everything looked … wrong. Where was everyone? The familiar faces: Malcolm who worked the smithy, Sheena who managed the stables. All he saw were dirty-clothed survivors from Scotia, their eyes tracking him as he reached the steps and climbed to the entrance.

Something was off. More than off, something was wrong.

He stood at the entrance and faced Gerat.

'What's happened?' he asked.

Gerat stood before him and folded his arms. He looked uncomfortable for a moment, and then his eyes hardened. Behind him Owen heard one of the large doors open.

'Don't fight it, lad,' said Gerat.

'Wh–'Owen tried to turn, but his arms were seized and something was pulled over his head, blocking his vision. Even as he struggled to break free he pulsed, *'Arno. Fly. Get away. Go!'* The Eagle reacted immediately to his distress. Owen heard a shriek and frantic shouting. *'That's it, Arno. Go. Get–'*

A fist drove into his stomach and he doubled over.

'He's talking to that damn bird of his,' shouted someone.

'Then shut him up,' he heard Gerat order.

Stars flashed before his eyes as something struck his head. Owen fell to his knees. He felt the impact of a boot to his back, and now he was face down on the wooden deck of the hall. More kicks followed. The breath was knocked out of him and he curled his body protectively. A boot smacked him in the ear and he jerked with the shock.

'Alright, don't fucking kill him.' The voice was muffled, like he was in another room. Hands grabbed him, pulled him to his feet and started dragging him … where? He couldn't make it out, he couldn't think straight. His legs wouldn't work and he just flopped into the arms of whoever was carrying him, his eyes closed and everything faded to black.

When he came to, it was in darkness. He could vaguely feel the sack or whatever it was still covering his head. His breath, hot and smelling of blood, washed back against him. He did not struggle or try to stand up, rather he tested his limbs, trying to understand the injuries he had received. He gently wriggled his fingers and his toes, and felt bindings on his wrists, tight and cutting. He shuffled his legs. They were not bound but hurt like hell in a number of places. He realised he was lying on the floor, on his side. He tried to lift his head and immediately regretted it. A wash of bile rose up into his mouth. He took deep breaths through his nose and started to swallow, gulping down the waves of saliva he was producing in abundance. Desperately trying to crush the panic. His throat stung sharply, but he was able to keep whatever was left in his stomach down.

Owen tried to take stock of his situation. He had a nasty lump on his head, a bunch of painful areas on his back and his legs, but his breathing was reasonably even, and nothing seemed broken, not even a rib. That was, all things considered, lucky. He ran a tongue along his teeth. They were all there. But there was something not quite right about his hearing. It was his left side, where the boot had connected, it felt … muffled. So that was him. Trussed up, beaten up, and likely locked up. But he was alive and in one piece, which meant something. But, and now he started to feel a rising sense of panic. *What the Emperor had happened here?*

Gerat had taken control. But why? What in the Seven Hells would that achieve? And more importantly, where was everyone else? That panic he had felt returned as fear. A cold dread. He had seen none of the other Highlanders. Were they all prisoners, like him? His mind raced, thinking about possibilities. And one thing kept repeating, one dreadful thought: his people would not have submitted, would never have submitted. They would have died first …

It was later, much later, that he heard movement and a door opening very close to him. It scraped the edges of the floor, not far from his head. That sound, it was familiar.

There were footsteps and hands gripped him, pulling him upright. It hurt. Then a hand gripped the sacking covering his head and, with a few head hairs in tow, pulled it off.

He blinked a few times, getting his bearings. Someone was next to him, holding the sacking. The room he was in was gloomy. A weak light, drab and sickly, filtered in from outside.

It was his room.

Standing by the door, his face in shadow, was Gerat. His arms were folded and he was watching Owen with open contempt.

'Owen.'

Owen was no fool. If he was alive, then the man wanted something from him. But he was in no way inclined to give it to him, whatever it was. He did not reply.

Gerat sighed and took another step into the room. 'Give him some water.'

The man next to Owen produced a skin and held it up to Owen's lips. He drank deeply, even as his scratchy throat complained. After a few seconds the skin was pulled away.

'Lad,' said Gerat. 'I understand. You are angry right now. I get it. No way round that. But you'll still listen to me. You've got no choice.' Another step and he hunkered down next to Owen and inspected his face. 'Got yourself banged up pretty good. Wasn't sure if you would come to. Taking a blow to the head like that, many folk never get up, some are never quite the same. You still the same, Owen?' He looked into Owen's eyes, searching. Owen breathed heavily through his nose, trying to keep his burgeoning anger in check. Gerat grunted and leaned back. 'Yeah, you're still there. Let's cut to it then. This place, Eagle's Rest, is no longer yours. It's mine.'

'What have you done?' demanded Owen. He had to know the truth.

'I did what I had to. You see, Owen, a place like this? Well, like I said, perfect. A safe place. A place where we can live peacefully. It was worth it, you know, that trek. It wasn't easy. We lost a few along the way. The old, the infirm. A couple of young ones. But it was worth every step. Soon as I got here, I thought to myself, Gerat, you can make this a home, a real home for your people. But there was a problem.' He rocked back and rubbed his hands together. He opened them up and looked at his palms. 'Your people were already here.'

'Gerat–'

The man stopped him with a shake of his head. 'I know what you are going to say. Plenty of space for everyone, right?' He smiled sadly. 'I could see that. But what did it matter? It still ain't no city, it ain't part of some great empire. It was one small, safe place, hidden from the world. And that,' he raised a single digit to force the point, 'that is why we had to make a change. Because all the folk here – folk – well, they weren't hiding anymore. You said it yourself. You are at war. And that means drawing attention.' He shook his head and sighed again. 'I couldn't have that.'

Owen was at a loss. 'Gerat, you've been at war since I first met you. I was the one who wanted no part of it.'

'True,' Gerat said, and placed a hand on Owen's shoulder. He squeezed it gently. 'You were right. War, fighting, resistance. What's the damn point, Owen? Everyone dies, nobody wins. We could never hope to win. All there is … all there can be, is survival.'

'And you are telling me what you had back west was survival?'

'It was. And it was shit. A slow, shitty death. I knew that. But it was all we had. My people, you saw them, they had nothing else. All they had was me to keep them together, to keep order. Without me and my lads they would have perished. But when you came, with your promise of something better, it gave us all hope. They were willing to give it a try.' Gerat rubbed his large hands over his face.

'But not if we continue to live in fear. We need space, room to breathe, freedom from always looking over our shoulders. We all want that. But you want war.'

'Gerat. They don't know where we are. They never will. It's not how we fight,' said Owen.

Gerat shook his head. 'Not yet, but the more noise you make, the more scratching you do, then they'll want to itch that scratch. They'll come. And we'll all die. Just like my daughter did. Not again.'

Owen understood now. Gerat was broken.

'Gerat, we can work this out. We can still make a home for you. It doesn't have to be here. Let me see my people, let me speak to Murtagh–'

Gerat shook his head. 'Owen. He's gone.'

'Where is he?'

'Want me to spell it out?'

Owen let his rage take hold, a cold, powerful anger. He surged forward, trying to get to his feet, reaching out with his tied hands to grab Gerat. He got his fingers around the man's throat before he felt a swift punch to the side of his head. He gasped, his hands twitched free, and Gerat scuttled back. His face was hard, murderous even.

'Careful, lad. I need you because you might come in useful. But I don't need you that much.'

'What have you done?' Owen cried.

'I've given us all a chance at a better life, a peaceful one. But your people, they weren't interested in that, they were all behind you. So I had to get make an example. Make my argument iron clad. Make sure there would be no resistance. So Murtagh, most of the men, they had to go.' He reached out and placed a fatherly hand on Owen's shoulder. 'It was fast. I'm not a cruel man, Owen. I made it quick, many were asleep. The others? We're keeping them safe.'

Owen shook his head, despite the pain. He felt tears streaming down his eyes.

'You fucker. You fucker.'

'I had to, I couldn't risk it. It was your people or mine. This world has changed, Owen. I told you, back in Scotia, people don't work together, they take what they can and if it means taking it from someone else, so be it. My people will follow me, and now they have something to call their own, a proper home. And I mean to keep it. And that,' he pushed himself up, 'is why you are still around. I figure we might get more of your people coming back. I need you around to keep them honest.'

'They'll fight you,' warned Owen. 'I won't order them to do otherwise.'

'Then they die. We'll just open the gates and let them walk right in. You want that on your conscience? That's up to you.'

Owen felt the rage suddenly leave him, drain away to leave nothing but a void in its wake.

'Gerat. You weren't this man. When I met you, you helped me, you hadn't given up.'

'Things change. People change. Look at you. As I heard it, all you could think about was vengeance. When I lost my girl, I died too that day.' He stepped back. 'We'll keep the hood off. Hosen here will bring you some food.'

He turned and started to leave, but stopped at the door, keeping his back to Owen.

'For what it is worth, I am sorry. I take no pleasure in doing what must be done. But look at it this way. Humanity gets to keep living. Surely that sacrifice is worth something?'

He stepped away and disappeared out of view. Hosen looked at him with a grim smile then retreated from the room, closing the door behind him. Owen heard something slide into place, a bar of some sort, and felt the rage return.

'You'll pay, you traitorous fuck!' screamed Owen. He charged for the door and bounced right off it. He fell to the floor, winded and in pain. He lay where he was, breathing deep. He needed to think. It wasn't over, it couldn't be, he needed to get out and fix this. But he wasn't getting out of here easily. They'd come after him. He needed to focus, think this through. Yet, no matter how hard he tried, familiar faces filled his mind: Murtagh, Naimh, and a score of others. His friends, his family. How could they do this? If he did get out, the first thing he'd do would be to find Gerat and stab him in his black and twisted heart.

CHAPTER FOURTEEN – MICHAEL

Father Michael shared a campfire with the Emperor, enjoying the peace, the gentle crackle of the flames. He looked up into the dark sky. A howl pierced the night's calm.

'How can they sleep with those beasts?'

'The Nidhal?' asked the Emperor.

'Yes, with their mounts, the vargr. It seems wrong to lie next to such wild creatures.'

'I would not like to sleep so close to such ravening beasts,' the Emperor concurred. 'But I suppose we judge the Nidhal by our standards. Their approach to life is very different from ours.'

'And there is logic to their method,' said Eilion, as he walked over to join them. 'Your Grace, the guards are set. Loras, my Watcher, has taken a view of the key approaches for a half mile in every direction.'

Father Michael only half listened to the exchange. It was the same report every night for the last week. At least they were making good time over firm ground. He glanced up at Eilion, the man was still speaking.

'They remind me of the Plainsfolk. They are a light cavalry force, used to hitting quickly and moving fast. By sleeping close to their beasts they can react quickly and be on the move within a matter of moments.'

The Emperor nodded. 'They make good raiders, I'd imagine.'

'Quite so, Your Grace. Able to strike deep into enemy territory. They could live off the land, harass a supply line and burn unprotected settlements.'

'That is all well and good, but how would they do in a pitched battle? We cannot hope to retake our lands with hit-and-run tactics. That will just tempt out a larger force, and we do not have enough of our own people to fight such an engagement.'

'True, you need discipline to hold the line in battle if it is to triumph.' Eilion looked at Father Michael, the disdain in his eyes clear. 'And I am not sure how the Nidhal would fare. But I am sure they will prove worthy of you, Your Grace.'

The Emperor picked up a twig and tossed it into the fire.

'Thank you, Eilion. If you see my squire, send him over. He should have my meal ready by now.'

The Gifted nodded and stepped away.

'Don't let him get to you, Father,' said the Emperor.

'Your Grace?'

'I am not blind to the words of those gathered around me. I simply choose how I will react to them,' the Emperor said with a faint smile. 'He is an arrogant man. I can see that. But much of it comes from an understanding of his Gift. He has been trained, raised up, to believe in himself. He is a proud man. Simply … forebear it, Father. We all need each other in these difficult times.'

'I understand, Your Grace. I will try to … rise above.'

'Well done, Father Michael. You are truly growing as a person.'

Father Michael wondered darkly when Eilion might do the same.

The following evening the two groups camped within the embracing arms of a curving bowl carved out of a hillside. It appeared to Father Michael this site had been created by some great gouging force. He studied the bowl as Cadarn and Bryce settled their eagles close by. He voiced his thoughts to Cadarn when he joined him.

The Rider nodded sagely. 'Yes. This happened a long time ago. An ice flow did it.'

'Emperor, that must have been a sight,' wondered Father Michael.

'We in the Highlands are no stranger to the ice. The winter we just experienced was harsh, no doubt, but try living that at our altitudes. The cold shapes the land and the mountains, and governs the rivers and streams.'

'You speak of it with reverence,' said Father Michael.

Cadarn smiled at him. 'I do. The Emperor may have my life and loyalty but my soul belongs to my homeland. There are greater forces out there than we can ever hope to master.'

'Like an eagle,' muttered Bryce, as he heaved his saddle on to the ground. 'This one was in a right bloody mood today.' He cocked his head towards his bird.

'It wants to hunt, to go for a stretch.'

'Aye, well. It can bloody wait for me. I'm for bed,' grumped Bryce.

'You can go scout the route tomorrow, that will stretch its wings,' offered Cadarn.

'You're all heart.' Bryce pointed over Father Michael's shoulder. 'Looks like you have some fans.'

Father Michael turned to see two of the Nidhal walking towards them. Both were unarmed, though they carried themselves with a swagger, a warrior's confidence. The stopped before him and nodded respectfully. One pointed at Father Michael then turned and gestured him towards their camp.

'I think they want you to go with them,' said Bryce.

'Yes, they do,' agreed Father Michael. And he reckoned he knew what might come next.

The other one put a hand to its mouth and mimicked drinking.

Oh. Perhaps not then.

'I believe you are to be an honoured guest,' observed Cadarn.

'I am not sure I should go,' said Father Michael. A night of drinking fermented milk had not been his intention.

'Oh, you should. It would not be a good idea to upset our companions. It is an act of diplomacy,' said Cadarn, his face straight and sincere. Behind him, Bryce was grinning.

Father Michael, looked around, hoping someone might object. Or conjure up a reason for him to decline. But none was forthcoming. Why would it? They were in the middle of a wilderness. Once more the Nidhal warrior pointed towards their camp. Father Michael knew he had no choice but to relent.

'I should tell the Emperor,' he suggested.

'I will do that,' Cadarn promised. 'Enjoy yourself.'

Defeated, Father Michael cricked his neck and adjusted his cloak. 'Very well.' He nodded at the Nidhal. 'Lead on.'

The Nidhal bobbed their heads and the second ran ahead, shouting in its guttural tongue.

'On second thoughts, I might stay up and see what happens,' said Bryce loudly.

It was a strange evening. Father Michael was indeed treated as if he were royalty. As he entered their camp, vargrs watched him with their usual interest as Nidhal warriors gathered around him and clapped him on the back, and he nodded and smiled as graciously as he could. He tried to recall his behaviour as an arena champion, how he lapped up the cheers of the crowds, wallowing in the adulation, encouraging it. He told himself it was a role, a game that he had played, and that this was no different. Father Michael had to play his part in this fledgling alliance. He raised a hand and smiled at the gathered warriors. A cheer of approval went up, and he was ushered to a spot by their fire. As he settled on to a blanket, a soft leather skin was handed over, the familiar stench of chaga assailing his nostrils. He tipped it to his mouth and took a tentative mouthful. The liquid was sour-tasting and fiery, and no better than when he had tried it the first time. He swallowed and made a face of appreciation. 'Yag. Yag!' he said, repeating the Nidhal word for good. Again, grunts and shouts indicated the Nidhals' pleasure. The evening continued with the Nidhal trying to teach Father Michael more words of their language. He dutifully tried and repeated the words, knowing full well he would forget most of them by the morning.

A haunch of meat was taken from the edge of the fire. This he accepted with greater eagerness, and as he devoured it, some of the Nidhal, younger ones by the look of it, gave him a display of their wrestling prowess. He watched them grunting and rolling in the dirt, their bodies sweating from the heat of the fire. He adopted a serious pose, judging their performance thoughtfully.

Their technique was awful. It was all brute strength, youthful spunk and bullshit posturing. He'd seen it a thousand times. But tonight they wanted to show off and seek the approval of the Tissan champion. So he applauded after each bout and continued to drink heartily from the skin, or its replacement. As the evening wore on and the alcohol took effect, he found himself relaxing, even enjoying himself. At one point he even got up and showed an eager-faced Nidhal how to grapple correctly. The Nidhal had launched himself at Father Michael with a mighty roar and ended up right on his arse. The watchers hooted with laughter and the Nidhal fighter, suitably shamed, retreated to the rear of the group. A second warrior, older, seasoned, stepped forward. It took Father Michael a moment to size him up and he decided to draw it out a little longer, so he allowed the warrior to grapple with him for a few moments. He could feel the strength in the Nidhal's arms, could smell the milk on his breath. Alcohol and overconfidence. It was always the same. Father Michael took him down with a sidestep, a punch to the kidney area, and a two-handed strike to the back of the neck. The warrior fell to his knees and the crowd's mood turned to shock. Clearly this had been their best man. Knowing it would do no good to shame this one, he held his hand out and helped the Nidhal up. Once done, he clapped him on the back and then raised the Nidhal's arm in comradeship. That improved the mood. Fighting done, he returned to his place and continued drinking.

He was unsure what time he returned to his own blanket, but his head told him it was at least two milk-skins too late.

Father Michael climbed down from the wagon he'd been sharing with Bron and Uther and looked into the dense treeline. It was the woods where they had first encountered Nutaaq. He remembered that moment well, yet he wished he could forget it. He wished he could dismiss the memory of his Emperor so distraught, so disturbed. But the scene now couldn't be more different. The trees were green and full of life, the sky was blue, and the afternoon sun continued to blaze as it slowly retreated to the horizon. What was past, was past. Did not Father Michael carry his own demons as well?

Waiting for them in front of the woods were Cadarn and Bryce, having flown ahead to rendezvous with another Rider.

'I have more messages for you, Your Grace,' said Cadarn, bowing to the Emperor.

'I am sure. We'll camp here tonight and you can share them with us.' The Emperor looked at Father Michael. 'Time to say goodbye.'

He made his way to the gathered Nidhal. This was the agreed parting of the ways. Father Michael and the others watched as the Emperor spoke some indistinct words. In response the Nidhal gave a single cry in unison, lifting their spears high above their heads in salute before turning and riding west towards the far mountains. The humans stood and watched them go.

'Just us again,' said Uther.

'Maybe not for long,' muttered Bron.

'Have faith,' said Father Michael.

'Oh, I've got lots of that,' said Bron. 'It's their weight of numbers that worries me.'

'They are on our side. They are our friends and allies,' argued Uther.

'Yep. So they are,' said Bron as he got to unloading supplies from the wagon.

Father Michael left them to it, and went to find the Emperor. He stood next to Cadarn, reading a letter and nodding thoughtfully.

'It seems the development of New Tissan and our fleet continues to go well,' he said, not looking up.

'Good to hear, Your Grace,' said Cadarn. The Eagle Rider looked up into the sky. 'If we continue at this pace, we'll reach the coast by the end of summer.'

'Your Grace,' said Eilion, joining them and standing to attention. 'Cardinal Vella sends her best wishes.'

'That is kind of her,' said the Emperor. 'She sent you a message?'

'Yes, she wanted to reassure herself of your safety. It is, after all, the responsibility of the Gifted to ensure it.'

'And I am grateful,' said the Emperor. 'Leader Cadarn just made an estimate of our likely arrival at New Tissan. I find myself eager, impatient even, to get back and see the progress for myself. How far to the first waystation?'

'We could reach it tomorrow evening, if we keep the pace the wagons are going at now.'

'And if we flew?'

Cadarn rubbed his chin. 'If you jumped on with me, and we unloaded everything else, we could get you home in four days. My bird would need to have regular stops to rest, what with carrying two of us, but there will be other Riders at the waystations. We could pass you along in relay.'

The Emperor nodded. 'It's something to think about. I find myself at odds. On one hand I want to get back, and on the other I have a responsibility to see my people home.'

'You don't have to worry about that,' said Cadarn. 'This is ground we have flown before. The others can follow Bryce.'

'Your Grace, I am not comfortable with this idea,' said Eilion gravely.

'Why?' asked the Emperor. 'Are you afraid that I'll fall out of the sky?'

'No, Your Grace. I am worried that you will have no protection from the Gifted taking this route.'

'There is no force that could pluck us from the air and on the ground we will have the safety of the waystations. And anyway there are no other threats. The Nidhal would have warned us.'

'Even so, I must counsel against it. The Gifted are charged with your defence and protection. If you are caught on the ground, one Eagle Rider is not sufficient.'

Father Michael thought Eilion appeared a little off balance, lacking his usual assured manner.

'Yes, I suppose,' mused the Emperor. He glanced at Father Michael. 'Father, what is your counsel?'

Father Michael shook his head. 'Your Grace, unless there are any dragons, wyverns, or bees up there, I can think of no safer place than in the air, and we encountered no dangers on the ground on our way here.'

The Emperor smiled. 'A pragmatic answer. Very well, I will think on it.'

The Emperor waved his hand in dismissal and the gathering broke up. Father Michael returned to the wagon where a cookfire was under construction.

'What are we having?'

'Stew,' announced Bron.

'It's always stew,' replied Father Michael.

'There's meat in it,' added Uther, as he gathered a skin of the fermented milk for the Emperor.

'Aye, and we've got bread too,' said Bron. Both foodstuffs were courtesy of the Nidhal.

'Exactly the same as last night, then?'

'I might add a little more seasoning,' said Bron casually.

'We could add one of those weird little fruits. The dried ones,' suggested Uther.

'I could. Just one, mind.'

Father Michael nodded his agreement. A little heat to the dish would be good. It reminded him of Erebeshi cuisine.

'Fine, I'll dig one out,' said Bron, taking a plate of meat from Uther and tipping it into the pot.

'How long do you think it'll be?' asked Father Michael.

'Depends how tough you want your meat,' said Bron curtly. He stood up and walked over to the wagon to collect a small hessian sack. Beautiful wandered over carrying another bowl full of vegetables.

'Straight in,' ordered Bron. He fished in a pouch tied to his belt and withdrew a small, red object the size of a baby carrot and threw it into the cauldron. He put his hands by his sides and leaned back. 'I suppose, the Emperor will want the meat tender, so you have a couple of hours.'

'Good enough,' replied Father Michael. It gave him time to exercise.

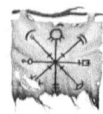

He walked a little way out of camp, stripped down to his britches, and got to his routine. Now that he no longer had a sparring partner, his routine lacked the extra edge. He could conduct his drills, go through the motions, stay flexible, practice the standard manoeuvres; they were not really the problem. It was the unpredictability of an opponent, the random chance, the split second reactions needed to anticipate then reconsider. Part of that, he acknowledged, was an edge that came with youth and vigour. Were others faster than him now? It was likely so. But he had years of experience to draw on, he just had to keep his body strong and healthy.

As he paused for a moment, he spied Eilion standing by the Emperor's tent. He could not hear the conversation, but the Gifted appeared quite agitated. In the fading light, Father Michael saw the Emperor make a cutting motion with his hand. Eilion's body became rigid as he pulled himself to attention. A few moments later he bobbed his head, saluted, and marched stiffly away.

'That looked interesting,' remarked Corporal Fenner, as he ambled over munching on a piece of bread.

'It did,' agreed Father Michael.

'It's never a good idea to upset the Emperor of all of Tissan. I imagine Eilion's future prospects of becoming a Cardinal have just gone sideways.'

'It is his duty to be protective. You can't blame the man for that,' said Father Michael. He rolled his shoulders and picked up a wooden sparing blade he'd had made by one of Nutaaq's brothers. 'Still, he is worse at diplomacy than I am.'

Fenner barked a laugh. 'Now that is the funniest thing I've heard all day.' He studied Father Michael, eyeing the blade. 'Do you want someone to spar with?'

'Are you offering?'

'Me? Hells, no! I'll go fetch Coyle. He's the only one big enough and stupid enough to even try.'

The sparing didn't last long, even after Wendell had waded in to try and even out the odds. Both men were exhausted, sweaty and beaten in just ten minutes, though Father Michael felt it polite to acknowledge that they had at least tried to make a fight of it. Beautiful promised that next time she'd join in to even the odds even more, and Wendell said he'd set up a book on how many seconds they would last.

When he had cooled off, Father Michael settled down to eat with Bron, Uther and the Emperor. He accepted a bowl of stew and as he chewed his first mouthful, he could feel the heat of the small, red fruit burn the edges of his tongue; not too much, but enough to make the stew interesting. He eyed his companions. Uther was already sweating, he had little tolerance for spices.

'Try some of the milk,' advised the Emperor. 'It will ease the burning.'

'That stuff? It tastes awful, Your Grace,' grumped Uther.

'Believe me, you'll get used to it,' laughed the Emperor.

'And you should keep taking small pieces of the fruit. It will build up a tolerance,' advised Father Michael.

'Quite right, Father. I suppose it is no different to any other kind of training. Pain can be controlled,' the Emperor suggested.

'It can, Your Grace. You can learn to put it to one side, in battle. It is about controlling your fear, embracing the rush that takes you when you face danger. It'll still hurt like shit afterwards– ah, apologies for my language, Your Grace.'

The Emperor waved his fork in the air to dismiss the apology, chewing vigorously as he did so.

'None necessary. Continue,' he said after a swallow.

'And of course there's poison,' said Father Michael.

'Poison?' asked Uther.

'You need to start taking poison.'

'What? I'm not taking poison!' Uther said, looking horrified.

'You need to, it is your duty.'

Uther looked at the Emperor for guidance.

'He might be right, squire,' laughed the Emperor. 'You need to taste my food. Make sure no one is trying to poison me.'

'That's why you have to build a resistance. I had to do the same in the arena. I had to take many different forms of poisons both natural and devised.'

Uther looked at Father Michael with desperate eyes. 'I thought that wasn't allowed?'

'It's the arena, you think there are rules?'

'You were poisoned in the arena, then?' asked the Emperor.

Father Michael nodded. 'I was, Your Grace, several times. It was a common trick. It was only the resistance that I had built up that slowed the effects, kept me fighting.'

'Do you think you can still resist such things?' asked the Emperor.

It was a good question. Father Michael scratched his chin and put his bowl down on the ground.

'Maybe, perhaps. I don't know. It takes time to build the resistance and then, like any other skill or physical ability, it takes constant practice to maintain. But sometimes …' He shook his head as the memory returned. 'Sometimes the effects were so bad, you wished you could just die, so it could end.'

'Well, there you are, Uther,' said the Emperor, sitting back. 'You'll need to get started.'

Uther, white-faced, bobbed his head.

'Yes, Your Grace.'

'Just as soon as we've worked out what actually is poisonous over here. Best you start building your tolerance to alcohol first,' said the Emperor, passing him a skin.

The next morning Father Michael awoke to the sound of eagles taking flight. He turned over and shaded his eyes as wings filled his vision and an eagle passed overhead. *Early start.* He pushed his blanket off and got to his feet. The camp was already breaking up and wagons were being loaded. The Emperor walked over, leading his horse.

'Good morning, Father.'

'Your Grace. Are you well?'

'Indeed I am.' He pointed at the two eagles now heading east. 'I've told Cadarn to meet us at the next waystation. He's to rest up, and wait for us to arrive. Then my intention is to fly back to New Tissan.'

'A good plan, Your Grace. There is no need for you to stay with us,' said Father Michael.

The Emperor's mouth quirked into a smile.

'I'm not sure that my Gifted would agree with you.'

'Eilion did not look happy, Your Grace.'

'He was positively sulking. Anyway, best we move out.'

Father Michael bowed and got to it. He hurried over to Bron's wagon and retrieved some bread to break his fast. He was still working his way through the dense chunk as they set off, him walking next to the wagon. The Emperor led, flanked by four of the Gifted. The other four marched at the rear. Clearly Eilion wasn't taking any chances now that they had no protection from the Nidhal. It was another fine day and the sun shone brightly.

He bid a silent farewell to the woods in which they had first encountered Nutaaq. It was six months ago, yet felt like a lifetime. So much had changed. The future was now full of possibility and optimism. He felt better in himself than he had in a long time, since before they had arrived in this new land. It felt good. He listened to Bron and Uther's chatter and watched the birds flit among the trees. Their path took them south towards the wide river that had taken the lives of the scout Reece and the marine Yentle. From there they would head due east, a simple journey.

One of the Gifted jogged by Father Michael, who watched as the man fell in next to Eilion, who led the front quartet. Eilion stepped out of the squad and looked back down the line. Father Michael turned around and saw that the second wagon had stopped and was falling behind. The marines had climbed off and were inspecting the underside.

'Looks like they've broken something,' said Bron, from his spot on the wagon.

'What do you think it is?' asked Uther.

'We should stop and have a look,' said Bron.

'No need for that,' said Eilion, as their wagon drew next to him. 'Corporal Fenner says they can fix it and will catch us up. We'll keep moving.'

Bron nodded and flicked the reins to move the horse along.

Father Michael stayed with Eilion and studied the wagon. The other Gifted walked back to speak to his comrades in the rear.

'Are you leaving someone?' Father Michael asked.

Eilion shook his head. 'They are soldiers. What more protection do they need?'

Father Michael conceded the point.

'Still, perhaps you are right,' murmured Eilion. 'Raspa!' He called to the Gifted who had bought the message.

Raspa jogged back.

'You and one other stay behind. Make sure everything works out as it should. Get Loras to commit the place to memory so we she can Watch you,' Eilion ordered.

Raspa nodded and turned away to speak to his comrades.

Eilion looked at Father Michael. 'Good advice,' he said, before returning to speak the Emperor.

Father Michael raised an eyebrow. Wonders would never cease. He continued to watch the marines as they toiled to fix the wagon. Fenner looked up and raised a hand, and Father Michael followed suit, wishing him well. The Watcher, Loras, had done … whatever she had done, and marched past alongside the other remaining Gifted. Raspa and his companion, Mercer, stood to one side as the marines continued their repairs. *Nice of them to help.* Father Michael shook his head and took his place next to Bron's wagon once more. A short time later they found themselves paralleling the river to their right. It was not as wide as where they had attempted to cross, nor was it frozen like last time. It flowed freely and vigorously, and it looked far more friendly and inviting. Father Michael wondered idly if there were fish to be had.

'We'll rest here for a moment to take some water,' announced the Emperor, as he slowed and dismounted. 'We'll be turning east now, and in six miles or so we'll find the first waystation.'

'Sounds good to me,' said Bron, stopping the wagon and stretching.

The Gifted halted and Eilion motioned to the two rearguard to join them in a gathering. Father Michael walked over to join the Emperor as he led his horse to the river's edge.

The Emperor tilted his head back towards the wagon. 'Father would you get my other–'

A shriek made them turn together.

Uther, his mouth open, was transfixed by the spear that had been thrust through his belly by Loras. She held the attack pose, her leg forward, arms outstretched. Upon the wagon, Bron was still seated, staring at the spear that was buried deep into his side. The Gifted bearing the spear pulled him off the wagon and on to the ground, pulling the spear loose as he did so. He then stepped close and drove it into Bron's throat, pinning the driver to the ground. Eilion and the other Gifted were walking slowly towards the Emperor and Father Michael, their weapons ready. Behind them Loras twisted the spear in her hands and withdrew it. Uther collapsed to his knees, his hands pressed to his wound.

Father Michael was in a ready stance before he even registered it. This was a challenge and his body knew how to react. Beside him the Emperor had drawn his sword.

'Eilion, what are you doing?' he shouted.

The Gifted slowed, forming a semicircle around the two men.

'Your Grace,' said Eilion raising a hand. 'I would ask that you lower your weapon and throw it on the ground.'

'And tell me why should I do such a thing?' the Emperor demanded.

'Because you are outnumbered and outmatched. I am not going to hurt you, but you must surrender to me,' said Eilion, calmly.

'Is this a coup?' asked the Emperor, in disbelief.

Father Michael was only half listening. He was already weighing his chances, planning where to strike. He was facing four Gifted, and two more were approaching. Without weapons or any element of surprise, it would be impossible to take them all before he received a killing blow. But by the Emperor's grace, he would go down fighting if it came to that. He singled out the Reader Leisha, on the left, her spear lowered towards him.

'It is not I, Your Grace,' Eilion continued. 'It is all of us. The Gifted have realised that a new way is needed. Our people need leadership, governance, wise counsel.'

'Yarn,' the Emperor spat.

'Yes, who will talk with you, when we return to New Tissan.'

'And what if I refuse? I am your Emperor, you are sworn to protect and obey me.'

Father Michael shifted his position slightly, gathering his strength.

Eilion shook his head.

'No, not any more–'

'Eilion.' Grieg, the Reader, looked at Father Michael and pointed. 'He's not going to come quietly, he is going to–'

Dammit. Father Michael covered the space between him and the Gifted in moments, getting inside the reach of the spear. He forced the shaft down and to the side with his left hand, throwing a jab straight into Leisha's faceplate, ignoring the pain in his fist as it connected. The Gifted staggered back but did not let go of her weapon. Father Michael followed up, taking hold of her helmeted head and twisting. Leisha grunted, trying to counter the force, but Father Michael was too quick, too strong and the Gifted fell. Father Michael swept up the spear and spun ready to engage. An explosion of pain to the side of his head made him stumble. He felt himself flailing, as another Gifted, spinning a spear high and horizontal, let the sharp end fly towards him. He caught a glance of the

Emperor swinging his blade high as two Gifted closed on him. Father Michael leaned back as lancing fire scored across his forehead. He was falling, his arms held wide, crashing into the river. As he splashed into the water the Gifted stepped up to the bank, readying his spear even as Father Michael was gathered up by the current. He heard a voice cry, 'Wait!' as an object flew towards him at speed. And as it struck, his vision went black and the river overcame him.

CHAPTER FIFTEEN – FILLION

Fillion travelled south, riding alone along well-maintained roads, relishing the time alone to take stock of events without the distraction of play acting to hide his true nature and intentions. Having taken his leave of Marmus, Ezra and the others back at Apamea, he had not stayed at the house, preferring to take a room at the Chalice. It was, he realised, an act that was out of character, but with most of Parliament in recess and scattered around the Heartlands, it would not attract much notice from the greatly reduced clientele. Kanyay was still in the west, and knowing him, would be in no hurry to return. Only the staff and a few others recognised him, and none chose to interrupt his quiet reverie. A bottle of wine and nobody to please but himself. After one night he had left for Patiir's lands to the south, following well-used roads bustling with good-natured traffic. There was no crime to speak of in the Heartlands, and a traveller could find respite among any number of impromptu campsites. Unless there was an inn nearby. He was too old to say no to a bed if it was on offer. And on those occasions, showing his belt of office proved most useful in negotiations.

The nature of the land changed. Where once benign forests and lush meadows had dominated, the road to the southern coasts became rockier, punctuated by steep hills, scrub, and hardier vegetation. But there were also vineyards, and numerous olive and fig groves, taking advantage of the bright sun and blue skies.

The settlements he passed were a little less formal than those further north, as if the climate had also affected the elven mind set, inducing a more relaxed outlook. White-washed houses gleamed upon the hilltops and pretty cottages clustered by the many small rivers and streams of sparkling, cool water, all winding their way south from the high country.

The place had a sense of ease about it, not like Apamea where everything was so damned … ordered. Here, the homes had an aged quality and they settled into their environment far more comfortably.

Steles by the road notified his entry into Patiir's lands. His fiefdom was huge and Fillion encountered several hamlets, a few larger villages, and at least one small but busy town, full of produce being bought, sold and transported north. This explained why his father-in-law wielded so much influence in Parliament. He was responsible for a significant portion of trade and produce that made its way north, trade that Fillion continued to pass in the form of wagons and carts hauling goods sedately along the road. On reaching the coast, he followed a paved road that took him the last two miles to Patiir's summer villa. It sat upon a gentle hillock, facing blue seas that glittered in the glorious afternoon sun. The villa was large with several outbuildings and it glowed pure white, reflecting the summer light, so that Fillion had to shade his eyes to look at it. He passed rows of vines, elves wearing wide-brimmed hats moved between them, tending them. Flanking him on the road were marble statues of elves, gods and beasts. If Patiir's home in the capital had been but one of a number of impressive residences, here he had his sense of power and position on full display. It only made Fillion feel so much more justified in his course of action.

He halted Amice outside the wide, pillared entrance and gazed into the shadowy interior. At first no one appeared to pay him any mind. Then a figure rushed into the light. Hedra.

'Sabin!'

'Hello, Hedra.'

The lad ran up to him and grasped Fillion's outstretched hand.

'We never thought you'd ever get here!' he said, his face one great broad smile.

'I've had to come a long way,' agreed Fillion. 'Where is everyone?'

'They are all inside. Come along,' Hedra urged, tugging at his arm.

'Alright, alright,' Fillion replied, laughing. 'Just let me get off my horse first.'

'Yes. Hang on,' Hedra disappeared back inside as Fillion eased himself off Amice and ran a hand through his sweaty hair.

Hedra reappeared with a female elf servant who bowed deeply to Fillion and took Amice's reins.

'The stables are behind the main house,' explained Hedra. 'They'll take care of her.'

'Good,' replied Fillion, slapping Amice gently on her flank. Hedra grabbed his arm again. 'Now, come!'

This time Fillion didn't resist as he was ushered into the cool interior of the villa. The specifics of its features passed him by, but he marked shadows, space, plenty of ornaments, and pools of water everywhere. He was led into a wide, internal garden flanked by arched corridors and dominated by a large fountain, where the sculpture of a sea creature, perhaps a dolphin, squirted a torrent of water from a hole in its stone head. Trimmed green grass flowed around small trees and flowerbeds which were colourful and vibrant compared to the more arid landscape beyond the walls. Nadena and Alica sat chatting on the lip of the fountain.

'Look who's arrived!' announced Hedra.

Alica made a squeak of delight and threw herself at him.

'Steady!' he cried. 'I'm still weary after my journey.'

Alica punched him in the arm.

'Nonsense, you should talk to your wife about being weary. She's just given birth!'

An unexpected thrill went through him. Fillion craned his neck to see her.

Nadena stood slowly and walked towards him. Her face was a picture of serenity. And in her arms she carried a small bundle, wrapped in white cloth.

'Husband,' she said, with a playful smile.

'Wife,' he replied, his own smile coming unbidden.

'Would you like to meet your daughter?'

Fillion felt goosebumps rise on his arms as she passed to him the swaddled infant. As he took the weight, he gazed upon a small, wizened face, its eyes closed, the mouth open a little, like the child was deeply worried about something.

He stared at it for a moment, trying to gather his thoughts, trying to work out what he was feeling. Before this moment it had all been just an unavoidable fact, a concept, an irritant, another obstacle to his mission that had to be factored in and overcome. The baby, it looked so … human.

'What, what's she called?' he asked.

'Well, we never got around to discussing names, did we?' Nadena smiled.

'No,' he said. He placed his middle finger into a grasping hand, felt those tiny digits wrap around and squeeze. He laughed in spite of himself.

'What was your mother's name?' Nadena asked.

Fillion looked up sharply. Another shock.

'Brynne. Her name was Brynne.'

Nadena nodded. 'Then meet your daughter, Brynne. Brynne, meet your father, Sabin. The elf I love. Who must promise not to miss any more birthdays.'

Fillion grinned. 'I will try. Brynne, if I cannot, blame your grandfather.'

He found he was rocking her, and in response her face had lost its worried look. She looked peaceful. Happy.

'I suppose you should go see him?' Nadena asked.

Fillion shook his head. 'That can wait. I want to sit with you, with my family for a while.'

'That's the right answer,' said Nadena.

'Sabin? Would you like some wine, something to eat?' asked Alica.

'Yes, to both.'

'Good. Come along, Hedra,' said Alica pulling her brother away. 'Let's give them some privacy.'

'Oh, yes. Right.' Hedra grinned and followed Alica.

'Should we not get her out of the sun?' Fillion asked.

'She is fine, I've kept her covered. Honestly, you are back but a moment, and already you are the fretting father,' she chided, gently.

'Sorry, I–'

She leaned in and kissed him. 'Don't be.'

Fillion pulled back, feeling a grin crease his cheeks. He looked down at Brynne. A little life. Innocent. Unaware of the world of monsters it had entered. A strange thought occurred to him. Could an elf be something other than the culture they came from? Was their nature ingrained, or could it alter with the experience of life? The answer came just as quickly. *Am I any different?* Then a surge of panic. He had completely forgotten. *What if?* He plucked at the cloth, pulling it gently away from her face but his reception at the villa had already given him the answer. Her ears were pointed.

Fillion walked on to the wide veranda at the rear of the villa. It was covered in marble flagstones, populated with the usual flowerbeds, and contained by a waist-height balustrade running close to the edge of a high cliff. Standing against it, a hand resting on the railing, was Patiir, a delicate wineglass held in his other hand, gazing out to a sea that was slowly darkening as the sun reached the edge of the western horizon. Fillion joined him and leaned over to look down on to a rocky shoreline where waves gently lapped against bare white rock.

'Careful, Sabin. You don't want to be teaching your daughter any bad habits,' Patiir warned.

'If she's anything like me, she won't need me teaching her to do this,' replied Fillion, reminded of his own reckless childhood clambering among the tall, spreading trees of Celtebaria. 'I'm sorry I did not come to see you sooner, but I had some other duties to perform.'

'And I would have been disappointed if you hadn't,' said Patiir with a smile. He touched Fillion's arm. 'Come, let's have a drink to toast the arrival of your daughter.'

He led Fillion to a table which held a pitcher of red wine with what appeared to be pieces of fruit floating in it. He placed his own glass down, lined up a second one next to it, and poured wine into both. He handed one to Fillion, picked up the other and raised it in a toast. Fillion followed suit. The wine tasted good. Sweet and cool. Better than anything he'd had before. Forgetting himself for a moment, he drained the whole glass.

Patiir's eyebrow rose. He picked up the pitcher.

'I imagine after weeks on the road, you would have built up a quite a thirst,' he said, pouring more wine into Fillion's glass. 'And then there is the burden of fatherhood.'

Fillion nodded his thanks and took a sip this time. 'I am a little overwhelmed, right now,' he said. And that was probably the most truthful thing he had ever said to the elf.

'I do not doubt it.' Patiir smiled, and placed an arm on Fillion's shoulder. 'As I do not doubt that you will be an excellent father to my granddaughter.' A firm squeeze, and he removed his hand. 'So tell me what you have learned and then I will ask no more of you for the remainder of our time here.'

Fillion took another, longer drink. This was it. 'You were right about the dwarves. And the humans. There are thousands of them working the mines. I could scarcely believe my eyes.'

Fillion paused as Patiir nodded, his face grave. He settled his glass on the table and turned out to look at the sea, his hands resting on the railing. 'Thousands.' He fell silent for a moment. 'Please, go on.'

'I travelled to the mines until we arrived at a plateau just before you enter the larger peaks of the mountain range. There was a small complex of warehouses, that's where I saw some of them. Walking around, virtually unguarded. There was one dwarf who appeared to own them all. He had no shame about his activities and was unconcerned by my questions.'

'That is of no great surprise,' said Patiir, drily. 'Please, go on.'

'There are several different mines feeding into the plateau. Each has its own human population. The dwarf estimated he had around twenty thousand slaves in total. Digging, breaking rocks, smelting the ore. His intention was to have them work in every aspect of his business.'

'And no doubt he said he would work them until they died?' asked Patiir.

'Yes, as a matter of fact–'

'It's nonsense!' interrupted Patiir, his voice rising in irritation. 'He might say that now, but when the dwarf counts the gold he is making from those human slaves his view will change. He'll start to realise that he does not want to lose such a huge workforce that he does not have to pay, barely has to feed. And you know what will happen? He will encourage them to *breed*. Their numbers will grow. And they will become uncontrollable.'

'The dwarves would surely not dare go so far ..?' asked Fillion.

'Oh, they might. Who can say? But whatever they may decide to do in the future, in the here and now this goes beyond a misdemeanour, or a minor misinterpretation of our agreements. This is no less than a betrayal of our pacts, our solemn purpose. The actions of just this one dwarf can undermine everything we worked so hard to achieve.'

There was a pause as Fillion watched Patiir pace back and forth along the terrace.

'What can we do?' asked Fillion.

'I will need to think on this but I have already prepared some of the ground. Some of my fellow Members will support my position.'

'Which is?'

'I will speak to Parliament and to the King. I will tell them what you have discovered and I will demand action. Marmus will be given a clear message to deliver to his race. They must finish what they started. Every last human must be put down.'

'Marmus will not like it,' warned Fillion. 'His tone on our journey back was defiant.'

Patiir nodded. 'I can only imagine the tension you must have felt. Sabin, I do greatly appreciate this service you have done for our kind.

You have begun a course of events that will have a dark ending. But you will play no part in that. Your war is done. I will ensure it stays that way. For you and our family.' Patiir turned and gathered up the jug. 'Your glass has emptied itself again. Let me refill it. For the moment let us put aside this matter, it is the summer and we celebrate new life and hope for the future.'

Fillion agreed with that sentiment. There was hope for the future. But if he had anything to do with it, it would look very different from what Patiir was expecting.

CHAPTER SIXTEEN – MICHAEL

Father Michael came to in darkness and in pain. He attempted to open his eyes, but found them crusted shut. He wiped them with the back of his hand and felt a sharp stinging sensation, the blow made by the spear. He felt liquid swirling around him and used it to splash his sealed eyes. The gunge loosened and he forced them open. It was night. He probed his forehead warily and came away with wet fingers. Blood? No, it was water. He was still in the water. It was night but overhead the sky was clear, and he could see well enough his condition. He was caught up in a fallen tree half-submerged in the water, the branches had snared and still held him in place. He tested his limbs, wriggling his toes, moving his legs, and then both of his arms. Nothing appeared broken and his questing legs touched the river bed beneath him. He tilted his head left and right, and was rewarded by a wave of nausea. He retched up some bile, which was carried away in the current. He once more explored his head, locating a tender bump on the side of his temple, where the spear had struck him. An absence of a cut suggested he'd taken the butt end. His probing fingers moved up to the top of his head, and against further pulses of sharp agony he traced out another lump, this time topped off with a fair amount of blood. He withdrew his hand smelling the iron on his fingertips.

It must have been a fair-sized rock that had been launched at him – it was probably that bastard Eilion. Father Michael wondered if his skull was actually cracked – he knew only too well that head wounds could still kill you hours after the blow was struck.

The flow of the water was behind him, keeping him pressed against the tree. He must be on the far side of the river otherwise they would have spotted him, and it was dark, so he must have been here a while.

His first priority was to get out of this damned water and figure out where the hell he was. The Emperor was held captive and needed him. There was nothing else for it. Father Michael took deep breaths, steeling himself for the pain to come, and started to work his way through and among the branches of the tree. He pulled, tugged and squirmed his way towards what he hoped was the riverbank, ignoring the tugs and scratches. Inching forwards the bank soon came into view, a dark mass against the backdrop of more trees and bushes. His footing became surer, and he forged to the edge to haul himself out of the water. He pulled his legs up and curled into a ball as another wave of pain came upon him.

After a moment, he forced himself to his feet. His clothes were sodden and heavy – he was still wearing his cloak. He took it off, there was no way he could do anything wearing such a heavy garment. He regretted its loss, but he was a practical man. He made his way downriver, pushing through the undergrowth and following the flow of the river. A wide stretch of the bank appeared, more open and clear of debris. Looking to the far side he could see nothing to impede him. He lowered himself back into the water, its cool embrace welcome this time, the cold keeping him focused. He continued on, against the current, trying to keep his footing for as long as possible. He had gone barely a few steps before he lost control and the current took him. Foolish to believe he could get to the far side so easily.

Helplessly he watched his chosen exit point move beyond his reach. Kicking his feet, he stretched with his arms and started to stroke gently, keeping his body at an angle to the flow. There was no point fighting it, he had to work with it. With no sense of how far or fast he was travelling, his head was spinning and he felt like he was going to pass out. *Just keep going, just keep going.* He spat water out his mouth, feeling the taste of blood on his lips. His head wound must have opened again. Eventually there was a lessening of the current, and the far bank now filled more of his vision. *One last push.* He kicked harder, swept with his arms with as much strength he could muster, until he could lower his legs and feel the riverbed beneath. Drawing close to the bank, he pulled his way upwards using protruding tree roots, keeping his eyes fixed on the ground ahead of him, willing himself onwards, his breathing ragged.

And then he was out of the river and back on dry land. He crawled forwards towards a large tree, with a thick trunk and wide roots spreading out from the bowl. Finding a space between two, he gathered his legs close and rested his back against the trunk. It was only then that he closed his eyes and gave into exhaustion.

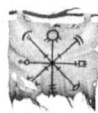

He slowly awoke to the sound of rushing water and birdsong, and felt sunlight on his face, warm, gentle, invigorating. His skin did not feel cold, and his clothes were no longer wet. Body and head still ached but he was still, at rest, pressed against the smooth bark of a tree. Father Michael stayed where he was, savouring the moment. He breathed deeply, evenly, taking in the scents of the land around him.

I am alive.

He slowly opened his eyes, blinking in the light of the summer's day. Truly it was a beautiful scene. The sun was low in the western horizon, just above the treeline on the far side. The fast-flowing water of the river sparkled and he could spy birds flitting over his head among the far trees. In the daylight he could see the river was perhaps thirty yards wide at this point, and the banks were not as heavily wooded as he had first thought. He closed his eyes once more then pushed out his arms, bracing them against the roots to either side. He levered himself up, pulling his legs back, feet flat on the ground. As he rose, he felt his body complain and the wound on his head spike with pain. He stood, his legs shaking at the effort, but he stood.

Turning around slowly, he tried to get his bearings. He was in a copse. Beyond that were more woods and rolling hills. He was at a bend in the river and he could see that further on it widened out and continued meandering to the south. What was next? He had to head east. East lay New Tissan. East lay the Emperor and the Gifted, and he had business with them. He walked slowly to the river, wincing at the pain in his head, and gently knelt. He reached out and cupped a hand to the water, bringing it up and to his mouth, repeating the motion several times, then placed his hand over his forehead. The blood there was dry and clotted. He ran a finger along the wound, it was long, almost the length of his forehead. Moving round to the lump on the side, it was sore, swollen, but as he'd thought, the skin was unbroken. At the least his wounds had been thoroughly washed clean. He tore a strip from one of his sleeves bandaged his head as best he could.

A gentle breeze played against his chest and he looked up in the sky. A sprinkle of clouds was starting to glow as the day began to end. He needed to get going. He turned from the river and worked his way through the copse and out the other side. East. If he was still walking in an hour, then perhaps he would do something about the growing hunger in his belly. Right now, it could wait.

'Father Michael?'

Father Michael's eyes shot open.

He blinked and started to push himself up off the ground.

'Easy, easy,' said the voice. It was a female's. It was familiar. Someone was sitting on their haunches in front of him. He sat up and rubbed his eyes. The crouching figure stood and stepped back, cradling a crossbow. Beautiful.

'Are you okay?' she asked, tilting her head to study him. 'Because you look like shit.'

'Ah. Yes. Yes … I–' And then it came flooding back. The fear and the anger. 'The Emperor. They have–'

'Yes we know. Fucking Gifted.'

Once more he made to rise. 'We have to find him.'

'We will,' she said firmly, and put out a hand to force him back down. 'But let's take a breath. Okay?'

Father Michael closed his eyes and did just that. He squeezed down on the panic he was feeling and took in a lungful of air. Recovering his calm he opened his eyes again and nodded at Beautiful.

'Well, alright then.' She turned, cupped a hand to her mouth and called out. 'Hey, fellas. You'll never guess who I just found!'

A voice shouted back.

'Is it a wine-seller?'

'Dream on,' replied Beautiful.

'Then I'm not interested.' That was Fenner.

Beautiful grinned and held out a hand to help him up. Father Michael accepted the offer, climbing to his feet and standing before her. An apple fell out of his pocket.

'Feasting like a king, huh?' she asked.

'It was the best I could do. I found a dead squirrel, but didn't trust it,' he admitted.

Beautiful nodded.

'Very wise. Never trust those little fuckers, alive or dead. C'mon.'

She led the way from the circle of trees where he'd taken shelter. Parked just ahead was the marine's wagon. Sitting on the bench was Fenner. A thought struck him and he felt his body tense. Were they in on it? These marines. Had they been sent to find him? *Don't be an idiot.* Beautiful could have just shot him in the head.

Fenner rubbed his chin as they approached. 'Emperor's beard! Sore head?' he said pointing at the makeshift bandage.

'I'm still standing.'

'Yes, you are. It's been three days now since you went missing. I reckon you'll make it.'

'Hey, Father,' said Wendell. He waved from his position at the rear of the wagon. His left thigh was bandaged and the leg was raised on a sack.

'Daft lad got too close to a Gifted, and got a slap for his troubles,' said Fenner.

'Bastards,' said Beautiful.

'Traitorous shits,' agreed Coyle, grimly, emerging from the trees on the far side, his crossbow held in a high port position.

'It was planned. They took the Emperor,' said Father Michael. 'We must do something.'

Fenner nodded, his face grave. 'We hoped that wouldn't be the case, but they went and did it, just like the Admiral predicted.'

'The Admiral? Lukas?' Father Michael frowned. What did the Admiral have to do about this?

'Why don't you hop on up here and I'll tell you about it,' suggested Fenner.

Father Michael didn't need to be asked twice. He was dead on his feet. He climbed up next to Fenner.

'Right you two, get back to it. We'll have time later for happy reunions,' Fenner ordered.

'Never a minute's rest,' Beautiful sighed loudly.

Beautiful and Coyle moved away from the wagon and Fenner urged the draft horse onwards again.

'I got those two as our flank scouts. Just in case. Wendell is the rearguard. When he's not falling asleep,' he added loudly.

'Hey! I'm awake. Here,' Wendell passed Father Michael a large chunk of bread and a waterskin.

Father Michael gratefully nodded his thanks and attacked the bread with gusto.

'Was it just you, or did anyone else get away?' asked Fenner.

'Only me,' said Father Michael, his mouth full of bread and water. He paused. 'They took Bron and Uther out.'

'Bastards.' Fenner was quiet for a moment, looking distant.

Father Michael swallowed and tore off another mouthful.

'I killed one of them. Leisha.'

'Good for you.'

'But I got knocked into the river. Someone lobbed a rock at my head.'

'Lucky for you you've got a thick skull.'

'I don't feel particularly lucky at the moment.'

'And lucky you were by the river,' persisted Fenner. 'If you went under they must've figured you were a goner.'

'What about you?' asked Father Michael. 'You said the Admiral told you this would happen?'

'Uh-huh. We got a message. It didn't say much. Just that we had to be ready.'

Father Michael thought about that and realisation hit. 'And you weren't there when they struck. You could've made the difference.' He felt anger start to swell.

Fenner put a hand up.

'Oh, I know where you're going with this. And you know it ain't true. We would never have been enough. The Gifted must've been waiting for the Nidhal to go before they made their move. Once that happened we were all on borrowed time. We had to change the rules.'

'It's what we do,' said Wendell, piping up from the back.

'We had to put some distance between ourselves and the *eight* Gifted,' continued Fenner. 'In a straight fight, they'd kill us all, no matter how many of them we might have been able to drop.' He reached out and took the waterskin from Father Michael. He took a long pull and wiped the back of his hand over his mouth. 'We faked our wagon breaking down. We didn't know if anything was gonna happen and we couldn't just start shooting without good reason. But I trust the Admiral's instincts and decided that we'd try and shadow the party, wait for the Gifted to make their move and then …' Fenner threw the skin into the back of the wagon, 'we'd come up with a plan. Fact o' the matter was, we weren't expecting Raspa and his buddy to stay behind.'

Oh. Father Michael coughed. 'Sorry, that was my fault. I suggested it.'

Fenner eyed him. 'That right, huh?' He snorted. 'I guess not much harm done. We just had to improvise, that's all. We were ready for a fight anyway, and as soon as I saw Raspa make a move, we were all over it. Not much a Gifted can do against crossbow bolts coming at them at point blank range. Still …' He cocked his head at Wendell. 'They went down swinging. We got lucky. Like you. And the way you tell it, I count three dead Gifted and two of ours lost. You gotta say that's a damned fine score. Better'n any we'd have a right to expect.'

Father Michael stayed quiet, he needed to think this all through. He had been angry at the marines for a moment, letting his emotions cloud the truth. They were right. There was more to this going on. The Admiral had sent word, and yet had not warned either he or the Emperor. Perhaps it was all just suspicion. That would fit with the old sailor's view on life. And did any others know? What of the Arch Cardinal? Surely any plan Cardinal Vella had concocted would have been smelled out by him? Another uncomfortable thought came to him – was it the Admiral making a power play and the Gifted were acting on the orders of Vella to protect the Emperor? *No, it makes no sense.* Even with his cracked skull, everything Father Michael had witnessed pointed to the Gifted as the betrayers. The marines were many things but they were loyal. And, now that he dwelled upon it, there was other evidence as well. Eilion had been opposed to the idea of the Emperor returning home by eagle. It made sense. It was not in the plan.

'How did the Admiral know?' he asked.

'That's a question way over my head,' said Fenner. 'He must've picked up on something. There was a reason he sent us along on this merry jaunt.'

'The Cardinal, he must have seen something.'

'I guess. You know what cracks me up? It's the notion that they probably got the order to do it the same time we got ours to do something about it. Now that, I believe, is what they call irony.'

'The Emperor,' he said. 'They wanted him alive.'

'Uh-huh.'

'So what does that mean?'

'Your guess is as good as mine, Father. That's politics and stuff. Not really my skill-set.'

'But he is alive,' Father Michael said firmly.

'If you say so.'

'Then we can take him back.'

'We could try.' The doubt in Fenner's voice was clear. Father Michael looked hard at Fenner. 'I'm just saying. The odds *are* better, but I got one marine who can only fight sitting down and, forgive me but have you actually seen yourself, Father? You are a tough son of a bitch, I know. But there ain't no way you are going toe to toe with anyone right now.'

Father Michael started to protest and then stopped himself. Fenner, frustratingly, was right again, so he remained silent.

'Now that's a face that says it wants to break something,' said Fenner.

It was not far from the truth. Father Michael wanted to break Eilion and all the Gifted. Break them for their disloyalty and for the shame they had inflicted on him. His first true test as a protector to the Emperor and he did not even have the comfort of knowing he had died defending him. He had lost. It had been all he had thought about for the last three days of walking. And it galled him. He had never lost, and now, for the first time, when it truly mattered, he had let the Emperor down, and it weighed heavily on him. Was it shame in failure? *Or is it my pride?* Truly, Father Michael could not decide which.

'What now?' he asked Fenner.

'We keep rolling on. It'll be dark soon. Why don't you rest up, join Wendell in the back. I'll get our resident healer to look at you when we make camp. You're no good to us the way you are, we need you back at fighting strength.'

Father Michael could not argue with that logic; rest would be most welcome. He stood up on the footboard and climbed into the back of the wagon. Wendell made space and Father Michael lowered himself down and gingerly rested his injured head against a sack. Within moments, he was fast asleep.

'Are you sure we can't make a fire?' asked Coyle.

'No,' said Fenner.

'Have you forgotten what we're doing?' asked Beautiful. She leant over Father Michael's head, inspecting his wound.

'It ain't dark yet,' complained Coyle.

'And what if they spot the smoke?' said Beautiful, pointedly.

Father Michael hissed as her fingers pressed down on the edge of the gash.

'Sorry, but it's got to be cleaned' she said.

'Father, you know why we are being cautious,' said Fenner. 'We've been heading east for three days. When we got to the waystation yesterday it was deserted. No birds, no Riders, but someone had been there just hours before. What that means, I don't know. Maybe the Riders were in on it, and have flown him back but I doubt it. Shit, maybe they think we were in on it. All I know is that there are several Gifted still ahead of us, moving in a wagon going to the same place we are, holding the Emperor captive. They must know by now that something is wrong because their comrades never caught up with them, which will have led them to the conclusion that we were the ones who took them out. So we're playing a game of cat and mouse here.

'I don't think the Riders were in on it either. But it's possible they have no choice now but to follow Eilion's orders. He has the Emperor,' Father Michael suggested.

'Right,' announced Beautiful, releasing Father Michael's head and stepping back. 'I've had a look, I reckon it's not infected so you'll probably be ok.'

Father Michael looked at her. 'Is that it?'

She shrugged and walked over to the wagon. 'That's just my opinion. But the wound looks clean,' she said and started to rummage among the supplies in the back. 'You feel any different? Smarter? Stupider?'

'I don't think so,' replied Father Michael.

'There you go then. Here,' she returned, clutching some strips of cloth. 'I got these bandages off the Nidhal. They've been boiled and some kind of plant paste rubbed into them. They swear blind it works.' She set to laying the strips over his head and under his chin. 'Besides, didn't I hear you got immunity to poisons and all that stuff?'

'Not to anything out here, I don't,' Father Michael said.

'Ah, you'll be alright, big guy,' she said, tying off the bandages and giving him a slap on the shoulder. 'Give it a couple of weeks and you'll be right as rain.'

Father Michael did not want to have to wait two weeks and, despite her optimism, he knew head wounds needed longer than that to heal completely. But he was grateful for her ministrations and held his tongue.

'Thank you,' he said.

Beautiful nodded her acknowledgement as she collected her crossbow. 'I'm going to take first watch,' she announced, popping a piece of cured oreq meat into her mouth and heading away into the lengthening shadows of dusk.

Father Michael looked to Fenner. 'Can we catch up with them?'

'Maybe. We got ourselves a few weeks to do it in,' said Fenner.

'And if we catch them, then we can take back the Emperor,' said Father Michael.

'That's highly debateable. They are still Gifted and they know we're coming for them but we'll sure as the Seven Hells try. And say we succeed, then what? Go back to New Tissan? It seems to me like there won't be a warm welcome for us there.'

'There doesn't have to be,' said Father Michael. 'He is the Emperor. The Gifted are still only few in number. When we return he will have command of all the loyal citizens of New Tissan. They will have no choice but to submit.'

'I guess you have it there, Father. Here,' He handed over some more of the oreq meat. 'We've got plenty of this stuff, and you'll need it to regain your strength. We'll need every ounce of it if we are going to beat those Gifted bastards in a scrap.'

Father Michael accepted the meat gratefully. Yes, he fully intended to do just that.

CHAPTER SEVENTEEN – CADE

Cade leaned against the side of the cavern partway up the track that wound its way to the Heights. From there she had a perfect view of the Downside Gate, the torches bright in their stanchions. It was almost time for the evening shifts to return. She pitied the poor bastards who barely saw any sunlight working those hours, even though she had done her best to get folk rotated. When the shifts came through the gate then it would be time for the Accounting. Regular as clockwork. Though her eyes were not good enough to see them all from here, it was clear there were fewer guards on duty these days. That made sense, Vidar's business was now spread so wide, he had fewer resources to police it. After all, the humans were a beaten, wasted race. There was no fight left in them. Right? Case in point, at shift changeover there were only a half-dozen guards watching the exchange of the mining tools. None went into the shafts anymore. Except Geir, you couldn't keep that bastard away. Up above, in the canyon, another six dwarves watched all the comings and goings. Six, for hundreds of humans. A crazy small amount. If that had been the case back in Aberpool, why, she would have complained to the warder. It would have been an insult to the thieving profession to be considered that low a risk.

Either way, Issar had done a good job. He had organised teams of watchers to track and report these details. Never the same folk twice, always making sure there was no pattern. Not that he expected the dwarves to be that observant, but why give them a reason to suspect? Quite the spymaster he had become. She picked at something stuck in her teeth and retrieved a small piece of unmilled grain. She flicked it over the path, raised her arms high and stretched. Right. It was time to kick things off. She turned and walked back up the path towards the cave. Ducking inside, she found Meghan deep in conversation with Issar.

153

'What are you two cooking up?' she asked.

Meghan looked at her and frowned. Issar looked guilty. But then again that was his resting face.

'We're just going over the reports,' Meghan replied.

'And?'

'No change,' said Issar.

'So why the long faces?' Cade asked.

'I'm just worried,' said Meghan.

'I'm not,' said Cade.

'That's because I do the worrying for you,' replied Meghan, finally raising a smile.

Cade grinned at her and settled down on her haunches. Issar passed over a beaker. Cade sniffed it and her nostrils stung. 'Your home brew?' she asked.

'Last chance to try it,' warned Issar.

'You know, if there was ever a way to prove they haven't broken us, this is it,' Cade mused. No matter how deep in the shit they were, someone always found a way to make booze. She took a glug and winced. 'Oh, sweet Emperor.'

Issar beamed proudly.

Cade let out a breath and gulped, trying to swallow the fire attacking her throat. 'Where – *shit* that's rough – where is Devlin?'

'Right behind you.' He settled down next to her and pulled the beaker out of her hand. He took a swill and swallowed, before handing it back to Issar with a nod.

Cade stared at him. 'Why are you not choking?' she asked, in disbelief.

'What? On that? It's just a bit of courage before the fight. Believe me, I've had worse,' he replied.

'I'm not sure I have,' said Cade.

'Either way. We're all set.'

'Everyone knows what they have to do?' asked Cade.

'As I said, all set.'

And just like that, they were about to start what could turn out to be the biggest, stupidest mistake of her life.

'You know, if this works. I'm going to retire,' she announced.

'If this works, then you're not going anywhere,' Devlin countered. 'This was your idea.'

'I didn't have much of a choice, did I?' she responded.

'I suppose not. But you must have realised. It was always going to come to this.'

Cade didn't respond. Truth was, she really hadn't.

'You have to admit, it's been amazing how everyone has rallied round,' said Meghan.

'They weren't in a position to argue,' said Issar.

'Even so. We are asking a lot.'

'They all had a choice. Die here or make a run for it,' said Devlin.

Cade grunted. Not much of a choice. And despite what Meghan was saying, there were plenty of folks who would still take this life over anything on offer out there. She couldn't blame them. But she sure as the Seven Hells wasn't going to die here because they didn't have the balls to do something about it. It was a good thing that she'd bought enough good will and plenty of muscle to keep the naysayers in line.

'Is there anything else we got to talk about?' she asked.

'Nope, don't think so,' said Devlin.

'Then I'll see you topside,' said Cade.

'Alright, then.' Devlin stood and proffered a hand to Issar, pulling the Erebeshi up. 'Good luck to us all.'

'Yeah, but let's hope luck doesn't have to come into it,' muttered Cade, pushing herself off the floor.

The two men left the cave but Meghan remained sitting on the floor.

'You worrying again?' asked Cade, putting her hands on her hips.

Meghan looked up and smiled.

'Me, worried? No. Hand up, please.'

Cade took her hand and hauled her up into an embrace. 'You aren't?'

'No. Not at all. Just look at how far we have come.'

'Not that far,' said Cade.

'Only because you never have perspective.'

'Do I want that?'

Meghan leaned in and kissed her.

'Yes. It might make you feel better about yourself.' She took Cade's hand and led her out of the cave. 'Who else could've organised all of this?' Meghan said, waving her hand across the cavern floor. 'Who else could've come up with a plan to get us out of here?'

'Right girl, right time.'

'Since when have you been so modest?'

'Since everyone started looking to me to solve their problems. I'm making this shit up as I go along, you do realise that, don't you?'

'Oh, I've known that from the start,' said Meghan laughing.

'Damn, I thought I hid that better.'

'Cade?'

A voice called softly from the entrance to the cave that held their water supply. Someone was standing just inside the entrance.

Cade stopped and looked inside. She couldn't make out who it was. She took a step towards them.

'Who's that?'

'Cade. What have you done?' asked the voice, quietly. It was a male voice that she recognised. She took another step.

'Gwillem, is that you?'

Gwillem stepped into the middle of the cave entrance. She hadn't seen him since he had lost his shit with her over the death of his wife. Which, she still maintained, was not her fault.

'What do you want?' asked Cade.

'I wanted to tell you something,' he said.

'Like what? I'm kinda busy right now.'

'That's what I wanted to talk to you about. Please do you have a moment?'

'We don't have time for this,' said Meghan, coming forward.

Cade put a hand up. 'It's okay, give me a minute.' She figured she owed the guy that much.

She stepped closer to him and studied his face. He looked better, his eyes clearer, more focused. 'You okay?' she asked.

He nodded.

'Yes, I just wanted to speak to you. I needed to tell you. I won't let you murder us all.' Cade saw the faintest flash of reflected light and threw up her arm in reflex just in time as she felt the sting of something sharp cut across her forearm. A blade. He grabbed her raised arm and thrust it back over her head, aiming to bury the weapon in her throat. She twisted just in time and the blade buried itself in her shoulder instead.

'You bitch! You murdering fucking bitch!' he screamed. Cade's knees buckled as he pushed down on the blade. She gripped his arms trying to force them away. Then Meghan was on his back, her arm wrapped around his neck. He reared back and pulled the blade with him in a spray of blood.

'Fuck!' cried Cade, clutching at her shoulder in agony.

Gwillem continued to backpedal, taking Meghan with him and smashing her into the cave wall. Meghan crumpled to the ground and he turned to strike her. Ignoring the pain, Cade scrambled up and fumbled for her boot, pulling her own blade free. She ran up to Gwillem and plunged it into his back. He howled and spun, backhanding Cade in the face. Her head whipped round and she staggered away. He was hot on her heels and threw himself upon her. She fell hard to the floor, the wind knocked out of her. His hands were around her throat and she couldn't breathe. She tried to pry his hands away but it was no good. As a pounding filled her ears, she thrust her left hand into his hair and pulled it back. His face, ugly and flushed, lifted a little. She felt spittle from his open mouth drip on to her cheek. And she saw his exposed neck. Her knife was still in her hand. She stabbed again, once, deep and hard into his throat. His eyes grew wide and his grip tightened. As her vision began to swim, she yanked her knife free and plunged it in once more, a wash of hot blood gushing over her hand. Finally, Gwillem's grip on her throat weakened and she was able to push him away. In the dim light he looked distracted, a little surprised. Then he collapsed on to his side, his lifeblood pulsing away and pooling on the cold stone beneath, and was finally still. She staggered to her feet.

'Meghan?'

Cade saw her still slumped against the cave wall. She scrambled over. 'Meghan?'

She did not answer.

'Hey!'

Cade leaned in close and cradled her cheek, pulling her face towards her. Meghan's eyes were open but unfocussed. She wasn't reacting. 'Hey,' Cade whispered. Then she looked down and saw the blade buried deep in Meghan's chest. 'No ...'

Cade collapsed to the floor, and felt a stab of agony in her shoulder. She put her hand to it again. It was hot and wet.

'Hells, Meghan, you had to be a hero.' She had damned well saved her life too. Another debt she never asked for and could never repay. Cade replaced her knife into her boot and then reached up and pulled Gwillem's weapon out of Meghan's chest. It was a single piece of metal, misshapen, wicked sharp ridges tapering to a sharp edge, a makeshift shank. She threw it away and it clanked somewhere in the dark.

Cade stood and staggered out of the cave.

'Ah, damn it,' she cried, as dizziness forced her to lean against the wall. She heard someone walking towards her up the path.

'Hey Cade. You're la–' Issar stopped. His mouth open.

'I look that bad, huh?'

'What the hell happened? Are you okay?' He grabbed her shoulders.

'It was Gwillem. He ...' Cade felt another wave of dizziness and her legs started to buckle. She felt Issar's arms around her, taking her weight.

'It's okay. It's okay,' he soothed.

She allowed him to take her to the side of the path, propping her up against the rock face.

'We've got to get going, we've got work to do,' she protested, weakly.

'Not like that, you don't, you're covered in blood,' said Issar. 'Where's Meghan?'

'In the cave. Gwillem killed her. I killed Gwillem.'

'Oh, my life ...' whispered Issar.

'Doesn't matter,' said Cade. 'We've got to get everything in motion.'

'Cade, you've been stabbed.'

'Nowhere vital. Trust me, I know about these things. Just bind me up.'

'Cade–'

'Just do it!' she hissed.

Issar swallowed hard.

'Alright,' he relented. 'Give me a minute, I'll be right back.'

He headed up the track and disappeared into one of the other cave mouths. Cade leaned back and closed her eyes. She tried to block out the pain. It would get worse when the excitement of the fight dissipated. She didn't have time for any of this. Damn Gwillem! His mind had gone. And now his insanity had taken the life of someone she had grown close to. Meghan had cared. Cared too much. It was not Cade's damned fault that Jessene had died. That was all on him.

'Here,' said Issar. She opened her eyes. He was carrying a pot full of water and had some pieces of cloth draped over his shoulder. 'Can you raise your arms?'

Cade lifted up her arms, feeling the sharp tug of the knife wound.

'Gods Below!' she moaned.

'Almost there.' He undid her tunic and tugged it over her head.

'For fuck's sake, Issar!'

'Sorry, Cade, sorry,' said Issar. He took a piece of cloth and dabbed it into a bowl of water, cleaned carefully around the wound and then rinsed the cloth in the water. She wiped her face with her hand as he did so and it came back darkly stained with Gwillem's blood. It was then that it hit home. She started to shake.

'Cade? You don't look good.'

'Uh-huh. Don't feel it either.' She was going into shock. She had seen it plenty of times before. She focussed on her breathing. Slow. Even.

Issar bundled up a piece of dry cloth.

'This is rough and ready I'm afraid. Hold this.' He pressed the cloth against the wound. 'Keep it pressed tight.'

'I know,' she muttered, placing her hand on the cloth. Issar set to wrapping more cloth around her shoulder and over to the other side. She let go when it tightened on her hand, and allowed Issar to finish off.

'Put this on.' He lifted up another tunic. 'Looks a bit big for you but it'll have to do.'

'Fine.'

With a bit of fuss, he got it over her head and uninjured arm. With a lot more fuss, swearing and pain, he got it over the injured one and down over the rest of her. Cade drew her legs up and braced her back against the rock. She slowly raised herself off the floor. Teeth gritted, she pushed herself into a standing position. She leaned back, puffing her cheeks and slowly blowing out the air. Issar handed her a beaker of water and Cade took a sip. Nice and slow.

'Issar. We need to get going.'

'Right. You good to walk?'

'Yeah. Just let me use your shoulder.'

She placed her right hand on him and together they moved off.

'We're late for the Accounting,' she said.

'It's already started,' said Issar. 'That's why I came looking for you.'

Cade stopped, took her hand from his shoulder and turned him around to face her. 'You mean they started without me?'

'Yes. Devlin's got it. Everyone knew what we had to do.'

'But I should be there!' she exclaimed.

'Only to watch, Cade. You came up with the plan. Others have to see it done. You're the brains, remember.'

'Now I know you're taking the piss.'

Issar laughed and firmly placed her hand back on his shoulder. 'Come on, everyone should be through the Downside Gate by now.'

As they continued up, they walked through the abandoned settlement towards the gate. It was an eerie feeling. They followed sounds of shouting and arrived at the Downside Gate. It was wide open. There were the six dwarves on the ground. All of them were dead and divested of their weapons. Five humans lay together, side by side. She stopped to inspect them. *Who the hell had time to tidy up?* They had crossbow bolts buried in them. None of the five were part of her inner circle, just foot soldiers.

'Let's keep going,' she said.

She was walking a little easier now that the shock was wearing off, so she let go of Issar.

Together they moved on to the chamber where all of the mining equipment was gathered. The place was a wreck. Carts had been overturned, racks had been emptied of anything that could be used as a weapon. There were more bodies too. The noise was greater here, filtering down the tunnel leading to the surface.

'Looks like we missed all the fun,' she said.

Her pace quickened. She had to see for herself. Had this really happened? As they moved towards the exit, the light wavered as black figures swarmed past the opening. The nearer they got, the louder the noise. And there was cheering, excited chatter and someone trying to shout orders.

She emerged into pandemonium.

All around her, the folk of the mine were celebrating; hugging, crying, laughing. Some just stood there, blinking in the light.

'Cade! Cade!'

She turned and saw Devlin forcing his way through the crowd. He was carrying an axe. Behind him followed a couple of her crew armed with crossbows.

'Devlin.'

His smiling face, flushed with victory, took in the bandages and he faltered.

'Cade. What the hell's happened?'

'It was Gwillem,' Issar said before she could answer.

'Gwillem?' said Devlin shifting his gaze quickly between the two of them.

'He killed Meghan,' added Issar.

'Oh, damn. Cade. I'm sorry.'

Cade shook her head. 'What happened? We good?'

Devlin didn't skip a beat. His manner shifted, turned business-like. 'You saw down below. We hit them at the shift change. The workers turned their weapons on the guards then led the charge to the Downside Gate. It was already open and we took them on the hoof.'

'Losses?'

'You saw them on your way up. We lost a few more up here. Geir organised a defence but we were too many.'

'Did any get away?'

'None that we know of. I sent runners down the trail and a group to the Upside Gate. I reckon we got them all.'

'We'd better had, or this will be shortest party in history.'

She looked around at the celebrating mass. People climbed over piles of rock, brandishing picks and shovels. Hundreds of humans, all experiencing the thrill of freedom. There would be time for celebration later.

'We need to get this lot organised. Get the wagons ready to roll.'

Devlin nodded and turned to their companions. 'Have the leaders rally their people and start scouring up what they need. Search the Upside Gate for food deliveries. Then get back to the wagons.'

Issar sketched a crude salute and he and the others moved off.

'This way,' he said to Cade, taking her gently by her good arm. They pushed their way through the crowd. On seeing Cade, there was renewed cheering and someone clapped her on the shoulder.

'Fuck, watch it!' she shouted, feeling faint again.

'Out of the way! Come on!' said Devlin, placing himself in front of her while Issar stepped forward to cover her injured left side.

They worked their way through the crowd to the track leading towards the plateau. Waiting for them were the half-dozen wagons that they used every day for deliveries. They were already crewed, and full with the usual shipment of ore-laden rocks.

'Everyone's ready to go,' said Devlin. 'I've got the usual folk driving the wagons and in the back of each one will be two of our best fighters. I got hold of most of the guards' crossbows and other weapons, but not all. Some of our people weren't ever going to follow our rules. Still, it's gone better than we could've hoped.'

'If you say so,' she said.

'Oh, one more thing. We got Geir. A bunch of guys were about to rip him apart but our crew got to him just in time.'

'Good. We need him.'

They reached the first wagon. Miriam sat on the driver's bench grinning broadly at her. Standing next to it was Geir, covered by another of their people.

Cade walked up and stood before him. He looked up at her, his face inscrutable.

'You want to live?' she asked.

He nodded.

'Then you do exactly as I say. We are headed for the plateau. We are going to take it. You will smooth the way. You try anything and I'll stab you in the throat.'

Geir's face turned a little red, his eyebrows knitted together. He nodded again.

'Get him on the seat,' ordered Devlin.

As the dwarf climbed aboard Cade turned to Devlin.

'No turning back,' she said.

'Never was,' he replied.

She looked down the line of wagons.

'Still not that many of us to take plateau,' she said doubtfully.

'They'll be enough. We'll have the element of surprise and the dwarves are too thin on the ground.'

'Just don't dawdle.'

'I won't. I'll get everyone organised here and then I'll bring the reinforcements.'

'We take the plateau, we take it all,' she stated.

'I know, Cade. Just take care of yourself.'

'I've had worse,' she muttered. 'Issar. Help me get up.'

She walked around to the back of the wagon. Geir's watcher reached down to take her good arm but it hurt nonetheless. She bit back on the tearing pain and climbed aboard, Issar giving her boost from behind. She settled herself and, using her free hand, slapped the wooden floor beneath her.

'Let's go!'

Miriam flicked the reins and the wagon jerked forwards, the pony settling into its familiar stride.

Cade looked at her companion. A man with jet black hair and a missing earlobe.

'Krste?'

'That's right, boss.'

'You know how to use that?' she asked, indicating the crossbow.

'Sure do.'

She flicked her head towards Geir.

'Anything looks or feels wrong–'

'He dies first,' Krste finished for her.

'Good.'

She settled back and closed her eyes. She was tired, and everything was starting to seize up. For a moment she thought about Meghan. *Goddammit.* Then her tiredness overwhelmed her and she slept.

'Boss.'

She cracked open an eye. Sunlight bathed her face.

'We're here.'

She blinked a few times and then got her bearings. They had left the track leading from the mountain and were starting to cross the plateau proper. She shifted her head to check behind her, and regretted it immediately as her shoulder protested.

'Boss, you're bleeding pretty bad,' said Krste.

She looked down on her front. It was stained red in a long irregular line running from her shoulder.

'You any good with stitching, Krste?'

Krste shrugged. 'Done my share, not the most delicate though,' he said, raising a hand of thick, grubby fingers.

'Do me a favour. When we are finished here, go find someone who knows about medicine and shit.'

'Will do, boss.'

They were approaching Vidar's complex, having skirted around the central buildings. There were a few dwarves going about their business, and some humans too. Clearly, nobody had gotten word to the plateau. As the convoy reached the main warehouse, Geir nodded at a pair of guards who were strolling by. They saluted and carried on.

Arriving at the entrance, Miriam applied the brake. Cade watched her place a hand behind her back to loosen a knife tucked into her trousers. Krste had his crossbow kept low, beneath the side of the wagon.

Young Evan walked out from the building, accompanied by a couple of others. He spotted Cade in the back and hurried over.

She stood up and got her legs over the side.

Evan blanched when he saw her.

'Don't faint,' she growled. She pointed at him to stand still and she gripped his shoulder for support and jumped down.

'What we got inside?'

'Usual. Two guards at the steps and two watching us working.'

'Fine.'

Cade raised her good arm and everyone started to climb off the wagons. They were covered from view between the wagon and the warehouse and weapons were carried without subterfuge. Krste and the other man carrying a crossbow came over to her.

'Krste, can I have that?' asked Cade, gesturing to his crossbow.

'Boss?'

'Your bow. Give it to me. You still got a knife?'

'Yes,' he replied, handing over his weapon.

'Then go sit up front, just behind the dwarf. Keep an eye on him. When we start, slit his throat.'

At that Geir turned to face her and opened his mouth to shout. The briefest cry of surprise sounded before Miriam leaned forwards and drove her thin-bladed weapon sideways into his ear.

'Or not,' said Cade, as the dead dwarf tumbled sideways out of the wagon on to the ground. She took the weight of the crossbow, cradled it in the crook of her arm, and strode towards the entrance. The others forming up around her.

The two guards saw them come in and raised their weapons.

'Take 'em down,' she ordered and several bolts flew. As the dwarves staggered backwards, others hurried forward to finish them off.

She continued on to the stairs as the fallen were stripped of weapons.

'Want support?' asked Miriam, running to her side.

'No. Clear the building but keep it quiet, we don't want the barracks alerted.'

The party, almost a score in number, turned towards the warehouse floor.

She climbed the steps steadily, deliberately. There was no need to rush.

On reaching the top she met Vidar walking out of his office towards the balcony.

'What the hell's going on?' he said, not noticing the crossbow Cade now held level against her hip.

She pulled the trigger and the bolt struck him in the belly. Vidar staggered backwards, a look of surprise and confusion on his face. Cade dropped the crossbow and walked towards him. He kept his feet and retreated, his arms questing behind to find the doorway. As his fingers found the frame, he spun round and moved inside. Cade leaned down and retrieved the triangular blade from her boot. Vidar made for his desk as Cade followed closely after. His hand closed around the dagger he had threatened her with weeks before. She lashed out and sliced his hand. He yelped in pain and the dagger fell to the floor.

Vidar staggered behind his desk and collapsed into his chair, his face red, his brow covered in sweat. The bolt was buried deep into his belly and blood was dripping on to the floor.

She pointed her knife at the wound. 'That's one of them slow bleeders. Takes an age to die. Real slow.'

Vidar's cut hand moved to his belly. 'What the fuck do you want?' he breathed.

'Me?' Cade took the seat on the opposite side of the table. 'Nothing much. An easy life mostly. Wine. Money. Women. Mostly wine.' She stretched her neck and winced. 'Right now, I got none of that.'

'You want money?' he asked, his face a mask of pain.

'I'd love some. But what would I spend it on?' Cade looked around the office. 'Might take this place, though.'

'What do you think is going to happen? You think you can escape?' Vidar growled.

'I'm certainly gonna try,' she said, brightly.

'Damn you, girl. Didn't I treat you right? Didn't I make your life better?'

Cade dipped her head. 'Yes, you did. Thanks a lot. Problem is, times change. A little bird told me the elves aren't happy and, business being business and all that, I doubt we had much of a future.'

'You won't get away with this,' said Vidar. 'Stop this foolishness and we can work something out.'

Cade huffed and raised her stubby, triangular-shaped knife.

'You know, I kept this a secret from everyone. Found it a long time back. It was my 'ace', my last throw of the dice. I think I always planned to save it for you. I daydreamed about shoving in your neck and watching the surprise on your face. But life has a funny way of ruining the best laid plans. I ended up killing a man with it instead. Is that irony?' She looked at him. He looked back.

'I think you would have treated us as well as any cattle could be treated. And when we became too old, too infirm, you would have put us out of our misery. Good for you. So,' she tapped the tabletop with the side of her knife, 'in appreciation, of all that you've done for us, for me, I am going to offer you a choice. Believe me, it's the best one you'll get today. I can get up and walk away. You can take your leave. No one will stop you. You can walk right on out of here. Not sure how far you'll get with that stuck in you but hey, hope springs eternal.'

He shouted, 'I won't last one mile, damn your–'

'Or,' Cade held a hand up, 'I can end you now. I'll do it real quick. A nice deep cut. You'll bleed out fast.'

'That's no choice,' Vidar whispered.

'Oh, believe me, it's a choice,' said Cade. 'One most folk don't get to make for themselves.'

'I don't want to die,' said Vidar.

'Neither do any of us but most of us don't get a say in the matter.' She looked at him and smiled. 'Choose.'

Cade emerged from the office, clutching a bottle of brandy. She'd found it and several other bottles in a cabinet. Sweet.

Issar and several others were standing at the bottom of the square, talking quietly. He watched as she clumped across to look down at them from the balcony.

'You alright?' asked Issar.

She waved the bottle at him. 'Gradually losing all feeling.'

'We were starting to get worried.'

Cade took another swig as Issar regarded her with disapproval.

'I've got Rula here, she's going to look at you,' he said, indicating the slight, blonde woman carrying a small hessian sack with her. Rula, the midwife.

'Get on up here then.'

Cade walked back to the office and opened the door, waiting for Issar and Rula.

'Don't mind him,' she said, indicating Vidar as they walked by her.

Rula shot her a concerned glance. Cade smiled back and followed her in, then took up her usual spot on the chair opposite Vidar. The dwarf stared back at her with dead eyes.

'What happened?' asked Issar.

'He decided he was going to die slow. Typical stubborn dwarf. I decided to keep him company. Least I could do,' Cade replied.

Rula put her sack on the table then inspected Cade, eyeing the bottle in particular. 'How much you had of that?' she asked.

'This? Um, half?' said Cade.

'Save the rest. Give it here,' she ordered, reaching out and pulling the bottle from Cade's free hand.

'Hey!' she protested.

'We'll need it for the wounds,' Rula said sourly. She put the bottle on the table next to her sack. 'Issar, help me with this.'

Cade swore as he peeled off the shirt, which was stuck to her skin with sweat and dried blood.

'You two weren't with the first group,' she mumbled. 'I take it that means the reinforcements arrived?'

'They did, we did,' said Issar.

They finished levering the shirt off and Rula got to work on the makeshift bandages.

'Everything working out?' asked Cade.

'It appears to be. We've got the plateau sealed off. Your crew did a good job, swept through the warehouse and joined up with the other works parties to pick off the dwarves scattered around the place. But they got into a shooting match over at the barracks. Got a bunch dug in over there.'

'Always knew it would be. Where's Devlin?'

'He's out there now. He wants to start sending out the squads to liberate the other mines while it's still daylight.'

Rula had finished unwrapping the sodden shoulder bandage and tutted when she saw the wound.

'How bad is it?' asked Cade.

'Jagged cut, not clean. It's gonna scar,' Rula stated.

'Adds character, so I'm told,' replied Cade.

'I'm going to stitch it up,' said Rula, reaching for her sack. Rooting through it she pulled out a pile of bandages. 'These are boiled clean. Better than what Issar patched you up with.'

'Hey, I was working with what I had,' protested Issar.

Rula eyed him with a scowl. Cade was happy that she'd been picked. They had a number of folk whose job it was to patch up the injuries gained in the mines and Rula was the best of the bunch.

Rula took the bottle of brandy in one hand and a cloth in the other. She cocked her head at Cade.

'You know what I'm going to do with this?'

'Waste it?' asked Cade.

Rula ignored her and poured a little of the brandy over the hole in her shoulder.

'Oh, fuck damn! Fuck!' Cade hissed. 'That stings!'

'That it will,' agreed Rula, leaning forward to run the cloth over the wound. 'Count yourself lucky. No one at the mines ever had any alcohol to clean their wounds.'

Cade snorted and watched as Rula pulled a leather wallet from the sack. 'Now for the fun part.' She opened the wallet and pulled out a needle and some twine. Cade moaned. This was gonna hurt.

Rula looked at Issar. 'Hold her down.'

Cade shook her head.

'You are so in the shit for this, Issar.'

'No need to thank me,' he replied and braced her back.

Twenty minutes later Cade, arm in a sling and supported by Rula, arrived at the centre of the plateau. A large number of people were gathered behind the bakery. A couple were propped up against its side, carrying wounds.

Devlin waved a hand and beckoned them over. 'You've looked better,' he said.

'No shit, and here was me thinking the alcohol was giving me a healthy glow,' Cade replied.

'I'll take a look at those,' said Rula, pointing at the wounded.

'Crossbow wounds,' replied Devlin as she walked by. 'But they should live. We left everyone else where they fell.'

'It was that bad?' asked Cade.

'The dwarves got their shit together faster than I'd hoped. Some of ours tried to rush the barracks and got their arses handed to them. Go have a look.'

Cade followed him to the edge of the bakery. From here she could see that others had taken up positions, from other buildings, all looking towards the barracks at the centre. A long, two-storied building that housed the guards and other workers from the plateau.

She eyed Devlin.

'You'll be fine. They aren't trying to snipe us. Saving their ammunition for any assaults.'

She edged closer and a crossbow-armed Tissan made way for her. She moved her right eye just past the edge. It gave her a view of the ground, some fifty yards away to the entrance of the barracks. There were a number of bodies on the ground, some of them dwarves. And there were more bodies by the door.

She squinted at the barracks. From this position it was difficult to see anything.

'Do we know how many are in there?'

'We don't, but they got bows at each upstairs window. And there'll be more downstairs at the doors.'

Cade pulled back and sat against the wall. 'We could just burn them out,' she suggested.

'That's what I thought too but then I heard about Geir.'

'What about him?'

'He's dead. And so is Vidar.'

Cade scratched her head. What was he on about? *Oh. Shit.*

'Sorry, I kinda forgot in all the excitement.'

Devlin pursed his lips. 'We needed one of them for intelligence.'

Cade chewed her lip. Devlin was right. They had discussed this. They needed a dwarf who spoke the Imperial tongue to tell them just where they were so they could plan a route out. 'Leave it with me. Anything else?'

'Most of our people are here now. We've got as many weapons as we could find and enough people to wield them. The dwarves here aren't going anywhere. I want to start the liberation.'

'Makes sense. You crack on with that.' She'd found maps in Vidar's office. And let's face it, she thought, they all knew which way west was. All the same, not having a guide was a problem. She took another look at the barracks.

'What are you going to do?' Devlin asked.

'I'm going to have a chat with our friends over there, see if anyone understands me.'

Devlin shook his head.

'Just don't get yourself killed,' he said.

'Believe me. I've had enough damage for one day.'

He placed a hand on her uninjured shoulder. 'Almost there,' he said with a smile.

Cade nodded, but did not share his enthusiasm. This was just the start. Devlin stood and ran off, barking orders as he went. A number of the crew peeled off to follow him. She sat back and took another look at the barracks. Then she turned to look at the companions.

'Alrighty then. Anybody got a white sheet and a stick?'

CHAPTER EIGHTEEN – OWEN

Patience.

For a while, Owen believed he'd had all the time in the world with his whole life mapped out for him. Just him and Arno, soaring through the skies, until they were both too old to carry on. But that was before Eagle's Rest, before Em. And now he felt he had no time to waste. He had purpose, a need to take the fight to the enemy. To rebuild what was left of humanity and to teach the bastard races of this land that there were consequences to their actions. And now, against all his expectations, he had been betrayed by his own kind. After everything. His own damned kind. There had been a few days, at the start of his captivity, when he had despaired. How could they achieve anything if they could not trust each other? They were doing the work of their enemies for them, squabbling over dirt, putting their self-preservation higher than that of the whole. But he had come through that, and now he was ready to pick himself up and carry on. There were good people out there still, fighting for all of them. He held on to that, kept it close to his heart. And he had a responsibility to those of his people still alive; to warn them that Eagle's Rest had been taken. And what of Arno? Had his friend escaped? Was he wounded? Had he tried some damn fool attempt to free him? Owen needed to know.

Patience.

He waited in his room, listening for the comings and goings of those outside his door; the voices, names spoken, the state of their occupation. He listened for any word of his folk outside the walls; nothing was said. He measured out the days by his meals, scant though they were. And he had worked out that when night fell, there was no guard on the door. Besides the food drops, no one came to visit him, not even Gerat. By his reckoning, it had been ten days since he had been confined. Time enough for them to have grown a little lax perhaps? It was time to find out. He sat close to the door, his ear pressed against it. There had been no sound for some a while, no light came from under the crack. He gently raised his hand letting it touch the latch, and applied upward pressure. It lifted and reached its natural apex. Applying a little force against the wood he felt it move, just slightly, a half inch, no more, before it met resistance. He pushed a little harder but the door would move no more. He held his position, ears straining for the sound of movement, of any reaction to his activity.

Nothing.

What had he learned?

The bar they had added to the door was not tightly fitted. The bracket it slid into protruded from the frame. It was, in all likelihood, a shit piece of work. A running jump or a well-placed kick or two would probably dislodge it. And wake everyone up. But that didn't matter, he had something to work with. They had done a bad job; the first bad decision. The second was putting him in his own room. He lowered his hand and released his hold on the latch when it fell back into place, and moved away from the door.

He made his way back to his bed and reached underneath the frame. His questing hand fell upon a leather package, and he pulled it forth. He sat on his mattress and placed the package on his lap. His fingers located the laces that held it together, undid them, and pulled the flap open so he could get at the contents. He had been an Imperial Eagle Rider only for a short time, but he had been a Highlander all his life. The package held his first ever tool kit, given to him by his father, so that he could maintain Arno's tack. All of the tools were smaller than the kit he flew with now. In those early days Arno was a still a growing bird. But this was all to the good. He ran his fingertips over lengths of wood and metal, felt the marks of time in the pits and ridges, and felt the sharp prick of his awl. That would do perfectly. He took hold of the wooden handle, shaped like a small apple, and pulled it out. The tool, used for punching holes in leather, had a length of six inches, the metal rod thin but sturdy.

Returning to the door, he settled down and went through the process again. As the door opened up, he released his grip on the latch and adjusted his position. He ran his left hand along the open gap until his fingers met the cold metal of the bracket and the warmer underside of the wooden bar. Now he had his bearings, he raised his right hand, holding the awl and probed with the tip at a slight angle, away from the door. As it met the bar, he pushed hard, rotating the handle to dig in the tool. Then, maintaining upwards pressure, he pulled the awl towards him, and the bar shifted. Not far, not by much. But then, it didn't need to. Owen repeated the action, upwards, digging in to get purchase and then a slight shift to the right. It was slow work. Sometimes the awl didn't take and the resultant 'clunk' filled Owen with dread. How could anyone not hear that racket? Moments of held breath, then relief followed as time and again no alarm was sounded. The door opened. Just slightly, just by a few inches. He sat there looking through the gap. It was still dark, yet slightly, very slightly, less so than his room. A little ambient light was making its presence felt along the passages leading off from the main hall above.

Owen remained seated on the floor. *Get up, you fool.* He went to his clothes chest, withdrew a cloak, a small knapsack which held some of his spare flying gear, and warm clothes for the nights ahead. He added a couple of apples that he had saved from the meagre meals given to him over his confinement. Donning the cloak, he squeezed himself through the narrow gap he had made and stepped out into the passage. He barred the door behind him. He knew where he had to go; this place held no secrets from him. In his hand he clutched the awl like a weapon. A weapon he wanted to use on just one person. And, if he were younger or a little more naive, he would have gone looking. But that was not his priority right now. Not this night. He had been made a fool of, but it was a lesson he wouldn't let go to waste. He turned right and made for the stairs that led to the hall.

Walking softly but with purpose, he climbed the stairs. In the hall, the embers of a fire glowed. There were people lying around the edges of the pits and among the tables and chairs, deep in slumber. A gentle chorus of snores filled the hall. He passed by a table upon which the remains of a meal were scattered. A hunk of meat on the bone sat in the middle of plate. He collected it and continued on to the doors, pulling the hood of the cloak over his head. Opening the left side he stepped through and into the night. A figure stood at the top of the steps, resting against a wooden pillar, wrapped in dark furs. The figure turned to look at him.

'You relieving me or Una?' asked a scratchy, high-pitched voice.

Owen made a show of raising the meat to his mouth and taking a bite. 'Una,' he mumbled.

A sigh.

'Fine.'

The figure turned away, no longer interested.

Owen tucked the awl into his belt and marched off down the steps, away from the hall, heading for the gate. The night was overcast, there was little natural light. From the hall, he would be lost from view. He paused for a moment and looked up. Should he? He couldn't help it. *'Arno? You there?'* He waited for a few seconds, looking for something: a call in the night, the whoosh of beating wings. Nothing. And it filled his heart with sadness. He tried to tell himself it meant nothing, that Arno could be miles from here, well beyond the range of his Gift. But in truth, the silence meant everything.

He reached the gate. It was barred shut. He looked up at the watchtower. It was manned – Una? The watcher turned at his approach.

'You're early,' said a female voice. Una, then.

Owen looked up. 'You want me to go?' he called.

'Like fuck I do,' came the reply.

He watched her climb down, and without a backward glance she started to walk away.

'Hey,' he called after her.

Una stopped. 'What?'

'Any water up there?'

'Uh. Oh, yeah.'

She pulled at her shoulder and raised an arm over her head. Una proffered a small waterskin. 'Here.'

'Much obliged,' said Owen. Taking another bite of the meat and throwing the rest away, he reached out and collected the skin. It sloshed, perhaps half full.

'It's a cold night,' said Una.

'Always is,' replied Owen.

He turned and took a grip on the ladder, climbing the tower to the viewing platform. He looked back. Una was already gone. Out along the trail it was quiet, still. He glanced back at the hall. Was Una talking to the guard? Would the actual relief already be on their way? So far Owen was less than impressed with their lax approach to security. Gerat had to know there would be threats out there, what the Hells was he thinking?

Owen descended the ladder and moved to the gate. He was minded to try and lift the horizontal plank from its brackets. It was a solid piece of wood and was properly a two-man job. The gate had been reinforced with extra bracing, one of the first jobs they had undertaken around the Rest when he had returned. He took the ladder next to the gate on the right-hand side and up on to the fighting platform – another addition to the original structure. Little more than a ledge over the gate, a couple of feet wide, it at least allowed defenders a chance to cover the ground ahead. A wooden crenellation provided protection and a field of fire. On the other side it was a drop of eight feet if he lowered himself over. He climbed on to the platform and went straight to the nearest gap.

'Thought you were replacing Una.'

Owen started, and looked further down the platform, towards a man, stretched out along its length. Damn. How had he missed him? Owen had been so focussed on the tower he had not spotted this extra watcher. They were being more vigilant than he had given them credit for.

'I was, I am.' Owen had to play this out somehow.

'Then what are you doing up here?' he demanded, as he pushed himself up into a sitting position, his back to the wooden screen.

'Just thought I'd pass the time. Check if you were still awake.' Owen's hand drifted down to his belt, his fingers closing on the stubby handle of the awl.

'Of course I fucking am,' said the man testily. 'Gerat knows I'm good for it.'

That voice …

Owen took a step closer. That voice was familiar. It had been a while but with every step, he grew certain. Dill. Older and craggier. He had not seen the man since way back, but Gerat had said he was still around.

'Much out there?' he asked casually.

Dill grunted and turned his head to look over the side, away from Owen, as he had hoped.

'Can't see a fucking thing. How Gerat expects–'

Owen pulled the awl free and closed the remaining distance stabbing forwards with the awl, straight into Dill's exposed neck. The tip slid in with little resistance, and Owen withdrew it for another thrust. But Dill stood and pushed him away, clutching at his neck. For a few absurd moments both of them looked at each other, Owen suddenly at a loss, Dill looking confused. He pulled his hand away and Owen saw a jet of blood. With a strangled 'urk' Dill came for him.

Owen drove the awl at an angle upwards, as Dill crashed into him. Owen felt it strike home even as he was driven backwards. He lost his footing and fell. Dill followed him down, his weight knocking the air out of Owen's lungs, his stinking breath washing over his face, his blood dripping into Owen's mouth. Owen gave him a mighty push and then Dill was gone, rolling off Owen and the platform, landing on the ground before the gate with a thump. Owen drew in air and started to cough. He pushed up on to his elbows and looked down. Dill wasn't moving. He climbed over the parapet, lowered himself over, hands holding tight to the edge, his arms taking his weight. At full stretch he released his grip and dropped. His feet hit the ground below and waited a moment to take stock. No injuries from the descent, no reaction to his landing. He started to run. Halfway along the ridgeline a bell started to ring. It was too soon. He increased his pace and started to descend. The trail was as familiar to him as the passages beneath Eagle's Rest, yet the fear of pursuit caused him to move faster than was wise on the narrow, stony path. *Get a grip, Owen. This is your land.* Moments later and he was down in the valley. He ducked off the trail and into a stand of pine trees, where he dropped to the ground and looked back. From there he could see the southern end of the gate and wall. There was a glow emanating from somewhere within the Rest. Lights appeared by the gate, bobbing and flickering. Owen allowed himself to calm down a little. It would be chaotic up there. It was a good possibility they did not know he had escaped, that no one had yet checked on him. Still, he had best move get a move on, there were folk up there who would be able to track him well enough. He had to go east, try and find some of his people before Gerat's found him. The Emperor only knew where they might be.

'Owen?'

He turned, his hand flying to his belt. The awl was gone. Lost in the flight.

'That you, Owen?'

Owen cocked his head and peered into the shadows of the trees. Three shapes emerged and came towards him. Two had bows, another held a blade.

'It's me.' There was no need to bluff. He recognised the speaker. 'Saul?'

The shapes drew closer, features defining themselves.

'Aye, it's me. Good to see you, lad.'

Owen started to smile.

'You too, Saul.' The second bow carrier drew closer. It was Anneli. 'I thought you were at the Rest?'

'I was,' she said with a grim face. 'There was no time, I just … ran.'

'No shame in that,' said Saul. 'Without her we might never have known what we were walking into.'

Owen nodded. 'There was no way you could have stopped it.'

'When they took over I was in the barn. I climbed on to Taru's bare back. There was no time to saddle him,' she said, her tone apologetic.

He nodded and clasped her shoulder, then turned to the last of the trio, Major Killen Roche.

'Major.' What was he doing here? He was supposed to be far to the east. 'I am happy to see you but a little surprised. How did you know?'

'All thanks to your bird,' replied Killen.

'Arno?' Owen's heart began to race.

'Woke up one morning, and there he sat looking at me, not ten yards away. Frightened the shit out of my camel. Always liked eagles.'

'Arno found you?' Relief washed over Owen. Arno had gone and looked for help. Damn but he had a smart bird.

'Found us and then showed us the way. It was obvious something was wrong so we decided to take a look. We hooked up with Saul and his people en route,' said Killen.

'We've had folk here a couple of days, keeping watch. If Arno came to fetch us it meant you were in trouble, and he didn't stop until we got here. Figured something was up when we saw that none of our people were leaving the Rest.'

Owen looked back. More lights were visible at the gate. 'Have we got someplace safe to go?'

Saul reached out and clapped him on the back.

'Yes, an hour's walk away.'

Owen nodded. 'Then let's go.'

The group moved back into the depths of the trees. Owen fell in at the rear, but Anneli pushed past him. 'We just got you back,' she whispered.

Owen smiled in the dark, yet he felt little joy. They didn't know yet, they didn't know that Murtagh and others were gone. He would have to tell them. And then work out a plan to kill the bastard who did it.

Owen was soon toiling. There was no trail to speak of, not from Eagle's Rest at any rate; it was pure cross-country slogging. He had to stop often to drink, but at least he had no fears of draining his single skin. His companions had plenty. Killen had even shared with him something from a small leather canteen that smelt rancid, tasted sour, and had a kick like nothing he had ever felt.

'You get used to it,' said the Major, with an apologetic shrug.

The hour felt more like two by the time the group climbed up a wooded rise that angled around to the south, skirting a high, steep-sided abutment of rock, the first expression of a larger mountain peak. As they rounded the corner a dark hole, like a yawning mouth, came into view, a relatively steep slope led up to it, a climb of perhaps forty yards. Owen knew where they were now. He had a clear memory of flying past this place countless times, and as a child exploring within. A stream flowed from the centre of the cave mouth, trickling energetically past the route they were taking; the ground was clearly marked by recent traffic, a matter confirmed when he placed his foot firmly into a pile of shit.

'Three going out and four coming back,' shouted a voice down to them.

'Since when did you know how to count?' Saul shouted back.

A shape emerged from the darkness and walked down to meet them. It was Larsen, a big grin on his face and his hand outstretched to grip Owen's.

'Good to see you, Owen. These three bust you out?'

'No need, he did it all by himself,' said Saul.

'And that's why he's our mighty leader,' said Larsen. 'Ain't that right, Owen?'

'I don't feel so mighty at the moment,' said Owen, scraping shit off his boot with a stick.

'We can fix that,' said Larsen, putting an arm around Owen's shoulder. 'Come inside and look at your host. Not that you'll see much, but you can sure smell 'em.' They climbed to the top of the slope and to the lip of the cavern mouth. Owen had to manoeuvre around a wall of boulders and large rocks, an effective barricade for any upwards assault.

'We put this together when we first got everyone inside,' said Larsen as Owen moved through into the cavern mouth proper. Outside, a pre-dawn light was filtering through and yet, even with that, he had trouble making sense of the space within. There were bodies all over the cavern floor, a lot of them too large to be human. He heard grunting noises amidst the snoring.

'My men … and their mounts,' said Killen.

'You've got everyone in here?' asked Owen.

'All of the Major's men, and my bunch and Larsen's,' said Saul. 'Damn near a hundred of us snuggled in tight with half as many camels.'

'We've got plenty of food, and water of course. This was the best place we could find to hide us all. Their hunters don't come this way,' Larsen added.

Owen looked at his companions, their faces so much clearer now in the subdued glow of a lantern. They made his sorrowful heart feel a little lighter.

'What about Arno?'

'He wasn't too happy about moving in with us. But he's about,' said Anneli. 'Probably with Taru.'

Owen looked back out of the cave mouth. He needed to speak to them all, to hold a council of war but he was also eager to be reunited with his bird.

'Everyone will be up and about soon,' said Larsen gently. 'Why don't you go call your bird? Then we'll get a brew on and we can talk.'

Owen nodded his thanks and moved into the open. He tracked back down the slope a little way and gazed upwards using his Gift to call out.

'Arno?'

Owen shivered a little in the shadow cast by the mountain. He was tired and worn out. But back among friends, he found his tension leaving him, the stress that had been keeping him alive, that had given him the strength to kill, had finally burned the last of his reserves. He needed to sit down. To close his eyes. To get some proper bloody sleep. But not quite yet.

'Arno, come here, you big dumb bird!'

He closed his eyes tight and rubbed a hand through his manky, sweat-moistened hair.

A screech announced the arrival of the eagle, sweeping in low from the west. Owen felt the displaced air blow against his face as Arno passed over his head, then continued on, describing a wide circle across the wooded slopes below.

Owen grinned and felt joy sweep away his fatigue.

'There you are, you little shit.'

'I hear what you're saying, Owen, but you know better than anyone, that knife-edge ridge is going to play havoc with any frontal assault,' said Killen. 'Without any kind of artillery, we have to rush the gates. We'll need a ram and we'll need shields. And they'll see us coming.'

'We'll lose people, Owen,' said Larsen, stretching his hands over a small cookfire. As well as the hunter, gathered in a small circle were Saul, Major Roche and his second, a dark-skinned Erebeshi officer whose name he had yet to commit to memory.

They were at war, they were always going to lose people. But Owen had to concede the point. Yet what Gerat had done could not go unanswered and no one had offered a viable alternative.

'What about a night assault? Take them by surprise?'

'They'll be on high alert now,' said Owen. 'They'll be expecting something.'

'I can't speak for your people but I've got some stealthy men who can get really close,' said Killen, nodding to his companion. The Erebeshi grinned and inclined his head.

'That's not a bad idea. Some of us could get real close to the gate, take out their guards and be in before they knew the shitstorm was upon them,' said Saul with a dark gleam in his eyes.

'We could try it,' agreed Owen. It would be a way of minimising casualties.

'We get the gate open, let in the rest of our people, capture the bastards and throw them over the damn side of the Rest,' agreed Larsen.

Owen bit his lip. A part of him wanted to do just that.

'We can't,' he said, looking at the expressions of those gathered round; Larsen's looked like thunder.

'Owen–'

He raised a hand. 'I get it. Believe me I do. But I've seen what they've been through, the lives they had. A road they had no choice to follow.'

'They had a choice,' said Larsen. 'We all had a choice.'

'And we all got lucky, we had people to lead us who were decent, who didn't lose their humanity when it all fell apart.' Owen reached out and gripped Larsen's shoulder. 'Larsen, you remember what Murtagh was like when I arrived? He didn't trust me. I was an outsider, not part of the group. But he came round.'

Larsen spat into the small fire they had gathered around. 'He wasn't a murderer.'

Owen shook his head. 'But that doesn't mean he wasn't a killer. You do what you have to do. To survive. Live or die. How many of us decided to take the easy way out? Not all of Gerat's people are like him. Not broken. I realised something, sitting in my room for days on end under guard, believing that everything was lost. I realised that Gerat and I are alike. He wanted to continue the war, to strike back. I didn't want to. I couldn't see the point. But he was driven, his anger burned bright and his light drew others. And then he lost his daughter. When Em died, I … lost myself too. And I became like Gerat for a while.'

'Not true, Owen,' said Saul. 'You're nothing like that bastard.'

Owen smiled. 'I know that. And I know why. Because of you, because of all of you. And because of that magnificent eagle out there. I always had my home, my friends.' He didn't know what else to say. He looked at each of his companions in turn.

'This world has become crazy, mad. It has turned against us. But the only way to keep going is to have faith in each other, to trust in each other to do the right thing. I'll not give up on all of those people in the

Rest. Some, perhaps most, can be saved. That's what we've been doing, isn't it? Save as many as we can?'

Saul scratched his ear. 'Damn it, Owen, you are a better man than I.'

Larsen rubbed his hands. 'If it was up to me? Well, you know, don't you, Owen?'

'I do,' said Owen. And there was no way he could blame the man for that, even if he was forced to stop him. 'But if we sink to their level then we are no better than Gerat.'

Larsen sighed. 'I'll follow your lead, Owen. Just promise me, that bastard will pay.'

Owen nodded. 'He will.' Of that there was no question. 'Major, can we take you up on your offer?'

'I'm not sure I was expecting our first engagement to be a civil war,' said Killen. 'But I suppose very little surprises me anymore. Captain Rashad?'

The Erebeshi inclined his head. 'I would like to see the ground.'

'I'll show you,' said Saul.

'Very good.'

'I want us to go in tomorrow night,' said Owen.

'And your plan?' asked Killen.

'You won't like it,' said Owen. He wasn't sure if he liked it himself.

CHAPTER NINETEEN – MICHAEL

'Fuck. There goes the chase, marines.'

Father Michael continued to sit on the wagon's bench as Fenner made the announcement. They had arrived at yet another deserted waystation. Fenner stood with his hands on his hips surveying the site, such as it was. Father Michael saw nothing more than the remains of a crude shelter, a firepit and a small midden heap.

Fenner turned and shaded his eyes, looking east. 'Yep, they are long gone,' he said quietly.

Next to him Coyle was on his haunches, studying the ground.

'I'd say there were five horses here,' said the marine.

'And looks like an eagle was over here,' called Wendell, limping his way back to them.

'What does this mean?' asked Father Michael.

'It means there ain't no way of catching them now', said Beautiful, who was standing by the wagon.

'They must have sent all the horses left in New Tissan,' said Fenner. 'If you include the two the Emperor had, that's a party of maybe seven riders now making their way east.'

'And what about their wagon?' asked Coyle.

'They won't be together now. That wagon will be going back by itself. Probably not even any Gifted on it.'

Father Michael stood and rolled his shoulders. His neck felt stiff and sore and he still got headaches, but he was healing.

'So they are riding back to Tissan,' he said.

'And they'll get there several days, maybe even a week or so, before us.'

Father Michael sat down once more. The last week had been

frustrating. Every day he hoped they had gained ground and would soon be able to act. To free the Emperor.

'We must press on,' he said.

'Well there's no point in turning back, that's for sure,' agreed Fenner. 'They know we'll be coming, mind you.'

'They won't know I'm coming.'

'You itching on taking them all on, Father?'

'I would if I had to,' replied Father Michael.

'That I would like to see,' said Fenner.

'But it will take all of us and a bloody good plan if we are going to defeat them.'

Fenner shrugged. 'Depends what you have in mind.'

Father Michael had nothing more to say. Until they got there, who knew what was going on in New Tissan? He'd have to remain patient.

'Does this mean we can have a fire tonight?' asked Coyle.

'Seven Hells, I don't see why not. Let's tear up that shelter and build a new fire. Can someone catch us something to eat?' ordered Fenner.

'On it,' said Beautiful.

'No reason for roughing it any more than we have to,' said Fenner, easing off his boots.

'Want me to peel some of those veg up?' said Wendell, already walking stiffly towards the back of the wagon.

'I'll unhitch the horse,' offered Father Michael.

'Thank you, Father,' said Fenner. He had also removed his socks and was rubbing his toes.

Father Michael saw Coyle already ripping apart the shelter. The prospect of hot food was probably the best luxury he could think of right now. He set off wearily to tend to the horse.

One week later, they spotted the eagle skimming low over the horizon, coming from the east. Fenner and Father Michael exchanged a look. Fenner pulled an earlobe.

'We should try and find out what's going on,' he said.

Father Michael nodded in agreement.

'Alright, look lively, you lot,' said Fenner. Wendell, keep your crossbow on the bird. It's the easier target. Beautiful, Coyle, find a spot, hunker down and give us a crossfire. Father?'

'Yes?'

'Look mean.'

Easily done.

Fenner halted the wagon and moved his crossbow on to his lap.

The waited quietly as the eagle drew near. The eagle stayed on a straight line, not even attempting a precautionary circling of their position.

'Not expecting trouble, this one,' suggested Fenner.

As the eagle glided in to land just a few dozen yards away, Father Michael recognised its distinctive wing colours. It was Nukka, Bryce's bird.

The Eagle Rider climbed off and strolled across to them, removing his leather gloves.

'Afternoon,' he called.

'Back at ya,' replied Fenner.

Bryce stopped just in front of the wagon. He looked right and left and then pointedly at Wendell who had taken up a firing position just behind the rear wheel.

'Good to see you,' he said. 'Could you do me a favour?'

'What's that?' asked Fenner.

'Could you all stop pointing your bloody bows at me?'

Fenner sat back and looked at Father Michael.

'What do you think, Father? Reckon we got time for this grouchy son of a bitch?'

'Yes, I believe we do,' replied Father Michael.

'Everyone stand down,' said Fenner loudly. 'Wendell? Let's get a brew going, shall we?'

Once a fire had been started and the water put on to boil, Bryce told them his news.

'I was hoping I'd see you. Cadarn told me to keep low, just in case.' He looked at the marines. 'I wasn't sure if you four were going to hightail it away. Wouldn't have blamed you if you had.'

'Not our style,' said Beautiful.

'Nor mine,' said Father Michael.

Bryce tipped his head in acknowledgment.

'Now, you I didn't expect to see. Heard you were dead,' said Bryce.

'Not yet,' replied Father Michael, drily.

Bryce nodded and paused a moment.

'That might change things. Maybe.' He turned back to the marines. 'As for you lot, you're not welcome in New Tissan.'

'There's a surprise,' muttered Wendell.

'What's happened?' asked Fenner.

'The Admiral. When the Gifted made their move, he got to *The Fist*, took it and the other men-o-war right out into the middle of the channel. And there he's stayed, refusing to talk to Cardinal Yarn and not listening to any of her threats.'

'Hah!' said Coyle, slapping his thigh.

'Good for the Admiral,' agreed Fenner.

'They even got the Emperor to tell him to come back in and he still refused, saying the command meant nothing if the Emperor was compelled to give it,' said Bryce.

'A bold move. No one ever denies the will of the Emperor, compelled or no,' said Beautiful.

'These are changing times,' agreed Bryce. 'Be that as it may, it cost three citizens their lives.'

Coyle whistled.

'Shit,' said Wendell.

'Yarn isn't messing about,' continued Bryce. 'That's how things are now.'

'How many has the Admiral got with him?' asked Fenner.

'Best we can figure, he's got skeleton crews and about a score of marines with him,' said Bryce. 'A lot of the sailors who might've been loyal were working on the new ships. There was no time for him to gather most of them.'

'Is that enough to retake the town?' asked Father Michael.

Bryce shook his head.

'It's the Gifted we are talking about here. There's about forty who can fight.'

'What about the other soldiers?' asked Fenner. 'There were plenty of armed men back there when last I checked.'

'The Gifted took care of that before they acted. Some officers had already been persuaded to turn and they ordered their men to stand down. Any loyalists that were going to cause problems were killed. The Gifted struck at night, many folk were killed in their sleep. There were some skirmishes. A few Gifted were killed, but at the end of it there were seventy soldiers and marines in the dirt.'

'Seventy?' said Beautiful, shock in her voice.

Bryce spat into the fire. 'As if we needed to help the bastard Elves do their job for them.'

Father Michael listened with a growing sense of dread. 'You said the loyalists were killed. What about the clergy? The Arch Cardinal?'

Bryce looked at him square in the eyes. 'He's dead. They all are.'

Father Michael rocked back, stunned. In just a few seconds his world had crumbled. His mentor, his saviour was gone.

'Why?' he asked. 'Why would she do this?'

'Yarn was being thorough with her coup. Best to make sure.'

'And what of the Emperor?' asked Father Michael.

'Cadarn and I were waiting for him at the waystation. Eilion told us that what had happened. He also said that the Emperor's mother was already a prisoner and that the Emperor had agreed to come quietly for the sake of her life.' Bryce coughed. 'I said to Cadarn, we should have just climbed on to our birds and tried to take them on. But the Leader said we had to swallow their crap.' He turned his head and spat. 'I didn't like it. But I did it.' He stretched his legs out and accepted a beaker from Wendell, taking a sip and making a sour face. 'Eilion knew he couldn't trust us, but he had the Emperor. He told us to fly back east until we found a Rider coming the other way, who could confirm it. Then we were to come back and pick up the Emperor and take him home.'

'That'll be where we found the waystation. With the horses?' said Fenner.

Bryce nodded.

'That was later. We were on our way back with the Emperor by then. The Cardinal had already despatched the horses to collect Eilion, no doubt she wanted all of her Gifted back. There are still a lot of unhappy people in New Tissan so they need the numbers.'

'Surely the whole population is up in arms?' asked Father Michael.

'Not everyone is as pious as you, Father,' said Fenner. 'You see your world destroyed, your loved ones slaughtered, it's gonna give some people pause to question their faith.'

Father Michael closed his eyes. He was struggling to understand how this could happen. How could anyone question divine right?

Bryce continued to talk. 'We picked up the Emperor and relayed him back to New Tissan. It was all true. The Empress was in confinement along with her advisor. The rest of the clergy was dead. A bunch of soldiers and marines were in the ground and everyone else was cowed. The Gifted are running things now but life is going on. Folk are still building, even the work on the boats continues. The only resistance is out on the water. And the Gifted have Watchers. There is nothing the Admiral can do. He doesn't have the numbers. Stalemate.'

'And the Emperor is what? Just doing what Yarn says?' asked Fenner.

'Seems that way. I haven't seen much of him since we got back,' said Bryce. 'The Emperor could command the people to rise up against Yarn, and maybe they would, but she's got the one thing that the Emperor doesn't want to lose. His mother.' Bryce took another slip of the tea. 'Gods, this tastes like shit. What are you putting in it?' He emptied the beaker and Wendell huffed his disapproval. 'Cadarn said that Yarn wants the Emperor alive and compliant. It'll keep the population in line. And there is the small matter of a horde of Nidhal on its way.'

'Yeah, doesn't matter how many Gifted Yarn's got, she can't afford to piss them off,' said Beautiful.

'And that's why I'm here,' said Bryce. 'I'm carrying a message to Nutaaq. Yarn wants to make sure there's no … misunderstanding when they arrive.'

'And are you going to deliver it?' asked Fenner.

'I am,' Bryce said gruffly. 'Cadarn, the other Eagle Riders, we are still loyal to the Emperor. Not to that bitch. Far as I am concerned, when she started killing soldiers, she crossed a line. The clergy, on the other hand–' He stopped and sucked air through his teeth. 'Ah, sorry, Father. Just telling it how I see it. If it's any consolation, they didn't suffer.'

Father Michael nodded absently, he did not have the energy or desire to be angry with Bryce.

'What do we do, then?' asked Wendell.

'We can't go back to New Tissan. We killed two Gifted,' replied Coyle.

'Feels good, don't it?' said Beautiful.

'We keep heading back east and link up with the Admiral, I suppose,' said Fenner.

The group went silent. Father Michael closed his eyes. *Sweet Emperor, what should I do?* He had sworn an oath, and he had failed. What was there left for him? Yarn controlled the Emperor and Father Michael had to follow the Emperor's bidding. Yet it was wrong. Surely the Emperor would not expect him to stand down? Father Michael felt the sharp claws of emotions that he had thought long gone. He felt the black oppression of despair creep its way back into his soul, just as it had done in the arena. He shook his head. No. He would not let it take him again. He faced a crossroads. Should he fight or retreat into nothingness. He had come close to that before, had lost himself for a time. And then the Arch Cardinal had saved him. He owed that man a debt. And perhaps, in the time spent out here, in the wilds, he had rebuilt his strength, his trust in his skills. He had seen the darkness in the Emperor, but he had also seen the salvation of Tissan in the Emperor's alliance with the Nidhal. Father Michael still believed there was a future and it was the Emperor's light, not his darkness, that guided the way. He knew what he had to do.

'I have to rescue her,' he announced.

'Who?' asked Wendell.

'The Empress. If she is free then Yarn will have no hold over the Emperor. And once I have her, then the Emperor will command his people to take back control. The Gifted will pay for what they have done.'

Father Michael looked at his companions. They looked right back at him, with various expressions, but no one spoke.

'I'll do it alone. It's my responsibility,' he said.

Fenner sighed and pulled at his moustache. 'I'll bite. You want us to try and infiltrate New Tissan under the noses of the Gifted and break out the Emperor and his mother, which will then spark a general uprising of the populace thus defeating the best warriors Tissan possesses and reinstating the rule of the Emperor and the Imperial faith?'

Father Michael rolled his shoulders. 'It's a start.'

'Your plan needs some work,' said Beautiful.

'The Admiral might be able to … tweak it a bit,' offered Fenner.

'Does that mean you'll help me?' asked Father Michael.

There seemed to be a moment of silent communication between the marines, as if they were making their minds up. Bryce coughed.

'What do you want me to tell the Nidhal?' he asked, looking right at Father Michael. 'Remember, there's a Gifted there too.'

Ellen? Of course, he had forgotten. Surely not her. She couldn't be a part of it. Yet … she was a Gifted.

'I'd like to think we can trust her but we can't risk it,' Father Michael admitted. He just hoped he was wrong. She wasn't like the others.

'She's one of them, of course we can't trust her,' said Beautiful.

'So, we don't tell them anything,' said Bryce. 'Shame that. A bunch of angry Nidhal would help our cause no end.'

'As long as Yarn controls the Emperor, the Nidhal can be of no help,' said Fenner.

'Then I'll head off in the morning and give her the message as planned,' said Bryce.

'If we ever see each other again, can you tell me what her reaction is?' asked Father Michael.

'Still think we might be wrong about her?' said Bryce.

'If we don't pull this off, it won't make any difference,' Beautiful sighed with a shake of her head.

Father Michael copied her sigh. 'Ellen will do as she is bid, no matter the outcome. I doubt I will see you before we act, Bryce.'

'Maybe,' said Fenner. 'I told you, the Admiral needs to hear this and to do that, we'll need you, Bryce.'

Father Michael listened in with a growing sense of purpose as Fenner explained their next moves. Moments before he had felt a sense of isolation, his path a solitary one. But perhaps he wasn't as alone as he had believed. The Emperor be praised.

CHAPTER TWENTY – FILLION

Fillion nudged Amice a little closer to the wagon. Nadena smiled and shifted her position along the padded driver's bench so that she was close to the edge. In her arms, Brynne was dozing. Fillion had noticed very early on that sleep was his daughter's favourite activity. He looked down at her face, a little chubbier, but still with that confused expression, like thinking was a painful process. When awake Brynne was even more confused and intrigued in equal measure. Every new sensation was a wonder to her and an opportunity to gurgle her delight.

'She's still here,' said Nadena.

'Just checking' replied Fillion.

'I know. You checked five minutes ago.'

'Really? It seemed longer.'

'Try sitting on this bench and see how slowly the time passes,' Nadena offered.

'You could ride inside,' he suggested, indicating the covered interior of the wagon bed that was adorned in pillows, rugs and furnishings. A mobile bedroom.

'And then you would complain that you couldn't see us. Honestly, Sabin, there's times I feel I have two children to please in this marriage.'

'Am I not allowed to be a concerned father?' Fillion asked, in mock outrage.

'Of course, but you can cease your vigil. We are perfectly safe from any marauding beasts. We are two days out from the capital. What could possibly happen?'

'Anything! Trust me, I've seen things.'

'And I haven't?' she challenged.

Fillion conceded the point with a scowl. She was right, but he didn't have to take it in good grace.

'Now, why don't you take your daughter, kiss her cheek, and accept everything is fine. Go stretch Amice's legs for a bit.'

She raised the baby high and Fillion, panicking slightly, his legs tightening against Amice's flanks, leaned sideways to gather her close to his chest. She wriggled in his arms and her eyes fluttered open. She made a gentle coughing sound that turned into a whine. Before it could turn into a full-blown whinge he kissed her forehead, rocking her gently, and started to hum a meaningless tune. Amice, without the guidance of her reins, continued calmly to keep pace with the wagon. After a couple of moments Brynne closed her eyes and passed into blissful oblivion.

'Nicely done,' said Nadena. 'I should get you to do that more often.'

'I suppose you can never start them too young. Get her used to being in the saddle now and in the future she'll be an excellent rider. Like her mother.'

Nadena opened her mouth in shock. 'Was that a compliment from the elf who hates to lose at racing? Are you feeling well, my love?'

Fillion laughed. 'It must be my excitement at returning to the capital.'

'Now I know you are sick,' said Nadena. 'Here …' She raised her arms and Fillion handed Brynne back over. She adjusted her grip and shifted sideways on the bench again. The driver, one of the staff from the villa, grinned at the baby.

'You know, you didn't have to stay with us. I would have understood if you had wanted to ride ahead with father. He likes to get a lead on matters before many of the others return.'

Fillion knew that, but he'd made a calculated guess that his gesture of familial support would go down far better.

'I think your father would have been annoyed if I hadn't stayed. Not that he would have said so in front of you,' he said.

'So, you do it just to please my father?' she asked, her face a mask of seriousness.

'You damned well know I don't!' he said.

Nadena smiled. 'Got you. You are so easy to get the better of sometimes, Sabin. But then that is why I like you. You're a simple creature at heart.'

Sabin started to say something but stopped, as he didn't quite know what to say. That indecision just made Nadena laugh.

'See? I am right. Simple.'

Fillion let out a 'bah' of indignation and sniffed loudly. Truth was he had no desire to return to the city. It would mean the summer was over, that the time with his family, his child, was over. And that he had to return to his mission. He could admit it to himself, even if he had trouble believing it, that he had enjoyed his time on the coast. Brynne was a delight and Nadena had maintained her serenity even on those nights when Brynne was in no mood to sleep.

He hoped, truly hoped, that when things started to come to a head, his daughter, blissfully ignorant of the seeds her grandfather had sown, would not suffer. She might be the one good thing, the only thing, to come out of all the slaughter and destruction.

'Sabin?' Nadena asked.

'Umm? Yes?'

'You looked miles away and that was one mighty frown on your face.'

'Ah, yes.' Fillion sighed. He had to remember, he was entering the pit of snakes and he must take control of his emotions once more. 'I was thinking about my duties.'

Nadena nodded, her face a little sad.

'It was always going to come, my love.'

'I'm sorry.'

'Don't be. You are the Servant to one of the most powerful Members of the Elves. I am proud of you.'

She shifted in her seat and made a face.

'I think I might go and sit in the back for a while after all. Brynne will no doubt want to feed soon. Why don't you go and bother Hedra and Alica? I can only imagine the two of them will be at each other's throats by now.'

'Very well. I'll come back a little later,' Fillion promised.

'I am sure you will.'

Fillion spurred Amice into a gentle gallop, chasing the next wagon in the caravan. He hoped the younger elves were asleep, he had thinking to do.

CHAPTER TWENTY-ONE – MICHAEL

They lay in tall grass not far from the beach. Father Michael could hear nothing but the sound of the waves running into the shore. It was a clear night and the stars shone brightly above. A breeze flowed from the east, bending the grass stalks above Father Michael's head. He knew his companions were close by, yet no one spoke, not even to make a joke or complain. It was unusual for the marines, but Father Michael had never truly seen them at work, and now, so close to their enemy, he could sense the change in their manner. They were totally focused on their business. Professional. Ahead of them was the channel that the fleet had sailed through to get inland. New Tissan was four miles to the west and it had added another five days to their journey to head south and east and then strike north once more. But they'd had to be sure that their path did not take them through any territory that a Watcher might be examining. As Fenner said, the last thing they'd expect would be the marines turning up in their rear. The wagon was hitched in some trees five miles back and the horse had been left to graze unfettered. They had walked on in darkness to reach this point, and there they had waited.

'I'd say it's about midnight,' whispered Fenner eventually, his voice muffled by the waves.

'Right,' responded Coyle.

Father Michael heard some rustling, some cuss words and then flint striking flint. A flash of light in the corner of his eye and he turned to see a fire catch and then flare in the darkness. Coyle raised it high and waved it three times, left to right. Then he lowered the torch and smothered the flame.

'Reckon they saw that?' asked Wendell, from somewhere behind Father Michael.

'We'll find out,' hissed Fenner. 'Now shut the fuck up and listen.'

It seemed like only moments when a dark shape passed overhead, silent, yet the force of its passing bent the grass against the wind.

'That's it,' ordered Fenner. 'Everyone up.'

As Father Michael got back to his feet and followed the others inland, another shape flew over their heads. The group quickly worked their way through the grass and into the open. Waiting for them were two eagles, unmistakable in the night. As they drew near, Father Michael spotted the dark shapes of their Riders, dismounted and waiting for them. It was Bryce and Cadarn.

'Corporal Fenner, good to see you and your people,' said Cadarn.

'Likewise, Sir,' replied Fenner, tipping him a salute. 'We weren't sure if it was just going to be Bryce showing up.'

'Like he'd let me,' replied Bryce.

'I'm with you. Smart thinking to meet us out here, Corporal.'

'Thanks. I guess I am right about Watchers on the Admiral?'

'You are,' nodded Cadarn. 'They know if any boat is coming from the town. And there is no one else out here with one.'

'We are in the clear, then?'

'Hopefully,' conceded Cadarn. 'The Gifted need my Eagle Riders, but they don't trust us. As soon as Bryce returned, he was questioned by a Reader.'

'Shit,' muttered Coyle.

'What did you tell them?' asked Fenner.

'The truth. I figured that they'd know if I was lying. I said that I saw you lot and told you that you weren't welcome in New Tissan, I also told them you were still going to try and link up with the Admiral. They were happy with that and sent me on my way,' said Bryce.

'Risky,' mused Fenner.

'That's the world we live in,' countered Bryce. 'I never mentioned you, Father. And they never asked. As far as they are concerned you are dead.'

Father Michael nodded. Yarn was still expecting something, but at least he could surprise her. 'Do they know you are up and about tonight?'

asked Father Michael. It seemed obvious to him that the Eagle Riders would be watched and their movements controlled.

'We are patrolling,' replied Cadarn. 'Yarn has us doing that every night now, just as a procedure. I just fixed it so Bryce and I would be together. None of the others know what we are up to. I'll tell them when we make a move. My Riders will join our cause, rest assured.'

'Good enough. Nobody said this would be easy, eh Father?' said Fenner.

'Nothing good ever comes easily,' replied Father Michael.

'Come along,' said Cadarn. 'Corporal, we'll take you and the Father back first and then come for the rest of you.'

'You're with me,' Bryce said to Father Michael.

Father Michael nodded and followed him over to Nukka. Bryce showed him where to climb up and then scrambled up in front of him.

'Arms tight around me, Father. But not too tight, eh?' said Bryce as he settled. 'My bird's a strong lass but you are a big son of a bitch, so when I tell you to drop, make sure you do it first time. She's got a lot of carrying to do.'

'I understand,' said Father Michael.

'By the way. Ellen, when I told her about what had happened, she seemed shocked. Genuinely. Then she got on with it. For what it's worth, I don't think she had any clue what Yarn was up to.'

Father Michael nodded.

'She asked about you,' said Bryce, taking up the reins. 'I told her you were dead. That actually bought a tear to her eye.'

Father Michael didn't know what to say. What could he say? Had anyone ever shed a tear for him before? Not that he could remember.

Next to them, Cadarn's eagle took to the sky.

'Here we go,' said Bryce. Nukka opened up her wings to their full span and with powerful downward sweeps they took to the sky.

'C'mon girl, get yourself up,' shouted Bryce.

Father Michael felt his stomach lurch and he closed his eyes, feeling the breeze against his skin. It helped to cool the sweat on his brow. If this was flying, then the Riders were welcome to it. He could feel the beast beneath him, feel the muscles tense and work, could imagine the effort it was taking to lift two grown men on its back. Then the sensation changed and the effort appeared to lessen. Father Michael opened his eyes, they were over water, heading north across the inlet. He looked over the wings as they beat gently, and beyond that the water, rushing past, glinting in the light of the stars. They were low, lower than he had thought they would be. That calmed him a little. Ahead, he could see Cadarn and Fenner. The Leader took them north until the far shore came into view and then he banked left, following the land westwards. After a few minutes, Father Michael found himself becoming accustomed to the rhythm of the wings, the breeze and the sense of peace it generated. In the darkness he felt himself relax. It was the calm before the storm.

The eagles banked again and there was New Tissan, a dozen lights marking its presence. But before that, approaching swiftly, the distinctive shapes of three large ships at station in the middle of the channel, each one marked by a single light at its rear. They were heading for the nearest. It was shielded from the far shore by the other two ships.

'Get ready,' shouted Bryce. 'Remember, I'll bank left. Let go of my waist. Don't fight it or grab me 'cos you'll bloody take the both of us with you!

Father Michael nodded – not that Bryce could see it – and released his grip.

When they were within thirty yards Bryce shouted 'Now!' and the eagle tilted sharply. Father Michael slid from his perch on the back of the saddle and experienced a few moments of freefall and an unexpected moment of silence before he struck the water side on. The impact was not too great but it still shocked him. He floundered for a few moments before he righted himself, paddling quickly and sweeping wide with his arms. Swimming was not his strong suit, and he'd been in the water under dire circumstances only too recently. A second splash nearby alerted him to Fenner's drop. He turned towards the sound and saw the marine bobbing in the water. Fenner raised a hand and swam over.

'You alright?'

'Yes,' replied Father Michael. 'What now?'

'I think we've been noticed. Come on.' Another light had appeared upon the ship and he followed Fenner, slowly stroking towards it.

'Who's down there?' a voice called.

'It's Corporal Fenner to you, I have Father Michael with me. Are you lot going to haul us up or let the sharks take us?' he heard Fenner shout as he reached the side.

'Depends. Are there sharks in there?' came a voice.

'Fuck off.'

Father Michael joined Fenner as a rope ladder was lowered. Fenner took hold and started climbing up.

Father Michael took hold of the ladder and hauled himself out of the water, using his arms to take his weight as he messed about trying to get his feet in the rungs. He reached the railing and a hand came under his shoulder, helping him up and over. He nodded his thanks to Fenner and straightened up. They were surrounded by a dozen or so figures, all of them armed. Several carried crossbows and wore the distinctive leather armour of the marines. They all looked wary and suspicious, their eyes flitting between Fenner and himself, their bodies radiating tension.

'Care telling me why you still got those pointed our way, Japes?' asked Fenner.

One of the marines pulled his crossbow away and stepped forward. He was a lad, maybe in his mid-twenties, skinny with two large front teeth, scraggly hair loosely tied back and a bandolier of knives across his chest.

'Sorry, Corporal, just a precaution, we're all a bit antsy. Okay guys, relax.' The gathered crew stepped back and lowered their weapons, the tension dissipating. The other marines joined Japes, leaning forward and sharing back slaps and shaking hands with Fenner. 'You kinda surprised us,' said Japes.

'That's the point,' replied Fenner.

'We honestly didn't expect to see you again. Hey, where's the others?

Is it just you two?' asked Japes, craning his head to look out on to the water.

'They'll be along. Watch out for them,' replied Fenner. 'Is the Admiral aboard? I'm guessing not.'

'He's on the *Fist*,' said another marine, pointing towards the ship floating to the left of theirs.

Fenner nodded.

'Right. You got a boat we could use? I'm fucked if I'm swimming over.'

This sprung the crew into action and with Japes calling out orders. A boat was lowered over the far side. Four crew climbed down into it and took up oars, a fifth took a position on the tiller.

Fenner tipped Japes a salute.

'Good work, lad. Now take care of the others and bring them across when they arrive. I'll send the boat back for them.'

'Aye, Corporal. Good to have you back, Sir,' replied Japes.

Father Michael followed Fenner to the side, as the corporal climbed down. Father Michael caught Japes looking at him askance. Father Michael looked back and raised an eyebrow.

'You're the Emperor's bodyguard ain't ya?' said Japes.

'That's right.'

'You look pissed.'

'That's right.'

Father Michael climbed over the side, leaving Japes gaping at him.

He reached the boat and settled next to Fenner at the front.

They rowed in silence across to the Emperor's flagship, *The Fist of Tissan*. Father Michael was reminded of the first night he had boarded this ship, carrying the heir of the Empire, leaving behind him a half dozen soldiers to their fate, brave men who had made the ultimate sacrifice doing their duty. And now he was returning empty-handed, without the Emperor. Seven Hells, he hoped he wasn't going to let those soldiers down at last. Yet he felt no less certain in his intent, no less driven. He had a purpose, and it was good.

As they drew near the massive man o' war, a voice called down.

'Hold and raise your oars. You got ten bows pointed at you.'

'Easy on the triggers lads. It's us from the *Pride*.'

'And? We weren't expecting visitors tonight.'

'Neither did we, then these two showed up, looking to speak to the Admiral,' replied the sailor at the tiller.

'And they are?'

'Corporal Fenner and Father Michael,' Fenner chipped in. 'Now enough of this shit. We want to see the Admiral. Now.'

A pause.

'Best come up, then,' replied the voice. Moments later another ladder was dropped down.

Once more, Fenner led the way and Father Michael climbed on board. He looked around the familiar deck, which was well lit by the light of the stars. He spied the pens that the eagles had been housed in and the landing platforms that hung over the sides. All were empty.

'Gentlemen.'

Father Michael turned.

Before them stood Admiral Lukas. He was carrying a cutlass on his belt and wearing a breastplate. Father Michael had never seen him so attired.

'Thought I recognised you two as you drew near. Just had to be sure though,' the Admiral said.

'Ready for a fight, Admiral?' asked Fenner.

The Admiral grunted. 'I can't afford to keep my guard down. Those bastards are coming. It's just a matter of when.'

'You mean the Gifted?' asked Father Michael.

'Aye, I mean them,' agreed the Admiral grimly. 'Come on, the pair of you, we need to talk.'

The Admiral led them to the second upper deck and along a short corridor which ended at his quarters. He stepped inside and moved about, putting a flame to a couple of candles. In the flickering light, Father Michael saw a large room with a table in front of a number of windows and to the left a collection of chests and cabinets. To the right was a bed, the sheets crumpled and piled up.

The Admiral set the candles down and glanced at Father Michael with an appraising eye. For his part Father Michael noted the Admiral's beard was longer, less well kept, but his hair was still tied up at the back.

'Take a seat, the pair of you,' he said, gesturing to chairs in front of the table. He walked around, undid his sword belt and laid it on the table before sitting. 'You chose a hell of a time to come back.'

'I can't argue with that,' said Fenner. 'Um, sorry about dripping on your floor, Sir.'

The Admiral waved a dismissive hand. 'Truth is, it's good to see you. I figured you were all dead.'

'We got your message in time. We did for two of them and we all got clear,' replied Fenner.

The Admiral smiled. 'Good for you. I'm glad something got done right.'

'The Father here almost didn't make it, but he's a tough son of a bitch,' added Fenner.

The Admiral turned his gaze to Father Michael. 'I can see you've been wounded, Father. Care to tell me what happened?'

Father Michael nodded. 'The Gifted attacked us when we reached the river. They killed Bron and Uther and took the Emperor captive. I managed to kill one of them before they took me out but … it wasn't enough. I got a couple of new scars for my trouble, as you can see.'

The Admiral shook his head. 'There isn't much you can do against several Gifted. Not even the Champion of the Arena,' he said, not unkindly. He looked back at Fenner.

'How did you get here?'

'Eagles,' said Fenner. 'Cadarn and Bryce brought us the long way round. It was the only way to get to you without being seen.'

'Good thinking. Are the Riders with us?'

'Yes, but there's not much they can do while the Gifted hold the Emperor.'

The Admiral grunted again.

'Isn't that the Hells-damned truth. I'm stuck out here, waving my arse at Yarn and her Gifted. But what can I achieve? Short of sailing away and leaving them to it. But I ain't for running,' he said.

'I hear you even refused an order by the Emperor,' said Fenner.

'It was no damned order from the Emperor, Corporal,' growled the Admiral.

'Is the Emperor harmed?' asked Father Michael.

The Admiral shook his head. 'It's difficult to tell, but he was standing when he spoke to me. He seemed surprised when I told him I wouldn't stand down. But he probably knew what Yarn was going to do, what she'd already done. Either way someone was going to die. It just happened to be innocent citizens.' The Admiral shook his head. 'You better not repeat this, but I am angry. Angry I didn't react sooner. I lost a lot of good men and women.'

'There was nothing else you could do, they acted so fast,' said Fenner.

'Maybe, maybe not. Maybe I should have moved before Yarn did. All I know is, if we sit here for much longer, the Gifted are going to come for us. I'm surprised they haven't already. I'll burn these damn boats before that happens.'

'I'm going to get him back,' said Father Michael.

'Who?' The Admiral looked at him with raised eyebrows. 'The Emperor?'

'Yes.'

The Admiral placed his hands flat on the table. 'Father. You are one man – an incredible fighter, I'll give you that. But you can't take them all on.'

'I never said I'd do it alone,' replied Father Michael. 'The Gifted have control because they have the Emperor. If we can get him away, then the people will rally to him.'

'And many, many folk will die,' said the Admiral. 'You think I haven't considered doing just that? But as I said, they'll see me coming.'

'They won't see me coming,' said Father Michael. 'I can go one on one with a Gifted and I can kill them. They are not gods. There is only one God. And my faith in him is absolute.'

The Admiral gave him a doubtful look.

'Listen, Admiral,' said Fenner. 'Isn't this the point? We either run, submit or we do … something! You said it, the Gifted will try for us. Besides, we owe them a fight.'

The Admiral leaned back, folded his arms, and inspected the pair of them. 'You're with the Father on this one?'

'We are,' replied the marine. 'We've got scores to settle.'

'Hmm.' The Admiral leaned forward, placed one hand back on the table and started to drum his fingers. 'We'd need to cause a diversion. Draw the Gifted away.'

'The Riders are looking out for a sign from us,' said Father Michael. 'Leader Cadarn knows what I intend to do. They can help.'

The Admiral slammed his hands on the table in unison. 'Alright, then. Fenner, you are getting your sergeant's stripe back. You're leading the marines.'

'Uh, great! Wait? What about Captain Rens?' asked Fenner.

The Admiral made a sour face. 'He was one of the ones who didn't make it.'

'Damn,' swore Fenner.

'Like I said,' continued the Admiral. 'You are now in charge of the marines. There weren't many left, apart from those already guarding the ships, and the handful I bought with me. I lost a dozen fighting a rearguard just so I could get away. I've got a score to settle as well.' He inclined his head towards Father Michael. 'I trust you can think of some suitable diversion to assist the Father here.'

'I reckon I can. But I think we are going to have to go all-in on this one. We only get one chance at this,' said Fenner.

'I have no doubt about that,' agreed the Admiral. He looked at Father Michael. 'What do you need?'

'I need to know that I can rely on you to die for this,' said Father Michael. Nothing less would do if his plan was to work. 'I do not wish to sound, ah, dramatic. But you have to buy me some time.'

The Admiral nodded. 'We understand that, Father. We've been doing that since this damned adventure started.'

Father Michael pursed his lips. *Good.* 'We are not waiting. We are doing this tonight. Let us plan the attack.'

Father Michael eased himself into the water for the second time that night. He was still damp from his earlier dip and he quickly adjusted to the change of temperature.

'You okay?' whispered Fenner, leaning over the edge of the row boat. 'Weight not too much?'

Father Michael tested the weight of the baldrick that was secured to his back. 'It's fine.' The baldrick held a shortsword. A sheathed dagger was tied tight against his hip.

Fenner reached down and patted his shoulder. 'Good luck, then. This should be fun.'

Father Michael shook his head. Not for the first time, doubting Fenner's sanity.

'I'll see you after,' he responded, and kicked off. He kept his strokes steady as he covered the hundred yards to the shore. He was fortunate the tide was with him. Having taken to the boat once more, they had used the cover of the warships to row to the far side of the inlet and then back towards the east. Father Michael was heading now towards the edge of New Tissan where, hopefully, there would be no Watchers to see his arrival. He thought about Fenner again, he had been a sergeant once but had been demoted. That didn't surprise him but he would like to find out the story behind that, once this business was done. If they both survived.

He looked back but the boat had disappeared. He was alone once more, and as he swam old feelings and expectations re-emerged from deep within. Going into the arena with no guarantee of success, against opponents that wished him dead. For his part, he welcomed the return of these thoughts; they were the experiences of a lifetime of combat and would serve him well in the night ahead. He was drawing near the southern shore now. He could see, a little further to the west, two distinct fires. The Admiral had told him that soldiers manned them, although he was sure the Watchers would be monitoring them as well. Even if those soldiers were loyal to the Emperor, the risk of discovery was still too great. The fires were along a stretch of beach where a few fishing boats were laid up. Beyond them, a few hundred yards away, were the new docks. When Father Michael had left they were the chaotic beginnings of a shipyard and a couple of jetties. Now, apparently, the docks were the focus, as the residents of New Tissan laboured to produce ships of a size and quality to survive the journey back to the old Empire.

Reaching the beach, he kept as low a profile as he could as the estuary bed rose. When he had no more water to keep him submerged, he forced himself up, and ran towards the long grass thirty yards away. Reaching cover he dropped down on his haunches and waited. After two minutes there was nothing to suggest anyone had seen him, so he stood once more and started his penetration into the town of New Tissan itself. Angling in from the north, he aimed for the square, where the Emperor had his quarters. Father Michael had no idea if that was where he was being held, but it seemed a logical place to start.

As he drew closer, he spotted a far larger number of dwellings than had been there before the winter. Stepping out of the cover of the long grass, he was in open, cleared territory. Much of it was demarcated by fields and enclosures. Cultivation was well on its way, as it needed to be to feed the thousands of imperial citizens. There was, he noted, no palisade surrounding the town. This had been discussed, and the work should have been completed. But perhaps the wood was taken for the shipbuilding. It made sense, there were no true threats, and contrary to the warnings of the Nidhal, he had yet to see any roving packs of vargr. Either way, it made his work easier. Moving swiftly through the fields and the pens of some of the domestic animals that had survived the crossing, he started to encounter habitations. And here he could tell that there were many who had yet to establish proper, permanent homes. Some were still living in shelters of canvas that had been shored up with timbers. He kept away from the main thoroughfare, but there were streets and lanes of sorts, some with crude walkways. As he followed them towards the town centre, and even with the late hour, snatches of conversation drifted through the night, a cough, snoring, the sound of a child crying and, here and there, figures moving in the darkness. Father Michael was no good at stealth and decided to just keep moving with purpose, and hope no one thought to challenge him. Why would they? He was already dead.

The crude homes began to be replaced by sturdier wooden cabins, larger storage sheds, and even some two-storey structures. He was close now. And perhaps now was the time he should think about using the shadows. He needed to find somewhere to get a view of the square and the Emperor's quarters. The choice was obvious. The temple on the eastern side of the square. It would give him a clear vantage point. The rear of the temple came into view. The Arch Cardinal had his rooms there. Would Yarn have occupied them? No, it was unlikely, she would have wanted to stay close to her fellow Gifted. But there was a doorway in the timber wall that had not been there before. Perhaps he should risk it?

The route he was following ended at a distinct space between the temple and the houses that surrounded it. He looked left and right, and with no one in sight, he sprinted to the doorway and pushed himself tight to the wall next to it. He withdrew his dagger, held it close to his chest, and reached a hand out to the latch. Gently raising the bar he pulled, and the door opened with little protest. He stepped inside, pulling the door back towards him and lowering the latch on the inside. He stood in the darkness waiting for his eyes to adjust. As the seconds passed he began to discern the layout of the room and its contents, as sparsely furnished as he remembered. In the far corner was the bed. It lay in a deep shadow, and he could not tell if anyone occupied it. *There's only one way to be sure.* Keeping his dagger high and ready to strike, he took a pace forward.

'Hello?'

Father Michael stopped. A male voice.

'Hello. I heard you come in,' the voice said.

He knew that voice.

'Are you here to kill me as well?' the voice continued, strangely good-natured considering the question.

'Father Llews?' asked Father Michael.

'Yes, it's me. And you?'

'It's Father Michael.'

The bed creaked.

'But you are dead.'

'Not yet.'

'Well, that's good news, yes, very good indeed.'

'What are you doing here, Father?' asked Father Michael. He felt no less tense for this encounter, he still had his work to do.

'I am now the only member of the priesthood left, outside of the Gifted, of course. So, the Cardinal decided I should take on the role of ministering the flock and maintaining the Temple. Not that I am very good with my hands, you understand.'

'She let you live?' asked Father Michael. He took a step forward and was able to discern better that Father Llews had sat up and moved to the side of the bed, his feet on the floor.

'Yes, indeed. It was most fortunate that when the Gifted took control, I was visiting the Empress. She pleaded for my life and the Cardinal thought fit to spare me.'

Father Michael hunkered down in front of Father Llews.

'Have you seen the Emperor?' he asked, eagerly.

The father nodded. 'Every day. He is permitted to come and see me. We sit and we pray together. We talk about many things.'

'And how is he?'

Father Llews paused for a moment. 'He is, ah, angry. He feels betrayed. Can one blame him? Those who swore their fealty have been found most wanting.'

'Not all of us,' said Father Michael.

'No,' agreed Father Llews. 'Some of us still know what it means to be in the presence of the divine.'

Father Michael thought. There was an unexpected opportunity here. He leaned in close. 'Father. I plan to free the Emperor and help restore his rule.'

'Then I must help you,' said Father Llews, with conviction. 'We must. It is our duty.'

'That is good to hear, Father. Very shortly, something is going to happen. I hope it will be enough to keep the Gifted distracted. But I must assume the Emperor will remain guarded.'

'Yes. There are two Gifted at his door at all times.'

Father Michael nodded. As he expected and he imagined he knew what Gifts they might have.

'And where are the others?'

'They are still quartered in their barracks behind the Emperor's cabin. They have extended it somewhat. I believe they wish to recreate their monastery from Nostrum. Pah!' said Father Llews. 'That will take them an age, and if we are returning to the east, I really don't see the poi–'

Father Michael placed a hand of Father Llew's leg.

'Father, please, there is not much time.'

'Yes, of course. What do you need me to do?'

Father Michael smiled. The plan's chances had just improved by a small degree. But that's what counted in a fight, an edge: sharp, precise, fatal. That's all he ever needed.

Father Michael left the Temple by the back door and crept around its southern side. He had borrowed a cloak from Father Llews. It was far too small for him but at least the hood gave him some kind of disguise. He pulled it over his head and stepped out into the square. The sword now rode around his waist. There was no point in trying to hide it, there were plenty of other armed men in New Tissan. He walked across the beaten earth towards the tavern on the far side. He passed by a platform that had been built in the centre of the square. A gibbet had been erected to one side of it, though nothing hung from it. That was new also. He wondered if that had been Yarn's doing. The tavern was shut, in darkness just like every other building in the square at this hour. He glanced across to the north and the Emperor's cabin. A solitary brazier burned outside the entrance, some distance from the porch. It was not for warmth, it was to allow the two Gifted posted by the door an opportunity to see anyone coming. He felt isolated crossing the square, and knew that their eyes would be upon him. He hoped he was far enough away from the light to seem nothing more than just another citizen. All he had to do was continue on. When he was within a few yards of the tavern, two figures stepped out from the side of the street next to it. Father Michael stopped. Already his hand was by his sword, already he was weighing odds. This close he could see these were two armed men, two soldiers of the empire.

'It's too late for that,' said one of them.

'What?' Father Michael mumbled.

'It's almost two bells. You think you are going to get a drink tonight?' the soldier continued.

Ah. 'I'm thirsty,' Father Michael said, trying to add what he hoped was a drunken sprawl to his words.

'Best you go home, big fella,' said the other soldier.

'Not sure where that is,' Father Michael responded. 'Maybe I can sleep here?'

The two soldiers looked at each other and shrugged.

'Fine. Just don't kick up a fuss and get the attention of one of those two over there,' advised the first one.

'Right,' said Father Michael, and tipped a salute. He stepped up on to the porch of the tavern and settled himself down on it, his back against the wall, pulling the hood over his head, well aware the soldiers were watching him.

'Come on,' said the first. 'So many damned drunks. Where do they hide all the booze?'

'I wish I could find it,' said the other one as they moved off heading towards the eastern exit by the temple.

Father Michael turned his head towards the Gifted. Neither had reacted but he still felt a prickling sensation, like he was being watched. He closed his eyes and waited, reciting a prayer to the Emperor. Much of what would happen next was out of his hands. His trust and faith was now in others and the grace of the Emperor. Truly, he had been meant for this. And just like that a bell started to toll. Moments later, shouts drifted from the north.

It had begun.

He did not know who would have raised the alarm, whether it was a Watcher or one of the pickets by the shore, but right now, they would be witnessing the *Fist of Tissan* and her two sister ships light a multitude of torches and lanterns. They would be seeing the ships weigh anchor, raise sail, and head out to the estuary and beyond. And they would be carrying word to Cardinal Yarn that the Admiral was leaving.

As the bell continued to toll and figures started to appear in the square, he looked north towards the barracks. He could see Gifted exiting the building and heading northwards. He turned his gaze back towards the Emperor's cabin. The two Gifted – one male and one female – were talking to one another just as the door opened and there, outlined in the flickering light, was the Emperor. Father Michael felt a surge of joy. He could tell the Emperor was arguing with the two. Another Gifted appeared, running towards the building, joining the others. More words were spoken and the Emperor was pushed back into the cabin and the door shut. *How dare they?* The third Gifted left the others and joined the general rush to the north, as more citizenry were being drawn to the sound of the bell. Now was the time. He regained his feet and stepped off the porch, joining others, just one of the crowd, and started angling his way towards the cabin. He could see a glow in the night sky a little to the north west. That was the true diversion. Fenner and his marines, swarming over the dockyard, putting torch to timber. The Gifted, all of them, couldn't ignore that. A parting shot from the Admiral, making sure he could not be pursued.

Father Michael looked towards the Temple. The door opened and Father Llews ran out. Seeing Father Michael on the move had been his cue. They converged on the cabin, Father Michael hanging back, staying to the side of the building where more folk were passing by to watch the spectacle. Father Llews was now on the porch, pleading with the Gifted.

'You must come! There was someone in my Temple. They were in my room!'

The Gifted looked at each other. Neither were moving.

'Go back, Father. We cannot help you,' said the male. Father Michael placed the voice, a slender Reader called Malik. His hunch had been right; if he'd tried to get close the Reader would have been alerted to his intent.

Father Llews reached out. 'But what if they mean to burn the temple too? We cannot allow that!' Father Llews was shouting.

The Gifted shared another look.

'It's probably nothing,' said Malik.

'I'll be quick,' replied the female, Father Michael didn't recognise her.

'Thank you, thank you,' said Father Llews, leading her away from the cabin.

Father Michael pulled away from the crowd and stepped on to the end of the porch, pulling off his cloak. He marched towards the remaining Gifted, pulling the dagger out. The Gifted was still watching his comrade, his head tilted to one side.

Malik jerked upright.

'Wait! He's lying!'

Father Michael saw the female Gifted turn even as Malik finally reacted to the sound of Father Michael's footsteps, but by then he had closed to with a few feet. In the light of the brazier, Father Michael could see the stylized metal plate that covered the eyes, nose and cheekbones. He could see the mouth open wide in surprise, as Father Michael kept walking and jammed the dagger straight into Malik's mouth. Using his momentum he pushed the Gifted up against the cabin wall, pressing his own body up against the warrior, leaning in with one hand against the chest and the other on the dagger. Malik struggled trying to force him away, gripping Father Michael's shoulders, moving his head left and right, as if that might dislodge the blade. Blood started to pour from his mouth, and Malik half cried, half gurgled his rage and panic. Then Father Michael stepped back, turned and drew his shortsword.

The Gifted by Father Llews lowered her spear and charged, shouting something unintelligible. Father Michael went to meet her. As the two closed the Gifted drove the spear straight towards Father Michael's midriff. At the last moment Father Michael swayed and chopped down on the spear, snapping the shaft near the point. The Gifted reacted swiftly, using her forward movement to move beyond Father Michael's reach. She turned and spun what remained of the spear over her head and brought it to a guard position, holding it like a blade. Father Michael took the briefest of moments to see this was a Speaker, the half-moon on her chin. *Finish her quick.* He charged in fast and she stepped back, twirling the staff and bringing it round her right shoulder, looking to brain him. Bad move. He raised his left arm, revealing the studded bracer beneath. As the shaft connected, he brought his blade in low, thrusting it up and into her exposed left armpit. She cried out and pulled away. Father Michael felt his own wave of pain from the spear shaft's impact, but it had been mostly absorbed by his armour. *Emperor she had hit hard!* But his discomfort would be nothing compared to hers; the nerve endings would be shredded, the agony terrible and the blood loss fatal. He eyed her as she cast the spear aside and pulled her own blade free with her right hand. The left was now useless. If she was to use her power to call for help, now would be the time. He wouldn't give her the chance. He closed again and she brought her sword low, in a horizontal arc. He dropped his blade, deflecting the blow and bringing it in a backhand slash across her throat. He felt the faint resistance, saw a flare of blood, felt something warm and wet splash against the skin of his check. She was finished. He resumed a ready stance, blade high, but she had no fight left in her. The sword was dropped and her hand went to her throat before her legs gave way. *I have to be sure.* He took a hold of her head, and tilted it back. Her eyes were nothing but black pools beneath the facemask. She did not resist as he drove his weapon into her throat. He picked up her sword, and quickly walked towards the cabin. He climbed the steps and saw Father Llews bent over Malik. He had removed the helmet.

'Oh! It's a Reader. Shouldn't be surprised I suppose. We were lucky, if their attention had been on you they might've reacted faster,' he said.

'They never react fast enough,' said Father Michael. That was how he was able to win. They never knew what was coming at them. Their arrogance blinded them to what he used to be, what he was still. But he doubted he'd ever be as lucky again. He pounded on the door.

'Emperor? It's me. Father Michael.' The door swung open and he was bathed in the light of a candle.

The Emperor looked at him in astonishment, his face clouding with confusion, before he finally broke into a grin. 'Father Michael, by my name, it is good to see you!'

'Emperor, come,' said Father Michael. He handed over the Gifted's sword. The Emperor took it and nodded. He was dressed in boots, trousers and a shirt. Good enough to travel in.

'Tigh?' asked his mother, Empress Alana, appearing from behind him. She was wearing a bed gown. Not so good.

'Mother, we are leaving,' ordered the Emperor. He looked at Father Michael. 'Where are we going?'

'Away from here. All of you follow me and stay close,' responded Father Michael.

The Emperor nodded.

'Your Grace,' said Father Llews to the Empress. 'I will assist you. Here.' He draped around her the cloak that Father Michael had been wearing.

'Oh, Father. Our prayers have been answered!' she responded.

'Come along!' Father Michael urged. There was no time!

'Yes, come on mother,' said the Emperor. 'Lead on, Father!'

Father Michael turned and took them directly south, away from the Gifted and the fires to the north. A crowd was streaming past them, eager to see. He caught catches of conversation, those speculating on what was happening: Who was attacking? Was it the elves? Had they finally found them? Was it the monsters from inland? Or was it the Admiral finally attacking? Father Michael bulled through them all using his size and drawn blade.

'Is that the Emperor?' cried one woman, as they passed her by. A man stopped in his tracks and pointed as they ran past, speechless. But by and large no one expected to see the Emperor running the streets in naught but a half-buttoned shirt, so they shook their heads and paid them little mind. Hitting the quiet street leading south away from the square, they gained more room and made better time. Father Michael looked behind for pursuit but saw none. The Empress was starting to tire but Father Llews held her hand and helped her onwards. The Emperor, breathing hard, glanced at Father Michael with a determined face. Father Michael allowed himself a brief moment of satisfaction. This was going to work. They continued on, passing through the outlying cabins and beyond to the edges of New Tissan. Just ahead in a patch of open land were several large shapes. One moved and spread its wings wide.

'Eagles!' cried the Emperor.

'Your Grace,' said Cadarn, bowing low as he emerged from the shadows. Three more Riders, all carrying their crossbows, followed him, their eyes scanning for trouble.

'I am truly glad to see you, and your Riders, Leader,' said the Emperor.

'I am sorry, we should have done more–'

'Nonsense! There was nothing you could do.'

'Guards?' Father Michael interjected, looking into the darkness. They weren't free yet.

'The pickets deserted their post when it became clear the action was at the docks,' replied Cadarn.

'Good,' said the Emperor. He also cast his eyes around. 'We are flying again?'

'Yes, Your Grace. Needs must. You are coming with me. The Empress is with Jenna.'

A female rider, Jenna, dressed in flying leathers, her blonde hair tied back in a long pony-tail, stepped forward. 'Your Grace, I have a better cloak than that for you.'

The Empress looked at her son, and then at Father Llews. He patted her hand.

'Go along, Your Grace. I'll be right behind you,' he said, reassuringly.

The Empress gestured to Jenna to lead on.

'Father Llews, we weren't expecting to see you, but we can have Raker here take you,' said Cadarn. 'Father Michael? You're with Bryce.'

'You and me again, Father,' said Bryce. He looked Father Michael up and down. 'So, did you make them pay?'

'I did what I had to do.'

'How many did you kill?' asked Bryce, as he led Father Michael to his eagle.

'Two!' the Emperor called over as he followed Cadarn.

'Seven Hells,' muttered Bryce, as he gave Father Michael a lift upon the saddle. 'We should just have attacked. You could have taken on the Gifted by yourself.'

'Not all at once,' replied Father Michael evenly, as he settled into position. A shadow passed overhead and Father Michael looked up to see more eagles.

'That's the rest of the crew,' said Bryce, taking his spot in front of Father Michael. 'Cadarn had everyone on standby. When things kicked off they launched. Didn't give Yarn time to tell them otherwise.'

'The whole squadron?' asked Father Michael.

'Yep. We're all deserters now. Depending on your point of view. Right, let's get the fuck out of here.'

Nukka sprang into the air and Father Michael lurched backwards for a split second before regaining his balance.

He looked to his left and saw the Empress on Lissa, seated behind Jenna, her cloak flapping with the rush of air. The eagles carrying Father Llews and the Emperor must be somewhere behind them.

'Do we know where we are going?' he shouted.

Bryce turned his head. 'We just figured we'd head west. Try and link up with the Nidhal.'

It was as good a plan as any. It would be the safest place if any pursuers were sent after them.

'How long can you keep up for?' he asked.

'My eagle will tire quickly carrying us both. We'll go for an hour maybe. Then we'll land, swap you over to the others in front of us and keep going in relay. We'll have to stop a little after dawn though, to give everyone a rest,' Bryce responded.

Father Michael closed his eyes. He felt tired. Not from the fighting. That was quick and clean. It could have gone much worse. It was the pressure, the burden he had borne in playing his part in the rescue. It had all depended on him. He had succeeded and was truly thankful, but now he felt a mental exhaustion. It was up to others now.

CHAPTER TWENTY-TWO – CADE

Cade rotated her shoulder. Still stiff, still sore. She pulled on her shirt and buttoned it up, yawning as she did so. Sleep. Now there was a thing. Three days in and she still couldn't get her rhythm right.

She stood up and adjusted her trousers. It was handy that Vidar had kept his bed in his office. Made things so much easier. She walked over to his desk and picked up a bottle. It was empty. Damn, she'd have to ration what was left a whole lot better. Come to think of it, she'd missed a trick earlier. She could've ordered all the booze on the plateau confiscated and brought to her office. That would've worked a treat. Oh well, hindsight and stuff.

There was a knock on her door.

'Yeah,' she said, replacing the bottle and reaching for an untouched jug of water.

Devlin opened the door and stuck his head in. 'Are you decent?'

'As I'll ever be. Bring 'em in,' she said. She walked round to take Vidar's old seat as Devlin ushered in the representatives of the other mining communities. Some shuffled in, others walked tall. Miriam brought up the rear.

'Hey, Winders, how's the head?' she asked.

Winders, the blonde one with the hair tied up she'd first spoken to outside the warehouse sported a bandage that covered his forehead. He reached up to touch it.

'I'll live,' he said, with a rueful smile.

'Glad to hear it.' Give him his due. When her crew arrived to help his people against their guards, he was leading front and centre. It wasn't the case with all of them.

She beamed at them. 'Right. What have we got to talk about today?'

'We can't stay here,' said Devlin.

Ah yes. Now she remembered. They were deep in enemy territory with dwarves all around, and no friendly Imperial armies coming to save them.

'Why not?' asked a woman with a long braid falling down her shoulders. 'There are no dwarves for miles. We can hold this plateau, can't we?'

'Yes. Easily,' conceded Devlin.

'How long could we last, though?' asked Winders, looking at Cade. Yeah, he'd worked it out.

'Based on an inventory of supplies, I say a good month with a bit of rationing,' said Devlin, folding his arms, 'before we started having to eat each other.'

'Excellent. What a happy time we'll have in our mountain fastness,' drawled Cade.

Rope-For-Hair sat back scowling.

'Oh and how long before they are expecting the next ore delivery?' asked Cade.

'Wagons should have left yesterday,' said Miriam from the back of the room. Turned out she had a head for figures.

'So maybe a week or two before we get any visitors?' confirmed Cade.

'Another food delivery will come in a couple of days,' added Miriam.

'That sounds like our window of opportunity,' said Cade, looking at Devlin.

'Yes. Send a vanguard out to ambush the food caravan. Take the wagons and supplies,' he said.

'Sounds like you've got this all planned out already,' said a man called Sent, a merchant who had more than a smattering of Plainsfolk blood in him.

'Time isn't on our side,' said Cade. 'And my man Devlin here isn't one to live for the moment.'

'And do we have a plan for leaving this place?' asked Winders.

'We are leaving as soon as we have those extra food supplies. We take all the wagons, all the weapons, food, blankets and anything else you can think of that might be useful.' Cade eyed the empty bottle.

'Just like that?' asked Rope.

'Just like that,' said Cade. 'We can't stay here. The dwarves will be mightily pissed. Seriously, what did you think was going to happen?'

'I suppose we all believed there might be some respite,' said Sent.

'No such luck,' said Devlin. 'This is just the start.'

'And what about those dwarves locked up in the barracks?' asked Winders.

Cade looked at Devlin.

'Up to you Cade. You promised they'd live if they surrendered.'

'I did, didn't I?' She puffed out her cheeks. Did her promises count? She looked at the gathering. Not much love for dwarves here. 'Torch them when we leave.'

A murmur of agreement rippled through the room.

'So where are we headed?' asked a long-limbed man, with the burr of someone from Aberpool.

'We are heading home. There is nowhere else to go. We have maps, we have some indication of what settlements are in our way. We move down through the mountains, out of dwarf territory, and back into Tissan. And we keep running,' said Devlin. 'Maybe they'll give it up as a bad job and leave us to it.'

Rope-For-Hair snorted.

'Not the best plan,' muttered Winders.

'Compared to the alternative? Not the worst, either,' Cade said, drumming her fingers on the tabletop.

'You remember what it was like getting here? The long march?' asked Sent.

'Yep. I remember. Took us an age. I get it.'

'And you want us to do it again? With barely any food and no protection? Most of our people are dead on their feet.'

'I said I get it,' replied Cade, trying to keep her voice calm and even. There was no point antagonising anyone, she needed them on side. 'Look,

I'm not going to coat this in honey. Many of us are hurting, broken. Is that any different from when we marched east? But look at us. We're still here! We survived. The weak? They are long gone. The old? They're gone too. Us that's left have taken everything they have thrown at us and we have kept going. For what reason? Did any of you believe this was ever going to end any other way than with us all dead? Come on, honestly?' She stood up and bit back on the pain in her shoulder. It felt like it wanted to tear open. She took a deep breath and ploughed on. 'You've all had two nights of freedom, and more food in your bellies than you've had for the best part of a year. Think on that. Stay here if you want, and if you come west with us then you are doing so of your own free will. It's your choice. The only real one you will have for a long time. You can choose to take a chance. Now, I'm not saying we aren't going to lose folk on the way. Maybe none of us will make it. But maybe some of us will. Maybe years from now, you can tell your grandkids about the great escape. How you took a chance and were ballsy enough to get away with it.'

'Bit late for grandkids,' Sent responded. He had a smile on his face.

Cade waved her good arm.

'I'm heading home. It won't be like last time. We still have the weather and this time we're not in chains. And we have a reason to keep going. If I die, so be it. I die on my terms. But there's two things I know for sure. If I stay here the dwarves will come. And I *will* die. Along with anyone else who stays. But, if I go …' She paused and slammed her palm on to the desk. 'I'm going to have thousands of fellow Tissans at my back, and we'll be fucking things up royally for any dwarves who get in our way. Now tell me that doesn't sound like fun.'

There were a few chuckles in the room. Devlin grinned. Miriam gave her the thumbs up. Winders stroked his chin. Sent shook his head in exasperation, and Rope continued to scowl.

'We'll be an army on the move. Make no mistake,' said Devlin. 'The logistics are a nightmare. To try and feed us all will be a monumental effort. There are some settlements marked on the maps. They are not defended, so I intend for us to hit them hard, sack them, and move on.

Beyond the Dwarf Nations we can expect no supply depots, no villages, no farms. All of them went long ago.'

'Then how do we feed ourselves?' asked Winders.

'We have to spread out, like a swarm,' said Sent.

Cade nodded. He had the right of it.

'Go on,' she said.

'It's like the Plainsfolk used to live,' he continued. 'The tribes had large hunting grounds. Going from place to place with the seasons. Taking what they needed to keep going then moving on.'

'I concur,' said Devlin. 'We stick together for protection when we are in dwarf lands. We take as much as we can and pile it on the wagons. Then when we get away, I suggest we split into smaller columns. Spread out over a wide frontage, sending parties out to forage and hunt. If we stay as a pack, we'll never find enough.'

'And, if you want, when we are back in the Empire, you can all head off on your own sweet way. I don't care. But until then, we back each other up and support each other,' said Cade.

'I'd rather we stay together,' said Devlin. 'We're stronger that way.'

'Maybe so. But I'll tell no one how to live their lives when we are free of this place.'

Over a few appreciative murmurs Cade walked over to Vidar's cabinet, the one that stored the liquor, and pulled out a bottle. She uncorked it and took a sniff. She really wasn't sure what it was. But she took a swig anyway. Her throat burst into fire.

'Emperor!' she declared. She heard Miriam snigger. Turning, she looked at the gathering. 'We are leaving tomorrow. Devlin has already put together how it will work and has written out a bunch of orders. No good me doing it, I can't write!'

More smiles.

She handed the bottle to Winders. He took a pull, gasped a little and passed it on to Rope, as his face flushed.

'Whoever stays, I wish you the best of luck. As for the rest of you, we'll make our own luck.'

Devlin stood. 'I'll be hosting a briefing downstairs in one hour. Thank you for giving me a list of your people and what they can do. I have already assigned them into works companies according to their skills. That work starts now. Go back and tell your folk. They will be reporting to their company leaders from here on in.'

The group stood and began to file out. Sent joined Cade. 'We have injured and we have sick,' he stated.

Cade nodded. 'I know. I am keeping six wagons back for them. That's as much as we can spare. If we find more, all the better. But we can't afford any dead weight. We can't afford to go slow.'

'Are you going to get better?' asked Sent, indicating her injury.

'What, this? You should see the state I used to get in after a wild night out in Aberpool. This ain't nothing.'

Sent smiled. 'Then I'll see you on the road.'

She tipped him a salute and he left the office. Devlin joined her and handed her back the bottle.

'What is that shit?' he asked.

Cade shrugged. 'Dunno. Could be medicine.'

'Could be poison.'

She took another sip. 'Now wouldn't that be a thing?' she declared.

'Good speech,' he said, taking the bottle back and having another pull.

'You think? It wasn't planned or anything.'

'Oh, I know that. Either way, you gave it to them straight.'

'Looks like most of them bought it.'

Devlin screwed his mouth to one side. 'Like they really had a choice. They'll fall into line. Our people are behind you. That'll help keep things together. As you said, when we get across the border, it'll be down to everyone to choose their own fates.'

'You know what I'd like to do?' Cade asked.

Devlin smiled.

'Open a tavern.'

Cade formed an O with her mouth.

'How did you know?'

Devlin laughed.

'Because in the absence of any left standing in the Empire, you'd be forced to build your own.'

'Damn it,' Cade said. 'You know me too well.'

Devlin shook his head.

'No, it wasn't that. Meghan told me.'

'Ah.' She hadn't thought about Meghan for a while. Hadn't wanted to.

'It's okay,' said Devlin. 'There'll be a time to mourn.'

Cade nodded. Sure. Mourning. She had never done that before. Wouldn't know where to start.

'You got everything you need?' she asked.

'I've got people taking charge, and found some others who have military experience. Divvied up our arsenal as best we can. Issar is organising some scouts. They are heading out tonight.'

'Wish I was,' said Cade. That sounded like the best job. Space to move, freedom.

'Not yet. Not even if you were fit,' said Devlin. 'We need you in one piece. Best I can offer is a place at the vanguard. But any fighting, you leave to me, for the moment at least.'

'Happy to!' she said, raising her bottle.

Devlin saluted and sauntered out.

Damn but he was loving this. Devlin had his own little army to play with at last. And what did she have? She wasn't sure. But it came with alcohol. So, all things considered, it could be worse.

Four days later she stood with her back to a waystation looking on to a canal. Behind her the noisy herd of Tissans were still streaming along the track leading from the mountains and joining the sloping trail down to the town below. Although some distance away, black smoke was rising from it, a pall fed by multiple sources. It climbed high into the sky, higher than Cade's position at the top of the ascending series of locks. Barges, now empty of crews, waited purposelessly along the canal. Their cargoes would not be reaching their destinations any time soon. All the mules had been taken, added to their growing herd. Tissan scouts ranged all over the surrounding territory, making sure no one could get away to carry word. She glanced back along the canal path, watching the procession. Twenty-five thousand souls. Who knew? Who could have thought the dwarves had saved so many? She surrendered to a brief moment of panic before she shook her head. 'Shit.' This was way bigger than she'd had in mind. How were they supposed to keep this rabble together? And then she looked back at the smoke. She chewed her lip. If that didn't announce their presence, she didn't know what would. But they needed the supplies. So instead of taking the route they had used a year ago to take them into the mountain, they detoured to hit this place. It was a risk. A big one. Devlin assured her that in a way, this would put the dwarves on the back foot, that their reaction to the breakout would be more chaotic as they tried to make sense of what was happening. She hoped so. They still needed to put some serious distance between themselves and whoever was coming after them.

She turned as Krste emerged from the building, his crossbow in one hand and a knife in the other. He was wiping it against the side of his trousers, leaving a red smear.

'You find anything?' she asked.

'They got food. They got drink,' he replied.

It's a tavern? Praise all the bloody gods. 'What are you waiting for? Get loading it on the wagon.'

'Yes, boss.'

She would have given him a hand but, well, she couldn't. Doctor's orders. When they camped for the night, she'd make sure the food was handed over to the quartermaster crew, now headed up by Sent. He'd worked out a neat little spot for himself, turned out to be quite the businessman. As for the booze, she'd keep hold of that. It was good currency. She walked back to the wagon and climbed aboard.

'Looks like a mess down there,' said Evan, who had been promoted to her driver.

'Looks like,' she agreed.

'Hey, boss!' called Krste, his head appearing from round the waystation door.

'What?'

'They got barrels in here!'

Cade pushed Evan.

'Ow!'

'You heard the man. They got barrels. Go help him.'

'Fine. Alright.'

She watched him jump off the wagon and jog into the building. Barrels. That meant ale. She looked down at the burning settlement again. The fighters would be thirsty. Bet they'd appreciate a refreshing drink when they got back.

She nodded, pleased with herself. Just keep the right folk sweet and the rest would follow. She looked back at the line of Tissans. What would you call them? Refugees? Escapees? An army? *Damn. But there were a lot of them.*

CHAPTER TWENTY-THREE – KILLEN

Killen had been dreaming of a feather bed. The sheets had been soft, the pillows yielding; his head had sunk into them and he had felt like he was supported on air. There had been a soft breeze on his face and he was pretty sure the frame had four posts, with a screen of suspended thin linen, rippling gently. And the smell. Fragrances long forgotten, odours of a life, of lovers.

Of a time before his bloody camel.

'Major?'

He opened his eyes.

It was dark, and the night sky was obscured by a screen of pine branches. A light wind rolled along the ground and with it a range of earthy odours. His pillow was his cloak, rolled up into a ball. He had picked a spot a little away from everyone else, wanting to enjoy a little privacy. Damn but if it hadn't been the best night's sleep he'd had for years.

'Major?'

'Hmm?'

'It is time.'

'Hmm.'

'Major?'

'Yes, Hassan. I am coming.'

The shadow that loomed over him bobbed its head and hurried off. Did that lad ever lose his enthusiasm? Honestly, he was exhausted just looking at him.

Killen pushed himself off the ground and adjusted his clothing, brushing off the collected burrs, twigs and soil. He picked up his cloak and shook it out before shrugging it on. Finally, he gathered up his sword and put the belt and scabbard over his shoulder to carry it in the manner of his soldiers when they moved while dismounted.

He took a moment to orientate himself before he stepped off towards the edge of the treeline. More cloaked figures were ahead of him, humped shapes resting on the ground or leaning against the trees.

'Major,' Rashad whispered from the right.

He turned towards the voice and saw an arm beckoning him over. Moving next to the speaker, he rested one knee in the soil.

'Captain. All is well?'

'I believe so. Our people took up position two hours ago. There was a change of watch ten minutes later. They sent out a small sweeper party that did little more than walk the edge of the ridge and back.'

'How many on the wall?'

'Five that we could count from here. The same as last night.'

'Very good.'

Killen had insisted on Rashad's reconnoitre even though it had delayed their assault and had taken much of the previous night, it had returned a clearer picture of the increased security arrangements within the settlement.

'Our infiltrators?'

'They are in place.'

'And your assessment on tonight's adventure?'

Rashad grinned. 'We are all looking forward to it.'

Killen shook his head. 'We are trying to avoid bloodshed, Captain.'

'Of course, Major. But you must forgive the soldiers. It has been some time since they have seen action.'

Killen had spent most of his army career behind a desk, and had never seen action, but this wasn't the moment to own to it. It was just like his scouts to be so excited. Killen supposed he couldn't blame them. And, in truth, he envied them their love of their work, their love of life. They accepted what they had and rejoiced in it. He might rejoice a little more if he had a vineyard in his life.

He lay his sword on the ground. They had but a short time to wait.

Almost seventy men and women were gathered in the woods around him, and yet he would never know it. He marvelled how quiet the night was. A gentle wind rustling the trees and an occasional cry of some night creature only added to the effect.

'There,' said Rashad. He pointed to the moon called Mercid. At this time of year it rose in the north; a bright white orb, it had only just started to wane. A dark shape passed across it. Slow, steady and then it was gone. That was the signal.

'Five minutes,' he said.

Killen felt a thrill of anticipation build. No, not a thrill, a knot of tension, in the pit of his stomach.

Owen let Arno guide himself towards the stone cairn at the end of the long spit of land projecting out from the settlement. The eagle landed lightly on the path and drew its wings in tight to its body. Owen climbed off and collected his gear. A spear and crossbow, both borrowed, the spear a little longer than he was used to, the point heavier. And the bow was larger. It would have been a pig to use in an aerial battle.

He looked into Arno's eyes.

'Go fly, Arno. I'll call you if I need you.'

Arno cocked his head and blinked. Owen stepped back and the eagle spread its wings once more, made one powerful sweep and launched off the edge, swooping out into sky below the spit.

Owen used the crude leather strap he'd attached to the spear to shrug it over his back, then taking the crossbow in both hands, he started to walk along the path. It meandered along the spit, besieged on both sides by hardy mountain grass and flowers. It was a testament to how little it had been used of late.

Aside from himself, few of the other Highlanders visited the stone cairn at the end. He had never asked them, but perhaps they felt it was not their place of remembrance. That only those born here should have the right to have a marker. He understood, but had always intended to assure them that they were all part of the Rest. Now it was too late. But when all of this was done, he would put a stone down for each of those killed. Unbidden, a voice entered his mind, his old comrade, Bryce. *'That's gonna be a big shitting pile o' rocks, Owen. It'll probably collapse and roll right off the edge.'* Owen smiled in spite of himself. Yeah, Bryce was probably right. How he missed his old comrade-in-arms.

The path was leading him into the settlement. He had walked the whole way unchallenged, just as he had expected. Gerat was no fool, but why would he expect anyone to come from this direction? A smart man might have given pause – this was the home of Eagle Riders, after all. The back of the hall was ahead, and he took the route around to the left of it, passing the smithy and on to the central square. The place glowed with light. Two flaming braziers stood sentinel at the top of the steps leading to the hall entrance. Another was sited right in the centre of the square. That was as good a place as any, so he made for the central fire. He walked easily, taking his time. He had already spotted the two sentries at the top of the steps and they had, at first, ignored him. He heard one shout out, but he chose to ignore the challenge. His gaze travelled down towards the gate. Unlike the square, there was no light. Why had Gerat not thought to put the braziers down there? Placed outside the gates they could have lit up the whole ridge path. Perhaps he had decided that the watchers' night vision would suffice. He turned his back to the central brazier, facing the steps. One of the watchers had disappeared inside. The other looked agitated, rocking from one foot to another, his spear describing a wide circle as he held it in a guard position. What were they expecting? That Owen was going to charge up the steps? He was more concerned about those behind him on the gate. It would be easy for one of them to take a shot. But that wasn't his problem to worry about.

He continued to wait. More people were appearing at the top of the steps, men and women awakened and keen to find out what was going on. Owen got a sense they were all on edge. Many were armed. Yet none came forward, content to point and whisper to themselves. Were they afraid of him? Finally Gerat emerged from the hall. In the light it was obvious. He was flanked by the guard and two others. One of them was Bedwyr.

Gerat came to the front and walked down the steps. Owen kept his crossbow lowered, but his grip was tight. He gently released his breath, easing his own tension. There was no need to make any silly mistakes now.

'Surprised to see you back, Owen.'

Gerat had his arms crossed, a sword was tucked into his belt, and he wore nothing but britches and a loose shirt.

'Sorry to have to wake you, Gerat. But I guess you were expecting me, what with all of this light.'

'Not necessarily expecting you, maybe your friends.' Gerat looked beyond Owen to the gate squinting a little. 'You come alone?'

'Only room for me on my eagle.'

'Yet I don't see it,' said Gerat, looking up and around.

'I came round the back way.'

'Ah. I should have thought of that. What do you want?'

'To give you a chance.'

'Didn't know we needed one,' replied Gerat. 'If I recall it was me giving you a chance. And you ended up killing one of my people. Now that's just ungrateful.'

Owen cocked his head. The gall of the man was truly unbelievable.

'We do what we have to do. You taught me that, Gerat.'

'Oh no, it wasn't me, it was the world, Owen.' Gerat looked back at his people, then smiled. 'What's this chance you're offering?'

Owen locked eyes with Gerat. *Here we go.* 'You sacrifice yourself and I let your people live.'

The smile disappeared from Gerat's face.

'That's fucking stupid of you, Owen. I seem to recall I have plenty of your people.'

Owen shrugged. 'The offer still stands. You come down here and face me in a straight fight. If win, I will spare your people,' Owen paused for a moment. 'Most of them.'

Gerat barked a short, ugly, laugh. Owen turned his gaze to those gathered near him, reading faces. Some looked fearful, some angry. 'Cover him,' commanded Gerat, walking down the steps. 'You want me to fight you?'

'You made it personal,' replied Owen.

'I do–' Gerat stopped and squinted, looking past Owen's shoulder.

Owen could hear muted sounds coming from the gate. A soft cry. That was the cue. He raised his crossbow and fired.

'Look!' whispered Rashad.

Killen saw the same shape as before flit across the face of the moon.

That was the signal.

There was subtle shift in the tension. He placed his hand on the pommel of his blade. They needed to move fast. In that respect, the light armour of the scouts worked in their favour. They had shed their usual layers of cloth and were wearing little more than trousers and tunics. He had grown used to not wearing his armour, especially in the Jebel, but now he wished he'd at least kept his breastplate. The kufeya was the only protection granted for his head. It felt thin and worthless right now.

'I see them!' said Hassan, excitedly.

Killen couldn't see a damn thing. There! Movement against the wall, shapes rushing towards it. What looked like a figure being hauled from the ramparts and falling to the ground.

'Major?' asked Rashad.

Killen looked at him. *Right then.* He stood and drew his sword.

'Everyone. To that bloody gate!' he bellowed and took off at full tilt.

He heard his force emerge from the treeline either side of him, and then they were all on the trail leading up the slope to the ridgeline. It only took moments for his breathing to grow harder, more laboured, as the burst of excited energy left his muscles. Others, mainly his scouts, started to outpace him, shouldering past as they reached the summit. As his right arm started to ache he noticed that his scouts all had their blades or bows strapped to their backs. Of course they did, why hadn't he thought of that? He felt the sweat start to bead up in his hairline, the heat start to pulse from his head. On the ridgeline itself the pain in his legs eased off with the gradient. Larsen was just ahead, his bow and arrow clutched in his hands. To Killen's side, Hassan was keeping pace, the lad's face shining. He grinned at Killen who could do little more than nod back. Many of his scouts and some of the Highlanders had made the gate, but it was still shut. Had something gone wrong? Had the surprise failed? What of Owen? Even as these thoughts sped through his mind the right-side gate swung open and his troops streamed inside.

'Yes!' he shouted, forgetting his position for a moment; luckily everyone was too engaged to notice.

A few seconds later and he had reached the entrance as well. He paused at the gateway to breathe and take stock, and found a body lying on the ground, one of the sentries. He stepped through and over it and into Eagle's Rest. Ahead of him a gaggle of scouts and Highlanders had formed a skirmish line. To one side, Saul and another of the Highlanders stood guard. On the parapet, Sadad waved down. He and the others were crouched faced inward, their bows ready. He spied another couple of bodies on the ground by the gate.

'Major,' said Rashad, giving him a salute as he approached.

Killen nodded.

'The gateway is secured. We have encountered a little resistance, but we are in good order.'

'Very good, Captain. Let's take the courtyard.'

Rashad bobbed his head and ran towards the skirmish line, barking orders. The gaggle of troops and Highlanders pressed forward.

'Major?'

He turned towards Saul. The man's face was blacked with char, lined with streaks of the sweat that had run down his face.

'Saul, did you lose anyone?' Killen asked.

Saul shook his head.

'We got lucky. They were too busy watching the show inside. Your men were up and over that wall faster than I could blink. Those sentries never stood a chance.' Saul bit the inside of his cheek, thoughtfully. 'I think we need to build it higher.'

Killen felt no small measure of pride in his people, even if he himself had done nothing more than run up a hill. But it wasn't over yet.

'I'm going in,' said Killen. 'Care to join me?'

Saul nodded and led the way. Killen followed. Hassan was still with him, his blade drawn. Killen returned his to its scabbard for the time being.

The way ahead was well lit by braziers. Between them and the light of Mercid, the course of the skirmish was clear. Several more bodies lay on the ground. None appeared to be Erebeshi. Ahead, his people were taking up position just in front of the hall. More were flanking around to encircle it. This was all as expected. Now it was just a case of whether they could be treated with or forced out. Fire was an option they might have to use, though it would be a terrible end. In the centre of the courtyard three more bodies. Here he stopped, remembering the plan; the lad's courageous and terrible gamble. Was Owen one of the fallen?

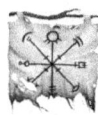

It was an instinctive shot, made from years of practice. Even so, he had had no time to take aim. The bolt took Gerat just below his right shoulder blade and he fell backwards on to the stairs. Folk started screaming and shouting. A few people made for the gate. Others ran back into the hall. Several came down the steps straight for him, pausing at Gerat who was blocking the stairs, squirming, his left hand clutching the wound. Owen took advantage of that pause, dropping his crossbow and retrieving the spear from his back.

Why had they not shot him yet? Maybe they never did anything without Gerat's say so.

'Fucking kill him!' Gerat screeched.

OK, that decision was made. Bedwyr and the other guard scrambled down the steps to meet him while others helped Gerat up. Owen set his spear against his side and went to meet them. As Bedwyr drew near Owen took a few running steps to close the gap and thrust high at Bedwyr's exposed neck. Blood flowed from the spearpoint as it pierced the skin. It was not a deep thrust, but enough to stop Bedwyr in his tracks. Owen pulled his spear back and described a wide arc left to right, causing the guard to jump away uttering a surprised howl of pain as the blade caught his arm. Owen started to retreat towards the brazier. He'd had to be quick with that first attack. Trying to keep two opponents at bay was hard.

He walked backwards, carefully listening for any flankers. There were all kinds of commotion going on down at the gate but he could not spare a glance. Bedwyr was following up on him quickly, ignoring the wound on his neck, an axe in one hand, a knife in the other. He was wary, far too clever to be reckless. Owen kept his spear low, feinting, jabbing and Bedwyr kept stepping out of reach. There was no panic or fear in his eyes, and he wore a grim smile. Bedwyr was a killer.

'You shouldn't have come back, Owen,' he said.

Owen didn't respond. The other one, with the sliced arm, was starting to recover, and was also closing in on him.

'Your friends? They all died screaming, pleading for their lives.' Bedwyr spat to one side. 'No fucking dignity.'

Did this fool really think baiting him would work?

The wounded guard rushed him, the glint of a sword raised high.

Owen jabbed fast at Bedwyr then swung round to meet the charge, whipping his spear low, like a branch, slamming it into the man's legs.

The man thumped to the floor, breath rushing from him in a gasp.

Owen struggled to turn as he wrestled his spear to a horizontal blocking position to catch the solid 'thunk' of Bedwyr's axe.

Gasping, he swung the spear down, striking Bedwyr's arm, seeing the gleam of a knife blade. In one fluid motion, he threw his weight into a clockwise spin that dragged the spear free of the grip of the axe, and slammed into Bedwyr's side.

The axe flew free as the knife blade came at him, Bedwyr slashing high as Owen ducked, ramming the spear butt to catch his assailant in the chin.

Bedwyr staggered. Owen had the spearhead round and thrust it into Bedwyr's stomach, twisting as he stabbed.

He pulled the spear out and the Scotian was on his knees, a look of confusion on his face.

Then, something else flashed across his gaze, a shift of attention in the quickly dimming eyes.

Owen spun round. Too late. The fist slammed into him. His nose exploded in pain as he rocked backwards. Stars danced in front of him. He tried to raise his spear. It was batted aside as a hand grabbed his jacket. He saw the second punch coming and tried to brace, but couldn't. As his legs began to wobble, he was aware that the pain had been less sharp. He supposed he was losing consciousness. Hands pushed him down on to his back. He felt his fingers still closed around the spear now pinned against his stomach.

A great weight fell on him.

'Think you are so fucking clever, don't you?' hissed Gerat. He shook Owen hard, lifting him off the ground then slamming him down. 'You should have fucking shot me properly!' Gerat shook him again and Owen's head swam. He couldn't think straight, he couldn't get his body to work.

'You want to see us all burn?' said Gerat. 'Then I'll burn this fucking place down.'

'Myra,' mumbled Owen.

'What?'

'Myra. You think she'd be proud of what you have done?'

Gerat stopped for a second and blinked. It was the reprieve Owen needed. He released his grip on the spear.

'Don't you speak of her. Don't you fucking dare!' shouted Gerat, spittle flying into Owen's eyes. Gerat lifted him up again, ready to drive him back into the ground and smash his skull.

Owen reached up and gripped Gerat's head, pressing his thumb into an eye. With his free hand he sought the crossbow bolt. His questing fingers found the shaft and twisted it.

Gerat howled and tried to push Owen off, but Owen held tight to the bolt. He felt the soft tissue of the eye give way. Gerat shook and thrashed and finally won free, scrambling away.

Breathing heavily Owen looked for a weapon. Bedwyr's axe lay just a few inches away. He picked it up and crawled after Gerat. The man was on his front, shaking his head, growling like a wounded bear.

Owen raised the axe high and brought it down on to Gerat's back. Once, twice, as Gerat bucked and writhed. A third chop and Gerat collapsed into himself, his spine giving way.

The growling become mewling.

'You are a disgrace. You don't deserve to live,' Owen hissed.

He raised the axe one more time and buried it into Gerat's head. The mewling stopped. Owen sat up. He struggled to take in air, his breath was ragged. The flickering light of the brazier cast shadows all around. The others he had fought were not moving. Were they dead? He could see others in the square. There was shouting. But it all felt detached, like he was in a dream. What was happening in the hall? He couldn't see. He didn't care. He felt too damned tired and there was nothing else he could do. Owen closed his eyes and fell backwards.

He heard some people draw close.

'He looks like shit. Is he alive? Is he still breathing?'

Another voice, oddly accented. A hand touching his forehead.

'Yes. He lives.'

'Owen?'

'Uh?'

'Listen, lad. This is going to hurt like a bastard.'

'Wha–?'

Owen felt his shoulders being restrained, gently but firmly. Then two hands rested themselves against his cheeks. He felt pressure and then screaming pain. He howled and he swore, as the pressure centred itself where his nose should be. He felt something shift and click. And then the pressure stopped.

'Alright, that should do it.'

The hands released his shoulders.

Owen opened his eyes and tried to blink away the seemingly endless flow of tears.

'Alright, lad? Owen?'

'Saul?'

The man's leathery face swam into view.

'Thought I'd just to go ahead and set the bugger now. You'll look real pretty for the next few weeks.'

'What?'

'Your nose. Not sure you'll ever have your good looks again, mind you.'

'My nose?'

'You still got your wits, Owen?' asked Anneli, placing a hand on his shoulder. She was hunkered down next to him.

'Um. Yes.' It was coming back to him now. He wiped his streaming eyes. 'We in?'

'We're in,' acknowledged Saul. 'Plan worked like a dream.'

'What happened?'

'Better we show you,' said Saul. 'Come on, let's help him up.' Anneli and Saul took a side each and gently got him on to his feet. A searing pain from the back of his head made him stagger.

'That's gonna hurt for a while,' said Saul. 'Almost cracked your skull open by the looks of it. Best you take it easy when we're done.'

Owen closed his eyes and waited for the pain and dizziness to pass. He felt unsteady on his feet, like the ground was swaying. He opened them again and took in his surroundings. He was in the roosting barn, his back to the wall.

'We thought we'd get you out of bowshot, just in case,' explained Anneli.

'Here,' said Saul, taking an elbow and escorting him to the exit. The door was open and he stepped through into bright sunlight. He hadn't noticed that in the barn. How long had he been out for?

Looking on to the courtyard, he saw a ring of soldiers behind a range of improvised barriers and screens. Others were occupying the surrounding buildings. There were bodies on the ground. The braziers still glowed. The doors to the hall were shut.

'Did we lose anyone?' he asked.

Saul shook his head.

'A few knocks, some cuts, and one arrow in the leg.'

Owen sighed in relief. That was good. That was very good.

'The bastards lost a dozen or so. And now we have them surrounded.'

'What're they doing?'

'Not much. They're taking the occasional pot shot.'

'And what are we doing?'

Saul placed a hand on his shoulder. 'Waiting for you.'

The three of them left the safety of the barn and moved at a pace towards the gate. Every step jarred Owen's head, and he winced with the pain. They slowed as they reached the square. Waiting for him was Major Killen, Captain Rashad and Larsen.

'Good to see you,' said Larsen, with a warm smile and outstretched hand.

'You too,' said Owen, taking the hand and gripping it tight.

'Well done, Owen. Got to say, that was a ballsy move,' said Killen.

'You are quite the fighter,' agreed Rashad. 'But you should try harder not to get killed.'

Owen shrugged. 'Believe me. I was trying.'

'Yes, that we can see,' said Killen, appraising Owen's nose.

'What is the situation?' Owen asked.

Killen pointed towards the hall.

'Your diversion worked perfectly. Once we gained entry, it was a simple matter to push on and take most of the settlement. Their resistance was light, uncoordinated. They withdrew into the hall and sealed it tight. A few shots were exchanged but for the most part they've stayed quiet. We now have them completely surrounded.'

'Gerat?'

'He's dead. Still on the ground where you left him,' said Larsen.

'Then they've got no one in charge,' said Owen. 'Chances are there might be one or two of his cronies left. And they'll be keeping the others in line.'

'What's the plan?' asked Saul.

'We going to smoke them out?' offered Larsen.

Owen shook his head. 'Not with our people inside. And let's not forget, they haven't used them to bargain with yet.' He turned and put his hands on his hips. 'It's time to negotiate.'

'Is that smart?' asked Larsen. 'Why do they get a second chance?'

'We can't be like Gerat. We have to be better than that. Like I said before, I believe that these folk just fell in with the wrong crowd, the wrong leader. They were just trying to survive.'

Larsen and Saul both looked sour but didn't argue the point.

'Major?' asked Owen.

Killen looked at Rashad then back at Owen. 'As you ask my advice, I would say they are beaten and they know it. If you throw them a bone, they'll take it.'

That's what Owen figured too. 'I'm going to talk to them.'

'Seriously?' asked Larsen, throwing his hands up in the air.

'You really have a death wish, Owen,' said Saul, with a sad shake of his head.

'At least let us give you some cover,' offered Killen.

'Fine,' replied Owen, 'but I need to do this.'

He turned and slowly made his way across the square. The others fell in behind him except for Captain Rashad who hurried forward barking orders in Erebeshi. Owen saw them draw bows and take a bead on the hall's entrance. He hoped it wouldn't be needed. His party stopped at the edge of the steps. He looked up at his home and started to speak. 'You know who I am and I am here to broker peace. I know you are scared. You think that it's over. In a way, it is.' He paused for a moment. A wave of pain and nausea washed over him. When he was sure he wasn't going to pass out, he continued.

'I know most of you haven't had any choices for a long time. That joining Gerat and following his lead was the only option left to you. And then you came here. You walked for a thousand miles and found a safe haven and people ready to welcome you. And instead Gerat decided to destroy that. Because of what you did, what you allowed to happen, good people died.' He paused. For a moment, even he doubted whether he should offer this. But then he remembered who he was, what he had sworn to do. He was still an Eagle Rider, sworn to protect the Empire, humanity itself. His father's face appeared in his mind, then Murtagh. Good people. What would they have him do?

'We are at war. But our war is not with each other. Our enemies lie to the east. Will I forget what you did? Never. But we are all that's left, and the fight must go on. We have to fight to reclaim our place in this world. To gain vengeance for everyone we have lost and loved. I give you one last chance. Rejoin humanity. Rejoin the Empire and fight!' Owen stood, listening to his words echo. He waited for a few moments more. 'You have five minutes to pledge your allegiance or we will take this place back by force. I hope you make the right decision.' Then he turned and made his way back to the others. He could see Larsen, his arms folded, looking grim. Saul, still shaking his head. Owen could sense the tension of the Highlanders and Erebeshi troops, the expectation of what might come next. And then a noise sounded behind him. And Killen's eyes grew wide.

Owen turned.

The doors to the hall opened and a man stepped out. Owen squinted. He didn't recognise him.

'Do you mean it? Do we have your word you won't just kill us?' asked the man.

Owen walked back up towards him. He could see the fellow was older, grey-bearded.

'Yes,' he said, simply. 'You do.'

The man looked back inside for a moment and then nodded. He took a step forward.

'Gerat lied to us,' said the man. 'He said you couldn't be trusted, that there was no other way.'

Owen stopped, momentarily confused.

Then, moving out from behind the greybeard and into the sunlight, came Naimh. She stood, blinking. As her eyes alighted on Owen, her face broke into a smile. Then more emerged. Women and children mostly. A few men, Malcolm the smith among them. Faces he had not seen in months. And there was Jenni. Oh Gods. She looked terrible.

Naimh walked down the stairs and he moved to meet her in an embrace.

He stepped back and stared open-mouthed. She was tired, worn out and dirty. But she was beaming and crying. He had to wipe his eyes as his own tears flowed once more.

Owen stood next to Jenni and around them were gathered the survivors of Eagle's Rest. Those that had been imprisoned and those that had fought to regain it. They formed a crescent around the burial cairn. The light was dimming, and the sun flared as it went behind the mountains to the west, their icebound tops glowing. He held Jenni's hand, and in the other a stone. This one was for Murtagh. Those around him carried others in remembrance of their husbands, fathers, brothers and sons. Naimh had told Owen how Murtagh had died first. Stabbed in the back. She had spoken, in faltering, sorrowful words of how Gerat had ordered most of the men, all but the youngest boys and male babes, slaughtered. And how he had imprisoned the rest of them until such time as they understood how things would be. How despair must turn into obedience and with it a chance of life. Naimh had seen the faces of Gerat's folk, had seen how they had given up, had accepted their fates.

'But we are Highlanders. Men or women, there is no difference between us. We would never have given up,' she'd said fiercely. 'Just like you didn't, Owen.'

And now they gathered. All the Highlanders left in the world, for all they knew. Fewer now, but more than he could have hoped for. Owen squeezed Jenni's hand then stepped forward to place the stone on the cairn. Another friend lost. A good man. His death would not be in vain. *I swear it*. He turned and made way for Naimh who touched her fingers to her lips and then placed them on Murtagh's stone. Together they made way for the others.

Once the act was done, he led his people back. On either side was an honour guard of Erebeshi, their faces solemn yet proud. These men and women from a faraway land, he had known them for only a short time but he knew all he needed to. They represented what was best of the old Empire. In the courtyard, Killen and Captain Rashad waited for him. The remaining members of Gerat's people were gathered nearby, under the watchful eyes of the rest of the Erebeshi troops.

Killen nodded a greeting.

'Owen. It's time. Your judgement?'

Owen looked at the sullen, ragged group. They looked utterly beaten. He spotted the greybeard.

'Are there any here you do not trust? Who were loyal to Gerat.'

The greybeard glanced left and right. 'There were some left in the hall with us. We did for them.'

Perhaps not so defeated as he thought. 'I told you, we cannot forget the past. I cannot and will not. And I cannot ask any of my folk to do so, but I will forgive you. You can go, or you can stay. If you stay, then every day you must try to make amends for what you let happen, what you let others do.'

There was silence. Gerat's folk looked at each other. Greybeard coughed and took a tentative step forward.

'We will stay.'

Owen felt his nose throb. 'Good.'

He turned and found Naimh studying him.

'Murtagh would not have done that,' she said.

'Oh but he did. For me,' said Owen.

Her eyes misted and she smiled wanly.

'What now, Owen?' asked Larsen, placing his arm around Naimh.

That question. *What now?* He looked into the sky, scanning the heavens in the fading orange and purple light. And there he was. His beautiful Arno, riding the last of the thermals. He looked back at his friends, at the Major and his soldiers.

'I'm done skirmishing with gnomes. It's time we took the war to someone who'll truly remember it.'

CHAPTER TWENTY-FOUR – FILLION

Fillion entered The Silver Chalice and found his usual booth was already occupied. Kanyay grinned at him, his sharpened teeth flashing in the candlelight.

'How do you do that?' Fillion asked as he gripped Kanyay's forearm in the traditional wood elf greeting.

'Do what?'

'Your teeth, they are so white,' Fillion said as he settled down opposite Kanyay.

'Ah, these?' said Kanyay, rubbing a forefinger down his field canines. 'It's a special bark I like to chew. It has a rough edge and some kind of oil in it. Very good.'

'You ever get toothache?'

'Never!'

Fillion was impressed.

'I should try that.'

'Come live with us awhile. I'll show you all manner of useful things.'

'I might just do that,' said Fillion. He picked up a full mug of ale that must have been waiting for him. 'This for me?'

'Yes. It's from home. Brought a few kegs back. Better than the grapeshit we normally have to drink!'

'I missed your craziness.' Fillion put the mug to his lips. The brew was thick and earthy. But it was good. He drank deep.

'And it is good to see a Heartlander with a proper appreciation of ale.'

'Did someone say ale?' asked Marmus, pushing into Fillion's side of the table.

'Ah, our dwarf friend. And now our merry band is complete,' said Kanyay, pushing a third mug his way.

Marmus picked it up and drained it.

Kanyay and Fillion shared a look. Kanyay raised a hand, gaining the attention of the barkeep. 'Three more.'

Fillion leaned back against the wall and looked at the dwarf. He could feel the tension radiating off him.

'Friend, Marmus. Are you well?' he asked.

'No. I'm bloody not,' replied the dwarf.

'Has the capital lost its magic for you?' asked Kanyay, his tongue firmly in cheek.

'The capital can go fuck itself.' Marmus turned to look at Fillion. 'The mines. It happened.'

Fillion blew loudly through his nostrils. A thrill coursed through his body.

'Oh no,' he whispered, keeping his elation buried.

'What? What has happened?' asked Kanyay, his gaze flicking between the two of them.

'He might as well know. I'm speaking to Parliament first thing tomorrow morning,' said Marmus.

'Sabin?' asked Kanyay.

Fillion sighed loudly, letting his shoulders slump as if in defeat. 'You know that I was sent to inspect the new workings.'

'Yes, you were overjoyed at that,' said Kanyay. Marmus scowled.

'What I was sworn to keep secret was the true motivation for my visit. The dwarves of that mine had a workforce made up of human slaves.'

'Oh, really?' Kanyay's wild eyebrows raised high, his gaze resting firmly on Marmus.

'Yes, we bloody had humans,' the dwarf growled.

'And they have rebelled?' asked Fillion.

'Yes, they bloody have.'

'Shit,' whistled Kanyay. 'And you didn't see that coming?'

'Obviously not,' hissed Marmus.

Three fresh mugs arrived at their table. They were shared out, and Fillion was surprised to find his first mug empty. He'd better slow down.

'Go on,' he urged.

'What more can I say? I know only the barest facts because no dwarf is alive to speak of what happened.'

'None?' asked Kanyay. 'Is that possible?'

'None from the mines. But there were others from the settlements they ransacked,' said Marmus.

'Ransacked?' Fillion feigned astonishment, acutely aware that any mass breakout would generate a tide of destruction.

'The first we knew of a problem was when our canals were hit. A swarm of humans overran our trade lanes and continued on to Bar-Ras. They killed anyone who did not flee, took anything that was not fixed to the floor, and burned the rest. It was only when those who escaped dispatched a party to the mine complex that they discovered the truth. Every dwarf slaughtered.'

'My life,' said Kanyay. 'Since when were you allowed to keep humans?'

'Since we bloody wanted to!' declared Marmus angrily. The other patrons grew silent, the gazes resting on the booth. There would be no keeping that outburst quiet. Fillion raised a placating hand.

'Peace, friend Marmus. Kanyay only asked what we all thought to be true. It does not lessen the terrible news or reduce the outrage.'

Marmus, his face angry, reached for his mug.

'Sabin speaks my words, Marmus. I feel sorrow for what has happened,' said Kanyay.

The dwarf sighed, and his shoulders sagged a little.

Fillion lowered his hand, the tension lessened.

'We lost hundreds of my kin,' said Marmus. 'Hundreds, to those bastards.'

'Where are they headed?' asked Fillion.

'West. The destruction they leave in their wake is easy to follow.'

'And you are hunting them, yes?' Kanyay asked.

'Aye, we dispatched a force. But that's as much as I know. I have tasked my staff to set up relay posts so I can get word on the situation as quickly as possible. By the time I received the first message, it was already two weeks old. The dwarf council did not think the elves or their ambassador were a priority.' Marmus looked pointedly at Fillion. It was obvious the dwarves had wanted to keep this quiet, but Fillion's words must have given Marmus reason to tell his masters that the elves already knew.

'How many humans are we talking about?' asked Kanyay.

'At least twenty thousand,' said Marmus.

'Twenty *thousand* ? By the Blessed Mother how did you hide that many?' asked Kanyay, shaking his head as he buried it into his mug.

'You can hide plenty within a mountain,' said Marmus gruffly.

Fillion decided to ask an obvious question. 'Do any of the Members know yet?'

'Aye, some do. Like they could keep their noses out of it,' acknowledged Marmus. That meant Patiir would be fully appraised.

'I'll be in the Chamber tomorrow,' promised Fillion.

Marmus nodded. He put his hands around his mug, looking into its depths. 'I've been told that I have a 'diplomatic' nature, more so than most dwarves possess. I fear it will be sorely tested tomorrow.' He let go of the mug and stood. 'As much as I would like to drain this place dry tonight, I think I best not. I will bid you both a safe evening.'

'See you tomorrow,' repeated Fillion.

Marmus scrutinised him for a moment, then took his leave of them.

'Diplomatic? I would hate to see what the undiplomatic ones are like,' said Kanyay.

Fillion smiled.

'They would probably remind you of you.'

Kanyay grinned wickedly.

'I think I'll enjoy tomorrow. It'll be fun watching Marmus squirm. Not that I'd say that to his face.'

'Best not,' agreed Fillion.

He glanced away to the door. This news was momentous, and he had no doubt that he'd been the instigator of the human breakout. A massive community of souls, heading back to Tissan. That they had created so much mayhem on the way only added to the sense of satisfaction he was feeling. But the question was, what would happen to them now?

Fillion rubbed his eyes. His head ached and he felt dog-tired. Too much ale, too little sleep, thanks to his little princess, and a head full of thoughts. He was seated on one of the many balconies that studded the circumference of the Parliament chamber – the place was so full of Members that all the Servants bar those with direct responsibilities within the chamber had been banished to the wings. Which meant Kanyay, in his recognised role of a Servant rather than ambassador, was seated next to him. Marmus was finishing up. Even though he was standing on the raised podium, Fillion knew that for those at the lowest level of seating, they could barely see his head. At least the dwarf's voice had no problem with carry. It echoed throughout the chamber, rising in volume when needed to counter the gasps of dismay his words generated. To Marmus's credit and Fillion's surprise, the dwarf retained his composure, and kept his words factual, short, and to the point.

'I can reassure the house that the Dwarf Nations will not allow this slight to go unanswered. We do not apologise for our decision to enslave our human captives nor do we shy away from the need to deal with the threat that they have become. That is all.'

Marmus left the podium to whispered conversations and the odd remark of outrage and returned to his regular position, an area set off to one side from the main seating of Members.

Kanyay nudged Fillion. 'He didn't do too badly, did he?' he whispered.

'He did the best he could,' conceded Fillion.

A number of Members indicated their desire to speak, but it was Patiir who had the privilege. At the Speaker's invitation Patiir stood, smoothed his robes, and adjusted his belt of office. He walked slowly, towards the podium, allowing the sense of anticipation to grow. For all knew that when Patiir chose to speak on these matters, his words carried the weight of the King's approval.

On reaching the podium, the elf placed his hands on the railings to either side and looked out upon those gathered.

'My fellow Members. My friends. I had not thought to ever speak to you again on the matter that has been put before us. I had thought that, a year ago, I would never need discuss the scourge of humanity in my lifetime. And yet, here we are. And it is a cold comfort that the reason for this is not of our making.'

He let that hang. Fillion looked down towards Marmus. The dwarf was stock still, staring directly at Patiir. It must be taking all of his self-control. Diplomatic, like he said.

'And what are we to do?' the elf continued. 'How do we respond to a marauding army of twenty thousand humans?' He raised a hand. 'And do not dissemble with the description. They may not be soldiers, but they are an army on the march. They will consume, they will lay waste. And if left unchecked, will thrive and *breed*. It is a fundamental fact of nature. Many, most of you, will have heard me say this before. I do not deny any species the right to exist, unless they have no means of controlling their baser instincts. Humans are one such species. And the dwarves, through their greed, their arrogance and their dissembling, have let them survive!'

A chorus of agreement echoed around the chamber. Fillion checked Marmus again. How soon before he stood up and stalked out?

'I say again. What should we do? I'll tell you what we were going to do. Yes, I have phrased that correctly. For just a few days ago I had an audience with His Majesty. And I told him what I knew of this matter. That I had gathered intelligence. And that we must, in the strongest possible terms, demand the Dwarf Nations end this insanity. That they must kill every single one of their slave population.' Patiir sighed heavily. 'And now it is too late. The beast is out of the cage. The beast that should not have been allowed to live. The King has already given his consent that we should send a diplomatic mission to the Dwarf Nations. Now that Ambassador Marmus has acknowledged the threat, we must take a different tack. The dwarves say they will deal with this. That they will hunt down these humans. They have after all a vested interest in exacting some measure of vengeance for those they have lost. But,' and he raised a pointed finger. 'I will not stand by and do nothing.' More cries of agreement filled the chamber. 'And *we* will not rest until we are satisfied the threat is removed!' Patiir, shouted over the din. Marmus was shaking his head. It was a slight, an insult directed squarely at the Dwarf Nations. The elves did not trust them to sort out their own mess. Fillion could see their point of view, the dwarves had bent, if not broken, their pacts. That they were the ones paying for it didn't matter. They had proven themselves less than honourable. And for the dwarves, he understood them well enough to know that their natural stubbornness would never accept the elves interfering in their affairs. Patiir's implicit threat to get involved would go down badly with Marmus. He would, to say the least, be royally pissed.

Patiir left the podium, and Member Tekla took his place. Not a surprise, Fillion had been sent with a hand-written message to her house late last night. She smiled beneficently at the seated Members as she took her position.

'I wish to thank Member Patiir for his rousing words. And I wish to formally second his motion. For I believe, though he may not have said the words, that there can be no doubt, we must be involved with this endeavour. The dwarves cannot be left to deal with this alone. We must send our own forces to assist in the eradication of the human threat.'

Again, more shouts of support amidst a sea of murmured conversations.

'And there he goes,' said Kanyay.

Marmus stood up and disappeared through a doorway. He left the Parliament to its devices, a procession of speakers echoing their support to the elven position. Fillion had to endure it all, it would be bad form for him to leave midway through such an important debate. Patiir would notice. It was not until a uniformed elf, a general who Fillion had never had cause to meet, took the platform and promised the mobilisation of a cavalry brigade within two days, that the Parliament appeared satisfied enough to call an end to the gathering.

Walking along the main concourse, Fillion could feel the energy that the meeting had generated. It was palpable in the way everyone carried themselves, the excited, urgent conversations. There was clearly nothing like a good slaughter to get these bastards going. He ought to be heading straight back to his own office but instead he continued on past, checking quickly to see if Patiir had returned. His door was shut. The elf was no doubt delayed by a host of colleagues wishing to share their support. He hurried on, heading further along the wide, sweeping corridor to arrive at the suite of offices belonging to Member Tekla. More ostentatious than many others he had seen, she had two extra Servants working for her, and subsequently the size of the room could swallow Fillion's own modest atrium three times. Long sofas trailed one wall and ended with a table adorned with bowls of fruit, and bottles of water and wine. Vines and flowers studded the walls and sunlight filtered in from several openings. Fillion always expected to hear harps playing from some hidden recess. Fortunately, the only occupant was Ezra. He smiled and stood up from his desk when Fillion knocked on the open door.

'Sabin. You are not with Patiir?'

Fillion made a point of looking around.

'You are not with Tekla?' he countered.

'Ah, well. I hazard the pair may well be in cahoots right at this moment,' replied Ezra, indicating that Fillion should take the chair on the opposite side of his desk.

'The question is, and I find myself intrigued by the possible answer: what deal did Patiir strike to get Tekla so squarely on side?' he asked.

Ezra raised an eyebrow. 'He didn't tell you?'

Fillion shrugged and raised his hands. 'It was late and I'm a father now. It means Patiir shows me a modicum of mercy when it comes to my working hours. I am taking care of his family after all.'

'I suppose, Sabin. Patiir must be getting soft in his dotage.'

'Not after today's display!' said Fillion.

Ezra, leaning back in his chair, chuckled. 'You have it right there. I have not seen him so animated for years. It is not his way. The dwarves have certainly got him riled. And,' Ezra wagged a finger, 'shame on you for being so brazen in your questioning. In her very office too.'

'My apologies, Ezra, but I assumed, as we appear to be in accord on this–'

Ezra raised a hand. 'Anyone but you, Sabin, and I would have chased you out,' he said.

Fillion tried to look embarrassed. He had to keep playing the game. He doubted Ezra had any real love for him.

'As we are alone, I'll answer your question. It is hardly something you couldn't work out for yourself given time. Member Tekla senses an opportunity. These events have generated some unfortunate, negative feelings towards our trading partners in the Dwarf Nations. After today, it will no doubt become even more unpleasant. And the dwarves will reconsider their trading conditions.'

'Let's not be coy, Ezra. They'll refuse to trade, knowing them,' replied Fillion. It was all starting to become very obvious.

'They might at that,' agreed Ezra. 'And Member Tekla will refuse to trade with them. Even though the intransigence of dwarves is well known, it is matched by their avarice. She will demand a renegotiation of certain deals, a revisiting of tariffs. Negotiations that will all end in our favour.'

'You sure they won't dig their heels in?' asked Fillion. Sweet Emperor but he hated politics.

'Perhaps at first but they will bend, given time. It costs us nothing. We are the injured party after all.' Ezra stood. 'Now, get you along, Sabin. Best we do not discuss this anymore.'

Fillion stood as well. He had what he wanted.

'Thank you, Ezra. I'll get back to it.'

'Sabin?'

Fillion stopped. 'Yes?'

'If I were you, I would change my drinking habits. At least for a while. The company you keep … well, it's not going to help your political career,' Ezra advised, condescending in his tone.

Like I care, you arrogant piece of shit. Fillion hid his anger, placed a palm against his chest and bowed. 'Thank you, Ezra. I understand.'

The Servant nodded and sat down. Fillion returned to the concourse fuming, trying hard to keep his face neutral. That bastard. Trying to tell him what to do. What *he* would like to do was punch Ezra in the throat. He arrived at his office and took his position at his desk. A Member sat in one of the high-backed chairs opposite.

'Member Kefe. It is good to see you,' said Fillion, forcing a conciliatory tone.

The elf, of an age with Patiir and sharing a home further down the coast, nodded his weathered face.

'Patiir is at it again, ay?' he stated.

'Excuse me, Member?' asked Fillion, trying to sound confused and slightly offended.

Member Kefe shook his head. 'Don't bother. I've heard it all before. Is he along soon?'

'I'm sure he will be here shortly, Member.'

'Then I'll wait here,' said the elf.

'As you wish,' replied Fillion.

Under the appraising gaze of Kefe he busied himself with correspondence. He thought about how he might approach Marmus. Would the dwarf even want to speak to him? He wanted to let him know what Tekla was up to. It wouldn't hurt to stir the pot. Perhaps he could stop by the embassy tonight – but that would be too obvious. Then his thoughts drifted to home – did he really want to be out late tonight? Little Brynne would be waiting for him.

'Sabin?'

Fillion looked up. Patiir was standing in front of him. 'Sorry, I was miles away.'

Patiir pursed his lips then turned towards the waiting elf. 'Member Kefe. I thought I might be seeing you.'

'Naturally,' replied Kefe.

'If you will bear with me but a few more moments.'

'Of course.'

Patiir continued on towards his private office. 'Sabin, a word, please.'

Fillion stood and followed Patiir in. He felt like he was back in the Imperial army, a junior subaltern just about to be chewed out for a mistake by his captain. He'd had a few of those. He closed the door behind him and stood at parade rest as Patiir arranged himself on his chair.

'Sabin. Your friendship with the Ambassador.'

Alright, not what he expected.

'Yes?'

'I will not deny, it has been valuable. But it must … cool, for a time.'

And another elf, telling him what to do.

'I understand, but would not an informal channel of dialogue prove useful?' he asked.

Patiir steepled his hands and nodded with approval. 'It is a good idea, one I had considered but discounted. Considering the position I have just declared, I cannot see how I can allow it. People would talk, and subterfuge is not your strong suit.'

Fillion tapped a finger against his lips as he tried to suppress a smile. 'How about Kanyay?'

'The wood elf?' Patiir paused for a moment. 'There is no reason for you to discard that friendship.' He nodded decisively. 'Yes. A good suggestion, Sabin. Use Kanyay as a conduit. Let him pass on to Marmus that he still has you as a friend. That you will work to mend the injuries of this business. We always need options.'

'Thank you, Patiir. I will be discreet and speak to Kanyay.'

'Good. Now, please send in Member Kefe. He is like a jackal, always looking for scraps of gossip and intrigue.'

Fillion smiled and opened the door. He had his channel to Marmus, and more importantly it was sanctioned. What better way than to hide his *subterfuge* than in plain sight?

CHAPTER TWENTY-FIVE – MICHAEL

'Father Michael?'

He opened his eye and blinked. Someone was bent over him but the sun, rising behind them, hid their identity.

'Father? You still with us?' said a familiar voice.

'What?' he said, pushing himself up on to his elbows. 'Yes.'

'Good. Here.' A hand was thrust out. He took it and was pulled up. And found he was looking into the eyes of the Emperor.

'Your Grace, are you well?'

'I am fine, thank you as always, for your concern. We are all fine, thanks to you.'

Father Michael shook his head. 'It wasn't just me. All of us here, and the Admiral and his crews, the marines too, they–'

The Emperor grinned, placing a hand on his shoulder.

'And they have been or will be thanked. Believe me. But it was you. You who came up with the plan. You who stepped forward to risk his life for mine. I am truly grateful. And I finally know what the Arch Cardinal, may he rest in peace, saw in you.' He raised his other hand which held a beaker. 'Now, here is some tea. It has been sweetened with what passes for honey here, so it is almost palatable. Get it down you. There is some food over there. We'll be heading off again shortly, we still need to put some miles between us and New Tissan.'

Father Michael took the tea and sipped. It was almost too hot but, it was indeed flavourful. He looked around the camp, such as it was. There were eight eagles settled in a loose ring around them and the Riders moved among them, readying for the next flight. There was a small central fire and he saw the Empress huddled close by it with Father Llews in attendance.

The Emperor followed his look. 'My mother has not enjoyed her first flight on an eagle. It has unsettled her somewhat.'

'I know the feeling,' Father Michael muttered.

'Hah! Well, you must be getting used to it. You were fast asleep when we landed an hour ago. You must have been quite confident in your ability to not slide off!'

Father Michael shook his head. He was damned if he could remember that happening. Yes, he was tired, but had he really forgotten?

'The Rider just pushed you awake and you climbed down and lay flat out, right here,' laughed the Emperor. 'I daresay you deserve the rest after your exertions of last night.'

Father Michael took another gulp of tea. He welcomed the sting of the heat.

'What are we going to do now? About New Tissan?' he asked.

The Emperor's smile faded and his eyes lost their warmth, were replaced by something far colder. Father Michael almost stepped back. He had seen that before.

'That bitch and her kin need to be brought to heel. They have grown arrogant and greedy. They destroyed my loyal priesthood and sought to control me.' He hissed through his teeth. 'They will learn what it means to defy their Living God. Father Llews has been most insightful into how we will regain control. The people need to be reminded just why we are here.'

Father Michael was silent. There was vehemence to the Emperor's voice. *So be it.* Yarn had declared her hand. Now she needed to pay for her crimes.

'Emperor?' Cadarn called, as he walked towards them. And like that the eyes changed once more and the smile returned.

'Yes, Leader.'

'Time to be off, Your Grace. We have still some way to go to put some distance between us and–'

Cardan's face grew grim as a shout echoed across the camp. It was one of the Riders, she was running towards them, her arms waving. Behind her, emerging from a copse of trees were three horsemen, galloping hard.

'Your Grace, we must go!' said Cardan urgently. 'My Riders will buy us some time. There may be more coming.'

Around the camp, Father Michael watched their companions readying for a fight. The Emperor raised a hand to his eyes to study the new arrivals.

'No.'

'Your Grace?' said Cadarn.

'I said no. Look. There are just three of them.'

Father Michael looked again as the three horses drew near. The Emperor was right. No others appeared.

'They are Gifted,' said Cadarn.

'Yes.'

'Bryce! Everyone. Get your weapons, form up on me,' shouted Cadarn.

Father Michael looked from the Emperor to Cadarn and to the others hurrying to join them.

'Your Grace?' he asked.

'Just three,' he said softly.

'Three's enough,' said Bryce hurrying past.

'I can think of a way to even the odds,' said the Emperor.

'Tigh? Tigh, what are we doing?' asked his mother, running towards him and taking his arm, an agitated Father Llews just behind her.

'We are taking back New Tissan, mother,' he replied. 'I will not run from the likes of these, again.'

In front of the Emperor, Cadarn was drawing up his Riders. 'All of you, form a line. Keep your crossbows trained on them. They get too close … well, just don't let them get too close.'

'They will not attack with so many weapons trained on them,' said the Emperor.

'They will,' replied Cadarn.

'As long as I get one of them in the balls,' said Bryce.

'I hope you get your chance,' said the Emperor. 'I believe I recognise them now.'

Father Michael agreed. The Gifted, seeing no attempt by the Riders to flee, had slowed their mounts. It was clear the creatures were exhausted. Eilion was in the lead, the others he soon recognised as Grieg and Loras.

'Three of our former comrades,' confirmed the Emperor.

The riders dismounted, still some sixty yards away, gathered their spears and shields, and walked towards them. The three Gifted stayed close to each other, their shields almost locking. They walked slowly, confidently towards the larger group. In response the Riders changed position, forming two ranks. The front rank dropped to their knees. Hearing no command, Father Michael surmised that Cadarn must have pulsed the command to his people. A notion of this moment struck him. But for a title and training, the Gifted and Riders were the same, they had the same powers. Yet here they were, two sides of a coin.

'That's far enough,' called Cadarn.

The Gifted halted about thirty yards away.

'Emperor,' said Eilion from his position in the middle. 'You are humbly requested to return with us to New Tissan. The Cardinal wishes there to be no more bloodshed and will pardon those who engineered this kidnap.'

'You can tell the Cardinal that I am touched by her concern.' The Emperor gently released his mother's hand and stepped to one side of the Rider's ranks. 'And you may also tell her that when I return, the Cardinal and the rest of you … aberrations will submit to my justice.'

Aberration? Father Michael saw the Gifted shift uneasily and look at each other.

'That will not happen, Your Grace. I give you one chance to come peacefully. Tell your Riders to stand down, get on their birds and never return. If you do not submit, we will take you anyway.' Eilion spoke calmly, as if it was the simplest thing in the world.

'Do you think you can take me by force? We outnumber you three to one,' said the Emperor.

'That does not matter,' replied Eilion.

'Try it, Gifted,' said Bryce icily.

'Perhaps you are right,' said the Emperor. He glanced at Father Michael, an odd expression on his face. 'I will offer a different proposal. You will face my champion in single combat to the death. If my champion dies, then I will come with you. If you die?' he smiled. 'If you die, your companions will make their own choices.'

Father Michael blinked. What was the Emperor doing?

Eilion did not respond for a moment.

'Your champion is?' he asked.

'You know,' replied the Emperor.

Eilion nodded. He stepped away from the small shield wall and raised his spear, planting its butt into the ground. Grieg and Loras looked at him and at each other.

'Eilion?' said Loras.

Eilion dropped his shield and removed his helmet, placing it by his shield.

'You don't have to do this,' said Grieg. 'Eilion. Our orders were clear.'

'I know what our orders are. Nothing changes. Except that one does not get to live,' he said lifting his chin towards Father Michael. 'Step away.'

Grieg and Loras backed up and took new positions behind Eilion. He turned to talk to them, though neither took their eyes away from the bows. Father Michael could hardly believe it. Was Eilion actually agreeing to fight him? This was no arena match. The fate of the Empire, of humanity, rested on this.

'Father Michael,' said the Emperor, bringing Father Michael back from his reverie.

'Your Grace.'

'Just in case you were unsure, you are now my champion. A new title to go with the many you've had before.'

'Your Grace,' Father Michael bowed his head. 'The title means nothing if I fail you.'

'If you die, I daresay it's over for us anyway.' He leaned in and clapped him on the arm, whispering in his ear. 'Don't lose.' The Emperor stepped back. 'Now, what weapons do you wish to use? Take what you need from any of us.'

Father Michael placed one hand on the pommel of the shortsword and the other on the dagger by his thigh. He'd keep both of those.

'What else do we have?' he asked.

'What you see,' said Cadarn. 'Everyone, stand down, make some room, but watch them,' he ordered. The tension seemed to ease a little, but Father Michael saw every crossbow was still levelled at the Gifted.

Father Michael looked at the eagles. 'Can I have one of those?' he asked.

'What? An eagle?' asked a red-haired Rider, Raker.

'No. The spear,' Father Michael said, pointing at the nearest bird.

'Oh, right,' Raker sounded disappointed as he jogged over to collect it from its leather fastening on the side of the eagle's saddle.

'Shame,' said Bryce, walking over to join him. 'I reckon an eagle might have given you an edge.'

'That would not be playing fair,' said Father Michael.

'Who gives a fuck about that?' replied Bryce. 'If only we'd been in the air when they showed up, we could have finished this already.'

'Here,' said the Rider handing him the spear. Father Michael nodded his thanks. Eilion would make it hard for him to get close, so he needed something with reach.

He weighed it in his hands. It was lighter than he would have liked. Eilion's would be heavier, though they appeared of a similar length. He took a deep breath and rolled his shoulders.

'I'll be as quick as I can,' he said, and walked towards the centre of the space between his people and the Gifted. He stopped, placed his feet wide and placed the spear butt on the ground. 'I'm ready.'

Eilion looked from his comrades to him.

'Very well.'

The Gifted carried his shield, but had not replaced his headgear. That was unexpected. *Ah, perhaps not.* Father Michael had killed Leisha with her helmet, Eilion was no fool.

Eilion walked towards him and stopped six paces away. 'You killed my friend.'

'She deserved it,' said Father Michael, raising the spear and swinging it high as he leapt forwards, aiming at Eilion's head, the spearhead coming round from Eilion's left. The Gifted leaned backwards and to the right, the surprise in his face evident.

He swung his weapon round to counter the attack, blocking with his spear's momentum, then quickly dropping his spearpoint to thrust at Father Michael's exposed chest.

Father Michael in turn used his forward movement to turn side on, allowing the point to slide past. They both stepped away and adopted perpendicular stances, facing one another. Father Michael glanced down at red stain appearing on his shirt. A cut, but not deep enough to be serious. The pain could wait.

He kept his body side on to Eilion, presenting a narrower target, his left foot leading, his right planted to the rear, knees bent, weight on the balls of his feet. He had seen Eilion fight plenty of times. He was very good with a spear, better than Father Michael. He kept his spear level at waist height, his hands wide apart, as Father Michael stepped right, so he followed, maintaining the smile, though his eyes were intent, never leaving Father Michael's.

Eilion thrust. Father Michael blocked, dropping his spear then raising it up for a quick stab. Eilion was already swaying backwards, anticipating the move.

Father Michael attacked again, thrusting up towards Eilion's head; it was blocked easily. Father Michael quickly reversed the shaft to butt Eilion's weapon away. He followed up with another head stab. Eilion's spear was in the wrong position to defend. He had him!

But then he felt pressure on the spearhead, forcing it away when it was just an inch from Eilion's face, sliding down the side of his breastplate, useless against the armour. *Damned Shaper!*

He stepped back to get away from his opponent's spear. They continued to dance around, the Gifted probing Father Michael's defence.

Eilion was just stringing this out now, waiting for him to tire. He had used much of his stamina in his night-time assault. But he was fitter and stronger than he had been in a long time.

He blocked a thrust, stabbed back. The spear was yanked forwards and he stumbled. Eilion was on him in an instant, sliding his blade into Father Michael's left leg. He shouted in pain as he felt a wash of hot blood spill down his calf.

He hobbled backwards swinging his spear in a wide arc. Eilion was already beyond its range. He didn't need to close, his Gift was doing all the work. Father Michael looked at his leg, a nasty gash in the lower side of his thigh. Nothing had been severed but the blood flowed freely. He was running out of time. He needed an edge, something Eilion couldn't counter.

'I thought I had killed you already,' Eilion said, moving slowly, easily. 'That rock I sent at your head should have smashed you. It would have any normal man.'

'I've got a thick skull,' Father Michael retorted.

'Thick, yes. I look forward to taking it back as a trophy. I look forward to being the man who finally bested the great Champion,' laughed Eilion.

There it was. It was his arrogance. His belief that he couldn't be bested. That he would live to be honoured.

And Father Michael knew what he had to do.

To beat Eilion he had to embrace the truth of his life. That there was a higher power than him. The Emperor. And he had pledged himself to his service.

Father Michael hefted his spear and threw it at Eilion. The Gifted leaned back and dodged the throw. And, for a second, he took his eyes off Father Michael.

Pulling his shortsword free Father Michael forced himself to close the distance, ignoring the tearing pain. Eilion swung his spear round, slicing along and through Father Michael's right side.

Against the white hot agony Father Michael kept going, his blade held high. Eilion raised his spear to block the downward strike of the blade, catching its edge and forcing it away. But Father Michael was there, his left hand closed on Eilion's throat. His forward momentum pushed Eilion back as the Gifted let go of his spear with his right hand and gripped Father Michael's left, trying to pry it off. Father Michael began to squeeze.

Out of the corner of his eye he saw Eilion finally drop his weapon and now both hands were trying to pull Father Michael's fingers away. *Mistake.* He brought his shortsword down at an angle, looking to stab into Eilion's neck.

He met a wall of resistance. His arm shook as he tried to force it down but he was making no headway. And then the blade began to turn. Slowly, by degrees, the sword twisted in his hand. He sought to fight against it. He tried to let go of the weapon, so he could get both hands round the bastard's neck. Yet the same force was keeping his hand gripped tight on the pommel. *Emperor but this Gifted has power!* He could feel beads of sweat burst on his forehead. Could see the sharp metal orient itself towards his body. The point wavered as he tried to redirect it. He was losing. He couldn't choke the Gifted and fight his own weapon. Father Michael closed his eyes.

So be it.

He opened them again and locked his gaze on Eilion. The Gifted was staring right back. His eyes were wide, but not panicked. He was focussed on using his Gift. At the edge of his mouth a smile started to form. He could sense his triumph.

Father Michael snarled. The blade would soon be at a point to drive down into the gap between the collarbone and shoulder blade, a killing space. He locked eyes with Eilion once more and relaxed his right arm, ending his battle with Eilion's Gift. The force of the Shaper's power, now with no counter force against it, drove the blade down past his collar bone deep into his right side, already opened and bloody.

Father Michael screamed. And he used it. He used the pain, rage and shock and channelled it into his grip. Eilion's eyes, his irises almost completely black, registered surprise and confusion. He increased his

269

probing of Father Michael's left hand and in response Father Michael roared and started to lift.

Now Eilion was panicking, Father Michael could see that the man was losing focus, losing control of his Gift. He surged again and Eilion was off the ground. Father Michael was shaking all over. His energy almost spent. His sword arm won free of the Shaper's power and he thrust his weapon vertically into the poorly protected groin area of Eilion's armour. Eilion screamed. Father Michael thrust again, and again, and started to feel the heat of blood on his hands. And Eilion was still screaming.

He let go and Eilion fell to the floor writhing in agony. Father Michael felt a wave of weakness wash over him. His vision swam and started to fade. He shook his head and fell to his knees next to Eilion. Taking hold of Eilion's hair, he raised his sword and pushed it into the Gifted's neck, where it stayed, quivering slightly.

Before him, Grieg and Loras had locked shields in preparation for an attack. Not much he could do about that. He turned towards the Emperor, tried to catch his breath but ended up coughing. The jerking of his chest was agony, his ruined right side flaring in pain. He put a hand towards it. All he could feel was wetness, hot and free flowing. He was done.

Father Michael swallowed. 'Your Grace. The field is yours.'

The Emperor, his face grave, nodded.

Father Michael closed his eyes. There was nothing more he could do. He had fought for his Emperor and had been victorious. His life had meaning. Now it was time for rest. He fell on to his left side and waited for nothingness. Yet he could still hear the words of those around him.

'My champion has won. Yours is dead. Now, stand down,' ordered the Emperor.

'No, Your Grace. With respect.' It was the female, Loras. 'Your champion is dead and your eight Riders are not enough to best us.'

'Submit now!' shouted Grieg.

'*We* will not!' responded the Emperor. He heard Cadarn ordering his people to prepare to shoot.

No. Father Michael opened his eyes, tried to push himself up, but he had no energy. All he could see was the sky and it was greying out. It was not supposed to end this way!

'Then your Riders die,' shouted Loras.

'They will not!' cried another voice, a female voice. 'Kill them!'

And as the world turned black he swore he heard the sound of thunder and the cries of monstrous beasts charging towards them. One of the Hells, it would seem, had finally come to claim him.

Father Michael's Hell was not as he had imagined it. He was accepting of his fate. He had too much blood on his hands, so much that even his rebirth and service to the Living God was not enough to forgive his sins. Yet his personal damnation was a strange sensation of floating, as if on a raft, upon a gentle but unrelenting sea. And there was the sound. Not of wave but of chanting: guttural, yet melodic in its way, droning on and on. He could not feel his body, if he still possessed one. At least he could not seem to move it. It was like he was frozen. A captive on this sea. At times he experienced intense bouts of cold and heat. Of pain. If he had no body then it must be his soul that was being tormented. For much of the time he would feel nothing, as if he were asleep. Then, awareness, if only for a few moments. He felt moisture, the sensation playing about his lip; so he did still dwell in his body. And then something being poured into his mouth. Liquid, something hot. He felt it in his mouth, and something touching his throat, forcing him to swallow. What punishment was this? He gagged but kept it down. It felt good. He drifted once more. And at some point, when a kind of wakefulness took him again, it occurred to Father Michael that the experience he was having felt very familiar and – as he could now recall – it was not something that should be happening to a dead man. He tried to move his lips and found a response. He prized them open and tried to ask a question. All he could muster was a gravelly hiss. Yet it was answered. Some kind of growling response that sounded like a word, yet not one he could place. A demon?

Moments passed. He felt pressure on his forehead.

'Michael? Can you hear me? Are you in there?'

It was a female voice.

Ellen?

CHAPTER TWENTY-SIX – CADE

'Where are we?' asked Cade.

'By a bloody great river,' said Issar.

'And you are in charge of intelligence? Is that right?' she asked.

'Tell me I'm wrong.'

'You're bloody useless is what you are,' muttered Cade. The river was called the Tuul after the town that marked its entry into the seas in the north. All stuff she'd never known before she'd had to learn to study maps.

They sat together, their backs to one of the wagon wheels. It was a warm mid-autumn day and the shade from the sun overhead was just on the comfortable side of cool. She chewed on a long blade of grass and surveyed the scene.

Stretched out along this side of the riverbank was a riot of people and beasts. Here and there she saw a few enterprising folk get fishing rods out. Good luck with catching anything with this racket carrying on. At this point the far side was maybe a hundred yards away.

'At least we get water,' said Issar.

'Not so good for getting across though, is it?' Cade observed.

'We'll find a bridge.'

They ought to. The maps said there was one nearby. There should be a load of them. The river marked the extent of the Empire. They cross the Tuul and they were home. *Home. Now there was a notion that she had not thought of for a while. The Rookery had been home. The cavern had been home. What was home?* She pushed herself up off the floor, her body no longer complaining with the effort.

She spat out the blade of grass, following it with a gob of spit. Coming up from the south was a cloud of dust generated by a group of horses – Devlin and his staff. She waited with her arms crossed as they drew up. Devlin was in the lead, riding upright and easily. He carried an axe slung over his shoulder, and wore a mismatched set of bastardised chain and plate. The dwarves may be short in stature but that was mostly in the limbs, they were a similar fit with the size of their torsos. Those following him were similarly attired. Cade had to admit, they looked the part.

'What's the word?' she asked.

Devlin stalked over, a frown creasing his face.

'We found the bridge. It's a mile south of here.'

'But?'

'They're coming.'

Cade nodded. It was always going to happen, she was amazed it hadn't happened sooner. 'How far are they?'

'Scouts say the main force is five miles out.'

'Shit.' Cade looked at the people by the river. 'They know we're here?'

'Yes. They're already skirmishing with our rearguard. They must know we'll be heading for the bridge.'

Cade rubbed her face. 'Issar? Where are most of our people?'

'North of here, Cade,' said Issar.

She nodded. 'Let's get them moving then.'

Devlin summoned some of his riders. 'Spread the word. Tell folk to gather their stuff and head south. No point in trying to hide it. Tell 'em the dwarves are coming.'

'That might spread a panic.'

'They'll need a little of that in their legs,' countered Devlin.

'What can you do?'

'My fighters will try to slow them down. We'll form a screen, hold them for as long as we can.'

'Understood. Let's go.'

Devlin climbed on to his horse, issuing more commands.

Cade wondered how everything could hold together before it collapsed. She had little faith in humanity as it was. Folk started to stir and move. Voices grew louder, urgent. Cade climbed on to the wagon and nodded at Evan. He nodded back, his face grim.

'Hey, Issar. You coming?'

'Reckon I am,' he said, already hauling himself up next to Cade.

'Come on, Krste, we're leaving!' Cade shouted to her bodyguard. He jogged up holding a couple of water canteens and threw them into the back. Evan set the wagon in motion and Krste swore as he fell back on to the ground. A second try got him on board as the wagon picked up the pace, joining the stream of people heading south.

Cade swayed and rocked with the motion, watching the crowd around her. Folk were starting to get strung out as those with stronger legs forged ahead. She looked back. How far back did the stream go? If the dwarves were mounted it would be a problem. A little way ahead she spotted a woodland and figures entering the treeline. Some of Devlin's skirmish troops, armed with bows. How close were the dwarves?

The bridge was also in view. It was already crowded with people. Directly ahead was a dirt road leading from the woods and continuing on westwards beyond the river.

'Evan. Park us up by the bridge,' she ordered.

Evan steered the wagon away from the crowd, wisely parking it on the southern side so as not to block the flow of panicked Tissans. Cade stood up on the driver's seat and looked east towards the treeline. The road was not straight, and disappeared from view a little way in. There were still some of Devlin's skirmishers on the fringes but they were pushing in. Gods Below but she had no way of knowing what was going on, or how much time they had. There was still a damnably long line of people coming south along the side of the river. It was plain that if the dwarves got here before they were all across, it would be a massacre. And then? Their pursuers could just cross over the bridge and continue the slaughter. Several supply wagons were starting to cross over, their drivers forcing their near-panicked mounts through the crowd. The bridge itself was barely wide enough to fit more than a wagon anyway, and she heard the scream of one woman who became pinned against the waist-high barriers that ran the length of the bridge. Further up she saw a man fall from the bridge into the river. She watched his struggle as the current took hold. He didn't look like he could swim and his head quickly disappeared under the water. Emperor help them if one of those wagons broke down on the bridge. They'd be done for. She spotted Sent at the head of their supply train trundling towards the bridge. She caught his eye and waved his wagon over.

'What's happening?' he asked.

'The dwarves are somewhere beyond those woods.'

Sent looked north and shook his head.

'We're too strung out, Cade.'

'I know,' she shouted, over the cacophony of tramping feet, crying voices and baying cattle. She shook her head. While they were blundering around all the dwarves had had to do was follow the roads. How else would they cross this river except by bridge? The nearest ford was fifty miles north. She looked at the bridge and then leaned over to look at its supporting beams.

'We need to stop the pursuit.'

'How?' asked Sent.

'We need to destroy this bridge somehow once we're all over. It's the only way we can buy time.'

Sent stood up and pointed. 'This is Tissan made. Look at the piles, early Empire. That's quality the like of which we haven't seen for many years.'

'Can we do it?'

He looked up at her. 'I know what you are thinking. Even if we got a score of axes on it, it'll take too long,' he stopped and rubbed his head. 'We could rip up some of the planks on top. Create a gap.'

Cade looked back towards the wood.

'We need to buy time. Sent, get across. Empty three wagons. Park them right by the bridge. And get a work crew ready, we'll need strong arms.'

Sent's eyes narrowed in understanding.

'We'll do what he can.' He clapped his driver and motioned him on to the bridge. She watched the supply wagons bully their way through the crowd who responded with angry shouts and raised fists. They'd be more pissed if that food didn't make it across.

'Evan. Get our wagon over there too. Issar, stay with him.'

'Where are you going?' asked Issar.

'I need to speak to Devlin. He'll be where the fighting is.'

'Be careful,' he warned.

'You know me.' She jumped off the wagon and started to jog.

'Hey, boss. Cade!' She turned as Krste hurried up to join her. 'Here.' He handed her one of the two cocked crossbows he was carrying.

She took hold of it and then the proffered bag of bolts.

'You might need it,' he advised.

'Hope not,' she replied.

They pushed on, following the road of beaten, rutted earth through the wood.

There was shouting up ahead, around a sharp bend in the road they found a number of horses, their reins held by a young dark-haired woman she didn't recognise.

'Devlin?' asked Cade.

'Just around there.' The girl indicated with her head.

Cade carried on with Krste shadowing her. The bend continued, describing a semicircle around a large depression in the ground, it was marshy-looking and full of downed trees. At its eastward facing side she could see a number of skirmishers in cover. They appeared to be trading shots with an unseen enemy.

She found Devlin crouched behind a large tree, clutching his axe in one hand. He was surrounded by his fighters and was busy issuing orders. A little way ahead of them on the road were the bodies of dwarf riders. A horse, a bolt sticking from its hind quarters, lay on the ground and was snorting in pain as it tried to get back on its feet.

'Hey! How's it going?' she asked, ducking down next to him.

Devlin looked at her in surprise. 'What in the Seven Hells are you doing here?'

'Taking a tour of the front,' she quipped.

'Not much to see. You should get back.'

'Just tell me what's happening.'

Devlin shook his head then pointed along the road. 'We ambushed them as they came down this road. They are now spreading out trying to outflank us in the woods.'

'How many of them?' she asked.

'Rearguard estimated about five hundred cavalry.'

'Emperor!' she hissed. She knew next to fuck all about military shit, but that number could annihilate them if they weren't stopped.

'He won't help us when they decide to keep us pinned down and ride around us,' he said, taking another peak around the tree. 'Fuck!' His head jerked back as a bolt shot past and disappeared into the bowl behind them. 'I've got my people spread in a line through these woods. We'll be able to hold them here for a while, but numbers will tell.'

'Like you said. They must know what's happening. They'll work out the best way to hurt us,' she said.

'Happy to take suggestions,' he said.

'Fall back to the bridge. I've got wagons waiting at the far side. You get there, how long can you hold them?'

'Hours. Until they bring up a mantlet or outflank us.'

'Do it,' she ordered.

Devlin reached out a hand and gripped her wrist. 'We're too strung out.'

'I know.'

'We'll lose–'

'I know! We don't have a choice. Pull your people back. We need them. I'll keep the bridge open as long as we can.'

Devlin's face was grim. He let go of her wrist. 'We'll start pulling back.'

'Good. Don't get yourself bloody killed.'

She kept in a crouch as she moved away. A grunt of shock made her look right into the woods. A Tissan skirmisher was sprawled on the ground, a bolt buried in his chest. Too damned close. She stood as she reached the horses and broke into a run, Krste keeping pace. They re-emerged from the woods. If anything, the crush of humanity trying to get across the bridge had increased. A large crowd was forming, trying to push through the funnel of the bridge mouth. She could see more than a few folk lying on the ground, trampled in the crush. How was she going to get through that?

'We need to clear a path.'

'I hear you,' said Krste. 'We might have to start swinging.'

She could see the wagons waiting on the far side of the bridge. Sent already had the right idea. One of the wagons had been unhitched and turned over on to its side, at a slight angle to the river, the Tissans flowing around it. Most of those crossing hadn't guessed what was going to happen next.

They reached the bridge and Miriam appeared from the crowd.

'Sent signals he's ready when you are.'

Cade did not know when she would be. How was she to know when to call it? Hundreds, thousands of folk were still on the wrong side of the river. The answer came quickly as, further north, she spied people begin to break from the mass heading south and enter the river. A great cry of alarm reached her, and the mass of humanity seemed to convulse and sway. Then it split apart as a group of cavalry hove into view, charging straight for the column, causing it to split into two. The dwarves were cutting off the escape route. Some chasing the northern half of the column and the rest coming south. Around her, word began to spread, and panicked Tissans started to push against those in front of them. Screaming and shouting swamped her hearing.

She grabbed Krste's arm.

'Come on, both of you.'

She led them around the expanding press of people trying to cross the bridge. With the loud snapping of wood, part of the side railings of the bridge fell away. A dozen people went with it into the water.

'What are we doing, boss?' asked Krste.

She wasn't sure. She was winging it.

'We need to stop that cavalry, or slow it down some!' she shouted.

They covered the ground, a hundred yards or so, and Cade stopped them. The cavalry was heading straight towards them, mixed in among the humans. She watched spears driven into backs, swords and axes beating down on others. The spray of blood. And people falling. The ground was littered with bodies.

'Here.' She stopped and dropped to one knee, took aim with her crossbow at an approaching dwarf, and let fly. She missed by a mile. Next to her Krste swore.

'Need to let them get closer,' he said.

Cade dropped the crossbow and tried to haul the string back. Her shoulder was better but even so it howled. She looked at Miriam, who stood behind her, a hatchet in hand. 'Reload this,' she said, passing over her crossbow and the bag of bolts. Krste was already locking his string into position. Cade kept low and counted. Best guess, a dozen cavalry working their way towards the bridge. One rider was only thirty yards away.

'Krste, that one!'

Krste stood and put the crossbow to his shoulder, squinting down its length. As the rider passed by he shot. The bolt hit the pony and it reared, throwing the rider to the ground. Cade reached into her boot and pulled out her blade. She sprung forward, sprinting towards the dwarf. Before he recovered, she leapt on to his chest, which was covered in thick leather and chain and started to stab downwards at the exposed flesh of his neck. The dwarf howled and flailed, pushing her off. She rolled away, expecting the dwarf to follow. Instead she saw Miriam standing over him, bringing her hatchet down on to his kneecap. The dwarf howled and arched his back in agony. Cade crawled back and drove her blade up and into the underside of his jaw. She rolled off him on to her sore shoulder.

'Fucking hell!'

Miriam offered a hand and pulled her up. She still carried the crossbow.

'I said to reload it!' Cade shouted.

'I don't bloody know how!' Miriam shouted back.

More people streamed by, as did the rest of the cavalry. Two were turning their mounts towards Cade's little group.

'Jump when they get near!' she ordered, bracing herself.

The riders jerked their reins and angled away north. What? A rider took a bolt in the back and slumped forward.

She turned and looked at Krste. 'Wasn't me,' he said.

Cade spotted figures emerging from the tree behind them. Devlin's forces were pulling back. The other cavalry pursing the northern half of the column had not noticed yet and was continuing to wreak havoc. It was time to move.

Signalling to her companions, she started to run back to the bridge. She waved at the fighters from the woods.

'Take them out! The riders. Kill them!'

On reaching the bridge she looked north. All the cavalry was withdrawing, leaving a carpet of slaughtered Tissans. A loose screen of skirmishers had formed up, likely dissuading them from operating alone against such huge numbers. That wouldn't last.

From the woods a group of riders appeared, heading at full pelt for the bridge. Devlin pulled hard and halted in front of Cade.

'That's it. They'll be after us.'

He looked at the crowd, and Cade followed his gaze. The numbers were starting to thin. And further back, there was a big gap where the cavalry had split the column. That was it, their window of opportunity. Already the northern mass of Tissans had seen the respite and was turning south once more, though many were still braving the waters.

'Devlin. Pull everyone back. I'm going to close the gate,' she said.

Devlin handed over his reins to another rider. 'Get the horses across and wait for me on the other side.' He dismounted and pulled his axe from his back. 'We'll hold them here. It's going to get messy. Don't wait for us. '

Cade nodded, slapped Krste and Miriam, and together they fell in behind the horses as they forced their way on to the bridge. Cade felt hot, sweating bodies pressing against her, was jostled by folk who barely registered she was there. Damn, but she could feel the panic. It was like some kind of sickness. It was all she could do to keep herself from losing it. Krste pushed past her, forcing others out of the way with threats and his swinging fists. As Cade fought to keep her balance, she looked over the edge of the bridge. It was a disturbing sight. As heads bobbed down the Tuul, it reminded her of leaves flowing down an autumn stream. There were so many.

She reached the far side of the bridge and pushed her way out from the flow of people. She found Sent waiting by the wagons, again, the draft animals already unhitched.

'You see what's coming?' she asked him.

He nodded.

'Get ready.'

Cade climbed on to a wagon that had already been turned on to its side. There it was. A large force of cavalry was coming from the north, emerging from the end of the woods. Devlin was concentrating his fighters into a shrinking ring around the far side, as Tissans pushed through the gaps. Hundreds more were trying to reach the bridge ahead of the cavalry. 'Shit.' They wouldn't make it.

She turned to look at Sent. 'Get them in place.'

Sent started to say something, but thought better of it. Good. There was nothing else to say.

She stepped back as the next wagon was rolled in front of the bridge. Indignant shouts greeted it as the last few fleeing Tissans struggled round the edges.

'Tip it over!' Sent shouted.

His crew got their hands over the wagon, and with a deal of shouting and grunting they hauled it up and over the side. It wasn't a clean seal. Far from it. People were able to squeeze through either side. Cade watched as more riders appeared on the road from the south, finally completing their envelopment. Devlin's fighters were now pushing over the bridge, while a knot of crossbow skirmishers held the far end, trading shots with the cavalry. The last wagon was pushed into place and turned over on the left side of the bridge exit, creating a crude barricade that had flank cover. Cade's teeth were picking at her lower lip as all that was left for her to do was witness the last of the Tissans fleeing to the bridge. Watch as the cavalry smashed into them, carving up people left and right. Bodies falling to the ground. And still they ran. At the far end, Devlin's group were taking heavier fire as the cavalry in the woods and the south dismounted and took up sniping positions. On the bridge, a skirmisher fell into the water. A thought struck Cade.

'Sent. We have a lot of people in the river. And some of them can swim.'

The Plainsman nodded. 'I know. I've sent some wagons south. We'll try and pick up as many as we can.'

'Alright.'

'She turned her attention back to the bridge. Devlin was falling back, keeping his people together. Fighters were scrambling around the gap on either side of the central wagon. They were carrying on, following the survivors. What were they doing? She needed them here! She cupped her hands and called to Devlin.

'Why are they running?'

Devlin looked up and waved a hand, pointing at the wagons. She shook her head and jumped down to meet him as he squeezed through.

'No need for everyone here, Cade. You only need a small detachment to hold this position. I'm keeping this lot here,' he said, indicating a knot of fighters who were now positioning themselves on and around the wagons.

'Let's take a look,' he said. Together they climbed back on to the right hand wagon.

'Keep your head low,' he advised. The bridge was momentarily clear. On the far side, a few surviving Tissans started to reach the bridge. In their wake were scores of bodies and the cavalry, pursuing scattered pockets and individuals, riding them down mercilessly. The cavalry by the wood and those to the south made no effort to close the distance, they were content to use their bows.

Cade watched as more Tissans fell to cavalry and crossbows. She counted those making the bridge. She counted every one. Twenty three. Twenty three made it through the barricade. Weeping, sweating and bleeding.

'That's it,' said Devlin quietly.

They watched in silence for a time. Cade lacked the energy to do anything else. The dwarves moved among the Tissans, finishing off those still living. Others took to building fires, setting up small camps just in the treeline. There was some kind of industry happening within the woods. She could hear the sound of chopping wood. Seven Hells, it seemed almost peaceful.

'What now?' Cade asked.

'We regroup,' said Devlin.

'How long will it take?' she asked.

Devlin scratched his beard. 'If the maps are right – and I ain't putting too much trust in them – a day and a half to the next crossing. And they might already have riders heading there right now. As I said, they might try and rush us here, but why bother? So, you get a day.'

Not enough. Cade looked behind her. 'Miriam, you've seen those maps. Is there anything west of here?'

Miriam thought intently for a moment. 'I recall we passed through a bunch of little places. Like where we got branded. There's bound to be a ruined village or something on this road.'

'Fine. Where's Evan. He buggered off?'

'He's way over there,' said Krste pointing to a small gathering of wagons and horses a hundred yards away.

Cade gazed at a broken line of staggering humans winding their way along the road and into the distance. From the south, more bedraggled souls, those that had made the river crossing, trudged to join the line.

'Who's running that lot?' she asked.

Devlin touched her shoulder. 'You, now get gone. Reach the head of the line and start telling people what to do. Believe me, they'll be grateful for it.'

Cade nodded. 'We'll keep on the road. I'll find a place to stop when it gets dark.'

'I'll stay here, keep them short-arsed bastards interested. If they don't try anything, we'll pull out at dawn tomorrow.'

Devlin squeezed her shoulder then beckoned over one of his fighters.

Cade stood, pointing at Krste and Miriam.

'Go fetch Evan. I'll be there in a minute.'

She walked across to Sent.

'So many dead.' He sounded distant, staring behind them.

'And we are alive.'

Sent inclined his head.

'Let's get ahead of this thing. When we set up camp, I want fires, and I want food distributed. No arguments.'

'Yes. I understand.'

'Good.'

She started to walk away.

'Cade?'

'What?'

'You know where we are?'

She grinned.

'Up shit creek?'

He smiled sadly. 'We are in Tissan. We made it.'

Cade looked at him for a moment. Made it? Made it how? Was dying here any better than dying in the mines? It depended on who you asked. Those they'd left behind, those still running for their lives, those who had been killed by spear or had risked drowning, they probably couldn't tell you the difference.

CHAPTER TWENTY-SEVEN – FILLION

Fillion adjusted his belt as he walked, giving it a downwards tug. He felt nervous. A state of being he had not felt since his first days in the capital. He had become so inured to playing his role that the day to day usually held no fears. And he supposed that perhaps it was because of the role he played, that his reaction was so extreme. It was not often that a Servant was summoned to accompany their Member to the Palace.

It waited ahead of them at the end of the boulevard, rearing into the sky on its pillars of living wood. He had once likened it to a spider, lording over its web. That perspective had shifted somewhat – now it felt more like a spider rearing to strike, and he was striding right towards it. Who wouldn't experience a sense of trepidation heading towards such a dangerous beast? It just so happened the danger only really manifested when you were inside the monster.

'Sabin, stop fidgeting,' commanded Patiir, marching beside him with his hands clasped behind his back, all purpose.

Fillion bit back a retort. He had to keep it together. Finally, after all the months of ingratiating himself into elven society, all the things he had had to endure, the constant play-acting, the feigned deference, the humility. It had all been for this one reason. To gain access to the Palace, to realise his last, great act of resistance. As they covered the last hundred yards he reflected on his first visit, his first reconnoitre really, to this place. Even then he had no real clear plan, only a dream. And reflecting on how daunted he had been by the towering monstrosity that confronted him, he really had never had any idea how he was going to achieve it. He had been winging it, improvising, and trying to keep alive ever since. And somehow, through blind luck, he was here. And he was shitting himself.

They arrived at the gate used for dignitaries. It was surprisingly unostentatious: two doors half again as high as an elf, framed within a wall of bark, were carved with simple fluting leaf patterns, and without any reinforcing bands. Like the city itself, defence was considered a foolish concept. They were still mighty thick, at least six inches of solid wood. And this was the King's Palace; a guard was stationed on either side of the entrance and a third bearing only a sheathed sword waited in front of the portal. This one, a female, stepped forward as Fillion and Patiir approached.

With her hand resting lightly on her blade's pommel she inclined her head in greeting. 'Welcome, Member. I will escort you to His Majesty.'

Patiir nodded in return and the guard turned to lead them inside.

They entered a small chamber. Fillion was momentarily taken aback. The walls and floor were bare wood, smoothed through time and passage and, with the application of some kind of varnish, shining, mirror-like. On a pedestal, a small glow-stone and the walls took up the light and intensified it. The result was space that defied the absence of daylight, it was so bright.

Patiir touched his arm, a small smile playing on his lips. 'Magic and nature have made this place. Nothing here should be so, but it has stood for millennia. Now, close your mouth.'

Fillion did so and nodded, his enmity briefly forgotten. Damn, but elves came up with some impressive shit. Embedded in alcoves set to the left and right were flights of stairs disappearing into the floor. Directly ahead was another portal, similar in design to the outside door though just as polished as its surroundings. The guard pushed at the doors and they swung inward. Beyond was another set of steps, climbing up and framed within what appeared a far larger chamber. Without waiting for invitation, Patiir strode forward, confident in his destination. Fillion followed, not into another chamber, but a gallery of sorts. The steps were carved out from the wood and, climbing upwards the space fell away below and around them, the entire space hollowed out to create a void. With no railings, Fillion found he was moving instinctively to the centre of the steps. There was more of this unnatural light, emanating from far above. He looked up and spied globes, like moons in the sky, throwing their cold light into the depths. He could not tell from here how they were fixed or suspended. Their destination was ahead at the end of the flight, atop a wide pillar of wood standing within the gallery. As they reached the top, the plateau revealed itself. It was, as far he could judge, a perfect circle perhaps twenty-five or thirty yards wide. The floor was smooth, though not reflective as the earlier chamber, and covered in swirling designs. Four guards stood at equidistant stations creating four points of a square within the circle, facing towards the centre. On the far side was another entrance which opened on to a short corridor feeding on to the circle and in front of that was a dais and upon that a throne. Wooden, naturally, but remarkably simple; it was of one piece, high-backed, with curving arm rests and a bare seat.

If anything, Fillion was a little disappointed. He thought of the Emperor's audience chamber and, well, there was a throne! Made of iron and gold and silver, and studded with precious jewels. And behind it a huge bronze representation of the sun, burnished bright, reflecting the sun's rays lancing through crystal windows set high in the ceiling. Fillion had only seen it once and the Emperor had not been in attendance, but he could well imagine what it would have looked like to be in the presence of such blinding grace.

Patiir motioned for him to stay in place and walked across to take position in the centre. Their escort stayed with Fillion. They waited in silence. By the set of Patiir's back, he appeared to Fillion relaxed and certain of his purpose. And why wouldn't he be? How many times had he been in attendance here? Fillion glanced across at the female elf next to him. She stood at parade rest, her hand still at the pommel. Her gaze was fixed upon the throne. Fillion placed his hands behind his back, letting them rest against his belt, his palms facing outwards, the fingers not touching. Against the backs of his hands he felt the hard iron of the blades through the cloth. They were, by necessity small, short stabbing knives, no good in an actual fight. He felt annoyed that his precautions in hiding them were wasted; the lack of even a rudimentary search meant he could have stowed something more meaningful. Trust the arrogance of the elves to believe they were free from danger. What would it take then? It would have to be quick, retrieving the knives on the move while going straight for the throne. Those guards were perfectly placed to close on any danger, but he was counting on a few moments of surprise his actions would generate. And then there was the elf next to him. He was worried about her the most. She looked too damned competent. His left index finger twitched, tapping against the metal. After a few moments, he realised what he was doing, and stopped. How was he going to get to the King? If she was any kind of soldier, she'd sense something was wrong, would see him going for the knives, and pull out that mean fucking longsword. There had to be another way to get closer to his target.

And, with perfect timing, his target appeared.

He hadn't even noticed his approach, had heard no footsteps coming towards the throne. Lujan, the King of the elves, seemingly glided on to the plateau. He wore a single silver robe the fringe of which dragged along the floor. And then he saw the others settling into a kneeling posture, their right knee bent, their left knee touching the floor, and heads bowed. Not the four guards, just his two companions. Unthinking, he followed suit. A few seconds passed and then a deep, resonant voice spoke.

'Really, Patiir. I do not expect an elf of your years to bend the knee.'

'But I pride myself that I still can,' responded Patiir.

'Quite so,' said the voice, a little lighter, suggesting amusement. 'Please, rise.'

And with that Fillion stood to finally regard the symbol of all his hatred. The King sat at his ease upon the throne, his hands resting lightly upon its armrests. His hair was a light brown, held back from his face by a finely wrought circlet that looked silver, but Fillion could not be sure at this distance. Other than that, the King was possessed of features that Fillion had come to regard as average. There was nothing striking about the elf, other than an air of quiet authority.

'And what is your business today, Patiir?'

Patiir indicated the centre of the plateau. 'May I?' The King inclined his head and Patiir took six steps forward. 'I wish to discuss with you the matter of our dwarf neighbours.'

'Ah, yes. Of course,' replied the King. He appeared remarkably relaxed, like it mattered little. Fillion would have thought it warranted more concern than was on display.

'It would seem that the dwarves have … lost control of their situation, my King.'

'How so?'

Patiir clasped his hands and rested them against his stomach. 'As part of our bargain, the dwarves took more, assumed more, than we had agreed to. As I reported to you previously, they had a human slave population which they employed in their mines. In and of itself, an issue I was willing to resolve through normal diplomatic channels–'

'Yes, I recall,' interrupted the King, 'but it would seem that the humans had other ideas.'

'Quite so, my King. They have revolted against their masters, and are now wreaking havoc through Dwarf territories.'

'And where are they headed?' asked the King.

'West. Heading home.'

'And I assume the dwarves are being less than diligent in stopping them?'

'The humans are many, and they appear organised.'

The King drummed the fingers of his right hand against the armrest. 'And I would deduce you have come here to ask for us to intercede?'

Patiir dipped his head in acknowledgement.

The King raised his hand to his chin.

'I had thought this business ended, Patiir.'

'As did I.'

'You know, I still recall when I was in the last campaign, before the humans. We appeared to be successful then.'

'They were driven from our lands. Never to be seen again,' agreed Patiir.

'I miss that time. I know I must refrain from such youthful desires, my position will not allow me to undertake such adventures, but I would have liked to lead my armies against the Tissan Empire, to see them routed once again.'

'I suspect these humans will linger.'

'And can we expect them to threaten us? How many can there be?'

'Our reports suggest thousands, perhaps twenty.'

'Warriors?'

'Few, if any.'

'Then they are a desperate remnant, driven by fear and the instinct to survive,' suggested the King.

'True. But the dwarves believed that too.'

The King flicked his fingers in the air, conceding the point. 'The dwarves cannot be relied upon to finish the job?'

'I would feel,' Patiir paused and looked up into the light-speckled roof of the gallery, 'more confident if there was an elven input into the matter. Just to make sure.'

The King smiled. 'Patiir. Your understatement belies your intentions. I know you well enough. You want this matter ended once and for all. There is to be no hope for this species? A second chance?'

Patiir shrugged. 'In a few hundred years perhaps a new society may arise. One with no knowledge of their past, a society we can guide and develop. But twenty thousand living Tissans? That constitutes a nation. A shared memory. Memory that would become dogma, a never-ending hatred. This we cannot allow.'

Fillion was surprised. Patiir had never suggested a future which involved humans before. But he doubted humanity would ever be allowed to evolve into something like the old Empire. The elves would be sure not to make that mistake again. He closed his eyes for a moment. Such thoughts weren't important. What was important was his rapidly shrinking window of opportunity. He had to do something before the moment passed.

The King dropped his hand back on to the armrest. 'You are right, of course. We must monitor the situation and act accordingly. A column perhaps, to offer assistance if the humans stray south?'

'Yes, my King. Something like that would suffice.'

'And twenty thousand you say? Then two thousand cavalry would do it.'

'No doubt.'

'I shall give orders. It will take some time for them to be in a position to assist.'

'We have time. They will eventually discover those survivors that the dwarves fail to apprehend.'

'Very good.'

Patiir bowed his head and started to step back. Fillion swallowed. He had to move. And that was when he realised the King was looking right at him.

'Is this your new son-in-law?'

Patiir stopped and glanced back at Fillion. 'It is indeed. And now the father of my first grandchild.'

'Truly? You mean the line of Kings will have to endure the endless badgering of your progeny? Step forward … ah, your name?' The King tilted his head in enquiry.

'Sabin, Your Majesty,' Fillion replied quickly. He took a single step. Was this it? He looked at Patiir, who beckoned him forwards. Fillion took the remaining steps as calmly as he could, taking a position next to Patiir.

The King leaned forward to better study him. Closer now, Fillion thought; he was close enough now to detect grey in the fringe of the King's hair. 'Where are you from, Sabin?'

'The west, my lord, the border country.'

'You fought in the war?'

'I did.'

The King nodded his approval. 'And tell me, how does the life of a politician suit?'

Fillion made a show of considering the question. He stood straight, placing his hands behind his back once more. His moment was coming.

'I will not lie, Your Majesty. I would not wish it on anyone.'

Patiir shot him a look, an eyebrow raised.

'Hah!' The King leaned back and clapped his hands on their armrests. 'An honest answer. Well done, Sabin. It fills me with hope!'

Fillion shifted a foot, positioning himself. 'Apologies if I was too blunt.' He hooked his fingers into the top of his belt. That guard would be watching him but hopefully she would see nothing threatening in his actions. Not yet.

The King shook his head. 'Not at all. Patiir, don't smooth out his edges, he is fine as he is.'

'I'll do what I can,' said Patiir with a wry smile.

'And Sabin,' the King continued, 'you have a child?'

'Brynne.'

'Brynne. A beautiful name,' the King said with a thoughtful nod. He smiled at Fillion. 'I ask you to do something for me.' He raised a finger into the air, his face turning grave. 'Raise her well, and make her understand that the things we do are sometimes terrible and awful. Tell her that peace is the true struggle. And when she is old enough ...' He paused and the smile returned. '... bring her here. I want to meet her. My children are already too grown and it would be good to enjoy the innocence of youth. Would you do me that honour?'

Fillion blinked. His hands were still in his belt. Why? Why had he not moved? He felt the silence, felt the eyes off all upon him. He bowed deep. 'The honour would be mine, Your Majesty.'

The King nodded and smiled. Then he stood. And as his rose, the party returned to their knees. In the quiet of the King's departure, Fillion's heart was pounding. *What are you doing? You bloody fool!* The King was leaving. His chance was fading away as he knelt in deference. He felt beads of sweat run down his back. His vision swam. Go. *Just get up and make a run for it.* But he couldn't.

And with the softest creak of leathers their guard stood. Fillion waited a moment, took a breath and rose. Patiir was looking at him with a smile.

'Shall we?'

Fillion nodded. His throat was too dry to speak.

'Member,' said the guard indicating the steps.

Patiir moved past and with long years of practice, led them all back out of the gallery, back down the steps, through the mirrored chamber and with a few words of thanks to the guard, back on to the boulevard.

'Are you well, Sabin?' asked Patiir.

'I am feeling a little light-headed.'

Patiir reached across and patted his shoulder, an unexpected gesture of affection.

'I would be surprised if you were not. I'll let you in on a secret. I remember when the King was a babe, I have seen him grow, have seen him march to war. I have counselled him, debated with him and once or twice even raised my voice.' Fillion arched an eyebrow. 'Yes, it's true.' Patiir laughed. 'And, for all I may look calm and collected, I always have to take a mental breath when in the presence of His Majesty. I think about who he is, and more importantly what he is, what he represents. For in him resides the bedrock of our society. Our culture, our continuity, the reason we have all that you see.'

'I'm glad you didn't say that to me before we entered. I think I would have soiled myself.'

'Sabin!' Patiir admonished, with amusement. 'There's your soldier's bluntness again.'

'Sorry.'

'Don't be. Our King was quite taken by you, wasn't he? Well done. That's a relationship worth cultivating.'

'Did he mean it?' asked Fillion. 'About wanting to see Brynne?'

'Oh yes, the King is not known for making frivolous requests. I believe he would be delighted to meet her.'

'I had better start teaching her some manners.'

Patiir waved a dismissive hand. 'And rob her of her father's charm? The young can afford to be honest in their innocence. Else what has this all been for?'

Patiir stopped a moment and regarded Fillion.

'Of all the service you have given me, the gift of my granddaughter is the most precious. I thank you for that, Sabin. The future of our family and its place in our world is secured by it.'

Fillion inclined his head. What could he say?

Patiir smiled, and stepped off. 'Now, let us turn our thoughts to the situation at hand. The disposition of the military campaign is not my affair but the Parliament must be informed.'

Fillion barely listened as Patiir droned on. He had his answer. The reason why he still had two unbloodied blades within his belt. The reason he still lived. It was because of Brynne. His little girl. How could he let her live among these people? Not knowing her true heritage, with no one of her kind to tell her the truth. She would become an elf, but would she age like a human? That was yet to be revealed. Would she be rejected, cast out? Or worse? She needed him. And he could not throw his life away. He could not leave Brynne alone. And his plans were in ruins. His vengeance left incomplete.

'Yes,' he muttered in response to some command by Patiir. 'I will do it right away.'

Fillion corrected himself. His vengeance was not incomplete. It had only just begun. The chain of events he had started in the north *was* his vengeance. He had instigated a rebellion. Hundreds of dwarves were dead, and there was a rampaging human army in the west. It was all due to him. And, with some work, he could do more. Much more.

Fillion felt his heart lift. He had a beautiful daughter to raise and a war to foment. And he knew where he had to start.

Fillion entered the royal library. He took a moment to inhale the dusky smells of dry paper and parchment. He was surprised to find he looked upon the interminable rows of books and scrolls with something like fondness.

'Sabin! It has been such a long time. What has happened to you?' asked the ancient library-keeper, Lenard. He held a single wax candle up to Fillion's face, and he pulled back a little as the flame got uncomfortably close to the tip of his nose.

'Fatherhood,' said Fillion.

'You have a child?'

'Yes. I did tell you.'

'Did you? My goodness. What is it?'

'A girl!'

'A girl? How old?'

Fillion stepped back. *Really?*

'Not even six months.'

'Oh.' Lenard pulled his candle back. And scowled at Fillion. 'Even so. Six months of learning lost!'

Fillion raised his hands and turned slowly to encompass the library. 'I have a lifetime to study all this.' It did seem a lifetime ago that Patiir had sent him to Lenard as preparation for his role of Servant.

'There are a thousand lifetimes of learning in this place,' warned Lenard, his liver-spotted hand pointed at him accusingly.

'Then perhaps you'll stop chiding and provide me with some guidance?' asked Fillion, with a smile.

'I can offer you all kinds, but I fear most of it is already too late for you. However, history, that I can give you.'

'I would like to learn about dwarves.'

Lenard laughed. 'I did wonder if someone might ask!'

Confused, Fillion scratched his head.

'Did you?'

'I do actually get out of the library on occasion, Sabin. And, as a student of history, I make it my business to know when it is in the making,' said Lenard.

'And what do you think I need to know?' Fillion was intrigued.

'You want to know if we have ever been at war with the dwarves,' stated Lenard, primly.

Fillion, impressed, nodded. 'I do.'

'I would be surprised if you didn't.'

'And can you show me?'

'Perhap. Perhap.' Lenard pointed over Fillion's shoulder. 'You ought to know by now where everything is. Head that way.'

'My thanks, Lenard.'

Lenard narrowed his eyes. 'If you can spare the time, when you are done, I have some chores you can help with.'

'I would be delighted.'

With a phlegmy cough Lenard retreated towards his shadowed table. Fillion raised his own two-pronged candlestick and headed into the depths of the circular library, following the aisle indicated by Lenard. After five minutes of rummaging through piled tomes and scrolls he hit upon a group that were truly aged. He put them at about nine hundred years old. Which meant they were written roughly at the same time as the last great genocide committed by the elves. He read through several before he found texts relating to the first meetings of the elf culture and the nearest dwarf clans to the north. At that time the Dwarf Nations were not federated in the same way they were now. Each clan vied for supremacy and land with its neighbours through a constant, shifting state of alliances and uneasy pacts. What was clear was that there were many skirmishes, and one or two genuine battles, before both sides sued for peace. It was evident from the writing that the elves had seen enough common ground and ability to negotiate that they decided against further aggression. That was as all he needed to know. Marmus had told him the dwarves had long memories. It was a good bet they could still remember a time when relations were frostier. He could build on that.

He stood, replaced the texts on to the shelving, and went to find Lenard.

Two hours later, after more humping and dumping than he had planned for, he arrived at The Silver Chalice. He was already late for his meeting, and worse than that, should have returned home for supper. There would be pointed looks and stilted conversation later. One thing he could also rely on was that Kanyay, once settled, would always be hard to shift. The wood elf had one of the booths, with a flagon and two cups in front of him.

'Have they run out of ale?' asked Fillion, taking the bench opposite.

'It was always going to happen,' said Kanyay with a sigh. 'But we have this.'

Fillion reached out and sniffed the flagon. 'Mead. I haven't had this for a long time.' He took one of the cups and filled it. 'Where d'you get it?'

'Marmus.'

'Ah. That makes sense.'

'I felt it only right that we show our solidarity somehow,' said Kanyay quietly, scowling at the rest of the inn's clientele. 'No one else is.'

'Considering the situation, you can't blame them,' Fillion suggested.

'Yes, I can,' growled Kanyay, tugging at one of his fetishes. 'Damned civilised elves wanted to tell folk what they can and can't do.'

'How is he?' asked Fillion. The dwarf spent most of his time ensconced in his embassy, almost like he was under siege.

'Today? He feels a little better.'

'Really? That's good.'

'You haven't heard why, have you?'

Fillion shook his head. Just recently he felt he was always one step behind events.

'They caught the humans.'

Fillion felt a cold chill of dread. *No. It can't be over.*

He put his cup down, slowly and carefully. 'Caught them?'

'Yes. A unit of dwarf cavalry intercepted them as they tried to cross the Tuul.'

'And?'

'It was a slaughter, apparently. The cavalry found them strung out along the eastern bank trying to reach a bridge. Cut that column in half, and wreaked havoc.'

'How many?'

'Not sure. But Marmus said they killed thousands.'

'Did they encounter resistance?'

'Plenty. There was some organised defence, some kind of military response. The humans took the bridge, got thousands more over it and held back the cavalry.'

Fillion nodded, hiding his intense relief behind his cup. Good. His plan could continue. He felt remorse for the Tissans that had died, but he needed to focus on the survivors and see it through.

'What are the dwarves doing now?'

'Marmus is unsure. His masters are royally pissed.'

'The dwarves are mobilising?' asked Fillion, drinking the mead. It was good. Almost as good as Celtebarian mead.

'Now that is a good question. All their cavalry is already in the field. If they mobilise it'll be infantry troops. They'll be walking after the humans. Might take a while.' Kanyay grinned into his mead.

Fillion sat back and rubbed his chin. 'I don't think our Parliament would like that.'

'I agree,' said Kanyay. 'Our cavalry will be on its way. I hear they have a wizard cadre joining them. I'm thinking of heading home and scaring up some riders. We'd catch those slaves before dwarf and elf alike.'

'You could pick up some more ale on your way back,' said Fillion, reaching for the flagon. A wizard cadre. That was a problem, no doubt riding those bloody great freakish bees of theirs.

'That's why I like you so much, Sabin. You put your concerns in the right order.' Kanyay leaned forward and held his cup out for Fillion to pour.

They touched glasses and drank. The small slip of paper that Fillion had been holding between his fingers was taken and slipped into Kanyay's tunic.

'Do I want to know what it says?' he asked.

'Up to you. But nothing that would surprise you,' replied Fillion.

Kanyay nodded. 'I suppose so. My good and trusting nature might be offended.'

'Then let's leave it at that,' agreed Fillion. The more Kanyay didn't know the better.

CHAPTER TWENTY-EIGHT – CADE

'You say that we have two, maybe three, days before they catch us?' asked Sent.

'If we are lucky.'

A murmur went around the gathered group of refugees Cade now called her 'council'. There weren't that many left from those who had been picked to represent the mines, mostly it was her inner circle. It was all a little moot now anyway. They were just one big churning mass of humanity.

She held her hands up to the small fire and warmed her fingers. It wasn't cold but she felt damned tired. The heat prickled her skin, and then turned painful. She held them there a bit longer before pulling away, the pain staying with her for a few seconds.

'So, what do we do?' asked Sent.

'We've made it back to Tissan. I always said that when that happened, folk would be free to choose their fates.' Cade lifted her fingers and blew on them. Around the group, a hundred fires glowed in the night. They hadn't found anything resembling a village or town, just burned-out husks. So instead, with the sun low in the sky, she'd ordered their ragtag column to stop by a large wood, and bid them build fires. It would help the stragglers, those who had made it across to find their way to them. After all of it, who were they hiding from? Until the dwarves got here, that is.

'That's not good enough!' said Winders, emerging from the darkness, a blanket wrapped around him.

'Nice of you to join us,' she said.

Winders stalked up to her and kicked her over.

'Hey!'

The small group erupted into chaos. Krste and a few others went for Winders, pulling him back even as he struggled to get to her. Others sprang to his defence.

Winders pointed at her from over Krste's shoulder. 'Not good enough, Cade!'

Issar got behind Cade, pulling her up. 'You alright?' he asked.

'Yeah, fine.' She brushed his hands off and pulled down her shirt. Adjusting the leather duster she had appropriated on their journey west, she cricked her neck. 'Everyone just calm the fuck down. Let him go.'

'Cade,' warned Miriam.

'Just do it,' she shouted.

She looked around. Their excitement had drawn a crowd. Faces loomed in the flickering light, some confused, others fearful. Very few looked hopeful.

Winders pulled his arms free. 'I wasn't lucky enough to be near the bridge, I was with many of my people further north. We tried to get to you, but it was too late. The dwarves cut us off. We were dying. So I told everyone to make for the water. They drove us towards it, cutting us down as we ran. We were slaughtered. And then folk started to drown.' Tears were rolling down his cheeks. 'You got us here, Cade. It's on you. All those deaths. It's on you.'

Cade flung her hands in the air. 'Fine! It's on me. If that makes you feel better about yourself, go ahead, fill your boots.'

'You left us to die!' he cried.

'We had no choice!' Cade snapped. 'You think we should have stayed and fought? When Devlin gets back I'll get him to explain what a shit idea that would have been. We saved as many as we could. They were always going to come after us. It was only a matter of time. You've got a couple more days. What you want to do next is up to you. I don't give a rat's ass.'

Winders deflated before her. His shoulders sagged and he dropped to the ground, his head hanging low between his legs.

'It's over, though, right?' asked a long-legged Scotian called Cline. 'We got across the border.'

Emperor but these people are stupid. 'What did you think was going to happen next?' Cade asked. 'We settle down and live our lives like we still have an empire? It's long gone.' Cade stretched her arm out – it protested. 'We are back across the border. But I doubt that will stop them.'

She looked at Sent, and then at Miriam. 'Either of you two, anyone, know how many we lost?'

Miriam shrugged. 'I was with you.'

'It's too early to say,' said Sent.

'Thousands,' said Winders bitterly.

'Everyone was strung out,' offered Cline. 'We still have stragglers coming in.'

'Supplies?' she asked.

'Are in a better situation,' replied Sent. 'The main supply convoy was near the bridge. We got most of the wagons across. That said, we are not going to have any settlements to sack now. We'll need to rely on foraging.'

'That suits your lot to the ground, don't it?' Cade asked.

Sent raised an eyebrow.

'Plainsfolk, you said it yourself. Used to the outdoors life.'

'Cade, I grew up in a house in a small town east of Brevis. When I started my business I lived in a larger house in Vyberg. I like soft beds, I like staff. And I don't have a fucking clue how to catch a rabbit, or plant a fucking radish.'

'That makes two of us, then,' said Cade.

There was a gentle ripple of laughter, a few smiles. And just for a moment, Cade felt the mood change. Now was as good a time as any to broach what she had a notion to do.

'I'm going to run something by you now. Something that maybe one or two of you have thought about as well.' Cade stood, because it felt like the right thing to do. 'I'm from Aberpool, ain't that right, Cline?'

'That you are,' said Cline.

'And, in the absence of anywhere else to go, I might as well head back there. Issar?'

'Yes?' he replied.

'You thought about Erebesh?'

'What about it?' he asked, looking a little confused.

'Going back there, you idiot!'

'Oh. Well. Yes, I guess so. You know, there was this lovely inn, right on the wharf at Tarut–'

'Yes. I'm sure,' interrupted Cade.

'I'd like to go home to Glendos,' said Miriam.

'I see where you are going with this, Cade.' Sent nodded.

She motioned for him to continue.

'It's been the plan from the start. It's time we split up. We have to widen our ability to hunt and scavenge. Like Devlin always said, if we stay in one mass, we make ourselves an easy target for the dwarves. And, if I have you right, you are suggesting that we split into our old nations, before we were united under the Sun banner.'

'Is that true?' asked Winders.

'Why not?' said Cade. 'If we all start going in different directions, it makes it more difficult for them to hunt us.'

'We might end up weaker. Is there not strength in the whole?' asked Sent.

'I can't argue with that. We split our numbers, we have less fighters for each group. But – and I'm just throwing it out there – what if one column, or two, gets away clean. What if they give up the hunt? I doubt they are keeping count.'

'That's grim, Cade. Real grim,' said Issar.

'There's nothing good about this. It's all fucked. But if you want to survive, this is the only way. Life has always been a scrap. And it's not going to change for any of us. But I ain't done fighting yet. So. Up to you. I'm heading west. Whoever wants to come with me, can. If you want to go your separate ways, you can. Sent, make sure they get a fair share of supplies, wagons and weapons. Anyone wants to kick off about it send them to me. No, don't send them to me. Send them to Krste.'

Krste grinned and gave her a thumbs up.

'Now go, talk among yourselves. Sort it out.'

With a sigh Cade settled back in front of the fire again. The group broke up around her, the conversation animated. There, she was done. She had nothing else to give or say.

'You were right.'

Cade looked up. Winders was still there, just on the other side of the fire.

'What was that?'

'You were right. To do what you did.'

'Uh, thanks?' Cade wasn't sure where this was heading.

'You had to block the bridge.'

'There was no choice.'

Winders looked hard at her.

'There was a choice. You made the right one. But I lost people I cared about, so I cannot give you my forgiveness.'

'I'm not asking for it.'

'No, I guess you're not.' He stood up.

Cade shook her head. She supposed she should be civil. 'What are you going to do?'

'I'm taking your advice. I'm going south, to Celtebaria.'

'That takes you awful near the elves.'

'I know. But that's my home. I haven't been back there for nigh on ten years. Not many of us left. They did a good job of wiping it clean. Maybe they won't notice me.' He turned to go and stopped. 'Thank you for getting us this far.'

'You're welcome. And good luck.'

Winders inclined his head and disappeared into the night.

'Morning,' said Devlin.

Cade lay in the wagon bed with her legs propped up on top of a crate of bottles. She opened an eye a crack.

'Morning.' He was looking down at her from his horse. His eyes had dark rings around them, and his beard was covered in dust. 'You just got in?'

'Yes. We pulled out a few hours ago.' He looked around, confusion on his face. 'What's going on?'

'Camp's breaking up.'

'I can see that.' He paused for a moment. 'I count at least three columns. One heading northwest. Another two heading south.'

'Uh-huh.'

He looked down at her. 'Spreading out?'

'Seemed like the right time.'

'We heading west?'

'I reckon,' Cade admitted.

'I thought we were going to coordinate things.'

Cade pushed herself up on to her elbows. 'Right now, I don't think I could coordinate a piss up in a brew house.' She squinted at him. 'Devlin, no offence but you look like shit.'

He smiled, almost apologetically.

'Yeah, but it wasn't that bad after all. The dwarves figured it out pretty quick. They pulled back and sent groups north and south, just like we expected. We're not sure how many were left watching us, but they didn't make a try for the bridge. We spent most of the night gathering in survivors from the river, and putting them on the road west.'

'Anyone left behind you?'

'Maybe. Left some scouts back along the route. Could be scores further down the Tuul. Best thing they can do is go it alone.'

Cade nodded. They might end up being the lucky ones.

'So, what about this lot?' pressed Devlin.

Cade sighed, climbed on to her feet and gazed around the massive encampment. As Devlin had said, a line of figures was heading northwest to the northern coasts of the Riverlands and two smaller columns running almost in parallel were heading south. The destinations were clear; one was for Erebesh, one for Celtebaria – Winders was at their head. Evan was stood at the front of the wagon, adjusting the straps on the ponies. Krste was taking a piss over the remains of the fire.

'Come on you two. We should get going,' she ordered.

'If my eyes are right, most of the survivors are still here,' said Devlin. 'Looks like people want to stick together after all.'

Cade huffed. 'Their choice.'

'So, are we staying on this road?'

'Might as well. The going will be easier and we need to get on. It'll take us close to the Highlands. That'll be nice. Always wanted to see them.'

'The dwarves will follow.'

'That's for you to worry about.'

Devlin grunted.

'Fine. I gotta start planning. Treat this like a withdrawal from combat.' He stood in his saddle and motioned to one of his riders. 'Hey, Rance, over here!'

Cade waved a hand. He was already off in his own head. Working things out. She climbed over to the driver's bench. Evan leapt up next to her, Krste hopped into the back.

'You set?' She studied the lad. Evan wasn't a boy anymore. He was as almost as old now as she was when she'd been thrown into that cell in Aberpool.

'All set,' he replied.

'Let's go.'

The wagon began to move, Evan guiding it on to the road. Cade swayed with the movement, feeling relaxed. Her mind, surprisingly, at ease. Up ahead she saw a convoy of wagons already on the road. That would be Sent. Getting ahead of the game. Good for him. Saved her having to think about it. As they rolled along, survivors picked themselves up off the ground, collecting sacks, baskets, items wrapped in clothing. They fell into line, joining a growing procession of walkers. Cade took a moment to reflect. They'd lost thousands just the day before. Someone said perhaps ten thousand souls had been left on the wrong side of the river. If that were true, it meant fifteen thousand were on the right side. She smiled contentedly. That meant fifteen thousand potential customers.

'Krste. How many barrels of ale we got left?'

'Er. Three.'

She sucked air through her teeth. She'd need to find more stock.

CHAPTER TWENTY-NINE – OWEN

Owen scratched at his nose, his finger running over the bump at the bridge. He spread his hand wide, drawing it down over his cheeks and chin, feeling the hairs of his beard. Having left it for so long, the thought of shaving did not entertain him at all.

'What do you think, Arno?' he asked. 'It's still me, isn't it?'

Arno cocked his head and blinked.

Owen smiled. Like his eagle gave a shit.

He ran a hand down Arno's flank and patted him.

'We'll hunt soon.'

He walked among the camp, passing Jussi and Ayolf. He stopped to inspect the lad's work, testing the straps of the saddle.

'Make sure you stow your spear nice and tight, Jussi. Don't want to see it falling out like it did last time.'

'It won't, Owen. And that was months ago!' complained Jussi. His voice was deeper, scratchier. Owen smiled as he turned to look at him. Puberty was taking hold, and Jussi was starting to fill out. Good thing that Ayolf had matured just as fast.

'I know, Jussi. But I'm never going to let you live it down. You almost skewered that camel.'

'And his rider won't let me forget it. You'd think I'd taken a shot at a family member.'

Owen laughed. 'Think of it this way – how would you feel if someone took a shot at Ayolf?'

'But camels aren't as smart as eagles.'

'You want to argue that with the Erebeshi?'

Jussi looked at the ground and kicked at the dirt. 'Not really.'

Owen clapped his shoulder. 'Smart lad. Now, get ready. We'll be off soon. Fly well and give the Erebeshi a reason to like you again.'

'Will do.'

'*And keep safe.*'

Jussi nodded, at the pulsed wish.

Owen moved on. He knew he treated the lad with greater care then the others. Jussi had seen enough to know to be careful, but he was still young. He just didn't want to fail him like he'd failed Em.

He waved at Erskine and Ernan. They'd returned a few hours ago, and no doubt would have liked more rest, but there was no more time. At least their eagles were fully grown, and both they and their riders were itching for a fight. The brothers had missed the events at Eagle's Rest and had been antsy ever since. They'd get a chance to work it out.

He walked through the camp. The eagles and Highlanders were billeted on the southern side of their camp, the scouts and their camels were on the northern side. Owen had his command group meet right in the centre. He settled down and greeted the young Erebeshi called Hassan, who was tending the small fire. This far out, there was no danger of being discovered.

'Hassan, you are well?'

'Very well, General,' he responded.

Owen grimaced. Since when had this new title taken hold?

'You don't have to call me that,' he said.

Hassan smiled. 'Of course, General. Very kind of you to say.' He handed over a small beaker filled with a steaming liquid. Owen held it under his nose, drawing in the scent of mint. Damn but they made good tea.

He took a sip. It had a thick, sweet texture.

'It's good.'

'Hassan.' They both looked up as Killen approached.

'Yes, Major?' responded Hassan.

'Got your kit ready?'

'Not yet. I was making tea. Here ...' He handed up another beaker.

'Thank you, son. Now get your arse back to your mount. We'll be riding soon.'

Hassan sketched a salute, stood, and jogged off.

Killen shared a look with Owen as he hunkered down by the fire.

'That boy, making tea when he should be sharpening his sword.'

'He's a fine lad, does his people credit,' replied Owen. 'Your people now, I suppose.'

Killen reached up and felt his face and the beard he sported, cut and shaped in sharp angles, tapering to a point just below his chin.

'I still don't get them, not completely. They have their own way of doing things. I doubt I'll ever fully understand.'

Owen raised an eyebrow. 'Major, have you seen yourself?' The soldier was dressed in his wargear, his breastplate over a linen shirt. Over this he wore the off-white robes of his scouts, and his leather helmet was encased in more linen, wrapped around his head and chin. On his arms he wore leather bracers, embossed with southern symbols and script. He now carried a curved sword tucked into his belt, rather than his issue cavalry sabre. And as for that beard ...

Killen raised both eyebrows in response. Owen saw him open his mouth to protest, then stop.

'I suppose. I just felt it important to honour their service.'

'I think they honour you, too,' replied Owen.

Killen grunted. 'Don't know why, they've carried me most of the way.'

'Not true, Major. I've seen you in action. You know your business and I'm grateful for it.'

Killen blew on his tea and took a sip. Owen watched him for a moment. There was something that he had been wanting to ask. Now seemed as good a time as any.

'Major, we've never had this discussion, but you know you outrank me?'

Killen snorted. 'I don't think that matters, does it, Owen?'

'I'm just an Eagle Rider,' Owen replied. It was the truth, after all.

'You also happen to be the leader of the last Imperial settlement left standing and the commander of her army. Sorry, *General* of her army,' he said with a sly smile. 'Trust me. You can keep that job. I'm happy with my scouts.'

'General. That again,' Owen scoffed. 'Don't feel like one.'

Killen downed his tea and raised the beaker. 'I've met a couple in my time. You're not doing too bad a job. Though they say you are only as good as your last battle.'

Speaking of which. Heading towards them were Larsen and Captain Rashad. He nodded to each in turn, and took it upon himself to serve them both tea. Rashad nodded gratefully, Larsen didn't look so sure.

'How are we doing?' Owen asked.

'We're ready,' said Larsen, taking a tentative sniff of the tea.

Rashad grinned at him and nodded. 'Our scouts have returned. The settlement is quiet. A few souls have raised themselves, but only to toilet. They have no sentries.'

Why would they?

'Major, your cavalry?'

'Once Hassan has himself sorted, we'll be ready to head out.'

'Then I think we are done. It's a pity we have no more Speakers here. It would have made coordination easier.'

Killen shook his head.

'Owen, welcome to the world of the Imperial Army. Those Gifted always stayed close to the Emperor. If we'd had them embedded, we might have stood a better chance in the war.'

'You never know, we might find more,' suggested Larsen.

Owen scratched at his elbow. 'Either way. We have the element of surprise. Let's make it count.'

He stood and the others followed.

'Good luck, all of you. I'll see you inside the settlement.'

He shook hands with each man, and watched them return to their commands. He took a seat and helped himself to the last of the tea. He sipped it slowly as the Highlanders loped off at a steady pace. A few whispered voices and the tramp of the feet in the soil was soon lost to the night. They had several miles to travel through undulating, lightly wooded terrain. The Erebeshi roused their camels and stepped off, and although he did not see it, he knew the group would be splitting into two parties. One heading north east, the other south east. He sat for a time. Enjoying the silence, even the solitude. His friends must have realised he needed some time to himself, and stayed close to their eagles. His decisions, all his actions, had led them to this moment. And he could not help but think of Gerat. The man had been a killer. Killed others so that he may live. And what was Owen now doing? He was condemning more of his people to death. Did he want to live? Yes. But the only way he could see that was to fight. And die. He placed the beaker by the fire and stood.

Now it begins. Finally.

He returned to the eagles, raising his hands to his fellow riders. They knew the signal and started to climb aboard.

'Arno. Time to get going.'

He reached Arno and climbed into his saddle. He went through his pre-launch checks. Everything was strapped in tight. His crossbow was loaded, his spear stowed. He settled his feet into the stirrups and leaned forward, holding tight to the pommel.

'*Up, Arno. Up.*'

Arno stretched his wings out and swept down, generating uplift. Together they lurched upwards into the night. It was cloudy, cool. Autumn had the land in its grip, and soon this place would start to feel the turn to winter. In these central territories the seasons were hard. They climbed for a few minutes, before he put Arno into a slow, languid circle, allowing the others to join him in their own time. As each rider arrived they placed themselves into a chevron formation: Owen at the front, the brothers each taking a flank, and Jussi taking the rear. They had worked hard on a sequence of manoeuvres and signals to make up for the brothers not sharing the Gift. Tonight would be their first test in conflict.

He turned them east. Though dark, Owen was confident of their destination. The target had a large open stretch of ground directly to its west, and a stream bordering it to the south; easy to identify from the air.

It would only take a few minutes before they would overtake his troops on the ground. Perhaps if they were looking up, waiting for the eagles to sweep by, they would feel comforted? In awe? Jealous? He'd felt similar emotions himself when he was a child, before he manifested the Gift. Ever since he'd been too damned busy to think about it.

Keeping low he spied a lighter patch of ground, and the trees gave way to an area of open heathland free of overgrowth thanks to the constant cropping of horses. Arno started to climb a little higher as he sped across the heath, reaching its far edge. Even in the darkness it was clear the treeline beyond the heath was marked with odd, angular shapes: dwellings, stables and storehouses. Owen and his squadron overflew the settlement and he took them on a wide curving arc west before positioning them in a lazy holding pattern. If Larsen and the others had not been looking for the eagles before, they would be now. He made sure they were an obvious sight, if one was minded to see. He doubted anyone from the settlement would be looking up at this hour.

Owen and the others waited patiently. There was nothing else to do until Larsen had his people ready.

'*Owen? I think I saw a spark!*' Jussi pulsed.

He stretched out and scanned the ground. He couldn't see anything.

'*You sure?*'

'*I think so.*'

He looked again. There! The briefest flare of light. Not far from the settlement's edge. He turned Arno to line up on it as that flare of light grew, turned into spluttering flames, then split into two, then split again, and again into smaller points of light, forming a spreading line. Almost thirty of their archers ready to loose.

Owen turned Arno again, this time to get out of the way of what was coming next. They banked sharply as the lit arrows were launched into the air, describing a high arc, reaching their apex and falling towards the settlement, scattering over the dwellings. Before they impacted, another wave was launched, and following that another, and another after that. The fire arrows were beginning to carpet the settlement. Many were striking trees, some hit the spaces between buildings, the flames burning out to no effect. Yet enough were starting to find their mark. Owen and his flyers were now over the settlement, high enough to avoid the arrows but close enough to witness their effects. As yet another volley flew, Owen could hear shouting, a rising level of alarm. Fires began to take hold. The settlement started to glow. Figures were emerging from the structures, running hither and yon. Another volley crashed down. A figure stumbled and fell. A scream rose up. And there, amidst the trees, he saw a corral, and a score of shadowed figures sprinting to it. He directed Arno toward it, and he spied a great number of horses. They did not appear overly panicked by the chaos. The gate to the corral opened and the figures streamed in. Owen altered Arno's course, back towards the line of Larsen's people. It was time for them to go.

Another volley.

Wooah!

A quick tilt of Arno's wings to dodge an errant pitch-soaked arrow of flame, and he was swooping over the Highland archers. If Larsen didn't get that message, he was in trouble. As he passed, he caught a shout.

'Let's go!'

They'd got the message.

He picked up height again and looked back. The Highlanders were up and running, sprinting across the open ground, heading for the safety of the far treeline. But they were not going to make it. They were never going to. It was the most dangerous part of the plan. To draw out the enemy they had to get close, to put them in harm's way. Owen levelled Arno out and raised his arms, high.

'*I see you, Owen,*' Jussi pulsed to him.

'*Good hunting, Jussi.*'

Owen turned Arno to the left in a tight arc heading towards the settlement. On his right flank was Erskine. Jussi took position on his left and beyond him was Ernan. The two brothers acting as wingmen, each following the lead of the two authentic Eagle Riders.

They dropped towards the ground quickly, gathering speed. As they passed over the tree line and back on to the heath, Arno levelled out again in a long, fast glide, the ground a blur beneath them. The rush of air competing against the noise coming from below. Owen saw his people and passed beyond them within moments. And there, directly ahead, framed by the now blazing settlement, were the riders. He guessed perhaps thirty of them. Nothing more than shapes in motion, but he didn't need to see them clearly to know what they would look like: wild-haired, bare-chested, inked skin, howling like madmen.

Wood elves.

And they had no idea what they were facing this night.

The eagles lined up and went straight at the horses.

'Hunt, Arno!'

Though he could not see them, Owen knew Arno's talons would be outstretched and homing in on his prey.

Arno struck, taking hold of a horse below in a powerful grip and dragging it away. His wings, wide and powerful, caused other riders to veer wildly out of the way, losing control of their mounts, crashing into each other. It was over fast. Owen looked left and right. The others were all with him. None of them appeared to have gathered any prey. Not a surprise, horses were not their usual target. Arno, however. He had been trained for this.

'Arno. Drop.'

A screaming, panicking horse fell through the sky into the darkness below. Owen did feel a little bad for it.

'Good lad, Arno. Good Lad.'

He raised his hands high. A second pass. He withdrew his crossbow from its holster.

This time he broke right, and Erskine, just a few yards behind, followed. They swept down into the churning mass of horses and riders as the elves tried to make sense of what had just happened. More riders were coming out of the settlement, and these were more prepared. Bows were already rising to track them as they sped over. But there was nothing for it and no time to worry about it.

'Hunt!'

Arno was way ahead of Owen. He crashed into a knot of riders, scattering them wide. Shouts and the wild shrieking of a horse accompanied the collision. Owen shot his crossbow into the press. He lay low in the saddle, letting Arno have his way. He looked right, Erskine was still with him. Left, fifty yards away, Jussi and his bird. Ayolf appeared to be struggling.

'Jussi? All well?'

'I'm not sure. We took a lot of arrows. I think … I think Ayolf is hurt. Maybe Ernan too!'

The lad was panicking.

'It's alright, Jussi. You're still in the air. That's a good sign. Head back to the camp. Take Ernan with you. We'll stay and support the ground.'

'Sorry, Owen.'

'Don't be, you did fine. Now get back and take care of your birds.'

Owen forced Arno to slow a little. He turned and gestured to Erskine, who urged his eagle to fly close. Jussi and Ernan carried on past.

Erskine drew level and looked towards him.

'Those two are heading back. We'll stay to cover!' Owen shouted across. 'Stay on my flank, keep close, do what I do!'

Erskine gave him a thumbs up.

Owen ordered Arno to climb and turn so he could better observe the fight. Time for the trap to be sprung.

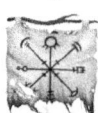

Killen had split his scouts equally. Rashad commanded the southern group, he the northern. Now they watched and waited. Beneath him his camel shifted and farted.

'Vile beast,' he hissed.

'We have a saying, Major,' said Sadad, quietly.

'Yes?'

'Better out than in.'

Killen sighed. 'Of course.'

Behind him Hassan stifled a giggle.

Killen straightened his back a little, trying to regain some decorum. They were just about to ride into battle. He hardly thought it time for humour. Especially as he was experiencing high levels of anxiety.

This would be his first cavalry charge. Ever.

He gazed out of their position just within a stand of trees, looking across the open ground. That at least was good. Fighting on camelback in woods was not advisable. He had no faith in the dexterity of his mount at the best of times.

'Major, I see something,' said Sadad.

A mass of stars flew into the sky and described a lazy arc before falling out of sight.

'That's the Highlanders,' Killen said.

More volleys followed.

'It reminds me of the solstice celebrations,' said Sadad, wistfully.

Someone murmured their agreement.

It was hypnotic, restful. And for the briefest of moments Killen and his troops could forget their deadly purpose. Then he saw dark shapes swoop low over the sky. The shower of stars ended.

'That's it. Draw scimitars!' He reached down and pulled his own blade free. He raised it high. 'Advance!' He kicked his camel's flanks and it slowly plodded forward, out of the safety of the trees and into the open. His soldiers followed and formed up a ragged line to either side. They trotted calmly forward, accompanied by snorts and grunts. Killen felt his breath start to quicken. From the settlement a mass of horses appeared.

And the eagles returned, spearing into the riders, and for a second Killen feared the worst. Then they rose. He watched open mouthed as a writhing horse fell from the sky. The shapes turned and engaged the horses once more. That was their cue. At a range of two hundred yards he lifted his blade.

'Charge!'

He kicked the flanks harder, urging his blasted beast to move. 'Come on, you shit. Move!'

At first it didn't not respond. But as those around him started to gather speed, it decided to join in. Very fast over short distances; the camels closed quickly. His scouts hollered and whelped in high-pitched ululations. Some shot bows into the melee. Killen just hung on for grim death. His camel pitched forwards, picking up an unexpected turn of speed and overtaking its fellows.

Bloody typical.

Keeping heads low, the mass of riders started to respond to their charge. A few arrows sped towards the Erebeshi troops, and some wood elves spurred their horses forwards to engage. Within moments Killen was among them. He swung his blade in a wide arc, slicing at a savage looking rider who ducked underneath it. Killen tried to turn to meet a counterattack, but the elf had already disappeared and his camel appeared hell bent on a forward trajectory. A spear was thrust towards him, and he quickly parried it away. A howling, bare-chested devil with snarling face and pointed teeth ran towards him. He raised his sword, but the elf was swept away as another camel careened past, taking him out. Killen continued on, trying to find something to hit. Then he met camels coming the other way. Rashad's group. He pulled hard on the reins. He needed to get a sense of what was happening. The camel slowed, and he urged it into as tight a turn as it could muster. Looking back, he saw a cluster of camels milling around, a sprinkling of riderless horses among them. A few elves were retreating towards the settlement, which appeared to be burning in several places.

'Captain Rashad?' he shouted.

'Major?' Rashad emerged from the press.

'Pursuit. Don't let up!'

Rashad nodded.

He swung his sabre over his head and called out something in Erebeshi. The riders responded, quickly regrouped, and set after the elves.

'Come on, then,' he commanded of his camel.

'Killen?'

He looked towards the voice and spied Larsen and the others approaching. 'Larsen. We have them on the run.'

'Good, we'll catch up. Be careful. These bastards don't die easy.'

Killen nodded and kicked his camel after his troops. Leaving the Highlanders in his wake, he trotted into the settlement. It was well illuminated; several buildings were blazing fiercely. Erebeshi and wood elves skirmished, both mounted and afoot amidst the flames. Many folk appeared to be ignoring the fighting altogether and sought to extinguish the fires. Perhaps they still did not realise the fight was done. He drew his camel up, and decided to dismount. At that moment a wood elf, a female, rushed him. In her hand a wicked looking short blade with a serrated edge. She held it high, holding it two handed. Killen reacted without thinking, stepping forward into a fencer's posture and lunging. The scimitar, not designed to thrust as well as his old issue sabre, was straight enough and sharp enough at the point to drive the weapon home. She pretty much impaled herself with her own momentum. The wood elf dropped her weapon, then pulled herself free. She staggered back, looking confused and bewildered and staggered away into the night. Killen watched her go, trying to register what had just happened.

He continued on through the settlement, nothing more than a village. Everything felt a little … unreal? This place had been alive with life but a few short minutes ago and now … it was destroyed, its people dead. His scouts had judged the population at around two hundred. The wood elves had a reputation that all those of able body would fight. It had been important to winnow the numbers before entering and this had appeared to bear fruit. All around him, as he walked the flame-lit paths, only wood elf bodies littered the ground. The surprise had been complete. A small group of Highlanders jogged past. He could hear shouting nearby, but no sounds of conflict. The battle was over and won. *So fast?* He stopped a moment just to take it in. He was hale, and a cursory inspection suggested no personal injury. All was well. He looked at his sword. There was blood on it. He bent low and wiped it in the grass on the verge of the path.

'Major?'

He looked up to see Owen striding towards him. 'Ah, Owen.'

'How goes it?'

'Captain Rashad has it in hand. Unless they have a massive force in reserve, I believe they have been routed.'

Owen nodded. 'Do you think any got away?'

'It's possible. Probable. Wood elves are formidable trackers,' Killen acknowledged. It would be hard to track down any survivors in the dark. And they were in no position to go chasing.

Owen nodded. His face turned to profile. He was studying a burning hut.

'It was an expected risk. But it would have been nice to stay hidden for a little while longer …'

Killen waited for Owen to return from wherever his reverie had taken him. Owen shrugged and looked at Killen. 'I think we are done here, Major. Round your troops up. I'll get Larsen to head out now. Burn what's left standing and then ride back to join us at the camp.'

Killen nodded. He watched Owen turn and stride away. There was a lot going on in that young man's mind. But was that really a surprise? Killen sheathed his sword and set off to start gathering his troops. Then he had better find his camel. With luck it had wandered into a burning barn and had roasted to death.

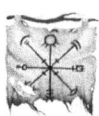

Owen stood by the small fire in the centre of their camp. He had stirred it back to life and waited as the water boiled and he received the tally of casualties. Jussi had been right, Ayolf had been hit, an arrow going straight through his right wing. It would be sore. But he could still fly as long as he was not over-worked. Ernan had also been lucky. His right leg had received the tip of an arrow that had struck his stirrup, the leather absorbing most of the penetration. His other Highlanders had all escaped unscathed, if you disregarded a twisted ankle. The Erebeshi had taken the lion's share of the actual fighting, and had lost a man and a woman. The first true losses in this new chapter of the war. Two humans lost weighed against two hundred wood elves. Was that a fair trade off? Likely not. And his small army would probably never face such favourable conditions again. But he'd take it. Every time. He would take it.

Now, surrounding him, were his commanders.

'Any sign of pursuit?' he asked.

'No,' replied Killen. 'I doubt we'll see any for a time. Even if there are survivors, it will take them a while to figure out just who the Emperor it was that attacked them.'

'I'm sorry you lost folk tonight,' said Owen, looking to Killen, then to Rashad.

The Erebeshi shrugged. 'We are soldiers, like you say. It is what we chose.'

'What's our next move?' asked Larsen, as he withdrew a small leather canteen from his knapsack.

Owen dug at the fire with a stick. 'I think perhaps we can continue with our guerrilla war for a little longer. We've stirred up a hornet's nest, and I believe the wood elves will strike out. They'll send their hunting parties looking for who did this. So we bleed them. For as long as we can, until they get wise.'

'Not a trait you hear about wood elves,' suggested Larsen. He took a sip and hissed.

'What's that?' asked Killen, nodding at the canteen.

'Here.' Larsen passed it over and Killen took a swig.

Owen watched his face. He adopted a thoughtful pose as he swilled it around his mouth. Then his eyes widened with alarm.

'Oh, sweet Emperor.'

Owen grinned at Larsen.

'Murtagh's home brew?'

'The very same,' said Larsen.

'Here,' said Rashad, taking the canteen from Killen. He repeated the action, and took a moment to savour it before swallowing. 'I like it.'

'Of course you bloody do,' gasped Killen.

Owen reached out and collected the canteen. He saluted into the air. 'Murtagh. Tonight was for you.' He sipped and swallowed quickly.

'Yes, he would have been proud,' agreed Larsen.

Owen passed the canteen back.

'As I was saying. We bleed them a little more. Until they get organised. Major? Can you lead them on a little chase?'

'I believe so.'

'Good. I'll have the brothers stay with you to provide intelligence. Larsen, take our people home to the borders. Look for ambush sites, but on our ground. I don't want you caught by wood elf cavalry. The Major will give them a more obvious target. Let them overextend, become fragmented.'

'And if they don't come?' asked Larsen.

'Then we go back and do it again,' said Owen. 'Major, I leave it to you to decide when to disengage. Don't sacrifice yourself, don't let them outthink you.'

'That's why I have Captain Rashad,' smiled Killen.

'He learns!' agreed the Erebeshi.

'And what about you?' asked Killen.

Owen threw the stick in the fire.

'I'll escort Jussi home, make sure he gets back safely.'

They all nodded. No one mentioned the obvious, that it was strange for the general to leave his men in the field. But, in this instance, he believed they understood why.

'Owen?' Miriam joined them and hunkered down next to Larsen. 'Jussi says he's ready to go, and the brothers have prepped Arno and fed him too.'

'Kind of them,' said Owen.

'Ernan was swearing like a bastard all the way through it. Whining like a baby,' she added.

Owen stood and brushed his trousers.

'Time to go. Well done, all of you. The wood elves are first. And when they are done, we move on.'

Owen left the group and went to find Arno.

CHAPTER THIRTY – FILLION

Fillion knew he was taking a dreadful risk, but there was nothing else for it. He slid out of bed and padded over to the window, looking out into the night sky. He had already been up once to visit Brynne. She had been a little fractious, and had been refusing to sleep. Nadena, taking the brunt of the caring, was exhausted and beyond waking by the sound of his quiet business. He dressed quickly, putting on a set of darker clothing, leaving his Servant garb in his wardrobe. He walked to his chest, opened it, and withdrew his dagger and belt. As he buckled it around his waist he paused to look down at Brynne. He could barely hear her breathing, but as he went to pull away she let out a little whine. He stopped and made a hushing sound, leaning over to trace a finger over her forehead. Her little hand reached up to clutch his. He held it for a few moments before teasing it free. Then he left his bedroom and made his way through the quiet halls of the house.

Everything was still, everything silent. Even the house staff would be asleep, the cook usually not rising until a false dawn tinged the horizon. He left through a side door leading into the courtyard and out on to the streets. He made for the wide plaza that contained the Parliament and the Temple. He did not try to skulk, that would have been too obvious, but he strode quickly through the quiet, climbing streets. Most houses were in darkness, though on several street corners lights blazed within small conical containers. These were mage lights, burning with some kind of enduring sorcery, the likes of which Fillion could not hope to understand. He passed by, walking confidently and with purpose. He did not think he was being tailed, but he had grown a little paranoid since his return from the north. And when he arrived on to the long avenue that would eventually take him to the vast, living palace of the

King, he did not cut across to the Parliament, but instead he made his way up the steps and into the Temple. Within the atrium he paused to look up at the statues of the gods; even now he felt himself a little awed. These beings were possessed of a power and nobility that caused him to question his own faith. Did the old gods of his Celtebarian heritage really step down before the Emperor? Or had they been conquered, made to kneel? That was a question he doubted he would ever have an answer to in this life. He considered passing on through to the many smaller chapels, pay a visit to his old friend, the god Mardock. But he had somewhere to be. He returned to the entrance and slipped out into the shadows cast by the large columns. He waited a minute more, just surveying the boulevard and the many buildings lining it. Taking in a sense of what surrounded him.

Across the way, the Parliament building was lit by mage lights slipped into brackets on each of its entrance archways. Each one was guarded by an elf of the King's guard. The mage light illuminated the building and the steps leading up, but did not blaze like regular fire. He saw no staff or functionaries amidst the archways or steps. Nor did he get any sense of being watched, no warning sign that he was indeed being followed. So be it.

He stepped from the Temple and made his way across the boulevard angling back towards the hill. He cut around the back of the Parliament and followed a leafy lane that brought him to the rear of the dwarf embassy. He stood in the shadows of the building opposite, some kind of trading concern. Its windows were black. A small door, set into the sheer stone blocks of the embassy, opened, and a cloaked figure emerged. It stood, head cocked, then raised a beckoning hand. Fillion hurried over and through the doorway. The figure followed and closed the door behind them. There was a scraping noise, and a flame was kindled which in turn illuminated a candle. The room, a small chamber, was revealed.

'What's with all the cloak and dagger shit?' asked Marmus, lifting the candle from a small table by the doorway.

'Huh?' asked Fillion, expecting a warmer welcome.

'If you had wanted to talk to me, you could have come round during the day.'

'But I thought that would be a little obvious,' suggested Fillion.

'You're a bloody Servant,' said Marmus, pushing past him and opening another door. 'This is politics, not war.'

Little do you know. Fillion followed him through into a pantry and beyond that some kitchens. Another candle burned on a sideboard, illuminating a plate holding a half-eaten piece of cheese and a mug.

'You want something?' asked Marmus, picking up the mug.

'No, thank you.'

'Suit yourself.' Marmus took a bite of the cheese.

'I am not supposed to be talking to you directly. Patiir felt that he needed me to distance himself from you,' said Fillion. His eye was drawn to the mug.

'Yes, that's ale. You want one?' asked Marmus.

Fillion nodded.

Marmus grunted and walked over to a keg resting on its side. He took a mug and placed it under the tap.

'What Patiir says, what he does, and what he believes can all be very different things,' said the dwarf. 'Look at me. I've shut up shop and hunkered down. It's what's expected. But you should see the traffic toing and froing from this place.'

He handed over the mug to Fillion. The ale frothed over the side and fell on to his fingers.

'Business never stops, Sabin. Wealth, power and growth. Nobody wants to see these things stop.' Marmus picked up his ale. 'I'm just playing the game.'

It dawned on Fillion that these politicians, even Marmus, did not fully realise the impact of their actions. They talk about war and wealth like it was all an exercise in points-scoring. They had no concept of the pain – the terror – that their 'game-playing' caused. There was no true consequence for them, because they had never had to wield the blade, never had to look into the eyes of an innocent as they bled out. If they did, Fillion knew, they might modify their viewpoint. He had seen how war, the physical act, affected people. It could make you hard or it could make you a pacifist. But it always left a mark, and sometimes it stayed raw and never faded away.

'Marmus. It would seem I continue to surprise you with my naiveté. I believe I understand. But if this is the way of things, I find myself content with my choices. I will not play games. Not with my friends and not when I see wrongs that must be answered.' Fillion raised his voice, injecting it with urgency and passion.

'By the forefathers, Sabin. What is it that has you so riled?'

'Don't you see? You are being manipulated on two fronts. Patiir wants what he says. He wants the humans dealt with and he wants the dwarves punished. He has the King's ear on this. And then there is Tekla. She doesn't give a damn – what she wants is to screw you over, she wants to make money at the expense of the dwarves, off the tragedy of your loss.'

'And they'll get neither,' growled Marmus.

'You think they'll give up? Marmus, I know what Patiir truly is. He is driven in a way I have never seen. I have read accounts, studied the histories. Patiir will not let this slide. You think that he'll stop with your assurances? He no longer trusts you. Tekla? She will see your trade diminished, dashed against the rocks of her ambition. This is the excuse they wanted.'

Fillion kept his eyes locked on Marmus. Was it getting through?

'Aye, an excuse, Marmus. You don't know what they are capable of. You think it ends with the humans? It will end with you!' He thrust his free hand out, reaching for Marmus. The dwarf stepped back a pace, batting Fillion's arm away.

'Dammit, Sabin. You sound like a madman.'

But Fillion could see something in Marmus's demeanour. He was shaken. He had to press on.

'Marmus. I'm sorry. I do not mean to scare you but I must be candid. Patiir has convinced the King that putative measures must be taken. The dwarves must be brought to heel, the dwarves must be subjugated. The dwarves must know their place. And if not, then they must be taught.'

Marmus was shaking his head and pulling at his beard.

'This is outrageous. It is nonsense, Sabin. Can you hear yourself? Do you understand the treason you are uttering?'

Fillion drew in a shuddering breath.

'Do I know that I put my life on the line? And that of my family? You think I didn't pause and think about my actions? I did and I knew that I could not live with the lie.' Fillion hung his head. 'Marmus, my friend. Do you believe the timing of the human revolt was by chance?'

He looked up at the dwarf. His face was unreadable in the shadows.

'What are you saying, Sabin?' asked Marmus quietly.

'I'm saying that I was but one cog in a much larger machine. I was sent to confirm what Patiir already believed to be true. And then he acted.' Fillion paused to down his ale. Let that information sink through. It was the best lie, the one that was virtually the truth.

'Sabin. Are you telling me your father-in-law deliberately engineered the breakout and subsequent massacre of scores, hundreds of my kin?'

'Yes.'

'That fucking cunt. That fucking shit,' whispered Marmus. He was starting to pace. 'How the fuck? What does he think he is doing? He wants a fucking war?' Marmus spun and grabbed Fillion by the shoulders, shaking him hard.

'How did he do it? Was it you? Have you betrayed me?' The violence coming from Marmus was palpable.

Fillion forced himself to stay calm, to not react, to deny his instincts to fight back.

'No, no. It was not I. Think about our traveling companions. I was not the only elf. Did they not travel with you? Could they not have passed the message on? Engaged one of your own with gold?'

Marmus gripped tighter.

'You think it was one of them? Ezra. Was it him?'

'I truly don't know.'

'I bet it was. That old shit. Never trusted him.' Marmus released his grip and resumed his walking. Fillion rolled his eyes and let out a breath.

That could have gotten messy. Marmus stopped. 'It galls me to think a dwarf may have been involved.'

'There was gold, I'm sure of it,' ventured Fillion.

Marmus stopped, looked at him sharply, then grunted.

'That would do it,' he said, then continued pacing.

'All a dwarf would need to do is pass a message written in the human tongue. They would never know what it said,' Fillion offered. But Marmus ignored him and carried on pacing.

'This is unprecedented,' he said, mostly to himself.

'With respect, it is not,' said Fillion.

'Go on,' said Marmus with a wave of his hand.

'Think on it, the humans were destroyed because the elves thought them challengers. There was another race. A thousand years before them. They were destroyed because the elves feared their nature. Who knows, perhaps there were more? My people have existed for a long, long time.'

'Don't I know it,' muttered Marmus. 'You say they have done this before. Why not destroy us when they had the chance? The Dwarf Nations were not federated in the way they are now. When we came west we were a fractured people.'

Fillion rubbed his eyes. The two candles were both smoky, made of cheap tallow. 'I truly don't know. Perhaps the elves were not united in their view of you? I'll tell you this, Patiir has been behind so much of the bloodshed, maybe he had to wait until he could gain the support he wanted, and drown out any moderate voices.'

Marmus laughed. It was an ugly sound.

'Moderate? One thing you bastard elves are not is moderate. Look at you all, living your perfect lives while decent folk sweat for their gain.'

Fillion decided he didn't want to be here anymore. He wasn't enjoying taking the shit for being the only elf in the room. And he wasn't even a damn elf!

'What will you do?' he asked, wanting to move things along.

'What can I do? I can march into the Parliament tomorrow and accuse

Patiir. That would go down well, wouldn't it? I have no proof. Only your word.'

'And that is not enough,' agreed Fillion.

'No. It isn't.' Marmus slammed a fist into the wall. Fillion actually jumped.

'If he thinks he is getting away with this ...' Marmus sighed. 'I am sending a messenger home. I will tell them what I have learned from you.' He looked at Fillion. 'This is not the first time dwarf and elf have come to blows, Sabin. In our first encounters it did not end well. But we are stronger now. Organised. You've seen our armies, have you not?'

Fillion nodded. 'A terrible sight.'

'Well imagine facing them. I'd like to see your arrows pierce our armour.'

'Marmus, please. I don't want it to come to that,' said Fillion.

'How else would you expect us to respond to such naked ambition?'

Fillion shook his head.

'I don't know.'

Marmus sighed. 'Neither do I. Short of trying to expose the plot. Imagine how that would go down.'

He stepped forward and placed a hand on Fillion's arm.

'Sorry to get so angry with you, lad. I owe you a debt.'

'You owe me nothing, Marmus. I just wish it had not come to this,' replied Fillion.

'Best you go home. Kiss your wife and your child and get some sleep. I have work to do, messages to send.' He picked up a candle and gently ushered Fillion back to the rear door. 'And tomorrow I go to Parliament and I will raise the matter.'

Fillion stepped through and stood in the lane.

'You will confront Patiir?' he asked.

'And he will deny it. But I am still a politician and my job is to represent the best interests of my people. What that may be, I have yet to decide. Farewell and goodnight, friend Sabin.'

'Goodnight.' Fillion pulled his hood over his head and turned away.

He walked the streets of the capital. His mood was sour. He could not understand why. Looking at all that he had so far achieved, no one would have credited it. He would have laughed in the faces of any who would have suggested such an audacious undertaking, and yet here he was. He had engineered the escape of the last of his people and he was now this close to creating a rift between the enemies of humanity. He had even stood in front of the King of the elves. Yet all he could think of now was his little girl. Asleep, innocent, and unaware that her father was responsible for the deaths of thousands. He gained a measure of cold comfort when he thought about Brynne's grandfather. Whatever Fillion might do, Patiir would always be worse and deserved to pay.

'The House recognises the Ambassador of the Dwarf Nations,' declared the Speaker.

Marmus stood up and slowly walked to the podium, looking neither left nor right, his face fixed firmly forwards. Fillion studied his posture. Marmus appeared formal, but there were no outward signs of tension. That was made up for by the hushed expectation around the chamber. Almost a thousand pairs of eyes followed the Ambassador as he mounted the steps and took his position. Stepping on to the box, he stood with his arms clasped behind his back and inspected the gathered Members of the elven kingdom. He took his time, his gaze travelling over the many elves, as if he were inspecting them, or perhaps appraising was a better word. Fillion wondered what Marmus had got up to last night after he departed. He doubted the dwarf had slept much. For his part, he had followed Marmus's advice to the letter and had slept far better than he had any right to. He leaned forward in anticipation.

'This should be interesting,' whispered Ezra, sitting on his right in one of the viewing balconies. He had insisted that Fillion join him, sharing the advantage of Ezra's senior position within the ranks of the Servants

– he now got front seats for the dramatic events he was helping to orchestrate.

Fillion nodded noncommittally. Marmus began to speak.

'Speaker. Members of Parliament. My colleagues. My friends ...' A pause to let that sink in. That last was dripping with venom. Fillion presumed that venom did not apply to himself and Kanyay. Maybe.

'The days of late have been difficult. I have found myself hemmed in, beset on all sides by those who hold us, the Dwarf Nations, in contempt for our actions. At best we have been accused of dishonesty, at worst betrayal.' Another pause as Marmus moved his arms and gripped the sides of the lectern. 'I have thought long about these accusations. There is, I have concluded, substance to those words. We did indeed take more than our agreement had stipulated. We did, in hindsight, make an error in our belief that the enslavement of the surviving humans could be controlled. We have paid for that mistake. It was not our intention to breed a new population of slaves nor did we possess any agenda beyond simple, honest business advantage. You, of all the races, should understand that. I say again. We have paid for that mistake. Paid for it in the blood of hundreds of innocent dwarf folk. Families, if you recall, who worked hard, to create and craft, to supply you all with the highest quality goods my people can produce. Communities dedicated to the pursuit of peace through commerce and partnership. We paid for it.'

Another pause.

'And who was it that marched with you into the west to annihilate the humans? Who was it that took up arms, bled and died alongside you? Many races did. But none with more commitment, none with more solidarity, and none with greater numbers than the dwarves. We were with you every step of the way. Until the end. We were there with you to see the destruction of an entire race. A blood-letting heretofore unheard of. We were there with you. And we shared in the burden of that terrible act.' He raised a finger in the air. 'But, I have begun to doubt the wisdom of our actions. I fear all we have done is sown the seeds of our own destruction!'

There was a collective intake of breath, then an outcry across the chamber as elves hissed their shock at his implication.

'Peace! Be at peace,' cried the Speaker.

'There are those of you who want nothing less!' Marmus shouted, holding his hands wide. 'You deny it?'

Damn but the dwarf was going for it.

Voices answered him from across the chamber.

'This is an outrage!'

'Proof. Give us proof!'

'How dare you accuse us!'

Marmus looked like he was grinning.

'Proof? I have received word that the breakout was orchestrated, not by the humans. But by someone working for a Member of this very Parliament. And that Member, I can assure you, was not working alone.'

'Lies!'

'Name them!'

Fillion's eyes opened wide. Shit. Would Marmus implicate him? But they were friends, weren't they? But Fillion could hardly use that as a reason. His mind raced, preparing to act with as much outrage as the gathering below him, already formulating his denials.

'You want me to name them?' asked Marmus, cupping his ear. Fillion was genuinely amazed. Marmus was like a dwarf possessed. He was bloody enjoying himself. 'You want me to name the elf who encouraged the humans to revolt? Who told them that they were to be slaughtered if they did not?' He pointed his finger at the front row. 'There she is! Member Tekla. And there ...' He moved his finger higher. 'Her co-conspirator. Member Patiir!' The chamber was in an uproar. Marmus was drowned out, his words meaningless. But the damage was done. And Fillion felt some of his tension abate. He was not implicated.

Fillion looked at Tekla. She had stood and was gesticulating at Marmus. He switched his stare to Patiir. He was surrounded by Members leaning in and speaking into his ear. For his part, he was studying

Marmus, stroking his chin, and for all the world looking as calm and collected as he always did.

'There is a game afoot,' said Patiir. He leaned back in his chair and regarded Fillion closely. 'What do think?'

Fillion shrugged.

'I don't know what to think. Our contact with Marmus was limited at best. Kanyay never suggested there was anything like this planned.'

'He was never going to be the most reliable of go-betweens,' said Patiir. 'Even so, I feel an element of regret. Perhaps I should have made more of an effort to keep talking to Marmus.'

That was a surprising piece of contrition from the old elf.

'What could we have done? Our position was clear,' said Fillion.

'True. We were the accusers. And their guilt was obvious.'

'And they did not have a leg to stand on. So they did the only thing they could. They tried to turn it around. Shifted the blame.' Fillion felt it best to be as supportive as he could.

'It's an ages-old tactic,' agreed Patiir. 'Yet it leaves them with nowhere to go. Marmus has effectively accused us, the whole elf race, of deliberately engineering a massacre as punishment for their actions.'

'What are the options?' asked Fillion.

Patiir raised his hands.

'You tell me, Sabin. I would think they are obvious.'

Fillion puffed his cheeks and blew out the air. 'We deny it. They, at best, withdraw all relations with us. At worst ...'

Patiir nodded. 'Go on.'

'War.'

Patiir remained silent, a faint smile on his lips.

'But that is unthinkable,' pleaded Fillion.

'It is unwanted, but not unthinkable, Sabin,' Patiir replied. 'I had no agenda beyond justice and reparation for their actions, as well you know.

I expected them to offer, with some resistance, payment of some kind. Trade deals and the like, hence Tekla's involvement.'

'May I sit?' asked Fillion, eager to show his exhaustion. Patiir nodded his assent. 'Is this situation recoverable?'

'Ah, that is the question. We have not had a situation like this for many centuries, not since we reached an accord with our woodland kin. I must go and speak to Tekla. Together we will seek an audience with the King. I imagine a summons will be issued shortly, but I prefer to stay ahead of that.'

'What will you tell the King?'

Patiir steepled his fingers and rested his lips against them for a moment. 'I will tell him that our position has not changed. That the dwarves brought this on themselves. And I will also say that I believe there is something else.'

Fillion leaned forward. 'Something else?'

'This is a desperate gambit that Marmus has played. Does the mandate come from the dwarf Council? He brings us to the brink. It is not like him. Therefore, he must have a motivation. The dwarves are stubborn, yes. They never forget a slight, yes. But he accuses us without evidence. So, again, I find myself asking: why? What does he know?'

'There was no plan, Patiir,' replied Fillion. 'We never wanted this.'

'No, we did not. Yet, something has convinced Marmus that our intentions went far beyond the truth of it. Marmus is pragmatic, a politician; yet his actions are far beyond rational.'

'That I agree with. It is not like him,' said Fillion. Though considering the truth, he felt Marmus had it spot on.

Patiir stood. 'We will discover the facts, in due time. But right now, I am accused of warmongering. It is something I must answer. Fillion, please stay at your post until I return. There will be any number of visitors.'

'Yes, Patiir. And what should I tell them?'

'The truth. I have gone to speak to the King.'

Fillion inclined his head and watched Patiir sweep out of his office.

He sat back and placed the palms of his hands on to his thighs. He breathed deeply. Events were starting to move out of his control. All he could do was look to nudge where possible, speculate, drop hints and generally stir as much as he dare. He could do that, yes. All in all, a good day.

CHAPTER THIRTY-ONE – OWEN

It took them the best part of a week to return to Eagle's Rest, Owen did not want to push Jussi and Ayolf too hard. He felt for Larsen and the others. Their trek was longer, and through gnome territory, though plenty enough of those bastards had been cleared over the last year. He liked to imagine the gnomes now thought the lands to be haunted. And what would the elves be thinking? It was an audacious strike, moving through Celtebaria and into the borders of the wood elf territories, but it had been worth every league they had travelled. He felt, for the first time in a long time, light of heart. Rationally, it made no sense to feel that way, but emotionally, he believed that finally they were doing something positive. They weren't running and hiding anymore. It made him feel more human. That they were reclaiming some lost part of themselves. *Hah!* Listen to him, Owen Derle, the great philosopher.

They flew along the ridge path, keeping low. They waved to the watcher in the gate tower and did a wide circle over the settlement. He spotted Jenni standing at the steps to the hall and Arno dipped his wings. She raised her hand in greeting.

A gaggle of children burst from the hall and ran down the steps, screaming and clapping cheerfully as Jussi swooped even lower than Owen. Someone was showing off.

'*Come along, you. Ayolf needs his rest.*'

'*He's the one chasing the praise, Owen!*'

He took Arno round to the roosting barn and he landed with practiced ease. Jussi joined him a few moments later. They got to work, stripping the gear from their birds.

'Need some help?' asked Jenni, from the doorway.

'It's fine, we're almost done,' replied Owen.

'Suit yourself,' she said with a brief smile. 'Where is everyone else?'

Her tone was easy and relaxed. And Owen knew it was completely forced.

'On their way back. It went better than we hoped. He knelt and undid a strap, yanking it free and hauling off the saddle. Arno did a little wiggle, happy to be relieved of the weight. Owen carried it away to the shaped shelves on the far wall. 'We lost two of the Erebeshi.' He placed it down and turned to look at Jenni. Her lips were drawn tight. She locked eyes with him, and he looked back, holding her gaze. This was the way it was now.

'And Ayolf got a hole right through his wing,' he said, deliberately ending the moment.

'Is he alright?' she asked walking over to his stall.

'He'll be fine,' said Jussi. 'Just a flesh wound. Still big and strong enough to get me back here. Weren't you, boy?' He pointed at the ragged area on his folded wing.

Jenni hissed through her teeth in sympathy. 'We got some coneys, if they'd like? They're hanging up just over there.'

'Great,' said Jussi. 'Hey, Owen, you go ahead, I'll feed them.'

'Good plan,' said Owen. 'I'll see you inside.'

He left Jussi fetching the rabbits, and together he and Jenni walked across the square to the hall. The children had disappeared back inside. A woman was carrying a basket down the steps. He could hear banging coming from the carpenter's workshop next to the smithy. He looked towards the gate. It was shut and barred.

'It's quiet around here,' he said.

'Not so many of us around,' she replied.

He supposed not.

'How are they getting on?' he asked, not needing to expand.

She shrugged.

'Best as can be expected. Some are trying harder than others. A lot still keep to themselves, but they contribute.'

'Uh-huh.' Three of them had gone with Larsen. They had fought. That counted for something in his book.

They climbed the stairs, and entered the hall. Inside it was cool and gloomy, the firepit was banked low and a kettle hung over it.

'Tea?' she asked.

'Ale?'

She smirked. 'Ale.'

He took a place at the nearest table. Jenni returned with a jug and two cups. She set them down, took a seat and poured out the ale. She raised a cup and Owen followed suit. Then they drank.

'It's good to see you, Owen.'

'It's good to be back.'

'But you didn't need to be the one to escort Jussi home. The lad is old and bold enough to take care of himself. He's grown up fast.'

'He's not that grown up,' Owen said, smiling.

'Perhaps not, but tell me anyway, why have you come back? And don't say it's because you're worried about us,' she said, wagging a finger at him.

Owen took another drink then set the cup down. He placed his arms out in front of him and laid them on the table, clasping his hands together.

'You know better than anyone how I feel about this place. How I feel about the war, those we lost. You are all following me, even though I promised nothing more than a chance for vengeance. Not victory. Just a way to make them bleed. But that attack on the wood elves ... we did well. I was pleased. But then I got to thinking. I want more. I want to win.'

Jenni picked up her mug, took a mouthful and then studied him over its rim.

'How do we do that, Owen? Leave it a thousand years and breed like devils until we have the numbers? You don't want to wait that long. So, tell me. What do you have in mind?'

Owen grinned. She was going to love this.

'We need allies.'

CHAPTER THIRTY-TWO – FILLION

Fillion nodded his thanks to the messenger, a young Servant employed by the Parliament, who carried a large satchel full of missives. Not such an unusual sight these days, what with things being as they were.

'Here, take these,' he said, in turn passing over a fistful of letters. Each one was addressed to another Servant of one of the Members, offering up small, often subtle insights into the mind of Patiir. It had come to him rather late, this revelation, that by association he wielded no small measure of influence. Since the troubles between elf and dwarf began he had been courted by plenty – always Servants and other functionaries – seeking information and leverage. Much of this he did with Patiir's consent, but there were some things he undertook alone. His time spent learning the Members, their loyalties, rivalries and agendas had paid off, and he knew who he could reach out to, who might welcome his discreet contact. He had to admit, he was enjoying himself.

'Have you heard?'

'Hmm?'

'Have you heard what has happened?' asked Ezra, framed by the doorway to Fillion's office.

'No. What?'

'It'll be in that pile.'

Fillion started to sort through the notes.

'Just let me tell you,' said Ezra, marching in and taking a seat.

'Come in,' said Fillion.

'It's the wood elves,' said Ezra, ignoring the sarcasm. Like Fillion, Ezra had found himself in the thick of things and was in his element. *Smug git.*

'What about them?'

'They have been attacked.' Ezra's face grave but his eyes flashing with excitement.

What?

'Who by?'

'Humans.'

What?

'How can that be? The slaves?' he asked.

'Who else can it be?' asked Ezra. 'They attacked a settlement right on the western borders of wood elf lands. Caused mayhem.'

Fillion scratched his head vigorously. *How? Why?* It made no sense.

'But they were headed due west. Don't tell me they made a detour.'

Ezra threw his hands up. 'Who knows? These are just the first reports coming through. It's all very sketchy and quite frankly damned confusing. They said they were hit by organised forces. Cavalry, fliers.'

'That's nonsense,' said Fillion.

'That's what I said,' agreed Ezra. 'You were there, you saw. No such force exists.'

'All the human armies were defeated, destroyed. And fliers? The Eagle Riders are all gone,' said Fillion, doing his best to not sound rueful. 'The reports are wrong.'

'Try telling that to Kanyay,' said Ezra.

Ah. Kanyay would not be taking this well.

'Where is he?' said Fillion as he stood up.

'He was last seen heading towards the Palace.'

Fillion squeezed his eyes shut. He could imagine what was going on.

'I'll need to go find him before he punches someone.' Fillion moved around his desk and made for the door.

'As long as he doesn't try to punch the King,' said Ezra

Fillion stopped. 'He just might.'

'Then I must see it,' Ezra announced, pushing past him.

Together they walked along the concourse, as crowded and purposeful as it always was. Many elves looked their way, some calling out questions relating to the attack. News, when it arrived at the seat of power, travelled fast, Fillion mused. He also wondered at this attack. It truly did not make any sense. The reports from the pursuing elven column, and what they had gleaned from the dwarves before they had stopped sharing information, was clear. The humans were heading resolutely westwards, trying to get as far away as they could. They had already lost so many, why would they risk any more? Perhaps some kind of splinter group or a diversionary force, deliberately buying time for the others? Or perhaps there was a simpler motivation, one he could easily recognise. They wanted to hurt the elves and the dwarves and anyone else they could find. Kill as many as they could before they themselves were cut down. He could understand that, though his desire to die in the process had receded somewhat. He had other responsibilities now.

He and Ezra were on the boulevard heading towards the palace. Coming the other way, under the escort of four palace guards, was Kanyay, marching sullenly in the chevron-shaped box created by the four warriors, their helmet face-pieces locked in place. Clearly they were not taking any chances. Ezra leaned into Fillion and whispered quietly. 'Let me do the talking.' He held his hands up to stop them, and in response the lead guard ordered the squad to a halt. 'I see you have found our friend,' said Ezra. 'We were just looking for him.'

'And now you can say goodbye, Servant,' replied the guard curtly. 'He was detained trying to demand his way into the King's residence with no invitation.'

'Surely not an arrestable offence,' said Ezra evenly.

'It is when you aim a punch at one of my elves.'

'Ah, regrettable,' said Ezra with a sympathetic nod. 'He is not in his right mind. He has had terrible news and wished to speak to the King.'

'Then he should have gone through the proper channels,' said the guard. 'Now stand aside. A week in gaol and he may well see daylight again if he behaves.' He made to step onwards but Ezra raised his hand again. Fillion could tell the guard's hackles were up. His posture changed, his back straighter, ready to fight.

'Indeed he should have, good sir, but as I said, he has received news that his people have suffered a devastating attack. By human renegades no less! Can you imagine? Tell me, did you fight? My colleague, the Servant to Member Patiir, was there. He can tell you all about the savagery of the humans.' Fillion knew, as did Ezra, that the Palace guard had stayed at home – they had no part in the fighting, and he also knew that it grated on them. The guard opened his mouth to speak but Ezra ploughed on. 'So you can imagine that both Member Patiir and my own Member, the good lady Tekla, have nothing but sympathy for our brother Servant's situation. Hence our haste in coming to you. Even now they petition to see His Majesty.' He reached out a hand and clasped the guard's armoured shoulder. A ballsy move, Fillion had to admit. 'You did absolutely the right thing in bringing him to us. And the King will, no doubt, be equally as concerned to see the representative of the wood elves to deliver his most heartfelt sorrow at the news. The King, after all, values the good relations of our woodland kin, no matter how … hot headed, they can sometimes be.' The guard looked at Ezra's hand. The Servant removed it slowly with a friendly smile.

Fillion watched and waited for the response, which was slow in coming. Ezra had effectively deployed his full arsenal of influence on this. The guard bored a hole into Ezra with his stare. The scowl behind his facemask evident from the squint of his eyes and the downward curve of his brows. Finally he nodded his assent with a shrug of his shoulders. 'Very well. You may have him. But be warned. If I see him lurking anywhere near the palace without an official invitation, he'll be in chains for a month.' He stepped to one side and motioned Kanyay forward. As the wood elf walked by he gave the guard his best shit-eating grin, his pointed teeth flashing white.

'Kanyay, play nice,' warned Fillion.

The guard led his squad away, muttering something about crazy wood elves.

Kanyay stood with his arms folded regarding the pair of them. 'I suppose you want my thanks?'

'Not at all,' said Ezra. 'We Servants need to look out for each other.'

'Be that as it may,' said Fillion. 'You do owe Ezra some gratitude. I would not have been so persuasive, and likely ended up in the gaol with you.'

Kanyay shook his head sourly. 'Fine. Thank you, Ezra.'

The Servant inclined his head graciously. 'You are most welcome. Now, perhaps you can tell us what you know of the tragic events that have unfolded.'

'Very well. But I need a drink,' said Kanyay.

Fillion was not surprised.

They repaired to The Silver Chalice, taking their usual booth. Ezra continued to accompany them, and as much as Fillion would have wanted to speak to Kanyay alone, he could not ignore the Servant's intervention. Once a flagon of wine had been shared out and Kanyay had drunk his first measure in one go, he became a little more talkative.

'A messenger came a little over an hour ago. A member of my own tribe. He had ridden for two days; his horse was all but dead under him. He brought tidings that struck my heart. The tribe of the Four Winds had been attacked, massacred. Barely half a dozen survivors escaped.'

'And it was humans, you say?' asked Ezra, leaning in close. Fillion noted he had not touched his wine.

'Aye,' said Kanyay bitterly. 'Humans.' He took another long drink, then slammed his cup down and wiped his mouth with the back of his hand. 'Humans that those damned dwarves let escape.'

'You are sure it was them?' asked Fillion.

'Who else could it be?' Kanyay collected the flagon and poured himself a third.

'But we heard something about fliers? Cavalry?' added Ezra.

Kanyay waved a hand. 'So he said, but that must be horseshit. There are no other humans left.' He took another drink.

'Kanyay, I am so saddened and sorry. If only we had acted sooner. If only we had made the dwarves see sense,' said Fillion.

'Too late, Sabin. It's all too late. I wanted to see the King, I wanted to demand he do something. To show his support, to act!'

'And I am sure he will,' said Ezra.

'You don't understand, old one,' said Kanyay, as Ezra raised an eyebrow at the epithet. 'The news has spread to the wood elf tribes. They, I, want vengeance.'

'We all want that,' agreed Ezra, but Kanyay was looking directly at Fillion and he knew what that meant. 'The King will order a larger mobilisation to hunt down these renegades,' finished Ezra.

'He doesn't mean them,' said Fillion, quietly.

'We'll hunt the humans down, be sure of it,' said Kanyay. 'It's the fucking dwarves.'

'Kanyay!' said Ezra, in shock, whether from the language or the implication, Fillion wasn't sure.

'My people know. They know because I do my part. They know it was the dwarves who are to blame for this. My people will want blood.'

'But Ambassador Marmus is your friend,' said Ezra.

Kanyay was looking at Fillion again. *Careful, Kanyay.*

'Yes he is my friend. And did I not also play my part for you, Sabin? For your Member? Did I not carry messages to him? Did I not speak for you?'

'Yes, you did, Kanyay,' said Fillion, trying to steer him away. 'But–'

'But nothing, Sabin. All your secret trysts and meetings with him do not count for anything. He says the elves are to blame, that they are at fault. Why he thinks that I cannot say, and I care even less,' Kanyay said angrily. 'The dwarves are to blame. My people will believe no differently.'

Fillion sat back. He glanced at Ezra. The old elf was looking right back at him. His face was set in an odd way, like he was looking at Fillion for the first time, like he was assessing him. *Dammit, Kanyay.* The wood elf had said too much. He had to fix this.

'I only tried to keep relations going, Kanyay. Neither I nor Marmus want a war. There has been enough bloodshed already,' he said passionately.

'And there'll be more, Sabin. Much more.' Kanyay drained his mug. 'I will not stay here any longer. My place is with my people. You can debate and argue, but we will prepare for vengeance. We will hunt down the humans and we will extract our due from the dwarves.' He stood. 'I do not blame you, Sabin. I do not even blame Marmus. But this path is set. Fare you well.'

Fillion rose and reached for Kanyay's arm, but the elf shook him off.

'Please, Kanyay,' said Fillion. 'There must be another way.'

Kanyay shook his head. 'If you wish, seek me out, ride with us. You would be welcome.' With that he stalked from the inn.

Fillion stood there for a moment, knowing the eyes of everyone were on him. He hoped Ezra took that final act as something sincere and honest. He heard Ezra stand up. The elf took position in front of him, his hands clasped behind his back. He looked stern.

'Well, friend Sabin. Can things get much worse?'

'I imagine they can,' said Fillion heavily. He looked at the table and tilted his head towards the wine. 'Will you join me?'

Ezra shook his head. 'I will leave you to your thoughts. I believe Member Tekla will want to know what our woodland kin are planning. I think perhaps, you might consider doing the same for Member Patiir,' he advised. 'I will see you later, Sabin.'

Fillion bowed gently and Ezra inclined his head fractionally, an odd quirk to his lips, and then he, too, departed. Fillion returned to his seat and experienced a vague unease. Had Kanyay said too much in mentioning the secret meetings? Surely not. After all he had only been doing what Patiir had told him to do.

He looked into his cup and with a rotation of his hands swirled its contents, watching a little whirlpool form. Then he brought it to his lips and tipped back the contents, swallowing it in one go. Things had most certainly come to a head.

CHAPTER THIRTY-THREE – MICHAEL

A week after his battle with Eilion, Father Michael was roused from his slumber by a very agitated Father Llews.

'Father Michael. We have arrived at the borders of New Tissan. I have come to collect you as requested.'

Father Michael nodded. 'Thank you, Father. I am in your debt.'

Father Llews waved his hands. 'Nonsense, nonsense. You must see this.'

Father Michael braced his arms against the travois and started to push himself up. Within moments two sets of large, muscular arms took hold of his and, surprisingly gently, took his weight. His two attendant Nidhal, one of whom was his old sparring partner Weguek, guided him upright. When he was steady, the older Nidhal handed him a crude but sturdy crutch. He looked at both his helpers in turn, and bowed his head. 'Naska. Naska.' *Thank you.* The Nidhal bowed theirs in return, then took up flanking positions just behind him as he turned to face the head of the column. Another Nidhal, this one skinny as a rake, his head, ears and nose covered in fetishes and bone piercings, hurried over and stood in front of Father Michael with a critical eye. It was Gantak, Nutaaq's head shaman. He leaned close to inspect the tightly wrapped bandages around Father Michael's torso. He reached out a digit and Father Michael tensed. The shaman growled and shook his head disapprovingly at Father Michael before pressing his finger on to the bandage. Father Michael hissed as the pain blossomed. Gantak appraised the dressing, obviously waiting to see if any leakage stained the cloth. Father Michael looked down. Nothing showed itself.

'Yag?' asked Father Michael.

Gantak sighed and growled out something. Then he looked Father Michael in the eye. 'Yag.'

'Thanks. Ah, Naska,' Father Michael replied.

Scowling, Gantak stepped aside and allowed Father Michael to pass, Father Llews hanging excitedly by his side and his two Nidhal following behind.

As Father Michael swung his way onwards, sweating with the effort of moving and fighting back the sharp, stinging pain in his side, he had to give it to the Nidhal's shamans. They had skill. No Tissan surgeon could have done what they did. Not out here in the wilds.

He made his slow progression along the Nidhal column, nodding occasionally to those he recognised. Most remained mounted, and kept their vargr in check when the creatures caught wind of Father Michael, any old familiarity lost to the scent of his wounded body.

A minute more's hobbling got him to where the Emperor stood, his hand resting against his mount's head. Next to him stood Cadarn. Hilja was a short way off to the side, a respectful distance being kept between her and the vargr. In the sky, the other eagles were patrolling in wide circles, riding the thermals.

To his other side was Ellen, her hands clasped behind her back, with Nutaaq a little way behind her. Of the Empress, there was no sign.

The Emperor turned as he approached, an eyebrow raised. 'Ah, Father. Stubborn as always. Good, good. You should see this.' He beckoned him forward and Cadarn made a space for him.

He took his position and looked out over the planted fields of New Tissan. The place looked empty. No one worked the fields. No one stood watch.

'What does this mean?' Father Michael asked.

'It means that they know we are here,' said the Emperor.

'My Riders report that there is a large gathering in the square,' said Cadarn to Father Michael.

'Where else would they be?' said the Emperor.

'They could have cut and run,' said Father Michael.

The Emperor shook his head. 'That is not Yarn's way. I misjudged her. In many matters. But I have never thought her a coward.'

'Your Grace?' asked Ellen, quietly. The Emperor stiffened at her voice but responded evenly.

'Yes?'

'Nutaaq wishes to know if we are going to storm the town.' She was tentative, almost apologetic in her tone. It had been that way since her return to the fold. As far as Father Michael could see it, the Emperor suffered her presence out of necessity. That she was the one who talked Nutaaq into riding to his aid gave her little credit. But she was a Gifted, and therefore tainted. Unfortunately she was also still the only one who could communicate effectively with their allies. Whatever she might be, Father Michael found he held no ill will towards the girl. She had not let them down.

'We will ride into town. This is still New Tissan, my capital. I mean to retake it, not raze it to the ground.'

'Yes, Your Grace.' Ellen turned towards Nutaaq.

'Come along,' said the Emperor, placing a hand on Father Michael's shoulder.

Together they slowly walked back along the line of Nidhal. Midway along they stopped by a large wagon drawn by two draft horses. It was a ramshackle affair with a hide roof covering the wagon bed. It had been given to Gantak as his home on the move, but had been requisitioned to house the Empress. She sat next to the shaman, a strange look on her face. Father Michael had already surmised she was still in a state of shock, especially at the rough living she had had to endure. And the smell.

'Help him up,' ordered the Emperor to Father Michael's Nidhal attendants. They did not need to understand the human tongue to know what to do.

'I'll see you inside,' said the Emperor. He walked back to the head of the column, where another draft horse was waiting for him. Both he and Ellen would ride at the head of the column.

With a fair amount of pushing and pulling, Father Michael was hauled up on to the wagon's bench and settled himself next to Gantak.

He nodded to the Empress. 'Your Grace, are you well?' he asked.

The Empress struggled with the effort to be gracious. 'Yes, quite well.

This nightmare will soon be over. Father Llews has told me that we will soon avenge ourselves.'

'I am sure,' said Father Michael, loyally.

Father Llews jogged past. A few moments later Father Michael could hear him climbing into the back of the wagon.

A horn sounded from the front of the line, and the vargr padded forwards. With a growl, Gantak shook the reins and the horses started to move.

Father Michael cursed as he was jolted back in his seat, a sharp pain in his side. He caught Gantak eyeing him.

'I'm fine!' said Father Michael.

Gantak grunted and turned back to his driving.

The column made its way along the track leading into the town proper. As they passed by the first of the dwellings, Father Michael scanned for any movement but he saw none. They penetrated further now, passing the larger structures, the houses, barns and workshops. And here, finally, he saw signs of life. Faces watching from the shadows, from half open doorways. Fearful, afraid. But why should they be? Their Emperor had returned.

Further in they went, and on the final stretch to the square, the column halted once more. Father Michael carefully took hold of the bench and leaned out to the side. He could see a gathering at the front. A number of Tissans on foot. He squinted. They looked like soldiers. They were armed at least. Words were being exchanged with the Emperor. After a few more moments, the column started again and the group of Tissans, fell into step with the Nidhal. Finally. Someone had decided now was the time to rise up in support of their lord.

The column filed into the square. As the wagon followed them in, he saw the Nidhal were forming a line, facing northwards, towards the Emperor's old cabin. The wagon rolled on and parked up behind the centre of the line. The following Nidhal and their mounts padded past to continue to extend the line to the other side of the square. But Father Michael only had eyes for what waited for them.

The Empress gasped and put a hand to her mouth.

'Oh my Emperor,' mouthed Father Llews, as he craned his neck around the hide coverings.

Father Michael looked for his helpers. He couldn't see them but he would be damned to sit here and wait. He lowered his crutch down, and then shifted his legs so they hung over the side. His teeth already gritted from the pain he started to push himself off. His arms shook as his weakened muscles betrayed him and he started to lose control. Just as he was going to tumble off the wagon, Weguek appeared and caught him.

'Aaaah, shit!' Father Michael cursed, as he grasped the Nidhal's shoulders.

'Yag?' asked Weguek, concern in his eyes. 'Tak?'

Father Michael took a few deep breaths.

'Tak,' he whispered. 'Yag. Yag.'

Weguek released him and gathered the crutch.

Father Michael took it, and made his way through the Nidhal to join his Emperor. He was surrounded by a clutch of armed men and women. Remnants of the Imperial army who must have survived the Gifted's purge. They looked pissed off and determined in equal measure.

Father Michael stopped by the Emperor's horse and looked on at the welcome gathering.

Yarn stood on the podium wearing her armour and flanked by two Gifted. A huge crowd of Tissans were arrayed to either side of the platform, and in front of them a line of a further twenty Gifted stood at the ready, shields locked tight to their chests and spears held horizontally. In front of each one, were two citizens of the Empire, a man and a woman, on their knees facing towards the new arrivals.

'Your Grace, you have returned to us,' said Yarn loudly.

'And I have not come alone,' replied the Emperor.

'Indeed not. I have been looking forward to meeting our new allies. Thank you for bringing them. We have much to discuss,' she said in a friendly tone.

'You have nothing to discuss. Though I will hear your plea for mercy.'

'I will plead for mercy, Your Grace, but not for me or mine. I beg you to consider what you face,' Yarn said, gesturing at the kneeling Tissans and then at the crowd. 'If you do not consent to return to rule with my guidance and counsel, then I am forced with offering you another lesson. One which I had thought you might have already learned.'

She nodded her head and the Gifted took a step forward in unison. Behind them the crowd shifted. Father Michael heard a wail. Someone began to sob.

'Each man and woman are parents to at least two children …' Yarn let the statement hang.

'I have three hundred Nidhal. I have Eagle Riders. I have loyal soldiers about me. You are outnumbered,' replied the Emperor.

'Numbers do not matter, Your Grace. If you attack, many, many, of your loyal citizenry will die. All because you are too blind. Because you are too arrogant. How many more have to die because of your selfishness, your greed. Is not an Empire's death enough for the line of Living Gods?' she spat.

Father Michael was shocked rigid. The Emperor was silent for a moment. Then he slowly, deliberately climbed off his horse. He pushed past Father Michael and went to stand midway between the two groups.

'Yarn. You are fool. You have played a desperate hand. You thought I might be cowed into submission at the sight of my beloved people under threat. You have it wrong.'

Father Michael was alerted to a ruckus coming from the eastern exit of the square. A few moments later a gaggle of marines burst into view. At their head was Corporal, no, Sergeant Fenner.

As his people took up firing positions, Fenner saluted. 'Admiral sends his regards, Sir.'

The Emperor raised a hand in acknowledgement.

'You see, Yarn? You see what your malformed Gifted brain has failed to understand?' he asked.

Yarn shook her head. 'Enlighten me with your wisdom, Your Grace.'

'My people love me. They love me so much they are prepared to fight and die for me.' He turned and pointed at Father Michael. 'Look. Look at the Father here. He embraced death willingly to save my life. He sacrificed himself to kill your best, the traitor Eilion. And yet, here he stands. Saved by the skills of the Nidhal and the love of his grateful Emperor. How many Gifted have you lost now? Your numbers are growing thin.'

Yarn folded her arms and shook her head. 'You are truly mad,' she said quietly.

'I am? Who is the one who thought she could defy her Emperor? Look at what you are threatening to do? You would kill innocents? To prove a point? You would slaughter them?' He took another step forward. 'I will not submit. I will order my warriors to charge and you will kill countless Tissans. And then you will die. And what will it all be for? My people love me. They follow me. If they must die, they die for me. Not for you.' He took another step closer. Father Michael tensed. The Emperor was getting too close.

'How much more blood do you want on your hands? Your gambit has failed. I will not stand down. I ask you again. How much blood?'

The Cardinal did not respond. She looked at the Gifted beside her. At those below. And at the crowd of Tissans who, in turn looked at her with anger and fear. The Emperor raised a hand and, as one, the gathered Nidhal nocked arrows and raised their bows.

The crowd let out a collective gasp.

Yarn sighed heavily.

'You would kill us all? All the Gifted?'

The Emperor barked out a laugh.

'Kill you? You think you deserve death? You deserve punishment.'

'Not all participated in the actions I ordered.'

'And none of them tried to stop you.'

Yarn lowered her hands to her sides.

'Very well. I will not see the people of New Tissan shed any more blood for a failed enterprise. You might wish to consider that … Your Grace.' She looked once more at her Gifted then hung her head. 'All of you stand down.'

Those on the ground shifted and looked at each other. One of the Gifted on the platform stepped up to her and whispered in her ear. She raised a hand, and muttered something Father Michael could not make out.

She looked up and faced the Emperor. Once more she gave the order. 'I said, stand down! Lower your weapons. We are not the monsters here.'

Slowly, one by one, the Gifted stepped back from the kneeling Tissans. They began dropping shields and spears, unbuckling sword belts and removing helmets. Then they clustered together. There were murmurings in the crowd, growing in volume. Those on the ground looked back at their captors, and realising they were released, helped each other up and hurried away from the standoff. Voices were raised, shouts against the Gifted and for the Emperor rang out. Father Michael sensed the people's manner was becoming ugly, promising violence. That was another thing he had learned in the arena.

The Emperor turned to Cadarn and beckoned him over. 'Use the soldiers and marines, take the Gifted into custody.'

'Yes, Your Grace,' said Cadarn.

'Also,' said the Emperor, looking hard at Yarn. 'I want you to separate the Shapers from the others. Take them to one side. And then kill them.'

'My Lord,' said Cadarn. 'Are you–?'

'Do it in front of the others. I don't care how you do it. Shoot them, I suppose. The marines have their crossbows. But not Yarn. Keep her with the others, for now. I want her to live.'

Cadarn hesitated for one moment and the Emperor turned his head sharply to look at him. 'Do you understand?'

Cadarn nodded. 'Yes, my Lord.' He called forward the gathered soldiers and marines. He raised a hand and beckoned Fenner and his command over as well. Father Michael listened in.

'We have to get control of this situation, quickly. Sergeant Fenner, please take command of the soldiers here. I will take your marines with me and put the Gifted in custody.'

'I should stay with my people,' protested Fenner.

Cadarn raised a hand.

'The Emperor has given me the responsibility. Just do it, Sergeant.'

Fenner, his face reddening, closed his mouth and nodded.

'As you say, Sir. Alright marines, follow the Leader here. Take good care of them Gifted. The rest of you lot, follow me. We need to disperse this crowd before things go tits up.'

The group of soldiers and marines split up and headed for the Gifted. Cadarn was barking orders at the marines who began to form a circle around the Gifted. Yarn and her companions dismounted the podium.

Someone touched Father Michael's left arm and he flinched despite himself. He looked down at Ellen. Her face was grave. 'I just wanted to say, I'm sorry. I would never have wanted this to happen.'

Father Michael nodded. 'I know, but if you had been here, you would have followed her orders. What choice would you have had?'

Ellen shrugged. 'It seems to me we always have a choice.'

'Perhaps you are right.'

Ellen smiled a sad smile. 'Anyway. I've come to say goodbye. I'm sure the Emperor will not want me around anymore.'

She turned to go.

He reached out with his free hand and grabbed her shoulder.

'Wait.'

There was no need for this.

'Emperor?' he called. 'Your Grace?'

The Emperor turned and Father Michael hobbled forward a few steps. 'What orders should Ellen pass to the Nidhal? I'm sure Nutaaq will want to know how things will play out now that you have regained your rightful place.'

The Emperor tilted his head and for a moment he looked angry and then thoughtful. He stared hard at Ellen.

'You are to inform Nutaaq that all is well. You are to tell him that I am grateful for all his support and that I invite him and his Nidhal to set a camp. Tonight, there will be a feast in his honour. I will bring the ale.'

Ellen nodded. 'At once, Your Grace.'

She turned to go and sent a grateful smile Father Michael's way.

The Emperor looked around the gathering. 'Father Llews?'

'Yes, Your Grace?' said Father Llews, scurrying up nervously from between two growling vargr.

'You said you knew the blacksmiths?'

'Yes, Your Grace. I have spent much time with them. I enjoyed watching them work.'

'Go to them. Explain to them the design of the collars. Take with you some of the soldiers to make the point. I want the first lot ready by tomorrow morning, as many as they can manage. She can have the first of them.' The Emperor pointed at Ellen.

'As you wish,' said Father Llews, bowing as he backed away. Father Michael watched him chase across to speak to Fenner.

'Father Michael,' said the Emperor, walking over to join him.

'Your Grace.'

'You have a sour look on your face. Do you not approve?'

'It's not my place to question your judgement, Your Grace,' said Father Michael.

'If only more thought that way,' replied the Emperor with a rueful smile. He turned to watch Father Llews chivvy along two soldiers. 'Now that we have returned, I find myself bereft of a council and indeed counsellors. I am lucky to have the good Father there. He represents the last of the Imperial religion – not counting yourself, Father. But I look upon you as something other. You are my strong, right arm.'

'Not so strong right now,' muttered Father Michael.

The Emperor laughed.

'Do not worry, you will have plenty of time to recover. Now, I must go and fetch my mother and take her home. Then I will get to work. I want us ready to sail in the spring.'

Father Michael watched the Emperor walk away. The Nidhal were already on the move, causing a fair degree of consternation among the townsfolk. Of course, this was the first time they had encountered the Nidhal. And they did take some getting used to. Weguek was hovering close by and Michael waved to him. He wondered if his tent was still where he left it. Otherwise he would have to bunk elsewhere. The Temple? No, he doubted he could take being so close to Father Llews. Perhaps Fenner could help. Ellen walked by, not noticing him in the milling crowds of Tissans and Nidhal. She was being trailed by two marines.

He sighed heavily.

CHAPTER THIRTY-FOUR – FILLION

Fillion walked along the concourse in no special hurry; the days had taken on a particular rhythm. He was busy, yes. Busier now than at any time he could remember, yet he felt adrift, as he had no investment in the work he was now doing. Every day was full of meetings, administering documents, fielding questions and looking after Patiir's calendar. The elven capital was galvanized in a way he had not before seen. There was a sense of purpose about the place. Not in any way a surprise, they were, in a very real sense, at war. Or at least preparing for one. The dwarf embassy had closed, and those within had returned home. That included Marmus. There had been no goodbyes, no messages, just a parade through the main route out of the city at midday. A line of carts carrying goods and supplies, clerks and embassy staff. Ahead and behind detachments of dwarf warriors, bearing all their arms and armour in a display guaranteed to make a point. And leading them all was Marmus. He wore his usual robes of office but, in keeping, he had a sword belted to his side and he kept the hand on the pommel as he rode past the Parliament. Breaking with his tradition of refusing to acknowledge those around him, this time he was free with his gaze, moving his head left and right, inviting those watching to make eye contact with him. That had included Fillion, as he stood at the bottom of the steps of Parliament, his mouth a little agape. There had been a brief locking of eyes, an almost imperceptible nod. And that was it. Fillion had turned to find Ezra watching him closely again. It was getting damned unnerving.

As Fillion neared his office, he caught himself sighing heavily. Marmus was gone, Kanyay was gone and it was lonely going to the inn each evening after his duties ended. It was nothing more than a habit, an attempt to recreate a more pleasurable time of his existence in the city.

But it never worked, and each time his stay was shorter than the last. So instead he would return home and take joy from his daughter. That little bundle was starting to grow now, and her inquisitiveness was matched only by the inordinate amount of feeding she insisted upon. Not something he could help with, that one, but he supported Nadena as best he could with giving Brynne as much attention as she wanted. And he was always there to put her down for the night, and again whenever she woke up crying in her crib.

As for his father-in-law, Patiir was tired, often exhausted. Fillion could see it in his eyes, the way he walked. Age, it would seem, was finally catching up with him. And why wouldn't it? His scheme and plans, enacted over many years, were unravelling, taking a course not of his making and certainly not for his profit. And he was more withdrawn. They worked together every day, conversed hourly, but it was far more formal than Fillion had been accustomed to. There was no warmth in Patiir now, certainly not at their offices and very little displayed when he returned home. What there was, it was perfunctory, like he was following a script.

'I have never seen him like this before,' Nadena had said to him one evening.

'It is the strain of his work,' he had replied. 'It is affecting us all. The King is not happy. He feels he has been manoeuvred into a situation not of his choosing. He may not be saying it outright but he blames Patiir and Tekla and the rest of their cronies. The King does not want a war, and yet one appears to be coming.'

'Then why not just stop it? Apologise to the dwarves, send help to the wood elves, finish what we started against the humans,' she had suggested, worry clouding her face. 'I hate to see him like this.'

'I wish I could do something but it's a little late for all that,' he had responded. 'The dwarves will not listen. The trade routes have been blocked, nothing more comes from the north. They have effectively sealed their borders. And the wood elves? Like they have ever listened to reason.'

'Then talk to my father, Sabin. Ask him to step down, retire. Let others take on the burden, he has done enough.'

'You think for one minute he would let this go?' he replied, with a shake of his head.

She had not replied. It was really not necessary.

As he stepped into the office, he started a little to find Patiir standing by his desk.

'Patiir, what have I missed? Did we have a meeting?'

The elf looked at him, his mouth tight, his lips thin. He shook his head.

'No, Sabin. I was waiting for you, though. Please go to Member Tekla's office. She has some documents I need.'

Fillion scratched his head. Odd that another Servant could not have delivered them.

'Very well, Patiir,' he said with a tilt of his head. He turned and stopped, looking once more at Patiir. The elf hadn't moved. 'Are you alright?'

Patiir nodded stiffly.

'Yes. Just collect those papers.'

'As you wish.'

Fillion marched off, chewing his lips. Damned odd.

It took him only a couple of minutes to reach Member Tekla's expansive offices where he wandered in to find Ezra the only Servant in attendance. He looked up as Fillion entered, and smiling broadly, stood to greet him.

'Fillion. Good to see you. I missed you in session this morning.'

'Yes, likewise. My apologies, my duties got in the way.'

Ezra waved his hand. 'No matter. Not much occurred today. Although, word has reached us that our column has made contact with a force of wood elves. They are well within the old borders of the Tissan Empire and hope to locate and destroy the human renegades soon.'

They had been saying that for a while now. Nobody seemed that bothered. It was all about the dwarves, all about the lost trade and the dwindling profits.

'That is wonderful news,' he replied dutifully.

'Indeed. I suppose Patiir sent you for the papers?' asked Ezra.

'Yes. Not sure why though,' said Fillion.

'Ah, these are important,' said Ezra tapping his nose. 'Come along, the Member has them on her desk.' He walked over to the door to her private office and waited for Fillion to join him. As he arrived at Ezra's shoulder, the elf knocked twice at the door.

'Come in,' came the muffled reply.

Ezra opened the door and ushered Fillion inside.

Fillion stepped through and bowed towards Tekla, who sat behind her desk. He raised his head and several things made themselves plain to him. First was that Ezra had come in behind him and had closed the door, second that Tekla had a face like thunder, and third that she was flanked by two of the Parliament's guard. His senses started to ring a multitude of bells, but he continued with the pretence.

'Member Tekla. Member Patiir sent me. He said you had something?'

Member Tekla was silent for a moment. Her eyes were following Ezra as he stepped around from Fillion's right shoulder and stood facing him. His face was grave.

'Servant Sabin. We have questions for you,' announced Tekla.

Fillion looked at Tekla then back at Ezra. 'Ezra?'

Ezra adopted a solemn pose, his hands clasped together. 'Sabin. It pains me to ask this. In fact, I believe it is not even a matter of questioning. I simply wish you to take this opportunity to be honest. To admit what you have done.'

Fillion made a face of confusion even as he slipped one hand behind his back.

'What are you talking about?' he demanded.

Ezra shook his head.

'Sabin, Sabin. Please do not make this any harder.'

'Ezra, I need you to tell me what is happening here. What is it you think you know?' he asked.

He needed to brazen it out a few moments longer, get the measure of the situation. One thing was already obvious, the chances of this ending well were heading south, and fast.

'Get this over with,' Tekla commanded.

Ezra smiled at him sadly.

'I think you know, don't you, Sabin?' He took a small step closer. Good. That made it easier. Ezra pointed a finger at him. 'You know, I wasn't sure, not for some time. It was obvious that this whole situation felt contrived. But I couldn't quite place my finger why this all happened the way it did. But, after a while, I stopped asking that question and just focussed on the who.'

Fillion wrapped his fingers around the hilt of the dwarf-made dagger, the gift from Marmus, the blade he had taken to carrying beneath the folds of his Servant belt, ever since the incident with Kanyay. A sense, an intuition had told him that it would prove useful.

'What are you accusing me of?' Fillion asked. The two guards had not taken any aggressive steps forward yet, but it was moments away. They both carried their spears, the tips just a foot below the ceiling of the office. That was a mistake.

Ezra's finger remained fixed on him.

'I accuse you of nothing, Sabin. I am already far beyond that. I simply state that it has become obvious you are the source of the unrest.'

'What …? Why …?'

'That is what we will find out,' replied Ezra. 'But by a sheer process of elimination, of reasoning, it becomes apparent that you are the only one with the information, the knowledge and the connections to make this happen. You, Sabin, are at the centre of this hideous web.'

'This is madness!' said Fillion. He took a step towards Tekla. 'Patiir will be outraged when he hears of this.'

In response, Tekla stiffened, Ezra placed a restraining hand on his shoulder, and the two guards dropped their spears into a horizontal posture.

'You think he doesn't know?' hissed Ezra.

That was it. The game was done.

He reached out with his free hand, placed it over Ezra's and twisted. Ezra howled as Fillion pushed him to his knees. He pulled the dagger free and took up position behind the Servant, placed the blade against his throat and took a grip of his hair in his fist.

'Sabin!' shouted Tekla, rising from her chair. The two guards stepped forward and Ezra raised his hands to ward himself.

'Stop.' Fillion ordered Ezra and pressed the blade against the elf's skin. 'All of you, stop.'

Tekla raised a hand and the guards, now just a yard away, pulled up.

'You can't escape, Sabin,' whispered Ezra. 'It's too late.'

'I know,' replied Fillion. He drew the dagger hard against Ezra's throat, feeling the bite. It didn't have to be clean, just effective. As Tekla made a yelp, and the two guards lurched forwards, Fillion pushed the now limp Ezra into the guard coming to his left, and launched himself at the guard on the right.

He was quick enough to catch the elf by surprise, not quick enough to stop the spear from catching him in his side. He let it pass by him, using his momentum to carry him onwards, focusing on the guard.

He rammed his dagger into the unprotected left armpit and twisted. The guard howled and his knees buckled. Fillion pulled the dagger free, his hand covered in jetting blood.

He spun to face the second guard and took sharp blow to the side of his head … he saw stars, felt a stinging sensation. He scrambled back a few paces. The second guard was already recovering from his spear strike. The elf lifted the weapon and slashed upwards, the spear slicing into Fillion's left arm. He let out a garbled shout and backed up, assessing quickly. His dagger against the spearman was no good. The first guard was still on the floor, writhing in agony. Tekla was rooted to the spot watching in open-mouthed fascination.

He went for her.

He dodged around the desk, yanked the chair to one side, and pulled her into him, wrapping an arm around her neck, the dagger pressed against her side. She made a squeaking noise but did little to resist. The guard moved towards them.

'Easy,' he said. 'Easy. You want her to die too?'

The guard's purposeful advance slowed. His eyes flicked to Tekla. Fillion felt something warm and wet running down his neck.

The guard said nothing but his posture changed, his pulled back a little.

'Tekla. Do you want to live?'

The slightest of nods.

'Then order him to drop his spear.'

A pause.

'Order him to drop his spear,' he repeated.

'Do it.'

The guard stood a little straighter. He did not respond immediately. He understood better than Tekla what was happening here.

'Do it!' A little louder, a little more forcefully.

The guard bent his knees, and lowered his spear to the ground, not once taking his eyes off of Fillion.

'Now his sword.'

Another nod from Tekla and the guard pulled his sword free.

'Place it on the desk and back up, over there,' said Fillion, indicating the wall to the right.

The guard put the sword on the desk and stepped to the side. Fillion manoeuvred himself and Tekla around the desk. He now had the door to the outer office to his left, and the guard against the wall in front of him. The sword's hilt was inches away.

He leaned in close to Tekla, placing his mouth next to her ear.

'Elf bitch,' he whispered.

He pushed the dagger into her side hearing her draw a deep shuddering breath. Letting go he took up the sword and met the charge of the guard bringing the blade in a whipping downward arc, catching the raised arm of the guard as he attempted to block the swing. The guard barrelled past, exposing his rear.

Fillion brought the blade up into a high horizontal position and thrust it deep into the guard's back. The armour in his breastplate was ornate but thin, more ceremonial than practical. It was no good against a thrust of heavy steel.

Fillion leaned in as the sword punched through. He pulled it free and chopped down on to the guard's head, a crushing blow against his helmet. The guard sprawled on the floor, motionless.

Fillion forced himself upright. He was breathing heavily and the exploratory hand he placed against his side came back slick with blood. He was hurt bad. He turned and found Tekla, on the floor, her back against her desk. She had her hands covering the wound in her side. She looked at him with defiant eyes.

'Traitor,' she spat at him.

'Long live the Emperor. Long live Tissan,' he replied. And as a look of confusion came across her face, he thrust the sword into her stomach.

Letting go of the blade he tried to take stock. There was nothing else for him here. All he could do was attempt an escape. But was that even possible? Surely someone must have heard the fight?

He pressed up against the door. Trying to calm his breathing, he listened for alarms, shouting, or the sound of running feet. Yet nothing came. Was he in luck? Perhaps he was. After all, he was just a Servant. Perhaps Tekla and Ezra had been arrogant enough to believe he would have meekly submitted to just two guards. *Fucking idiots.* His wounds would soon start to make themselves known. He had to move fast. He looked at his clothes. They were stained with blood. He'd have to deal with that in a moment. First up, he retrieved his dagger and then set to cutting strips of material from Ezra's robes of office. The first strip was for his head. It was then he realised the extent of the damage, his fingers finding a large flap of skin hanging down over his ear. He closed his eyes, trying not to think about it. He pushed the flap of skin upwards and laid it back into place. Tilting his head he then wrapped the strip of material around his forehead, tying it off against his good side. He took another strip and repeated the action. His thoughts were about keeping the pressure on the wound. Perhaps it would dry in place, his blood clotting. He knew these were the wishes of a fool. But he daren't face the reality until he was away.

Once done he applied a similar process to his left arm. The gash was not as bad as he had feared. His arm would stiffen up but should be usable. Then he switched to his side wound. It was a nasty one no doubt, yet something he could deal with. He placed a wad of material against the area and then wrapped strips around his waist to hold it in place. It was as good as it was going to get.

Now, what next? He untied his Servant's band. It was already severed in places as it was. He took Ezra's and wrapped it around his waist, a little higher than normal, to help disguise the bandages. He cinched it tight with a heartfelt 'Fuck!' and tied it off. *Right.*

A wine cup sat on the desk. He drained it of its contents. He didn't need a mirror to know he looked like shit. Though there happened to be several scattered around the office – Tekla had, he supposed, been handsome enough in her way to be vain about her appearance. She was an elf after all. He took a moment to look into the nearest one. He really did look like shit. On the plus side, it was late in the evening with fewer elves to avoid. But it would only take one to raise the alarm.

He walked over to the door and, dagger in hand, opened it into the outer offices. He scanned over the room and his eyes alighted on Ezra's desk, or rather what was behind it; resting on a hook was his cloak. A hooded one. He moved quickly, collecting the cloak and returning with it to the inner office. He pulled it on and tied it off. It was designed to be a little roomy for an elf, so in his case it was tight across the chest. But it would suffice. Then he pulled over the hood – thank the Emperor for the hood. It was not only big enough to cover his head, it was also big enough to cast his features in shadow. Perfect. Now he had a chance. He cast one more eye over the scene of decidedly messy bloodshed while he placed the dagger into the unusual hiding place behind his new belt.

He turned, opened the door once more, and closed it tight behind him before moving through the offices. Stopping at the double doorway he closed them shut as well. The message clear; no one was in attendance. That should buy him some time.

And then he left, hurrying purposefully along the concourse. He realised his life as he knew it here was at an end, he would not be treading these paths again. Did he feel remorse, a sense of loss? All too damned late now. His luck held. He passed a few elves on his journey, but with his head down, his arms in the wide-brimmed sleeves, as if he had an urgent errand to perform, no one stopped him to enquire about his business. It was, after all, Parliament. Where else could one feel so safe? He smiled, someone would be in for a surprise later. He reached the porticoed entrance way, with its many portals leading to the outside. The steps down were well lit and he could spy the top of a spear leaning out from one such portal. Onwards. He continued under one archway, passed a guard to his left and right and was halfway down the steps before he took another breath. And then he was on the boulevard and heading away from Parliament, the temples and the Palace. *Good fucking riddance.* They had their chance to kill him, and they had screwed up. So, what next? His feeling of accomplishment passed as swiftly as it had arrived. *Home.*

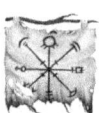

Fillion returned to the town house as quickly as he could. The wound in his side was hurting like a bastard and the crude bandage tied around his waist was quickly wet to the touch. The wound would need sealing or stitch work. Likely his arm too. He didn't want to think about his head. Either way he was never going to look so handsome again. Like it mattered. This was the end game. He had one last thing to do. Then the outcome, the future, was no longer his to influence. He felt a warm trickle along his forehead and wiped away the blood before it fell into his eye. If this had been daytime …

He arrived at the archway entrance, the gate was open, as it always was, and lights were burning in a number of windows. It was after supper. That meant the family would be spread throughout the house. He looked to the stables. Perhaps he should?

No. Fillion continued on and reached the front door and went to open it but changed his mind. Instead he went to the side door which led through the kitchens. He entered and was met by the smell of cooked meats. Even in his dire state, he felt his stomach rumble. A sure a sign as ever that he wasn't dead yet. The kitchen was light and a fire burned in the grate. To one side he saw the cook cutting fruit. He waved in his general direction, bid him good evening and hurried forward before he could reply.

Thankfully, the dining room was empty. He took a moment to catch his breath. Blinking rapidly, he withdrew the knife. *How do I do this*? There were two choices. One was bloodier than the other. But what did he want to achieve? Nadena or Brynne. What did he want? Did he love her? Truly? Or was it their daughter? Could he have one without the other? He clutched his head, it hurt just to think. He tucked the dagger back into his belt and pushed himself away from the wall, fighting a wave of nausea and carried on through the house, heading for the drawing room. The door was slightly ajar, a light within, but there were no voices. He checked left and right, trying to sound out if anyone else was nearby. He raised a fist and knocked gently on the door.

'Yes?' the muffled answer was Patiir's.

Fillion pushed the door, stepped swiftly through and closed it behind him. He turned and found the elf sitting in one of the two chairs by the gently burning fire. He nursed a glass in his hands.

'Have you … oh,' he said when he realised who was wearing the guard's cloak. To give him his due, Patiir did not miss a beat. 'You are not supposed to be here, Sabin.'

Fillion took a step forward and pulled the hood away from his head.

'And it looks like you know why,' finished the elf.

'You should have sent more men,' said Fillion.

'Evidently,' agreed Patiir. 'Though it looks to me that you are almost finished.'

Fillion took another step.

Patiir raised a hand. 'What do you hope to achieve by coming here?'

Fillion stopped and thought about it. He had been running on instinct up to this point but now he experienced a moment of clarity – it was a sound question and one he realised he had the answer to.

'I came to this city with no hope and only one purpose. I wanted to kill your King. I could think of no other act by which I could take my vengeance. But then I met you, and your daughter showed me kindness, and I found myself in another world.'

'Why would you wish to kill our King?' asked Patiir, looking genuinely puzzled.

'I said your King. Not mine. You killed mine.'

Patiir shook his head, still looking confused.

'You killed him back in Tissan and most of his family as well. But not all. I saw to that,' said Fillion feeling a flush of satisfaction. 'An heir lives.'

Patiir made an O with his mouth and his eyebrows sunk low as he frowned.

'You cannot be. A human? No. You are an elf.'

'Half-elf.'

Patiir waved a hand. 'Those aberrations are a rarity. Those that breed with humans are outcasts. You cannot expect me to believe you are a human. I do not forgive you for your actions, Sabin, but you are not a human. You are sick. The horrors of war and your injuries have left you damaged, like so many others. You are ill and you need to be put away for your own good.'

Fillion took another step forward. 'Hear me now, elf. My name is Captain Sabin Fillion of the Imperial Scouts. My father was Celtebarian. My mother was an elf. She left me to return home when I was a child so I turned my back on her kind and devoted myself to serving my Emperor. My last mission was to see the last living heir to the Empire safely to Aberpool. Once there he would join a fleet, waiting to sail to the west. I completed that mission.' One more step and he was face to face with Patiir. 'Look at me closely. Am I lying? You said I was no good at subterfuge. Tell me, where was I found? Lying in Aberpool surrounded by Imperial troops. My troops.' Fillion spat blood on to the floor and smiled. 'Tell me. Am I lying?'

Patiir snorted. 'And what? You gave up on killing the King and decided to foment conflict between dwarves and elves? You are an arrogant fool if you believe that will work.'

'It will work, Patiir, the groundwork is already laid. And when the guards come they will find you slain, and lying next to you will be a dwarf-forged blade,' Fillion drew the dagger and plunged it into Patiir's stomach. The elf let out a little cry and dropped his glass. It fell on to the thick rug, but did not smash. The red wine stained the white weave, as did the droplets of blood. His hands covered Fillion's trying to force them back, but Fillion leaned forward, pressed hard, and sawed the blade to the left. Patiir's mouth had formed another O and he fell back into his chair, the dagger sliding out of the wound.

There were tears falling from Patiir's eyes as he looked down at the red mess staining his robes, and then up at Fillion.

'Sabin? What have you done?'

Fillion leaned down and pressed the blade against Patiir's chest, against his heart.

'I have killed you, Patiir, and now I will kill your family. And the blame lies at your door. You did this when you sought the slaughter of my race.'

Patiir, shook his head. The denial in his eyes was clear.

'No, not them, not my daughter, not your child–'

'Yes.' Fillion pushed the blade hard and deep into Patiir's chest. He gave a sigh, his arms dropped and his head fell backwards. Fillion let go of the blade's grip and stepped back. He studied Patiir; a blood-soaked ragdoll. Once the most powerful elf outside of the court, the architect of millions of deaths, the ending of two, maybe more races. And now just … gone.

Fillion spat on him – another thick gobbet of blood and mucus. Vengeance had, in a way, been served. Yet it was a cold comfort to him. This was better. It truly was. But he had not expected to live and the mission had changed. To make this convincing, to make this the enterprise effective, it had to be done right. And now he had to live. He reached down and pulled the blade out. He didn't have to enjoy what he did, nor would he. *I do this for all who are lost.*

Over the coming minutes, Fillion stalked the house. He was a tide of death. Old Rabi who had shown him nothing but kindness, taken from behind, his neck snapped. The cook bent over his mixing bowl, the blood from his open neck spilling over the fruit. Hedra asleep in his bed, it was over quickly without pain for him. Alica was in the bath house, she always liked to bathe late in the evening. Her screams were muffled by the water as he pushed her under even as he stabbed her in the back, red spreading across the pool. Nadena, when he stepped into their bedroom, was also fast asleep. And curled in her arms was Brynne. Fillion stood and watched them breathe; his wife, her features calm and at rest. His daughter, that face, that look of permanent confusion, a tiny hand pressed against her tiny nose. He closed his eyes, listening to the rhythm of their life. And he reflected on all that he had done. In the house behind him there was a slaughter and nothing he could do would change that now. This pretend life, it was over. He had ended it. It was always going to end, one day. That die was cast a long time ago. He took a step forward. But he looked again at his sleeping daughter and stopped. *No.* There was another way.

He hurried back through the house and out the front door to the stables. Inside he saddled both Amice and Nadena's horse, Naleth, strapped in a hunting bow and arrows and placed saddlebags on her mare. Grabbing a second set and placing them his shoulders, he led both horses out to the courtyard. Precious minutes spent when every moment he expected to hear the sound of armoured troops running down the street. He ran back into the house, and then deliberately slowed his pace, walking softly back into the kitchens where he filled the saddle bags with bread, cheeses and meats, adding two waterskins to the load. Finally he pulled a long knife from the chopping board and slipped it into his belt. Then he was back through the house and into the drawing room, where he placed the dwarf dagger beside Patiir's body. As he straightened up one of the waterskins bumped into his side.

'Fuck!'

The pain reminded him what bad shape he was in. He just had to hold it together a while longer. He returned to the bedroom carrying a lamp he taken from the kitchen. Nothing had changed within. His wife and child were still unaware of the horrors he had committed. He stepped quietly to the side of the bed, dropped the saddlebags on the floor, and sitting down on the edge, gently touched Nadena on the shoulder. She let out a little moan and made a pained face.

'Nadena.'

'Uh.'

'Nadena, please. Wake up.'

'Uh?' She cracked open an eyelid. 'Sabin.' Then she closed her eye again.

'Nadena. Wake up.'

'What is it?' she said, the irritation clear.

'Look at me.'

She opened her eyes and blinked in the light. It took her a few seconds.

'Sabin.' She stopped. Her eyes grew wider and she shifted upright. 'Sabin! What has happened to you?' she said, reaching up to his face. 'Is that blood?'

'Nadena,' Fillion touched her cheek. 'Do you trust me?'

'Yes, but what–'

'Nadena. Everyone is dead.'

Nadena looked at him blankly. 'Sabin. Why is there blood all over you?'

Little Brynne shifted in Nadena's arms and woke up. She gurgled a little and coughed.

'Nadena. Our family are dead.'

She picked up Brynne in her arms and held her protectively.

'Sabin. You are scaring me.'

'I am hurt. I have been stabbed. I got away but I could not save them.'

'Who?' she whispered, gently rocking.

'You father. Your brother. Your sister. They are all gone.'

'No.' Nadena shook her head and closed her eyes. 'No.'

'Nadena. Look at me. We have to go. More of them will be coming.'
She opened her eyes.

'More? Who?'

'Dwarves.'

'This is nonsense,' she said firmly. 'You have taken a fall. You must
have been drinking with your friends again.'

'It's true. And we have to go. Now.'

'I don't believe you.'

Fillion started to lose his patience. There was no time for this.

'Dammit, Nadena. I am not drunk. Go look for yourself. Look at what
they have done.'

She stared at him. It was like she was looking at a stranger.

'Very well.'

She laid Brynne on the bed beside her and climbed out.

'Show me,' she commanded. She stood stiffly, brushing down her
nightdress.

Fillion pushed himself off the bed and led her downstairs. He took
her to the drawing room.

'Inside.' He said reaching out to touch her arm. 'We have to get ready
to go.'

She looked at him with that oddly detached expression and brushed
his hand away. She opened the door and stepped inside. A moment later
he heard a gasp and then a gentle, plaintive whine. Fillion turned and
walked back upstairs. He was starting to find it difficult to move. His
body was finally starting to give into the shock.

He went to Nadena's wardrobe and pulled out some of her riding
clothing and threw it on to the bed. Next to he went to the drawer and
gathered up things for Brynne; blankets for her body and squares of cloth
for her toilet. He shoved these into the saddlebags. He heard someone
enter the room behind him.

'You are bleeding,' Nadena said quietly.

'Uh?' Fillion looked down. Some spots of blood were gathered by his feet. 'There's no time to deal with it,' he said.

'Yes, there is,' she replied moving to the same drawer he had been in. She pulled out more of Brynne's cloth. 'Move those to the side,' she said, pointing at the waterskins. Fillion did as he was bidden. He watched as she made a square of the material and placed it against the hold in his side. Tears were rolling freely down her cheeks.

'Hold it in place,' she said pressing the cloth tightly to the wound. He clenched his teeth against the pain and moved his hand to take hold of the pad. She collected another piece and refolded it into a long strip which she placed over the pad and then tied off around his waist. All this she did with the same practiced ease she had displayed caring for the wounded soldiers returning from Tissan. The way she had nursed him, all those months ago.

'Did you see?' he asked.

She nodded.

'I'm sorry. I couldn't save them,' he said.

'And the others?'

'I checked. They are gone.'

Another nod.

'We have to get away from here. A dwarf assassin took me as I walked home. I must have scared off whoever was in here.'

'Is help coming?' she asked.

'I don't know. I hurried home. It's all I could think about. I had to get back to you. I was … too late.'

'Where are we going?' she asked as she pulled off her nightgown and quickly dressed. She was all business now, even as the tears still flowed.

'I don't know. I was getting the horses ready. I don't know where's safe.'

'Go downstairs. I'll bring Brynne,' she said.

Fillion nodded. Picked up the saddle bags and left the room. He found the horses waiting patiently in the courtyard and he flung the saddlebags over Amice. He went back into the stables, finding a flint and tinder, some other useful items. As he stowed them away on Amice, Nadena appeared, carrying Brynne.

She hurried over and handed him the baby before climbing aboard. She held her hands out and he held Brynne up for Nadena to take her.

'We should go to the King,' she said.

'No,' replied Fillion. 'We must get out of the city. We are being hunted. Nowhere is safe.'

Nadena nodded vacantly. It was safe to assume she was still in a state of shock. It made it easier for him to direct her. He waited until she was settled and climbed on to Amice.

'Stay close,' he ordered.

He led them out under the archway, on to the lane and away from the townhouse. He wanted to put Amice into a brisk trot but the sound of her footfalls seemed inordinately loud. So, against his better judgement, he walked them slowly through the sleeping city, past rows of neat and orderly dwellings, leafy squares and gardens and under the many mage lights burning on street corners. They saw no one until they approached the gates marking the western boundary. It was well lit and Fillion counted three guards on duty. He knew there would be another half dozen in the guardroom set in the top of the gate, the standard number that he had taken the time to find out about a long time ago, when he was first learning all he could about the city and its security. There was no sense of alert, no air of tension as they closed with the gate. He nodded to the single guard, on the city side.

'An early start,' stated the guard in a friendly tone. His spear was resting lightly on his shoulder and underneath his helmet, he was smiling.

'Don't I know it,' replied Fillion. 'We have just heard that my wife's mother is unwell. We are heading west and I wanted us to get as many miles under our belts as we could. With luck we'll reach my wife's mother's home by dusk today.' He flicked his head towards Nadena. 'She does worry about her.'

'Is the little one warm enough?' asked the guard, looking at Nadena as she rode past him, her head bowed low.

'Oh, she is a tough one,' replied Fillion quickly. He was past the guard and had to turn to look back. His side was howling.

The guard looked at him and raised his free hand.

'Safe journey.'

Fillion returned the gesture and as he passed beyond the gate, he nodded at the guard to his right. A few moments later and Nadena was through as well.

Fillion breathed deeply. If she was going to have done something to raise the alarm, then would have been the time. Yet she continued to follow his lead. He took his hand off the knife at his belt. He hadn't even noticed he had reached for it. He waited for her to draw level.

'Nadena. Are you well?'

Silence.

'Wife?'

She looked up.

'Are you well?' he persisted. Nadena's look was unfocussed, confused.

'Sabin?'

'Yes, it's me.'

'They killed my family.'

'I know, my love.'

'I've lost them all,' she whispered.

He reached over and gripped her wrist.

'Not all. Not all,' he said.

'She smiled wanly. Then looked down at Brynne and hugged her close.

'Where are we going, Sabin?'

'A long way from here. Somewhere we can be safe.'

'I want to go home.'

'I know.'

Me too.

Fillion knelt by the stream and removed his bandage. He hissed as he pulled the sticky material away from his wound. Underneath it was a red mess of dried and congealed blood. He gently probed at the edges of the wound. *Fuck*. That shitting hurt. He took the bandage and submerged it in the water, working it together to clean it as best he could.

'You need to let me see to that,' said Nadena.

Fillion looked up and smiled at her. She sat under a tree, nursing Brynne. The two horses were nearby, heads down, both drinking.

'Did we pack a needle and thread?' he asked.

'I did,' she replied. She lay Brynne down on the ground and walked across to him, rummaging in her pocket. She produced a small leather wallet. He recognised it as the one she carried with her back from Tissan.

'Try and clean that wound,' she said. He did as he was bid and used his bandage to dab at the hole. He looked up and watched her thread a thin piece of twine through a needle head.

'That is going to hurt,' he said. He really didn't want that needle going anywhere near him.

'Yes, it is,' she agreed. She sounded like her old self. The elf he had first encountered on the wagon train.

'Shouldn't you let a round wound heal to the air?' he asked hopefully.

'Look at it,' she ordered.

He stared down at the wound. The area around it was much cleaner so the extent of the damage was now clear. There was an opening four inches across, a jagged long line, roughly horizontal. Somehow he had got it into his head that he had been punctured, not slashed.

'Alright. Not as bad as I thought,' he admitted.

'Bad enough. Your face is white. You have lost a lot of blood. I don't know how you haven't passed out by now.'

'I had to stay awake. I had to get us out of there.'

Nadena bit her lower lip. 'You can stop cleaning. Lie down on your side.'

He adjusted his position, brushing some detritus away from the ground, and lay down on his side.

'How is your head?' she asked.

'Worse than my side.'

'Then we'll look at that next.' Her tone was formal, businesslike.

She started work.

'Shit. Ow. Shit!' He felt, sharp stinging pain, the like of which he could barely take.

'Sabin. Peace. You swear like a dwarf.'

'Can you blame me?'

'No.'

Another sharp stab of pain. He felt his flesh being tugged together.

'Where are we going?'

'West.'

'Why not south?'

'Because they would expect that.'

'The dwarves?'

'Yes. And their allies.'

'Allies?'

More stabbing and tugging.

'Ahhh,' Fillion sucked air in and out through his nose for a few seconds, waiting for the pain to subside. 'Yes. There was no way they were working alone. How could they be?'

'Who would support them, Sabin?'

'I don't know. But they jumped me in the Parliament. They killed Ezra, Tekla. Two guards.'

'And you fought them off?'

'Yes. And you see the result. I escaped with my life, barely.'

'How many were there?'

Damn but she was persistent. 'Where?' he asked. Perhaps he could use his exhaustion as a cause for his confusion.

'At the Parliament. How many attacked you?'

'Uh. Two I think.'

'You killed them?'

'Yes. I told you that.'

'And there was one at our house?'

'At least.'

He felt a final hard tug and Nadena leaned in close, using her teeth to bite off the twine. At last, the pain subsided.

'Thank you,' he said.

She rocked back on to her haunches and cocked her head with a quizzical look, her eyes unfocussed.

'It makes no sense,' she said.

Fillion grunted in response.

'None of it does.'

She shook her head. 'That's not what I mean.'

'What do you mean, then?' he said, pushing himself up slowly. He felt dizzy and closed his eyes, waiting for it to pass. When he opened them she was looking at him intently.

'Why they attacked you in the Parliament. That place is so well guarded.'

Too clever by half. That was Nadena.

He sighed heavily and shrugged. 'I truly cannot answer that, Nadena. I have been too busy trying to keep us alive.'

She nodded.

'Yes, of course. You did all you could.'

That was better.

'I didn't do enough,' he said softly.

Nadena bit her lip and tears started to form in her eyes.

She turned her head away and wiped a hand across her brow. He watched her chest expand as she took a shuddering breath. Then she reached out and took a small pot from the satchel. Unscrewing the cap she placed her finger into it. It came away covered with green ointment.

She turned towards him again.

'This is going to sting,' she said with a strained smile. 'But it will protect you against infection.'

'I remember,' said Fillion. She had used the same salve on him on the wagon journey to the Heartlands. A long time ago.

As she ran her finger over the stitches and the ointment penetrated the wound. It hurt like a bastard, just like she had promised.

'Is Brynne alright?' she asked.

He looked over to his daughter. Little arms waved in the air and little legs waggled under the wrapping.

'She's fine.'

'We were so lucky,' said Nadena. 'That assassin, whoever they were. They left Brynne and I until last. I understand that they would want to kill my father. I know what it means. But to kill all of us as well? They stalked the house, one end to the other, finding my family. We could have been the first to die.'

'But you weren't,' said Fillion.

'Let's take a look at that head,' she said.

Now this was the part he had least been looking forward to.

'I wish you wouldn't,' he said.

'No choice.'

'Alright. Do it,' he sighed.

She reached up and began to unwind the bandage. He closed his eyes. Her intake of breath was all he needed to know.

'That bad, huh?'

A pause.

'Yes.'

'Fixable?'

Another pause.

He felt the pressure of her finger and he shied away. She uttered a 'Tsch.'

'You ear is almost hanging off. The blade sliced you in the head and down. Another inch and your ear would have been cut clean off. That would have been better, in a way.'

'Because?'

'Because I am going to have to try and stitch this back in place.'

Wonderful.

'Just do it, Nadena. Just get it done.' Perhaps after that the questions would stop, and they could finally move on.

CHAPTER THIRTY-FIVE – CADE

Cade studied the map. The detail was poor at best. They were still on the road. A road at any rate, she wasn't sure which one it was. How many weeks now? Months? At least two. Either way the winter was almost here. The skies were grey today and a westerly wind blew cold air down from the mountains far to the southwest. She climbed off the wagon and walked over to Devlin and his people. They were clustered beneath a small copse of oak trees, the branches swaying gently, shedding leaves over people and horse alike.

Devlin was bent over a patch of cleared earth. He had a stick and was pointing at a number of pieces of stone and moss forming some sort of pattern. She had become accustomed to seeing these impromptu creations. All very military.

Devlin looked up at her approach. He was quite the grizzled commander now. He still sported his stolen armour, still carried the axe on his back. He also bore a leather patch over his left eye and a nasty scar running vertically down from his forehead on to the top of his cheek. It was still sore, red and puckered. He nodded at her and continued his briefing. She listened in, trying to look interested; it was the done thing, apparently.

'This valley affords us the best defensive opportunity we've had for a long time,' he said prodding the largest piece of moss. 'We would be fools not to use it.'

He pointed at a line in the dirt that Cade presumed was the road.

'After this, our scouts say we will reach the Brevis Sea, and from there we have to make a decision. Follow the water, head south for the Highlands or head north to the Riverlands.' He looked up at Cade. 'Either way, we have to do enough damage to get a clean break. We can't take any more winnowing.'

Wasn't that the truth? Two months of running and fighting, running and fighting. Folk were dead on their feet. Cade knew that most folk were beyond caring. They were just putting one foot in front of the other. The column was harried daily by dwarf outriders, waiting for their moment to swoop in on a group of stragglers. They were like a pack of wild dogs, looking for weakness in the human herd. Barely a day went by when their numbers weren't thinned. Hundreds dead. It meant the column had to group closer together for protection, but it also slowed them down.

Devlin commanded a group of fighters who were more than just brawlers now, they were hardened and canny. Laying traps, ambushes and the like and, when necessary, forming a skirmish line at the rear of the column, going toe to toe with dwarves. It had become a weird game, almost. The dwarves had followed them further than Cade had expected them to. Stubborn bastards. They must be as strung out as the Tissans, they certainly didn't have enough numbers to crush the humans, but they weren't letting go either.

'Cade?'

'Hmm?'

'What do you think?'

'Yes. Great plan.'

Devlin stood back and folded his arms. Those around him grinned. 'Which part?'

Cade sighed.

'Oh, the bit where we win. That's my favourite.'

'Yes. About that,' said Devlin shaking his head. 'I think we've reached a point where we need to end this. The dwarf cavalry has been bleeding us for too long. But they have not been reinforced. I'd estimate there are no more than two hundred left in pursuit.'

'Why's that?' Cade asked.

'Maybe they went after the other columns first? Who knows? Either way, we should take this opportunity.'

'And see what comes next?' she asked.

Devlin nodded.

Cade grunted. 'You are starting to sound like me.' She hunkered down and studied the plan in front of her. 'Talk me through it again.'

'You know this is a dumb idea, right?' asked Miriam.

'What do you mean?' asked Cade, though she knew exactly what Miriam meant.

'Why are we looking to start a fight?'

'Because.'

Miriam looked at her as if she was mad.

Cade shrugged. 'Look, I'm bored, alright?'

'Bored?' Miriam threw her hands up in the air. 'You are bored? Why didn't you just say so? There was plenty of work going with organising stuff.'

'That's your job, and Sent's and the other folk. Isn't that right, Issar? Issar?'

'Yes, Cade. Whatever you say. But can I ask, what am I doing here?'

'It's a fight, isn't it?'

'Cade, I don't like fighting.'

She waved his comment away. 'Devlin assures me we've got a really good chance.'

'Of dying?' asked Issar, straight-faced.

'Issar, were you always this negative?' she asked, adding extra levity to her voice.

'Yes.'

'Bah. Seriously, it'll be fine. Besides. I wanted the old crew back together again, just one last time. We make it through this, and I reckon we'll be in the clear.'

'That's bollocks for a start,' grumped Anyon.

'Have I ever let you down?' she asked. *Hah!* They couldn't argue with that. It was still true though. Most of the faces here had been with her since the start.

Issar shook his head and picked up the crossbow.

'How many are there?' he asked.

'Devlin reckons two hundred, max,' Cade replied.

'We're outnumbered, then,' observed Issar.

'Quality counts,' said Cade, waggling her finger.

She stood up from their little cookfire and walked around the side of the wagon, inspecting the damage, a rear wheel missing from the right axle. The animals were unhitched and grazing off to the side. The wagon was parked on the side of the road. A second wagon set a little bit beyond, this one in working order. Trent sat by another small fire, making busy with fixing the first wagon's missing wheel. Including herself, ten Tissans made up the party. A nice, easily digestible number. Krste stood a little way along the road facing east, looking for trouble.

The road continued past them leading up a gentle slope and out. The valley sides were thickly wooded and steep. The valley was quite broad where it started a half mile further east, but it quickly funnelled. A perfect choke point. The road itself, and the grass and bush verges to either side, were trampled with the passing of thousands the day before. And now they were the only humans left in the valley. Just as it had to be. The dwarves weren't stupid, they'd see this valley for what it was, and would make sure of it before they entered it. That meant someone had to be the sacrificial lambs. Cade wondered just how it transpired that it ended up falling to her? Wasn't she, like, the leader of this bunch? Hadn't there been a time when she had been indispensable? Less so now she had plenty of other people running everything. But still, she'd told them to run everything!

'Ah, shit,' she muttered to herself. Who was she kidding? It had to be her, because it was the only way to keep everyone else in line. They might start questioning her life choices. Or worse still, start thinking about stealing her booze stash. She couldn't have that. Nope. It was yet again time for Cade to step up and show everyone what's what. There was only one way this plan was going to work and that was to show the dwarves exactly what they needed to see. A group of humans, left behind in the wake of the column. And it had to be real. No bullshit, no set-up. She walked over to Krste. The man looked deeply worried.

'What's up?' she asked.

'I got a prickly feeling in the back of my neck. Like I'm being watched.'

'Hmm.' Cade looked back along the road, and either side of it, at the trees that crowded the valley sides. 'You probably are,' she said quietly.

'Huh?' he said, giving her a nervous look.

'You hear that?' she said.

'What?'

'That sound,' said Cade. A gentle rhythm like a distant thunder, or perhaps drumming. Either way it was growing heavier.

'I'm feeling something under my feet,' said Krste.

'That'll be the vibration of two hundred ponies charging towards us,' she observed, taking a moment to look up into the sky. It had brightened a little, and the wind had died down.

'Can we head back to the wagons?' asked Krste, a hint of nervousness in his voice.

'It's not like you to run from a fight,' she said.

'I'd rather fight from back there,' he replied.

She grunted. 'Go on, then, bugger off.'

'You not coming?' he said, backing up.

She crossed her arms and planted her feet.

'Nah. Better if they get a good look at me.'

Krste looked doubtful. He started to walk back towards her. Nice of him.

'I said bugger off. I'll probably be fine.'

Krste clearly didn't believe a word of it but nonetheless jogged back to the others. The rest of them had also picked up on the impending shitstorm and were reacting. Crossbows and spears were pulled out from the wagons and the second one was being drawn up to the first to make a better defensive position. Trent dropped the wheel he had been working on and he and Anyon picked it up, rolled it back to the axle and levered it back into place. There was no point in pretending anymore. The dwarves were coming whatever happened.

As the seconds ticked by and the sound grew louder, Cade started to question her decision. Maybe it was the cold, unsettled feeling in her stomach that made her feel like she wanted to throw up. Or the screaming voice inside her head, telling her to stop being so bloody stupid. It wasn't too late, she could still run. But that wasn't her style, was it? She could talk her way out of anything. Couldn't she?

That screaming voice reminded her of the scars she now carried. *Oh yes. Those.*

From further down the valley they started to emerge, even as the sound lessened. A ragged line of ponies broke free of the tree-lined slope on either side of the valley floor and a larger knot came walking slowly along the road. They had spotted Cade, a juicy target unprotected and unarmed. They expected a trap and stopped their charge in response. They were fifty yards away when she raised her hands.

'Morning! Any of you lot speak our language?'

A hand went up from one of the lead riders and the whole horde reined in. Cade felt the tension in her butt cheeks lessen just a fraction.

'Just wanted a chat, that's all,' she shouted, in her most neighbourly voice.

There was a conversation among the dwarves. Several riders were sent into the trees on either side, picking their way up the slope, looking for any surprises. A few moments later a single dwarf kicked his pony forwards and closed the distance to something like ten yards. Cade kept her hands up and smiled. The dwarf looked a little ragged, his kit was worn, and both he and his pony were lean. Life was as hard for them as it was for the Tissans. A state of affairs Cade could use. He laid his loaded crossbow across his saddle, reached up and undid his helmet, an all-in-one piece that had a faceplate, revealing a dirty, beardless face. Oh, it was a female. She had never seen one this close before.

'Hey there,' Cade said brightly. 'Been quite a chase, huh?'

The dwarf did not respond immediately, looking past her to the wagons and beyond. Scowling, she sniffed and spat. 'What?'

'What?' replied Cade.

'What do you want?'

'Oh, just felt this might be a good time to get your view on something.' The dwarf shifted in her saddle and stared hard at Cade.

'See, it's like this,' said Cade continuing on gamely. 'I was wondering, if, considering it all in the round, whether you might entertain the notion of calling it quits?'

The dwarf muttered something in dwarvish. 'Quits?'

'Um. Agreeing to call it all off. It's been quite a slog and you're a long way from home. You've been killing us, and we've been killing you. And we are on foot. It's damn tiring.'

The dwarf smiled but there was no warmth to it. She turned and looked back at her companions.

'We don't have to walk,' she said, returning her gaze to Cade.

'True. But, and I'm spitballing here, you have no more help coming. Now, that offers an opportunity,' Cade lowered her hands. 'Instead of you killing more of us and us killing more of you, we can just … part ways. We'll just carry on heading west. A long, long way west. You won't hear from us again. That's a promise. And you lot, you can turn around and go home. Anyone asks, you just say, job done. You found as many as you could, killed us all, and now you'd like your back pay. Everybody wins.' Cade crossed her arms, awaiting the response.

The dwarf tilted her head and her eyes narrowed. It looked to Cade she might just be considering it. The dwarf glanced back at the gathered riders. Was she the one in charge? Cade didn't think so. In confirmation, the dwarf faced her and raised her helmet above her head. 'Wait,' she ordered, as she lowered and buckled it back into place.

'Absolutely. Happy to,' Cade stepped away with a deep bow. The dwarf turned her pony round and cantered back towards the others.

Cade turned and walked slowly back to her group, half expecting a bolt in the back.

Issar looked at her from behind the nearest wagon. 'You're not dead.'

'Nothing gets past you.'

Issar pointed beyond her. 'They are talking.'

'Talking's good,' she said, reaching the wagon.

'And now one of them is gesturing at us.'

'OK. Is it a friendly gesture?'

Issar took a moment.

'Nah.'

'Typical,' muttered Cade. 'You try and play nice.'

She reached up and Ralph passed her a loaded crossbow.

Cade turned to watch the front rank of cavalry close up.

'Think they are scared we might attack?' asked Miriam, from the cover of the wagon bed.

'Shitting themselves.' Cade settled down on one knee and readied her weapon. The cavalry line looked set. She heard a barked command and spears were lowered.

'Don't shoot until you can hit something,' Cade ordered.

'That's me buggered then,' said Issar quietly.

Ponies in the line became restless. But the cavalry did not charge.

Cade listened to more orders, each sounding more frantic than the last. There was a lot of activity now, but it still wasn't focussed on them. She grinned and turned to look at Issar.

'There you go, bang on t–'

A shout made her turn. They were coming. The front line of cavalry launched into a canter which quickly became gallop. The line started to lose coherence as the riders angled towards the front wagon. Cade hunkered down as the noise of horses started to overwhelm her hearing. She heard shouting from above her. The ponies and their riders swarmed around the wagon. Cade raised her crossbow and took aim at a dwarf who had reined his pony hard to the left and was levelling his spear right at her. Her bolt took the pony in the neck and it reared in pain, throwing the rider back. She'd take that. Cade shifted around the wagon wheel and scuttled underneath the wagon. Issar was already there.

He pushed over a preplaced loaded crossbow and she threw her spent one aside. There was no way she'd get the string in place for a reload under here. It's not like they'd have the time anyway.

She looked back towards the second wagon, seeing its occupants were now engaged, trying to ward off the probing spears of the surrounding cavalry. Trent was swinging a hammer and yelling, while the woman next to him went down with a spear in her belly.

She heard scuffling above and someone fell to the ground with a 'whump' in front of her. It looked like Trent. She drew a bead on a rider just beyond the wagon, hitting them in the arm. The dwarf dropped his weapon and steered his pony away.

'This is going to be over real soon,' said Issar.

'Any more bows?' she asked.

'All gone.'

Cade pulled her knife out.

'Not staying here to get spiked,' she said, poking Issar in the ribs. 'You coming?'

'I have a choice?' he muttered, picking up a hatchet.

Cade pushed her way out and up from the protection of the wagon. In the whirling melee she set her sights on a rider a few yards away with their back to her. She ran hard and vaulted head first, crashing into the dwarf. She hit the rider's breastplate and she felt her nose crunch against it. The rider went forward with the impact and Cade used the moment to get her legs on to the pony's flanks. Then as the dwarf started to react she reached up, grabbed the helmet and yanked back, exposing the unprotected knee. She stabbed hard, quickly, repeatedly. And then she let go and pushed herself backwards off the horse, twisting and rolling to fall flat on to her front, arms braced to push herself up.

A horn sounded from somewhere, three short sharp blasts. She scanned the battle looking for another target. But that horn had made an impact. Some of the cavalry were disengaging. She spun around wary of an attack, but none came. The horn sounded again – three more times. And now all the cavalry were moving, heading east, back along the valley. Cade took a moment, found a discarded spear and ran back to her wagon. She found Issar crouched low, clutching his head.

'Issar?'

He looked up and waved her away. 'Got clubbed by spear as soon as I stood up. Fell right back down like a sack of shit.'

She switched her attention to the aftermath. There was no movement from the far wagon, just a few bodies scattered around it. A dwarf was crawling along the ground. Next to Issar lay Trent. Cade knelt by him and felt for a pulse. Nothing.

'Issar. Grab your hatchet and take care of that one,' she said indicating the injured dwarf.

'Right.'

Cade climbed up on to the wagon and spied the cavalry's retreat. She could only see a few in the treeline but the sound of combat was unmistakable.

A groan turned her attention towards the wagon bed. Miriam lay on her back, clutching her stomach, a wet red stain covering her shirt. Cade knelt and gently prised Miriam's protesting hands away. Cade sighed. The hole was big and deep, Miriam would bleed out soon enough but it would be a shitload of pain every second.

'Cade?' asked Miriam through gritted teeth.

'Sorry, Miriam. No coming back from this.'

'Finish it, then,' said Miriam.

Cade nodded. Brave woman. She'd always backed Cade. She deserved better.

Cade reached up and stuck her blade into Miriam's neck. She leaned back as the blood spurted out. Not that hard, not that much.

Miriam's eyes went wide for a moment but quickly lost their focus. Cade stood up wiping her blade on her arm. The battle was continuing. She wasn't sure if that was a good sign.

'What are we going to do now?' Issar called over wiping his hatchet on the grass. Behind him Anyon emerged limping.

'Let's get some bows and go help. If the dwarves win, they'll come after us anyway. You good to fight?'

Anyon waved. 'Yeah, I still got two good arms.'

'OK, go find something to shoot with.' Cade jumped off the wagon.

She was the only one to walk away unscathed. Her luck was holding. Then she felt her nose throbbing. She reached up to inspect the damage. It felt swollen. *Maybe not.* She ducked under the wagon and pulled out one of the used crossbows. She found a bolt bag, fished one out and set to pulling the string.

A long horn blast sounded followed a moment later by another.

Issar walked over to join her. 'I can't see them.'

She looked up as the string caught the trigger. 'D'you want to take a bet on what that means?' she asked.

'I might,' said Issar.

Anyon joined them, carrying a crossbow in one hand and using a spear as a crutch in the other.

'Let's go take a look,' Cade suggested.

The three of them set off along the road, going slowly so that Anyon could keep up. That was fine by Cade; she was in no hurry to get into another scrap.

They could still hear some kind of ruckus ahead.

Cade shared a look with Issar.

Riders appeared from further down the valley, sticking to the road.

Cade and the others stopped. Unbidden, all of them raised their weapons. Just as quickly Cade lowered hers.

'Horses,' she said in response to Issar's sideways look.

'Ah. Good news, then.'

They waited on the road as a group of horses slowed their pace as they closed the distance.

Devlin, on the lead animal, pulled his mount to a stop. He had blood on his face and breastplate.

'You alright?' he asked.

'Depends. Does a nosebleed count?'

Devlin glanced at the other two. 'You all that made it?'

Cade nodded. 'Your timing was a little tight,' she said.

'It was the best we could do. Go check on the rest,' he said to his companions. As they rode towards the wagon Anyon plonked himself on the ground and lay down. Devlin dismounted and joined Cade and Issar. He looked pissed. 'You knew I had to keep everyone back to avoid discovery. It was always going to be tight. And it was a damn stupid idea, you being part of this ambush.'

'Like you keep saying. It kinda worked, though, didn't it?'

Devlin removed his gloves. 'Yes. It worked. Their attack on you helped us get close enough to stop them reacting in time, which meant they couldn't bring their numbers to bear.' He rubbed his tired eyes. 'We shocked them into a retreat. I lost half my people doing it but I reckon there's not more than fifty of them left.'

'Nice work,' said Cade, slapping him on the shoulder. 'Look at us.'

'Still standing,' Issar said quietly. 'Shame Meghan's not here.'

Cade sighed and ran a hand through her hair. It felt greasy and gritty. 'She won't be the only one. We got a long way to go yet.'

'That's a question worth asking,' said Devlin. 'I reckon we've bought ourselves some breathing space after today. But we need to figure out where to go now. I know you said about the Highlands but I'm not sure we want to be caught up in there when the winter hits. We aren't prepared and many folk have no idea how to survive.'

'Stay in the lowlands?' said Issar.

Cade nodded.

'Maybe we head to Brevis then? It's in the Riverlands,' she ventured. She hadn't paid much notice to it going through but it was the least inhospitable of the environments they could spend their time in.

'You make a good point. You got fishing, you got hunting. There was agriculture there. We should be able to scare up the resources to keep us going for a while,' said Devlin.

'At least we want to get over the river. There must more bridges across it. We'll have to skirt the Brevis Sea,' said Issar.

'I heard there are islands. Shame we couldn't get to one of them,' said Cade. 'Got to be defensible, right?'

Devlin nodded appreciatively.

'Good thinking, that. Definitely worth considering.'

Cade appreciated the compliment. She felt no need to mention the vineyards she'd heard tell of. That would just be a happy bonus.

Devlin turned back to his horse, pulling himself on to the saddle. 'I need to head back and gather my people. They follow orders well enough but some of them are still a little hot-headed.' He raised a hand and beckoned to his riders by the wagon. 'Do you want me to leave a couple with you? Help with sorting out the wagons? Provide some extra protection, just in case?'

'Yeah. That would be good,' agreed Cade.

Devlin nodded. 'I'll see you back at the column, then.'

'It'll probably be after dark,' said Cade. They had a long way to go to catch up.

'After dark it is. Issar, save me some of that gut-rot of yours.'

Issar raised his leather sack.

The other riders returned.

'All dead or far enough along not to make a difference,' said one of them to Cade.

She raised a hand in thanks. 'Come on, Issar. Let's find our horses and get them hitched. Hey Anyon, stop playing dead and get off your arse. Start collecting weapons.'

'Right,' said Anyon pushing himself off the ground.

Issar sighed heavily as they walked back to the wagons.

'What's that for?' asked Cade.

'Just happy to be alive.'

'You're welcome.'

Issar grunted and looked at her.

'You know, it was a smart move, as well as a stupid one.'

Cade nodded. 'I know. But you give folk a different perspective, a new life, they kinda forget how they got there. They start getting ideas about how they could run things better. You need to keep your reputation to keep them honest.'

'Quite the politician, Cade, making your own legend.'

She supposed so. The fact of the matter was, she needed them all. If they didn't stay together, they'd have gotten picked off one by one. Death by a thousand cuts. She'd just proved once more that she was one of them, taking risks, putting her life on the line for those she led. That would buy her credit. Hopefully more than enough to find one of those vineyards. They had villas attached to them. With comfortable beds, fountains, sofas and great big, airy, well-stocked wine cellars.

She was, after all, a simple soul.

CHAPTER THIRTY-SIX – FILLION

Fillion rocked in the saddle. He felt cold, feverish. Sweat beaded his forehead. He pulled his cloak tighter, trying to extract some warmth. It did no good. He swallowed, his throat was sore. His muscles ached. Whether that was due to his wounds or to the infection he undoubtedly had, it didn't really matter much. Every step that Amice took jolted him. She was barely going walking pace but everything hurt. He closed his eyes and felt his body sway. He was miserable. He felt lonely. After the nightmare of agony that was Nadena's repair job on his head she had fallen into her own silent funk. At least the relentless questioning had subsided. She had asked the same questions over and over again. It was like a damn interrogation. He supposed he couldn't blame her. She was trying to make sense of what had happened. It hadn't helped that his head was aching like the worst hangover imaginable.

He closed his eyes for a moment, trying to remember what it felt like to be hale. Now he just shook all over. For two nights he had borne this fever, huddling by the fire. He was next to useless and their food was all but gone. He had expected to be able to forage, to hunt. Piss all chance of that at the moment. Luckily for all of them, Nadena was more than capable, finding fruit, plants and even some meat. She did what she had to do to make him comfortable and focussed her energy on Brynne. Fillion didn't begrudge her that; his daughter needed it more than him.

He opened his eyes again and shifted in the saddle, wincing as he did so, and checked on his family. Nadena was directly behind, nursing Brynne. She looked up at him, but she remained silent, her face blank. He turned back, glanced along the edge of the treeline to his right. There was plenty of forest to hide in, all he had to do was keep them moving westwards. Eventually they would break free of it. But they would have to circumvent the wood elves. Unless he invoked Kanyay's name, that might buy them tolerated, if not safe, passage. But any wood elf they encountered could just shrug their shoulders and take them captive anyway; capricious, unpredictable bastards that they were. He wondered what Kanyay was up to now. Had the elf returned to his people? He found he genuinely missed him. His was seized by a coughing fit and he collapsed forwards. His lungs screaming, his throat scratching and his head hammering. He turned his head and spat out a thick gobble of mucus. He lay his head against Amice's neck. It was warm and smelled comfortingly familiar. He didn't have the energy to push himself upright, so he just lay there, trying to breathe deeply, waiting for his body to stop protesting. It seemed like several minutes before he heard Nadena call to him.

'Sabin?'

'Yes?' he mumbled.

'We should stop soon.'

He cracked open his eyes. It was certainly darker. Had he fallen asleep? It had been midday when he had last checked.

'Yes. We should find somewhere.'

He placed his hands on the saddle horn and forced himself upright. He groaned loudly. There was a small river running nearby, they had been deliberately following it, he knew it would eventually join the Tuul. He angled Amice towards it.

Half an hour later they had set up camp and Fillion had somehow kindled a fire. The effort had pretty much finished him off. Nadena could have done it but he had insisted, leaving her to take care of the horses and Brynne. Now he lay beside the fire and fed the flames from a pile of dry wood he had collected.

'I'm going to look for some food,' Nadena announced.

'It's a little late?' he said.

'I thought I saw an apple tree a little way back. Might be some nuts too.'

'Alright,' he said. He was in no position to argue.

'Mind Brynne,' she ordered, and settled her down next to him.

Brynne's hands reached up, he waggled a finger in front of her, and she grabbed it.

He heard Nadena walk off but he only had eyes for Brynne. She was gurgling in delight and he felt himself smile.

He awoke to darkness and heat. Even so, he felt his body shivering. He tried to get his bearings. The fire was in front of him and it blazed vigorously. Far more than it should.

He looked for Brynne, she had been right by him. Where had she gone?

'Nadena?' he called.

'I'm here,' she said. He looked down towards his feet. She sat there, looking him, the shadows and light warring for her face.

'You shouldn't build the fire up so high.'

'Why not?' she asked softly.

'You know why. We mustn't draw attention to ourselves.'

She ran a finger along her cheek. 'Oh, yes.'

Damn but she was getting more withdrawn. 'Where's Brynne?'

'Nearby.'

Nearby?

He pushed himself up.

'Nadena, what is the matt–?'

She put a finger to her lips and moved towards him, crawling on all fours, on the far side of his body away from the fire. She stopped as she drew level with his chest. He twisted and lay on his back as she loomed over him.

'We are going home.'

'What? We can't,' Fillion responded. Her mind had finally given in.

'We are going home.'

'Nadena. They'll find us if we do. It's not safe.'

Nadena smiled gently, leaned forward and ran a hand over his forehead.

'No, they won't,' she said.

Fillion screamed as he felt the blade slide into his wound. He thrashed in agony, but Nadena pressed down on his head and leaned in with her body. He tried to reach her other arm the one that held the blade but as he clutched for it she drove it in deeper. He cried out again. His remaining energy drained away and he stopped struggling.

He felt the blade slide out but there was little pain now. Nadena started to stroke his head again. He found it hard to breathe.

'Why?' he whispered.

'I am your wife. I know you better than anyone, my love. I have learned to tell when you are lying.'

'I'm no–' He stopped himself. What was the point?

'None of it made any sense. The deaths. Your behaviour, making us run like this. But I worked it out, Sabin. There were no dwarf assassins.' She paused and her hand halted its gentle caresses. 'It was you. I don't know why – I don't care why – but you were the one. You killed our family.'

Fillion looked into her eyes. They were sad. So very sad.

'Yes.' What else could he say?

'I know,' she said.

He saw a flash of reflected light. The knife held in her other hand. It was the one he had taken from the kitchen. He couldn't even remember losing it. She pushed it into his chest and the pain was sharp and quick. He heard his sigh and his vision shrank. As the light faded he thought of Brynne.

And then, nothing.

CHAPTER THIRTY-SEVEN – OWEN

Winter. Why did he spend all of his time travelling during winter? Owen's teeth started to chatter. He wrapped the woollen scarf around his face. It was crusted with ice on the outside. His gloves were similarly covered in a layer of white. At least he could still feel his fingers, although they were so well encased he couldn't feel much of what he was picking up anyway. He gathered the fallen wood in his arms and clumped his way back along the shore line to the camp. The wind was a brisk north-easterly and their west-facing aspect on the small peninsula gave them shelter from the worst of it. The shore was covered in shingle, coated with spray, polyp-covered seaweed and other bits of detritus. The sea was a murky grey, churning with white foam and utterly uninviting. Overall, it was damned grim. He turned away from the water and struck inland. The clearing was only a few yards from the shingle and the gathered trees were little more than lichen-covered skeletons, lacking any sense of strength or any particular height. But he'd been able to clear away enough of the thinner branches to string up the canopy, sloping diagonally like a pitched roof. Made up of treated cotton, it just about shielded Arno from the elements. He'd also been able to weave together a surrounding framework of more pliable branches from further inland. The fire, small but lively, was as close to Arno as he could get it without spooking the eagle. Arno was pretty relaxed around flame, but he was still a beast with thousands of years of survival instinct bred into him.

Arno eyed him suspiciously as he approached.

'Yeah, I know. I'm in trouble. Sorry.'

Arno's forbearance has been nothing short of legendary but there was no way Owen was sleeping next to the bird when he was in such a bad mood. So, he shivered by himself on the far side of the fire. He hunkered down and dropped the wood, adding it to the semi-circle of earlier collections so it could dry out a bit before he added it to the flames. Well banked up it would give them as warm a night as possible. He laid his hands in front of the fire and waited for the heat to penetrate. He gave a little sigh, he could definitely feel his fingers. He rubbed his gloves together. One more trip. Then that would be enough. He stood and faced the sea. In the dismal, grey distance, he could see a dark smear spreading along the edge of the horizon. It was land. They'd leave at first light and should reach it within a couple of hours. Owen had to balance resting Arno against the draining cold. The eagle had done well. They'd left the coast of Scotia two days earlier and had embarked on an island-hopping adventure across the Drifa Straights. Most were not on any maps that Owen possessed or had seen, he just knew what others had told him. On the whole they were barren rocks, but there were some, like this one, that was large enough to have some proper vegetation. The larger ones even had some game. He looked at the shelter. It would be a pain in the arse to get that down. And, if they actually made it back here again, it would be good to just shift back into it. Yes. He'd leave it. They only had one shot out of here so why make Arno take the extra weight? As he wound his way along the beach he smiled, feeling his lips crack beneath the scarf. He'd have been in some shit if he had tried that under Cadarn's command.

That night he risked sleeping on Arno's side, having first fed him and built the fire up nice and high. It was a welcome relief to fall asleep bathed in heat. He awoke slightly later than he had planned, but dawn was a slow, deceptive affair this far north. The skies were still so dark, and the cloud cover so thick, he could only guess where the sun actually was. He pushed off his bedroll. The fire had burned down in the night and the insidious cold had crept back in.

'Arno. I think it's time to go.'

His eagle was awake and restless. He had been aground too long. Owen forced himself into activity and got to preparing Arno for flight. He fumbled his way around strapping on the saddle and the other assorted bits of gear. It must have taken another twenty minutes before they were finally ready to start. He led Arno away from the shelter, out from the clearing and on to the beach. The wind was gusting almost easterly. That would make things a little easier for the eagle.

They took to the air and Arno turned towards the north. Owen hunkered down. *It's cold. It's so bloody cold.* There was little else for him to do but shiver. He had all his flying gear on with the extra furs he had bought along and it still wasn't enough. With his spare scarf wrapped around his head, his vision was reduced to a small slit of light. There was nothing to see anyway. He closed his eyes.

And awoke.

Just ahead, no more than a few miles, was a coastline, ragged and saw-toothed, stretching east and west. *Drifa.* He could see no beaches as such. It was all high cliff peninsulas and inlets, bordered by forested slopes of tall, evergreen trees. The land was covered by snow and as they skirted the edges of the coastline, he saw the spreading branches droop with the weight. Many of these inlets cut deep into the land. He had no clue how far they had drifted westwards but, from everything he had heard, it was within those high-sided inlets where he would find what he sought.

Picking one at random he lined Arno up and they slipped in, passing between two towering cliffs, covered with those tall trees – spruces, not pine. He kept them centre of the inlet skimming across the water. It was a lot calmer here, away from the open seas. He spied a pod of large sea creatures working their way north. Were those whales? He had never seen any before. They looked huge! They swam, lazily, breaching the surface and then sinking back under. One let out a spray of water. For his part, Arno paid them no mind and soon outpaced them. The inlet must have been all of a mile long, if not longer. What did the Scotians call them? *Fjords.* The land on either side looked friendlier now, the slopes leading down to rocky shores. The trees climbed high and a flock of birds emerged from the left, startled, perhaps, by Arno's presence. There were no giant eagles this far north. At least, none he had heard of.

The fjord's end was swiftly approaching and revealed nothing more than what he had already seen. It was too much to hope that they would get lucky straight away. He took some comfort from what he had seen so far. If they needed to camp, the territory looked far more forgiving than the islands to the south.

'Which way Arno?' The eagle offered no suggestions. *'Let's try east.'*

Arno gained height, following the climbing treeline north before cresting on to a series of tree covered hills and snowbound peaks. Just ahead he saw a pounding, fast flowing, white water cascade back down the slope. He had not spotted where it entered the inlet. Arno turned right and Owen started to guide him to the start of each fjord in turn. On the fourth try, Owen thought he saw a shimmer of something. Turning Arno south he angled downwards, barely clearing the trees.

There.

It was a ship. Long, thin, with a single wide mast, the sail furled.

It was tied up against a short pier that led on to the shore and a wide wharf, flanked by a shallow sandy beach. He knew very little about sailing matters but he was surprised the boat was still in the water at this time of year. They flew over the boat and out to the water, getting a better look inside. There were banks of benches but little else. He turned again to cruise over the ship. *Ah.* There were buildings here, two of them, just set back from the beach within the trees. He had not seen them before because the roofs were covered in the same thick branches. Something was off about them. At first he couldn't place it. Then they were past them and Arno was climbing again. Owen wanted another circuit to work it out but it struck him. *The size, it's the size!* That's why it looked all wrong. The huts were larger than they should be. *Obviously.* What next? He thought about how best to announce his presence. He wasn't sure at all about any customs or etiquette. But he reasoned most people didn't like strangers just showing up and barging through the door. He got Arno flying in a loose gentle circle, just over the water beyond the pier. He flexed his hands, rolled his head and tried not to think about how damn cold he was. He spied none of the sea creatures below in the water. He saw very little of anything. There was no movement in what he could see of the site. No smoke curled into the sky, no industry was present by the wharf.

'I think we have made a mistake, Arno. We'll have to try elsewhere.'

He looked out along the fjord to the open sea. Perhaps he'd give it another hour then he would put down for the night. Find them a nice protected site like this. Arno swung north passing by the settlement one last time.

Standing on the wharf was an ogre.

What else could it be? It was half again the height of a tall man and its shoulders were broad. Its hands were tucked into a leather belt and it was studying Owen. Arno flew over him and the ogre looked up to watch him pass. Owen waved a hand in greeting. The ogre did not respond.

That shouldn't be a surprise. He had, at least, found what he came for. It was time to say hello properly.

Arno landed on the beach surprisingly gently, his talons sinking into the sand. The ogre hadn't moved. Owen hauled his stiff, frozen limbs off the saddle and slid clumsily to the ground. His eyes alighted on his spear, and then they drifted towards his crossbow in its holster. Not that it was loaded. He made a face. Neither of them would do him much good if things went south.

Instead he steeled himself and walked across the beach to the wharf, stepping on to its crudely cut planks. He raised his hands high, palms facing outwards. He really wasn't any threat whatever way you cut it. He was no Shaper.

He was close enough now to study the ogre properly. He had been right about the size. It was big. Bigger than any man. But it wore clothing not dissimilar to his own; a mixture of thickly woven wool and animal skins. Its feet were covered in leather boots with fur sprouting out from the inside lining. Its belt was wide and thick, encompassing an impressive waist. Only its hands and head were uncovered. The hands were gnarled, thick fingered, and covered with rings. His head was where the true difference emerged. The skin was white, very white, like it had never seen the sun. It had an overly thick neck, marked by wide veins. An equally wide chin, clear of any hair was flanked by sets of mutton chops that had been allowed to grow almost six inches. The nose was large, bulbous and flaring, way out of proportion with the rest of the face. The forehead was very high, almost angular, it possessed no eyebrows. And the hair on its head was dark, almost ebony, sweeping back in what Owen could best describe as a mane. Then there were the eyes. They were red. Not bloodshot. Red. They almost glowed. Perhaps at night they did. If anything marked them out as no close cousin to humanity, this was it.

Trying to radiate a sense of confidence he in no way felt, he pulled his hood back, unwound the scarf and then removed his flying mask. He kept his eyes on the ogre watching for a response. As the mask came free he expected some kind of reaction.

Nothing.

He raised his arms once more, clutching his headgear and took another step forward.

'Good day,' he said with forced lightness. 'My name is Owen. And you are?'

The ogre, motionless, unreadable, stared at Owen.

Its mouth opened, thin lips cracking apart, a wide maw appearing in the white, bony landscape of its face. Huge teeth appeared: uneven and sharp. And hanging from the incisors, what looked like small pieces of flesh. Owen's imagination started to run riot.

The journey was short, perhaps ten minutes before they arrived at the village, or stockade, Owen wasn't sure. They crunched through the snow, following a clear path amidst the trees, leading north and east. The land levelled out a little, like they were in natural bowl set into the hillside.

There he discovered a crude wall surrounding a collection of huts, animal pens and a large central building set back against the hillside. He thought of Gerat's settlement in Scotia and found there was no comparison. This place looked like it had a sense of permanence, for all its lack of any cultural identity. Everything had a function, but no sense of craftsmanship about it.

Then there was the smell, an overpowering odour of fish. He'd got it on the shore too but here though, the place seemed to radiate it. It was awful. They arrived at the gate, little more than a screen that could be lifted into place. Right now, it was open, and the screen rested against the stockade wall. They continued inside. It was gloomy, like the sun never penetrated the tree cover, everything frosted in ice. Why was there no one else around? They passed by a long, windowless hut, crudely constructed with large gaps between the timbers. A noise, a whisper, a gentle bump. He studied the hut and for the barest moment he swore he saw a set of eyes watching him, but just as quickly they withdrew into the darkness, leaving him doubting what he had seen. The eyes had been white. The ogre continued without a glance. It led him to the central building, which was not backing against the hill as Owen had thought. Instead it merged with it, projecting out from the slope which was steeper, not far from vertical at this point. The effect was not so much a separate structure, it appeared more like an entrance, a vestibule.

The ogre pushed at the large, unremarkable wooden door in the centre and walked inside. Owen was greeted by one of the most offensive smells he had ever experienced. A mixture of sweat, decay, the stench of viscera, of bowels loosed at death and of course, the ever present fishy odour. He felt an urge to gag but placed his gloved hand in front of his face, drawing in the more reassuring scents of old leather and eagle. *Damn, Arno but I'll never complain about your stink again.*

He was right about the entrance. As his eyes adjusted, objects emerged from the dark: scattered sacks, detritus, discarded weapons, items used for fishing and sailing. The ogre continued on towards another portal, this looked like the access to the hillside itself. Large enough to accommodate the ogre, it was simply a cave mouth. Large boulders and rock protrusions flanked it and Owen could well imagine how it looked before the wooden structure was added to it. The light filtering in from outside did not penetrate within the cave but was replaced by large yellow candles. One such sat on a rocky ledge just within the entrance. It was smoky and gave off a weak light. A short passageway opened into a large cavern, with a high ceiling and several exits leading off. It was much warmer in here, musty and oppressive. More candles burned in niches and the smoke wafted its way lazily upwards with no discernible airflow.

And they were no longer alone.

Ogres filled the room, lounging upon skins, leaning on benches, or sitting at tables spread throughout. Most went bare-chested, having shed their tunics and skins in the stifling warmth. And their white skins were covered in tattoos, swirling chaotic messes of concentric circles and rings, embellished with finer detail between them. Just to his left an ogre lay on its front as another used what appeared to be a piece of bone to pierce the skin. The ogre holding the bone looked up at him with a blank expression before dipping the bone into a bowl of black ink. For a moment Owen had trouble spotting the difference, but he quickly separated the females from the males. Their breasts hung free and their hair was braided at the back. He passed one lying on the ground, propped up on one elbow. She was feeding a male, holding a chunk of ragged meat, letting him tear pieces from it.

Owen struck something on the floor and as it rolled away, he saw it was a long bone, partially gnawed, stringy pieces of sinew left trailing along its ends.

Emperor protect me. I have entered the Seven Hells.

Ahead of him the ogre had taken station before a platform and upon it was a high-backed wooden throne decorated with bones. And upon it sat another ogre. A female, though it wore a loose, leather tunic that covered its breasts. She looked at Owen with unblinking eyes. Owen could see a little better now and could pick out more of the feminine features. The forehead was smoother, a little more sloped. The eyes were longer, elongated, like a cat's. And the muscles in her arms looked leaner. Two slivers of bone were threaded through her nose and her ears dropped low with the weight of two metal circles piercing the lobes.

His ogre guide started to speak. It was the first noises Owen had heard any of them utter. Its words were low, guttural and clipped. Each word ended with a throaty click. It finished and bowed its head, taking a step back. If there was any doubt, it was clear the female on the chair was in charge. She continued to look at him and Owen could not shake the feeling he was being sized up as her next meal. She opened her mouth, and ground out two words.

A command? He waited for the seemingly inevitable seizing of his body and dismemberment, ready for the pot. Instead a curtain, set back from the platform twitched aside, and a cloaked and hooded figure stepped out from it. The figure moved to stand to one side of the platform and bowed low. It was much smaller than the ogres that surrounded it.

The female spoke again and the figure responded in kind. It recovered from its bow and turned to face Owen. It removed its hood.

'You are either very brave or very stupid. I have yet to decide which,' the figure said.

It took a moment for Owen to realise his mouth was open. Standing before him was a woman. She was thin-faced, with a pinched nose, high cheekbones and long grey hair brushed back tight against her head, falling in a braid like the female ogres. Her eyes, he decided, were blue. And on her face was a tattoo. Not in the style of the ogres. It was in the shape of a Reader. *Damn me.*

'You are a Gifted?' he said.

'Obviously. And you came by way of an eagle. So you are a Highlander.'

'Yes.'

'Imperial?'

'I was … I am.'

'Interesting answer,' she said.

The female ogre, uttered a few, short words. The Reader inclined her head once more and replied. Owen could tell her clipped words were not as precise as the ogres, the clicking in the throat not so harsh.

'My lady wishes to know why you are here. A predictable request, don't you think?'

'I come to parlay.'

The Reader raised an eyebrow.

'You are looking for sanctuary? A last desperate bid to find a safe place to hide? As I understand it, you should not exist anymore.'

'Not sanctuary.' He looked around the chamber and spread his arms wide. 'One can find many ways to survive, even in the most dangerous of places.'

She smiled thinly.

'Your point is made. Very well. You come to parley. Who do you represent?'

'The Empire.'

'The Empire is gone.'

'But her people are not,' he replied.

'Perhaps. But I doubt they are many.'

'That is true. But the war continues, nonetheless.'

The ogre spoke again and the Reader responded. This time the ogre reacted with a grunt and looked Owen up and down. She smiled and spoke.

The Reader nodded. 'I have informed the queen that you are a representative of the Empire. She finds this amusing as she knows the Empire has been destroyed. She helped do it.'

'She didn't finish the job.'

'For both our sakes, I will not translate that.'

'Either way, I am here to speak terms.'

The Reader smiled again.

'I think that is a little strong. But you are fortunate. You are in the presence of one of the more forward-thinking monarchs of Drifa. She always felt the deal struck with the elves was a poor one.'

'What did she receive?'

'They were allowed booty. As much as they could carry. But were forbidden their usual prize. Slaves. No humans could be returned to Drifa. They could only be used as fodder during the campaign.'

'Fodder?'

'Humans have many uses. Even when they are too broken to work.'

Owen felt himself shiver, despite the heat. 'And yet you are here.'

'Ah, I was … taken, before the war. Nothing has changed in that regard. The ogres continue to prey on those of the other races. Their palates are unrefined. Meat is meat.'

'There are other humans here?'

The Reader dipped her head.

'Most will be broken, without will. You will find dwarves, gnomes and even elves here too.'

A thought occurred to Owen. 'How many humans are on Drifa?'

'I don't need to be a Reader to know what you're thinking. Don't even bother entertaining that notion.'

The ogre queen barked out a single, short word.

'My lady grows impatient.'

'I come seeking an alliance. I come to ask for her help, the help of the ogres.'

'An alliance? To do what? Wage war against the mainland? I believe I already have the answer.'

'Even so, that is why I am here. The ogres are known as fearless and mighty warriors. With them by our side, we can take the fight to the enemy.'

'Not their enemy.'

'Not yet. But tell her anyway. The Tissan Empire offers an alliance to the ogres of Drifa. We hold no grudges. We only wish them to fight by our side.'

She sighed, shot Owen a pitying look, and turned to the queen. The ogre listened impassively until the Reader had finished. There was a silence and then the queen broke into laughter. It was hard to tell but the constant grunting, hooting and the heaving of her chest suggested as much. He glanced around as the gathered ogres started to join in. It was not unlike being in the middle of a pig sty at feeding time. Still, there was nothing like laughter to win friends.

The queen quieted and gestured the Reader to hear. She spoke again, watching Owen. The Reader turned towards him, her lips pursed.

'The Queen is intrigued. Probably because she has been bored for some time and you have entertained her. I have one question. And I will offer you my sympathies before you answer it, as I doubt you have anything that will stop her having you for supper. What could you possibly offer the queen to convince her to go to war against the twin empires of the elves and the dwarves?'

Owen paused. He considered just what he was dealing with, what he had seen, what he had witnessed in his short time among the ogres. It was, by any stretch a terrible bargain, something he would not wish on his worst enemy – if they had been human.

He met the ogre queen's gaze. 'Slaves. I offer you slaves.'

The Reader stroked her chin and turned to share his answer.

The queen stood. She ran a finger down her ear. And smiled.

CHAPTER THIRTY-EIGHT – MICHAEL

Father Michael stood on the aftcastle of the *Fist of Tissan* and enjoyed the bright spring sunshine. The weather had been set fair for a week, and back on land a riot of flowers had bloomed and the fields and forests were full of birdsong. He lowered his gaze to look up on the gathering of ships that had been assembled for the voyage home. They were now all afloat in the centre of the estuary, spread out in a line facing eastwards. There were the six surviving ships of the original Imperial fleet; The *Fist*, its two sister ships, and the three sturdiest merchantmen. The latter had been refitted and strengthened to survive another long voyage and all of them had been beached and their timbers cared for. Joining them were six more craft, native to this new world, they lacked the finery and finishing detail that the Tissan ships had. They were built to be simple, sturdy, and strong. He was impressed by how quickly they had been constructed. The good folk of Tissan had worked their hearts out, and the Nidhal, though lacking the technical experience, were a willing and energetic addition to the workforce, lending their strength and numbers to the task. They were already working on the next batch of ships that would join them in the relocation effort. It would take a long time to transport the majority of the Nidhal nation who were willing to relocate but that was the intent. Their bowels were designed to carry the vargrs and their riders, each ship now holding twenty-four vargr and the food and water needed to keep them alive. The morning had been taken up with the ships drawing alongside the docks, lowering their ramps and cajoling the creatures on. Many had not been happy with this prospect and at least one Nidhal had died. Father Michael wondered just how these creatures would deal with being cooped up below decks for six weeks.

He was glad that he did not have to find out. The *Fist* would carry only humans, some horses and its complement of eagles.

'Father?'

Father Michael turned to see Ellen standing behind him. His heart fell a little whenever he saw her now. She wore the iron collar around her neck, and a simple woollen shift, but at least she was unshackled. Her fellow Gifted were seldom accorded such freedom. Their minds were needed, not their bodies.

'Ellen. It's good to see you. But I thought you were on the *Pride?*'

'Nutaaq was meeting with the Emperor. We are heading back now. I just wanted to say hello and goodbye, I guess,' she said with a shrug.

'We can still exchange messages. The Riders will pass them on.'

'I suppose,' said Ellen. 'If we are close enough I'll try and pulse you.'

'Is it just you over there?' he asked. Ellen had remained as the principal interpreter between the Emperor and Nutaaq, even though there were many folk, and a few Nidhal, who had taken to each other's language. Communication was much better between the two races, although he felt mutual understanding would take longer.

'Yes. I guess I am lucky. Nutaaq is a better master to work for than some I might name.'

Father Michael raised an eyebrow at the less-than-subtle barb.

'Nutaaq likes you,' said Father Michael. It was the Nidhal who had insisted on keeping Ellen close. The Emperor had acceded to the request, but he had not been happy.

'He is a good man, um, Nidhal. Anyway, I should be going.'

Father Michael nodded.

'Take care. I will see you at landfall.'

Ellen hesitated as if she wanted to say something else. Instead she took a step forward, took his hand and squeezed it.

'*Thank you.*'

She let go and ran to the left side of the ship where Nutaaq and his two brothers were waiting to disembark. Father Michael looked at his hand, feeling a little shocked. A simple act of affection, yet something he had barely ever experienced.

'There she goes,' said Sergeant Fenner, appearing at his shoulder. 'Odd seeing a Gifted running about unguarded.'

'We have Nutaaq to thank for that,' said Father Michael.

'Thank? Well I guess that depends on your point of view,' observed Fenner. 'I reckon Nutaaq keeps her around because he respects you and knows you are fond of her.'

Father Michael felt his cheeks flush but fortunately Fenner wasn't looking at him.

'Still, she's a good lass and always looked uncomfortable about the other Gifted,' Fenner mused. He tucked his thumbs into his belt. 'I heard you mention landfall. You know where we are headed? No bugger tells me anything.'

'I heard that we are heading back to Aberpool,' said Father Michael. He had heard it by being in the same room as the Emperor and the Admiral. A silent observer.

'Makes sense. I was wondering if we might head for Vyberg. Or North Haven.'

'That would bring us closer to the enemy,' replied Father Michael.

'Ah, and that's a bad thing?'

'The Emperor wants a base of operations. Take and hold some land before working east. He hopes we can build up numbers before pushing on. There is no point in provoking a fight before we are ready.'

'Glad to hear it. Emperor knows, I'm all for a scrap. But how many we got here?' he raised a hand and started pointing at his fingers. 'Three score marines, fifty soldiers, eight Eagle Riders and not forgetting you, Father. You are a walking platoon all by yourself. Even so, you add that to the hundred and forty vargr cavalry, and another thousand very grumpy footslogging Nidhal.'

'It's a sizeable force,' said Father Michael.

'Aye, well, if you want to go raiding, it's a grand sum. But not enough if we are pushing inland, with no support, no supply lines. That's on a different scale.'

'And that's why we need a firm base, greater numbers and the Imperial roads cleared of any blocking forces behind us, Sergeant Fenner,' said Admiral Lukas walking up behind them.

'As you say, Sir,' grumped Fenner.

'You would rather have stayed back in New Tissan?' asked the Admiral, his eyebrows raised.

'Seven Hells, I would not.'

'Of course you wouldn't. Besides, I wouldn't have let you,' said the Admiral. 'Father Michael has the right of it. There's no point striking until we are ready. Otherwise it's just another bloodbath.'

'Admiral, the Nidhal, will they be enough?' asked Father Michael.

The Admiral shrugged.

'They have numbers. If we can get enough of them over without being compromised, why not? The elves will not be expecting them. We could give those bastards such a beating they'll be suing us for peace.'

'That'd be nice,' agreed Fenner.

'Me? I'd rather see them all dead. It's only fair after all but I'm old-fashioned like that. And the Emperor hopes we may not be alone. We made it out. Maybe some others have survived too. If we can link up with other groups, then our chances will improve,' continued the Admiral.

Father Michael looked out over their ship thinking about that possibility.

The Emperor had gone to watch Nutaaq depart and now he walked across to join them. In tow was Father Llews, a vague smile on his face, and behind them was a Speaker, wearing a similar shift to Ellen's and the iron collar about his throat. This had a chain attached to it and the end was held by one of two soldiers.

'Gentlemen,' said the Emperor, as he climbed the steps. He wore leather trousers, a white tunic and his sword was buckled around his waist. His simple approach had won much favour with the people, one that he had cultivated on their expedition. He looked up in the sky as an eagle passed overhead. Father Michael followed his gaze. It wasn't lost on him that the Highlanders had avoided the punishment inflicted upon the other Gifted. Yet they carried within them the same, what was the word? *Mutation.* Yes. That was it. An affliction Father Llews had started to preach against. It would seem loyalty could earn mercy, even gratitude. And that felt right and proper to Father Michael. So why did he still feel a sense of unease?

'Admiral, I believe the weather is set fair and the wind is with us,' the Emperor stated.

'I believe you are right, Your Grace,' agreed the Admiral.

'Then I give the order for us to set sail.'

'Right you are, Your Grace,' said the Admiral. He turned and nodded at his first mate. The mate cupped his hands and bellowed out orders. The crew scrambled into action, the sails were dropped and the anchor was hauled up from the depths. Father Michael looked out across the fleet as the other ships were beginning to follow their lead.

'Keep it in the middle of the channel, nice and steady,' ordered the Admiral to the helmsman.

'Aye, Sir,' replied the helmsman.

Fenner nodded at Father Michael and left to join his squad on the main deck, gathered watching New Tissan slide away.

The Emperor placed a hand on Father Michael's shoulder.

'Father, we have done it. We are finally going home!'

'Congratulations, Your Grace,' replied Father Michael. 'Your first victory is against the Fates themselves.'

The Emperor made an appreciative face.

'Yes, I like that. You have become quite the erudite, Father. But it is as much your victory as it is mine. Without you, I would not be standing here. The Tissan Empire would not be embarking on its great resurgence if not for you and the actions of all my loyal sons and daughters, many of whom have given their lives. I swear to you, in the bloody days ahead, their sacrifice and all the sacrifices to come, will be rewarded. The Empire will be restored. Enjoy your moment, Father. You have earned it.'

Father Michael smiled and closed his eyes. The Empire restored. The Emperor returned to his throne. Was it not worth it? Worth all of it?

Every drop of blood shed. Every life taken. Father Michael opened his eyes and looked back towards the trailing vessels, and saw Nutaaq's ship, the *Pride of the Emperor,* just behind theirs.

And he thought of Ellen …

The End

About the Author

Alex Janaway is an Army officer based in Saffron Walden with his wife and two magnificent, if somewhat wilful, cats. When not pounding keys he can be found at the cinema or the pub rolling dice and moving small painted metal figures across a table. Alex is a world-renowned tabletop gamer having been victorious at the Warmaster World Championship held in the Olympic Stadium in May 2018. Because of his legendary wins, he is known on the Warmaster Podcast as the GOAT (Greatest Of All Time).

Alex also writes for computer games including the BAFTA nominated *Merlin: The Game*.

His military and gaming experience have undoubtedly helped to shape the gripping authenticity of the epic struggles related in his End of Empire series.

If you have enjoyed this book, please consider leaving a review for Alex to let him know what you thought of his work.

You can find out more about Alex on his author page on the Fantastic Books Store. Why not sign up to our newsletter to get advance notice of forthcoming publications – including Alex's third book in his End of Empire series: Resurgence. While you're there, please browse our delightful tales and wonderfully woven prose!

www.fantasticbooksstore.com